The Miranda Complex

Volume 3:

The Man Behind The Curtain

Barry Smolin

Three for the Zoo,

they who endured the night rumblings

CONTENTS

This Insubstantial Pageant

1

"Remember, what you think you see isn't necessarily really there," advised Gina Dichlich with authority because she'd dropped acid before, "but on the other hand it might be—"

The three of us were sitting in her chipped-beige Dodge Dart, Gina and I in front, Manny in back, parked in a lot outside the Shrine Auditorium where the Grateful Dead were playing that January night in 1978.

Another winter in Los Angeles.

I sported a long sleeve Dodgers shirt, wearing it proudly even though the Dodgers had lost, yet again, to the Yankees in the last World Series, a humiliation they'd repeat the following October.

Fucking Reggie Jackson.

"—So question everything," continued Gina, "I'll make sure you don't do anything stupid or dangerous."

Manny and I were planning to try LSD for the first time and Gina had offered to refrain and be our chauffeur and escort through the cosmos.

"For the first time in my life I'll be the only straight person," she said.

We laughed a little bit longer than the joke warranted as the kaleidoscopic rainbow air was starting to vie for our attention.

Manny Shepherd and I weren't into the Grateful Dead at all, but we'd heard it was easy to find acid outside their shows, so Gina pulled into this makeshift parking lot which was actually an elementary school playground, and then Manny and I just started strolling the vicinity with open ears and eager eyes. Gina waited in the car.

Within minutes we encountered a man of the trade—a pearly-faced guy with incandescent sky-blue eyes and a scraggly flaxen goatee who was quietly offering "shrooms, acid, bud"—and we made a transaction for two blotter hits having no idea if we were being ripped off or not but going on jewboy faith that we'd be dosed to the highest heavens.

"Lay it on your tongue, dude," Manny said as the vendor moved on.

"Rock and roll," I goofed like a lame-ass Caucasian and partook of the holy wafer.

We smiled together and waited for the effects to begin manifesting.

"Do you swallow it?" I tasted the tiny square.

"Every time, lover."

"Nyuk nyuk nyuk."

"I think you just let it dissolve on your tongue."

"Maybe we should have waited till we're back at Gina's car. She could've showed us the right way."

"Too late now obviously," Manny said, "Dude, we are already tripping. We're just not feeling it yet. We will be. In a major way. We can't turn back now. It's a one-way ticket. Cray-zee. LSD is just something you hear about second-hand or see in bad movies."

"Not anymore," I said and stuck out my tongue with the blotter hit still on it, "It's really happening, dude," and we slapped hands.

A parade of hippies—some originals, some recent converts—surrounded us, all of them smiling with unabashed eye contact.

"I don't feel anything," I said.

"So I've heard," Manny said, "Haha . . . psych."

8

"Why I oughta," I raised my fist.

"You looked like you were in a TV show just now when you said that," Manny inhaled a laugh.

"Well, you laugh like the creaky door in horror movies."

"Dang, dude, I can't help it. I inherited it from my dad. We're a family of creakers."

"Creakers and what's-it-calleds."

Manny creaked, "Totally."

"Everything still seems normal," I looked around at the astonishing number of beautiful girls around me.

Dang, dude. Girls.

"Nyeah, I think it takes like half an hour to come on," Manny said, "Let's go back to Gina's car while we're still coherent enough to find it."

"Roger Wilco," I sounded like one crying in the wilderness.

We journeyed long, longer than was necessary, to find Gina's Dart.

"Underway?" Gina asked when we finally got back into the car at the end of our daunting quest.

"Affirmative," I stuck out my tongue to show her the spitlings of paper still left there.

"Flagrant. I saw you guys walk right past twice and I was busting up both times. I said, 'They are tripping.' Like out loud."

"Thanks for stopping us."

"It was too funny. And how are you feeling?"

"Like I want to kiss you."

"You are not allowed to do that."

"Dang, Miss DICK-LICK, you are a bad mother shut your mouth."

It hadn't been a full half-hour before the hallucinogenic symptoms of something else happening all around me started expanding my peripheral vision and everything looked the same whether my eyes were open or closed.

"Uh huh," Gina said, either in response to my having called her a bad mother shut your mouth or else to the obviousness of the glazed otherwise in our eyes, "Remember, what you think you see isn't necessarily really there, but on the other hand it might be. So question everything. I'll make sure you don't do anything stupid or dangerous."

That's where the deja-vu ended. Or started. Or something. I lost track.

"You guys want to walk around and check shit out? There's a lot to look at here. It seems to me you're already feeling it-it-it-it-it-it-it-it-it," she fake-echoed and then cackled like Janis Joplin.

"Yeah, cool," Manny said as we all got out of the car, "Let's go rustle us up some big tittied women."

"You're not gonna be rustling up anything but your own demons tonight," Gina said and locked arms with Manny.

"Hey, I'm jealous," I said, locking her other arm.

The three of us strode the lot and environs thus entwined.

"We're off to see the Wizard," I sang.

"The wonderful Wizard of Oz," Manny held the z.

"Totally," I said.

"So that would make me . . . Dorothy?" Gina said.

"You've got the necessary vagina," Manny said.

"Who's to say Dorothy's not a boy in drag? Maybe that's the reason gay guys love Judy Garland. But whatever dudes I'll concede the vagina thing. And you are?"

"Scarecrow," Manny said.

"I want to be Scarecrow," I said.

"Nah, dude, I'm Scarecrow. You be somebody else."

"How about the Tin Man?" Gina said.

"I am the great and powerful Oz!" I roared like in the movie, "Pay no attention to the man behind the curtain . . ."

The Necessary Vagina would be a great title for something.

We didn't have tickets to the Grateful Dead show.

We were just wandering the cosmos, tripping on lights fantastic.

The community of Deadheads was a glimpse into a world unchanged.

Clothing, hairstyle, vibe, Weltanschauung, all tapped into the ancient ecstatic ethos.

It didn't feel dated. Instead it felt perpetual.

An ongoing manifestation of the Cult of Dionysus.

Nor were the Deadheads a monolith, by any measure.

Some of them were brilliant. Some of them were brainless dolts. Some of them were beams of light and creativity. Some of them were incarnations of the gnarly darkness. Some of them were en route to truth and beauty. Some of them were merely hiding from home. Some of them came for enlightenment. Some of them sought only oblivion. Some of them were there to get laid later. Some of them weren't sure of their own whereabouts. All of them though were enraptured by the music.

There were kids at school who were Deadheads and they dressed and acted that way, so it was not totally unfamiliar to me, though I never really hung out with them. We actually ended up running into that crowd later in the evening because, as it turned out, we got into the show for free.

As we walked past one of the Shrine's side exits on 32nd Street a door opened and this very tall freaked out messiah waved us in.

"Greetings, fellow travelers. Come partake of the splendor," he said as we made our way through the surprise portal and into the Shrine.

"Dude, we just got in for free," Manny said. "It's the fuckin' Grateful Dead, but, dang, dude, it's free."

"And we're tripping."

"Everybody's tripping," Manny looked aglow at all of us.

"Here," Gina said, pointing to the stairs, "I think it'll be easier to find a place to sit in the balcony. Can you deal? It won't matter that we don't have a ticket up there I bet. Everybody is wandering the aisles down here."

I thought there was a chance it could become claustrophobic up in the balcony but on the other hand the prospect of the view was alluring, plus Gina was correct in her wager that it'd be easier to find a seat up there, and Manny agreed, so we followed her up.

The faux elegance of the Shrine had this grandiloquent cheeseball throb to it that excited my senses with all of its Jupiter redness and geometric woodwork.

It was while sitting there spacing out on the Shrine ceiling chandelier before the show started that I first realized I was probably in the process of falling in love with Diana Hitchcock and I thought, like, dang, dude, this again.

Engagement with girlness is just fucking unavoidable.

No matter how many times I swear off them.

Love calls you by your name, as Reb Leonard sings it.

Every fucking time.

Dang, dude.

"Hey whiteboys," we heard a voice and turned.

That term applied to just about everybody at the show with the exception of the guy who'd said it, with dreadlocks and crooked John Lennon glasses, Waldo Banks.

"How's it going?" Waldo said.

"Pretty good," we all overlapped.

"Ready for liftoff?" Waldo smiled and flapped his hands like bird wings.

"In a major way," Manny said.

"You guys tripping?"

"We are thus engaged, yes," I said.

"When'd you drop?"

"I don't remember," Manny said.

"Time doesn't exist," I said.

"Or at least not the way we usually think of it," Manny added.

"You guys are tripping," Waldo eeked and held out his hand for slapping, "Have a good show, dudes, happy travels," he said as he trailed away from us into the hippest heavens.

"Love how he didn't acknowledge me?" Gina said.

Manny leaned over and rested his arm on my shoulder, "Nyeah, didn't he try to hit on you at a party or something and you—?"

"—kneed him in the balls, yeah," she said, "And he whined like a little bitch."

"Ouch," Manny closed his knees.

"That sucks you have to deal with shit like that all the time," I said.

"Uh, yeah," she said, "it does indeed suck. All girls deal with it pretty much all the time. Always some fucking asshole implying, 'Come on, bitch, you know you want it.'"

"Except Ethel Mertz," Manny said, "I don't think she had to deal with it."

"Nyeah, even Ethel got her ass harrassed," Gina said, "even fucking Ethel Mertz. I promise you. You think William Frawley didn't try to get his hands up in Vivian Vance's business? Waldo fucking deserved it, dude."

"Well, I value my sweet tenor voice and do not wish to sound like Neil Young when I sing," I said, "so I will not, even in my trippingest trippingmost . . ." and my eyes closed at the sight of this comet coming right at me.

"Will not what?" Gina jarred me loose from the cataclysm.

"I don't remember what I was thinking," I said.

"Will not try to hit on me maybe?"

"Come on, bitch, you know you want it," I said like a pimp.

"Eat shit and die twice. Promise."

"I promise. I will not try to hit on you. I might try to hit on Manny, but not you."

"You know the bitch wants it."

"Wants what?" Manny returned from a farther galaxy to respond.

"Nothing," Gina said, "Go back to your own dimension, golita."

I'm not sure how much longer it was before the house lights went out and the kaleidoscopic rainbow air filled with hoots and howls and stomping feet.

"Grateful Fucking Dead!" shouted a girl to my left somewhere.

Bass thumpings and guitar noodlings and tunings went on it seemed an eon and a half.

I was used to bands who hit the ground playing.

A blast of feedback elicited a shout from the crowd in the dark.

"Imagine our surprise at finding out some of this stuff doesn't work," Bob Weir addressed the undulating fans.

"What're they gonna open with?" I heard a dude say behind me.

The band started playing before whomever he asked could answer.

The Deadheads knew it in 3 notes.

"Bertha!" that same girl to my left somewhere shouted.

Everything was blurry swirling.

The present was far away, like a disassociation.

I couldn't tell what was prediction and what was memory.

I had a hard run to the toilet in order to vomit after I got home from the Deirdre Lux/Mr. Hill wedding reception back in September.

The ceremony was private, but the reception took place in the rec room of a condo complex overlooking the Ventura Freeway.

Lorelei Lux was the maid of honor. I'd never really seen Lorelei in a dress except at the odd bar or bat mitzvah. It was difficult to imagine her wearing anything other than those skintight jeans I could never get my hand all the way into.

"You look beautiful," I said to her before I got drunk.

"Thank you," she looked away.

"Mazel Tov," I offered as she moved on and I wondered if that exchange bothered her as much as it bothered me.

In the center of the room was an elaborate fountain of champagne into which one only need submerge one's plastic goblet and bring it forth to one's lips and thus imbibe. I pretended it was mead and I was a knight in the royal court.

Sir Lancelot Link, Secret Chimp.

The room was filled with my rivals. They coveted both my supremacy in the knighthood and the attentions of m'lady. None would have either. I was ready for their onslaught. I stood among the mead and foodstuffs, vigilant of the surrounding peril and awaiting m'lady's advent.

It was some time after I'd finished my third plastic goblet of champagne that Diana Hitchcock approached to lower her own plastic goblet into the fountain, that blushful Hippocrene.

"Hey, whiteboy," she said.

"You can call me Lance, you know."

"I prefer whiteboy."

"Well, sure thing then, negro."

"Hey."

"Sorry. I meant negress."

"Hey, that's racist," she said and glared for an agony of an instant, "And sexist."

Then she smiled and we clicked plastic glasses.

"Ha . . . psych," she snickered.

I hadn't fucked up.

I would fuck up eventually, but not that night.

"It's nice to see you," I said.

"You just saw me yesterday at school."

"Yeah but," I blushed.

Diana dipped her empty plastic goblet back into the fountain.

She knew she had me.

"It's nice to see you . . . *again*," I leaned in toward her.

"What do you think of Ms. Van Poole so far?" Diana referred to our new Drama teacher, Mr. Hill's replacement, because, obviously, he couldn't return to school given the fact that he'd just, you know, married one of his students.

Diana backed away and I debated the consequences of having a fourth plastic goblet of champagne which I ultimately, in retrospect, deemed to be worth the unpleasant payback at the end of the evening.

I let the bubbly fill my flagon once more.

"I like her," I said of Ms. Van Poole. I did, too. Ms. Van Poole was smart. She was funny. She was cute. That's all I ever need to trigger my crush-whore tendencies.

"It's only been a couple of weeks, so who knows," Diana said, "We'll see what she picks for the Fall drama. But yeah, she's mostly cool. Yeah. Yeah yeah."

I didn't have anything else to say to her and she appeared to be experiencing the same lack, so we just kind of nodded and parted ways, I to the other side of the champagne fountain, she to a trio of men who, I figured, were friends of Mr. Hill.

The champagne told me they were looking at her sexually and I found I was, just enough to notice, jealous.

My immediate response was to fill my plastic goblet a fifth time.

I fantasized about walking right up to her and kissing her while she was talking to those guys, but I feared my wobbly legs and careening equilibrium would fail me and I'd end up doing one of those formal function faux pas accidental pratfalls that gets talked about for years afterward.

"Remember at Deirdre and Mr. Hill's wedding when Lance Atlas got drunk and fell face first into the wedding cake?"

I did not want to be the protagonist of that story.

It was during my 6th plastic goblet of champagne that Diana returned to refill her own plastic goblet and I moved toward her and kissed her flush on the mouth and I'm fairly certain she kissed me back with a modicum of passion.

"You are drunk," she said upon our completion of the kiss and she patted my chest.

"I am very drunk," I said and we started kissing again.

After we finished that second kiss she said, "It would be different if you weren't drunk," and she walked away for the rest of the evening.

I remember starting my seventh plastic goblet of champagne.

Apparently Mimi and I ended up getting a ride home from Sharon Rose who, according to my sister, kept begging me the whole way not to throw up in her car.

I do remember my father that night, clad in jockey shorts and a white undershirt, seated in the big black chair watching television, eating his favorite sliced bananas and sour cream late night snack when we walked in the front door.

"Been drinking?" He looked into my crossed eyes, rolled his own eyes, and pointed in the direction of the bathroom.

"Better hurry," he said as I fled down the hall.

I managed to reach the toilet just in time to puke liquid the color of Gina Dichlich's chipped-beige Dodge Dart.

2

Test me, test me
Why don't you arrest me?
Throw me in the jail house
Until the sun goes down

The Dead were still rolling through their first number.

Time was folding in on itself and somehow shit from 4 months ago felt as present as Manny and Gina and the rippling swarm of Deadheads undistractedly attuned to the visceral rhythm of the only music they cared about.

Manny was sitting in his seat, bobbing his head, eyes closed. His hands were dancing.

Gina was up and moving to the music and, man, her ass in that miniskirt was just, like, dang, dude.

"Where are you?" she leaned into my ear.

"Right here," I said, "I've never been more precisely right here," and pointed to the floor.

"You feeling good? Positive vibrations?"

"Totally," I said, "I am like immersed in the whole *megillah.*"

"Like Magilla Gorilla?"

"Like Squiddly Diddly," I said.

"Snoop And Blabb."

"Quick Draw McGraw."

"El Kabong."

"Lippy The Lion and Hardy Har Har," I sang.

"Huckleberry Hound," Gina drawled.

"Yogi Bear."

"Yes, Mr. Ranger, sir. I promise I will not steal anymore of of those pic-a-nic baskets."

"Man, I keep seeing Squiddly Diddly everywhere," I pointed in several directions.

"That's 'cause you're immersed in the whole Magilla Gorilla."

The Dead were doing a song I recognized, the old Rascals tune "Good Lovin'."

"It's weird to feel part of something this big," I said.

"What, like this tripped out audience?"

"No, all the multiverses, dude. I'm seeing like Hindu iconography and shit."

Gina smiled at me.

"Keep flying, baby. I wish I was up there with you," she said and turned her attention back to the music.

I was melting with love for Gina Dichlich but her preference for pussy dampened my hope, and Diana Hitchcock kept orbiting the perimeter of my consciousness so that I could almost feel her standing next to me and I knew how perfectly right that would be. Yet I was wary of another heartbreak and/or pain in the ass because it's always one or the other.

I've got the fever, you've got the cure

I sat down next to Manny and he opened his eyes.

"Where you been?"

"All over, dude," Manny crossed his arms, "And you realize we're not even peaking yet. This is just the come on."

"Can't you see just like every fucking molecule?"

"Every fucking atom, man. I can feel the solar neutrinos passing through my body nonstop."

"Yeah yeah, right on."

We slapped five.

"Grok the fullness. Thou art God," Manny gestured like Mesmer.

Manny was tapping his foot in time to the music which was absolutely bopping along like a sleigh ride down a rocky hill.

In fact I felt the oogly fearful ache that extends from intestine to anus I always get on roller coasters and rocket ships.

The sensation of falling through space in some indeterminate direction forever absolutely alone.

A long lull between songs gave rise to jungle screeches and hyper-awareness of body odors, of musk and patchouli and man-sweat and menstruation.

"We're trying to get everything working as you can plainly see," Weir explained the delay.

One of the roadies said, "OK, let's try this, Hello lo lo lo lo," and his voices echoed thus to the rapt congregants and they hooted in reply to the holy tones.

Across the span of darkness I thought about Miranda Savitch, whose vagina I would probably never lay tongue on.

Gone are the days when the ladies said please

The Dead were singing of brown-eyed women and I thought of the myriad lasses I'd fancied thus endowed. Miranda Savitch. Dolly Ferris. Lorelei Lux. Candy Stoner, whose sister Desirée, equally brown-eyed, had taken my virginity, which surprised me because I had long thought my virginity would fall to Taryn Rust who'd taught me everything except fucking and who also had very big brown eyes.

I remember the night I thought I was going to fuck Taryn Rust, though.

It was just a couple of days after the Deirdre/Mr. Hill wedding.

I had gone into Aron's to buy the *Talking Heads '77* album.

The sound of the thunder with the rain pouring down outside made Aron's an even more tempting refuge than usual.

"It never rains in September," Taryn Rust was saying as I walked in from the deluge.

"Well, guess what? Now it does," yapped this little gnome of a dude behind the counter, "Check your assumptions and paradigms at the door, boss lady. Panta Rhei, dig?"

"Don't you be impertinent with me, you little scalawag or I'll have you hung from the highest yardarm," Taryn came back like Captain Bligh immediately and pointed at his rodentine face, "Keel haul this man!"

I caught on that they were doing shtick when Taryn used the word scalawag but at first I thought they were being serious.

"Oh, hey," she said when she saw me and moseyed over, "How's it going?"

"Pretty good," I said and smelled her hair as we half-hugged.

Taryn's hair smelled like pine cones.

"Wearing out many grooves lately?" she asked.

"My share," I said.

"I bet. That Talking Heads album is great," she pointed, "I can't stop listening to it."

"Yeah, I heard 'Psycho Killer' on KROQ and knew it was something I should check out more of."

"Hey, look, here's a treasure in the $1 bin if you don't have it already," she moved a few bins down and pulled out Elvis Costello's *My Aim Is True*.

"I've heard a couple of songs from it."

"Well you should get it," she said and handed it to me, "It's only a dollar."

"Do you guys have the new Tom Waits record?"

"Yeah, it's here, but we don't have it out front yet. It doesn't officially release until Tuesday."

"Can I get one?"

"We haven't put price stickers on it yet."

"Pllleeeeeeease?" I gave it my best flirt.

"How about if I take one out of the store after work and you come pick it up at my place tonight?"

"You can do that?"

"Dude, I'm the manager."

"Coolness," I said, "What time?"

"I dunno, um, 7?"

"I will be there. And thank you."

"No problem. See you later."

Presuming we were going to have sexual intercourse that night—because we'd sort of done everything but—I had to decide whether or not I was going to buy condoms to bring with me to her place.

At first I thought yes definitely because what if she doesn't have them.

But then I started to picture myself going into 7-11 to get them.

I'd probably do like a Woody Allen buying porn at the beginning of *Bananas* type thing. Like buy a can of Cactus Cooler, a Hershey bar (with almonds), dental floss, a Bic 4-color pen, one of those erasers that smell like fruit, a 3-pack of Trojan condoms, a roll of Kodak Instamatic film, a pack of cards, a Dodger cap, Vaseline, and a copy of the *Herald-Examiner*.

But having neither the money nor the courage to enact that scenario, I turned to Manny's ongoing mantra, "Practice non-attachment."

I agreed to a deal with myself that I'd show up without condoms, and when the moment of fornication arrived, if Taryn had condoms, great, we'd fuck, and if not, fine, we wouldn't.

I determined to be happy with either outcome. Plus getting the new Tom Waits album was totally worth it.

When I arrived at Taryn's place, I was surprised to find a guy there with her, sitting on the couch. I recognized him but didn't know his name.

They were listening to David Bowie's *The Man Who Sold The World* album, which, in addition to being one of my favorite albums of all time, also reminded me of when Miranda Savitch gave me the Lulu version of the title song for my bar mitzvah.

"Hey, Lance, this is my boyfriend Arthur," Taryn gestured over to the sofa.

"Artie," he said, "How's it going?"

"Pretty good," I said, "Nice to see you," I waved.

Artie was a music geek who also worked at Aron's. I had talked to him about Moody Blues album covers once while he was ringing me up, but I don't think he remembered that conversation. I actually don't remember it very well myself other than that it happened. I don't know why the topic had even come up because I sure as hell wasn't buying a Moody Blues album or anything.

"So, here it is," Taryn handed me the Waits album.

"Excellent, thank you."

"My pleasure," she said.

I wasn't sure what I was supposed to do. Just leave?

Taryn bailed me out with the offer, "We're just kicking back listening to Bowie. You're welcome to hang if you want, get high, whatever."

"Nah, I think I'd better head home," I said trying vainly to mask my chagrin and bewilderment and slight nausea.

"You sure? I've got this new weed from Bigelow called Shaolin Temple because it makes you feel like Grasshopper getting monk-slapped by Master Po next to a koi pond."

"Nahmcool. But thank you again. I really appreciate it. I can't wait to hear this."

"Dig it, man. Glad I could help you out. I'm always happy to get great music into the right ears."

"That's what it's all about," Artie barked in agreement.

"How much do I owe you?" I asked.

"Nothing," she waved me off, "It's a present."

"What? No," and I tried to hand her a $10 bill.

"Nuh-uh," she pulled her hands away, "It's yours. Really. I mean it," and then she lowered her voice almost to a whisper, "I'm sorry."

"For what?"

"You know."

"Nice to see you," I said to Artie again and then turned to Taryn whose eyes were void of fire, and said, "I'll see you when I look at you."

"An indisputable truth," she nodded.

I nodded back and left her place for what I figured was probably the last time. My stomach had never felt emptier.

Dang, dude.

Devastation before Troy.

I dragged myself home totally bummed out.

The storm had cleared but the air was still cool for September. I'd heard on the radio we were about to get another heat wave. Santa Ana winds heading our way. I was already feeling it in my nose and eyes and scalp. The dry itch. The emotional abrasion. The skin crawl.

When I got to my bedroom I put Side A of *Foreign Affairs* on the stereo and lay in the dark with a multifaceted sadness.

I actually cried a little bit about Taryn, the goneness of the promise, her turning away, the hugest letdown. She'd always been into me and then suddenly she wasn't. And I felt just how very much she wasn't.

But I was also moping over Dolly, missing her, wanting to hear her voice and engage her toying banter and feel her hand on the back of my neck and our mouths engaged in the best frenching of all time.

And you're looking for someone to take the place of her . . .

Dolly had been gone a month and I hadn't yet received a letter from her.

Who we were together had become a blank.

I did get a letter from Songwriters Showcase saying they liked "Rain On Me" but that I needed "some more songs like that one" for them to give me a slot in the showcase and to "please audition again when you have more material to share."

I showed the letter to my parents who were enthusiastic and proud but all I could think about was that Ben and Ian didn't like the other songs.

"That's great, they liked your song," my dad enthused, "You only need one hit and you never have to work again, just one."

Ben and Ian didn't like any of the other ones, I kept thinking.

"That song is pretty. I've heard you playing it on the guitar," my mom said, "It's almost like a children's song."

"Yeah," I said, "it is. Or at least it's about childhood."

"You should write more like that, just like they said," my mom encouraged.

"What, children's songs?"

"Mmm, more like songs about childhood."

"Childhood is mostly about dealing with boredom."

"Then write about that. I remember how often you used to complain that you were bored when you were little."

"Yeah, I was, a lot."

"And what would I say to you?"

"Take two sticks and drum on your belly," I repeated my mom's longstanding remedy.

"Write a song about that."

"Take two sticks and drum on your belly?"

"Yeah. Or something about a kid who's always bored."

"That's what *The Phantom Tollbooth* is about," I said.

"So, yours will be a song. That's different from a book," my father chimed in. "Take two sticks and drum on your belly," he sang, dancing two steps forward and two steps back, clad in black socks and threadbare white Jockey briefs, cigarette, as always, a-dangle, a makeshift melody that I realized was in fact a cool idea for a song.

When Side A of Waits ended I turned on the light in my bedroom and took a break from the album in order to work on this song I ended up calling "Take Two Sticks."

I went for a walk up the block so that I might inhale the sacramental herb and summon the Muses.

There were a number of sexually attractive women who lived on my block and I hoped I might catch sight of one or two as I ambled. That always spruces up an evening stroll.

One time Buzzy Lagniappe and I came up with this idea for a porno movie called *Neighborhood Gigolo* about this dude who fucks all the women on the block. We had a distinct elaborate scenario for each lady, each one, of course, based on an actual foxy mom.

"*Neighborhood Gigolo, or The Meandering Philanderer,*" I proposed as the title.

"Dude, it could be like a series. Like, *Neighborhood Gigolo II: Caught In The Act.* And it'd be all these scenes of husbands walking in on them. And like either the husband joins in for a threesome or the two dudes fight and it turns into a kung fu movie for a while."

"Too bad Bruce Lee's dead. Could've been a second career for him."

"Dang, dude. Kung Fu porn."

"*Neighborhood Gigolo III: Older Sisters,*" I said.

"Of course. Penelope can star in it."

"Me and her up on the garage roof, dude," I said, "I'm game."

"Dude, shut up, that's my sister. *Neighborhood Gigolo IV: Me & Mrs. Jones.* Your mother can star in that one with me."

"Dang, dude."

"*Neighborhood Gigolo V: Battle For The Planet Of The Apes.*"

We both laughed.

"That'd be flagrant, dude, for real, if it was all the same houses and characters and shit from the other movies in the series but everyone is wearing ape costumes while they're fucking."

"Nyeah, I think it should be real apes, like on *Lancelot Link, Secret Chimp*, only we get apes who are trained to fuck in human positions on cue."

"Totally," Buzzy was busting up, "Doin' it homo sapiens style."

I missed him being like that. Like laughing at stuff, getting it, riffing. It was unusual for that to happen anymore.

The smell of the still-cool night air jogged loose the usual blockage.

I got home and pounded out an old-timey melody on the piano, inspired by what my dad had been improvising, and constructed some lyrics that followed boredom through the four seasons.

It came easily, like Taryn Rust once upon a tryst.

One of the few times I have ever written the music and the lyrics at the same time. They arrived in unison.

When the grass grows long and yellow
And the sky spreads out big and blue
When the world feels far away from you
Here's something that you can do:

Take two sticks and drum on your belly
Take two sticks and drum on your belly
Take two sticks and drum on your belly
A-rat-a-tat rat-a-tat
Boom boom da-boom

When the grass grows white and withered
On a ruined rainy day
When the world wears gloominess and gray
Here's something that you can play:

Take two sticks and drum on your belly

Take two sticks and drum on your belly
Take two sticks and drum on your belly
A-rat-a-tat rat-a-tat
Boom boom da-boom

When the grass goes dead and empty
And the snow falls from the sky
When the world's a winter lullaby
Here's something that you can try:

Take two sticks and drum on your belly
Take two sticks and drum on your belly
Take two sticks and drum on your belly
A-rat-a-tat rat-a-tat
Boom boom da-boom

So then when the grass grows green delicious
And the sky spreads out shiny new
When the world feels special made for you
You'll know just what you can do:

Take two sticks and drum on your belly
Take two sticks and drum on your belly
Take two sticks and drum on your belly
A-rat-a-tat rat-a-tat
Boom boom da-boom

My mom and dad came dancing in when they heard me playing the song and made me start again from the beginning.

"See, I told you," my mom said, "That's wonderful."

"You know your great Uncle Sam was an old-timey piano player in Cleveland back in the day. He would've loved this song," my dad said.

"Nyeah, it turned out pretty cool."

"Write some more like that."

I went back into my room to listen to Side B of *Foreign Affairs* and was in less of a funk due to the emergence of a new tune that I wanted to play again later if my parents weren't asleep yet.

A riddle's just a ticket for a dreamer

The Waits album was just so saturated with sadness, the vocals, the lyrics, the melodies, the arrangements, all resonant with my pensive spirits. My kind of shit.

Some nights my heart pounds just like thunder don't know why it don't explode

And of course the music reminded me of Miranda because every god damn fucking thing in the world reminded me of Miranda.

Most vagabonds I know don't ever want to find the culprit
That remains the object of their long relentless quest
The obsession's in the chasing and not the apprehending
The pursuit you see and never the arrest

But it ended up being Dolly who commanded the bulk of my sadness that night.

Dolly who was very far away.

A foreign affair juxtaposed with a stateside
And domestically approved romantic fancy
Is mysteriously attractive due to circumstances knowing
It will only be parlayed into a memory

But Dolly was in France, thus ye olde daimon hopelessness derailed any possibility of getting off to thoughts of that.

Taryn was now gone from the pantheon too.

Lorelei had rejected me.

Diana was still way below the surface.

Gina was a dyke.

I had no one to commune with.

The cupboard was bare.

I tried to conjure up a scenario wherein I'd attempt to convert Gina Dichlich to heterosexuality through my prodigious well-taught cunnilingus skills, like I'm eating her out but she doesn't know it's a guy and is having orgasms, but even that failed to get a rise out of me.

I fiddled with limpness.

I'd hit sexual zero.

3

Is there anything a man don't stand to lose
When he lets a woman hold him in her hands?

Manny was holding his head and groaning.

"This is horrible," he said, I supposed in response to the music.

It was some kind of country tune.

"Ugggh," Manny agonized.

"What's going on?"

"I long for the zero," Manny said.

"Well, I can dig that, dude. A while ago I was falling through space forever and my only thought was wishing to be torn apart by solar winds."

"Yeah, man. Annihilation would be preferable to what I'm hearing right now."

"You guys doing ok?" Gina shouted over the music.

"We're cool!" I strained back, "Manny's not really digging the country vibe!"

"I like it!" she said and went back to dancing and I definitely watched her ass for a really long time so that I didn't even notice the Dead had segued into a different hippie hoedown until Manny started groaning again.

"What is it with this cowboy shit?" he said and held his head.

Taught me good, Lord, taught me all I know

Mr. Megiddo was my Period 1 teacher again in 12th Grade. AP English instead of American Lit, but still Mr. Megiddo. That's all that mattered. Being in the room with Mr. Megiddo. Everything else was the cigarette after.

"I think I recognize everyone here," Mr. Megiddo said on the first day of class. "Except you," he pointed at the girl sitting to my left (where normally Claire would have sat but Claire wasn't in Period 1), a fair-skinned lass with tawny hair pulled back into a tight ponytail and a severe but comely face,

"What's your name?"

"Emily."

Mr. Megiddo scanned his roster.

"Emily. Wolf?"

"Yes."

"Are you new to Fairfax?"

"Yes."

"Where did you go to school before?"

"Hamilton."

"Hami sucks," Buddy Feigenbaum coughed.

Mr. Megiddo ignored the giggles.

"Do you like to read?"

"Oh yes."

"Who's your favorite author?"

"Spinoza."

"Spinoza the philosopher?"

"Yes."

"That's pretty heady stuff for someone your age."

"I like heady," she said, and several kids starting laughing.

"I bet," Buddy Feigenbaum murmured to Claude Moss.

"Blowjob," Whitman Rust pretended a yawn that became real.

"Flagrant," Claude Moss started yawning too.

Emily turned to look at the hecklers behind her and then turned back to face Megiddo.

"I like heady," she opened her mouth wide in a contagious yawn.

"Good," Mr. Megiddo said and addressed the class, "because we are going to be getting heady in here on a daily basis."

"Heh, getting heady," Buddy pantomimed fellatio.

"The texts we encounter in this class are going stretch your capacities for analysis and sharpen your insights into what and how literature means."

He knew how to lean on a pause for just slightly longer than was comfortable.

Megiddo continued, "When we talk about figurative language we are not going to be saying that the similes and metaphors and personifications are there to make the poem more interesting, or the way I hear some of you putting it, 'so you'll feel like you're there.' When we talk about figurative language in AP English we are going to be looking at how the similes and metaphors and personifications are there to convey or reinforce meaning or a theme in a poem."

He pulled a manilla folder from the top of his desk and began distributing a mimeographed poem to us.

"Art in general and poetry in particular is like an organism," Megiddo went on, "Just as every cell in your body contributes to your ability to function in the world, just as every beam and strut in a building contributes to the structure's ability to stand without toppling, so too in poetry does every word, every chosen image, every phrase, every metaphor, every allusion, contribute to a poem's ability to have cohesion and integrity and maybe even mean something."

He scanned the mimeograph for a moment.

"What do we make of this poem by Thomas Hardy? 'Neutral Tones,'" he then read the poem out loud.

We stood by a pond that winter day,
And the sun was white, as though chidden of God,
And a few leaves lay on the starving sod;
– They had fallen from an ash, and were gray.

Your eyes on me were as eyes that rove
Over tedious riddles of years ago;
And some words played between us to and fro
On which lost the more by our love.

The smile on your mouth was the deadest thing
Alive enough to have strength to die;
And a grin of bitterness swept thereby
Like an ominous bird a-wing....

Since then, keen lessons that love deceives,
And wrings with wrong, have shaped to me
Your face, and the God curst sun, and a tree,
And a pond edged with grayish leaves.

That line *The smile on your mouth was the deadest thing/ Alive enough to have the strength to die* right in the middle of the poem grabbed me immediately.

Following his recitation, he hung with the silence immediately after.

"What's this poem about?" he asked us.

"Lost love," said Miranda Savitch.

"That's the result, in hindsight, yes, but what's it about? What's going on in this poem?"

"It's about a couple breaking up," Gina Dichlich said.

"The break-up itself?"

"Just before the break-up. The moment he realizes it's over," she said.

"The moment who realizes it's over?"

"The speaker."

"Yes. Let's start using that language when we talk about literature," Megiddo said and looked around at us. "Some of you know that moment. Realizing that it's over," and there were a few nods around the room in acknowledgement. "What does that feel like?"

"Sad but also kind of dead," Emily Wolf said.

"Removed. Like you're watching it from the outside," Gina Dichlich added.

"And how does Hardy convey that feeling, that deadness, that exhaustion?"

Nobody answered.

Megiddo nodded his head and let the discomfort linger.

"Look at the language," he finally rescued us, "Look at his diction, the choices he's making. The meaning is everywhere. *We stood by a pond that winter day*," he read. "That first verb. Stood. He could've had them walking or strolling but instead he chose a verb of stasis. So right away the motionlessness is present. And then the pond. Of all the bodies of water he could have chosen, he uses pond. What is it about a pond in the context of the poem? Why not ocean or river or lake even?"

"A pond doesn't flow. It's still and self-contained," Emily Wolf said.

"Good. Very prone to becoming . . . what?"

"Stagnant," Miranda said.

"Yes," Megiddo answered, "and then at the end of the line we learn it is a winter day. Again, of all the four seasons he could've chosen, he places the poem in winter. Why winter? I know this is a more difficult question for you season-deprived Angelenos."

"Nature dies in winter," Miranda said.

"Yes, or goes dormant. You see how Hardy has packed that first line? Stood. Pond. Winter."

"*And the sun was white,*" Manny Shepherd quoted the next line.

"Good. What kind of color is white?"

"White's not a color, technically," said Miranda.

"That's an argument for another day," Megiddo said. "What's a good adjective, then, to describe white?"

"Bright?" Claude Moss offered.

"Does that fit the tone and the theme of the poem?" Megiddo asked.

"No," Claude said.

"Neutral?" I said almost as if Megiddo was handing us the answer (which he was also good at).

"Yes. The most intense ball of energy in our vicinity, the source of our ability to be here at all, has gone white, neutral."

"It has lost its fire," Miranda said.

"And of all the trees growing in England, Hardy chooses to use the ash tree. Why ash?" Megiddo went on.

"What's left after the fire has burned out," Jim Lord said.

"Yes, ash is the residue of fire. Right."

The smile on your mouth was the deadest thing
Alive enough to have strength to die

There it was.

That was the couplet that latched on.

I thought they were the most perfect lines of poetry I'd ever read.

I knew that exhaustion.

It happens every time eventually.

"Imagine if the only energy you had left was the energy to die," Mr. Megiddo said. "Her smile is the state of their relationship. And the *ominous bird a-wing* in line 12. Hardy doesn't have to tell us outright what kind of bird it is, does he? What is it?"

"A crow," said Manny.

"Close. But more ominous than a crow even."

"A raven?" Jim Lord tried.

"Also close. There's a better one," Megiddo prodded.

"A vulture," I said.

"Yes. Exactly. Why?"

"They come around when something's dead."

"Dead? Or?"

"Dying," I said.

"Yes. If you're walking parched in the desert like some movie cliché and you look up and see vultures circling? They know something you don't know," Megiddo said and the class laughed. "Remember, this is just before the break-up. This is that unbearable sense of not feeling it anymore yet still going through the motions. Moribund love."

Some of us knew what Megiddo was talking about, some didn't.

Moribund Love would be a great title for something also.

"Then that last stanza," Megiddo said, "Pulling us into the present. *Keen lessons that love deceives.* How does love deceive? What's the big lie love tells us?"

"That the other person loves you back," said Miranda Savitch.

"Well, suppose the other person does love you back. What's the bigger lie love tells us?"

"That it lasts forever," Emily Wolf knew.

"Right," Mr. Megiddo pointed at Emily "When you're first in love there is no question that the passion is eternal."

"And then it isn't," said Emily.

"Yes," said Megiddo. "We are always betrayed in the end."

"That's depressing," said Sharon Rose, lifting her head from her notebook (in which she'd been doodling 3-D boxes all period).

"We are always betrayed in the end," Megiddo went on, "betrayed not by our beloved but by love itself."

"Wow, he gets right to it," Emily Wolf whispered to me.

"Oh yeah," I nodded, "He changes my life daily. This room is currently my favorite place in the world to be. Other than the Tar Pits."

"I love the Tar Pits," said Emily.

"The center of Los Angeles for me," I said, "Ground Zero."

"Maybe we've seen each other there."

"May be," I shrugged, knowing I'd never seen her before.

Her eyes were on the yellow side of brown.

Dang, dude.

She hooked me instantly.

The crush was immediate and massive.

Emily Wolf was Martian smart.

Emily Wolf was into Mahler, Proust, and Spinoza.

Emily Wolf was someone I could talk the shit out of.

Emily Wolf had the type of face I'd describe as shiksajew.

You knew one of her parents was a Yid but definitely not both.

She had big white *goyishe* teeth.

Emily Wolf had the kind of intensity that would probably become unbearable after a while.

The desire to kiss her very hard on the mouth rendered that eventuality irrelevant however.

Another of the lies love loves to tells us.

I had a free Period 4 which I spent in the Library most days.

The librarian Mrs. Tisk knew me by my first name because I was always in there checking out books.

In Mrs. Tisk's lexicon you were either a 'turkey-butt' or a 'jack-ass' if you misbehaved in her library.

"Don't be a turkey-butt," she'd snipe at some kid who'd been ignoring her warnings about quieting down, "Now tshh."

The 'tshh' sound was her way of shushing us. Sometimes 'tshh-tshh' if we were being particularly disruptive.

I was looking through this huge compendium of American universities which ranked the schools in a variety of categories.

"Don't you think there should be a category for Available Pussy? That would be incredibly helpful," said Jim Lord, sitting across the table from me.

I laughed and said hey and Jim was laughing too as we gave each other five to say right on.

"Gentlemen," Mrs. Tisk clucked from her desk, "A tshh to the wise should be sufficient."

"Sorry," Jim said not quite loud enough for her to hear, "I meant Available Vagina."

"Mind your tongue," I said.

We giggled some more.

"Lance, I mean it," Mrs. Tisk got personal.

I nodded my head in understanding.

"You have a free Period 4 too?" Jim asked.

"Yeah," I said. "Thought I'd look at college stuff even though I don't have much choice. Where are you applying?"

"Just UCLA and USC," he said, "I have to stay in town."

"Me too. I'm going to live at home, so it'll either be UCLA or Cal State Northridge for me."

"What about USC?"

"My mom's a Bruin. I can't."

"Ah."

"Yeah. We couldn't afford it anyway. I'm sure I'll be going to Northridge though so it doesn't really matter."

"What makes you say that?"

"Mr. Wood told me my grades in math and science would lower my GPA too much to get into UCLA."

"Fuck him."

"Nah, he's right. I mean, I'll apply to UCLA. But I'll be going to Northridge."

Jim Lord was also in my Period 5 Government class with Mr. Bassett.

Buzzy Lagniappe was in that class and he managed to finagle a seat next to Heaven Sender, his years-long obsession.

Buzzy was trying to hang in with us but it was a struggle.

Sometimes he was grounded in the consensual and other times he was busy talking to Flippy Killbones about the house next door. Occasionally he'd switch over right in the middle of class.

This one time . . .

"You're not real, go away," Buzzy said.

"Buzzy?" asked Mr. Bassett.

"Yeah."

"Who's not real?"

"Flippy Killbones."

"Who's that?"

"The fat kid from *Willy Wonka & The Chocolate Factory.*"

"Augustus Gloop is the fat kid from *Willy Wonka & The Chocolate Factory.*"

"Oh, then a spider, a spider."

"A spider."

"Yes. He lives in my head. But he's not real. I was just reminding him of that fact."

"The fact that he's not real."

"Yes."

"I see," said Bassett, not knowing what to make of Buzzy's lucid madness.

"He forgets sometimes," Buzzy added.

"That he's not real."

"Yes."

"Very good," said Bassett, grasping, "now who can tell me about gerrymandering and franking privilege? Or better yet, what is a Writ of Certiori?"

Sasha Sherlock was still making up fake *Twilight Zone* episodes and talking about them as if they were real.

It took the least goading.

You just had to set him up.

"Sasha, you remember that *Twilight Zone* episode where this Martian lands in a backyard and there's this naked woman sunbathing?" Jim Lord asked.

"Martians Have Needs Too? Yeah, I love that one," and Sasha took it from there.

"You're talking about the one that starts out with the woman in her bedroom changing out of her clothes and wrapping herself in a towel while listening to a news report about an unexplained disturbance in the sky. She goes outside into the backyard and unwraps herself so she can lie naked on the towel. Once she's on her stomach sunning her backside you see the shadow of the Martian enter the picture which makes her turn around and look at him and she goes, 'Are you the new pool man?' and the Martian makes these screechy clicking sounds and the naked lady goes, 'God fucking damn it, I told them I needed someone who spic-a da English.' And then she goes back to sunning herself. As the Martian's shadow gets bigger and closer, the Twilight Zone music comes up, and Rod Serling's voice comes on, 'Meet Carol Partridge, a lady of leisure, who came out to enjoy

44

the noonday sun, only to be taken on an orgasmic ride to the Twilight Zone . . .'"

"What happens when they come back from commercial?" Jim asked.

"Then it's just all anal probing and full-on Martian gangbang. The Martians all come on her at the same time, and, dude, their cum is green."

"*Twilight Zone* was in black and white," Jim Lord said.

"Yeah but you can tell it's green."

"Green eggs and cum," said Buzzy Lagniappe who I thought wasn't listening.

"I do not like it, Sam-I-am," I said.

"Sam the ice cream man," said Manny Shepherd.

"Oh, man," I said, "I wonder what happened to that guy."

"Dinosaur Times," Manny reminisced.

"The shit," I said.

"Anyway, that's the episode you're talking about, right?" Sasha said.

"Yes," Jim Lord said, "You have a good memory."

"When it comes to *The Twilight Zone*, hell yeah. It's my Bible," Sasha boasted.

Period 6 was Play Production, my 2nd class of the day with Ms. Van Poole because I also had her for Stagecraft Period 3.

Moe Roth had taken over for Dolly as stage manager.

Moe was an unusual Jew in that he actually knew how to operate machinery and fix things.

Lorelei Lux was keeping pretty constant company with this goodlooking goyboy named Tom Studdard who was in charge of building the sets.

Tom Studdard wielded tools like Thor.

Tom Studdard held spare nails in his mouth while hammering.

In 7th Grade wood shop, while the rest of us were making boxes and hat racks, Tom Studdard made a fucking breakfast room table and 4 chairs.

Tom Studdard had like no ass whatsoever.

Tom Studdard went on camping and fishing trips to the lake with his nana and papaw.

Tom Studdard's parents still had a picture of Pat and Dick Nixon hanging in their den over the wet bar.

Tom Studdard competed in the All American Soap Box Derby in Akron, Ohio when he was a kid.

Tom Studdard could've played Ben on *The Waltons*.

He seemed an unlikely fit with the anomalous whatness of Lorelei Lux.

Had he tried to get his hand in her pants yet?

Had he smashed flat against the iron curtain?

It'd only been a month since Lorelei and I'd broken up.

Maybe he'd as yet been spared the barrier.

Or maybe he'd conquered it.

I couldn't tell.

One cool new edition to the thespian crew was Xeno Cortez, who had switched into Drama after spending the previous 2 years playing several different instruments in both Jazz Band and Orchestra and singing in the choir.

"Hello, Munchkins," was his generic greeting, always, upon entering a room wearing his signature leopard-skin fez.

To Xeno Cortez, following the yellow brick road was a pilgrimage, a mission, a sacred vocation.

"That's all I'm doing all day long," he said really stoned at a party once, "following the fucking yellow brick road, baby. At the end of that road is the source wisdom of all the world's spiritual paths. The ultimate truth. The one essence. The man behind the curtain. Cosmic reality. The place we've been all along."

Diana Hitchcock was back in school and returning to Drama, so that was also a sort of new addition but not really because she'd been in Play Production before only not when I was also in it so it was new for me.

We were all anxious to hear which play and which musical we'd be doing.

"I haven't decided yet," Ms. Van Poole said, "I kind of want to get to know your talents, a sense of what you're made of. Find out what we've got to work with. Then pick material that will make the best use of your strengths. That's all I know at this point in space."

4

Yet more equipment glitches led to another long pause between songs and a hush fell upon the Shrine as the Grateful Dead road crew fiddled with the gear.

Manny was davening like a Chasid in a rhythm and a tempo that precisely anticipated the groove of the next Dead tune, one of the few I knew because guys would play it on the guitar at parties sometimes.

Set out runnin' but I take my time,
A friend of the devil is a friend of mine,
If I get home before daylight,

I looked over at Gina who was still standing and her ass beneath that miniskirt was terribly tantalizing to my lysergic lupine gaze despite her lack of all interest in dick, my own specifically.

I could tell she was enthralled by the music, just totally into it.

Manny tapped me on the shoulder.

"Dude, have you been seeing the kids playing in the village?"

"Huh?"

"The kids playing hide-and-go-seek in the village."

"Uh, no," I said, my eyes trying to keep track of Gina's ass and my mind torn between the music and Manny's hyperreal hallucination, apparently so visceral he presumed I had to have been seeing it too.

"One of those kids playing hide-and-go-seek was Jesus, dude."

"You saw Jesus as a little kid."

"Yes."

"Playing hide-and-go-seek."

"Yes."

"That's a great image, dude," I started laughing.

"Jesus playing hide-and-go-seek," Manny started laughing too, "on an elementary school playground."

"Red Rover Red Rover, let Jesus come over," I barely sputtered out and Manny cackled like a madman.

"Oh shit," he wheezed, "Dude, imagine being friends with a kid in elementary school who grew up to be the Messiah."

"Yeah, what if you didn't get along with Jesus when you were kids? Like saying 'Jesus, you suck!' when he lost at tetherball or something."

"You know he'd remember that shit," Manny said.

"Yeah-and like after he became the Messiah he'd come up to you and say, 'Who sucks at tetherball now, bitch?'"

"Totally, like, 'I'm gonna play tetherball with your everlasting soul, asswipe, and then zap you with lightning or send you down into the fire of eternal damnation on the banks of H-E-Double-Hockey-Styx, as in S-T-Y-X. Dig?'"

"*I'm sailing away*," I sang in my highest tenor and it sounded really weird against the Dead playing "Friend of the Devil." "I feel like we've talked about this before," I said.

"Same with me," Manny concurred.

We paused in a joint effort to retrieve the specific memory.

"Like Jesus as a little kid playing around with all his Caucasian friends," I said, "Something like that, right?"

"Yeah yeah," Manny said, "or at the very least we both dreamed it."

Manny had broken into this wide yawn.

"Yawning is gagging," he said.

"What?"

"Yawning is just really a form of gagging."

"Not really."

"Just like a really mild form. Totally. Yawning is gagging, dude," Manny insisted.

"I love you, Jerry!" yelled the girl who'd yelled earlier.

"Jerry heard me," she bragged to her show pals.

"You can tell the boys are having fun up there," one of her friends said, when in fact they were clearly having a terrible time with the equipment glitches and looked vaguely pissed off.

"Totally," the girl agreed, and in a rubbery time shift that felt interdimensional I became aware of Mr. Megiddo distributing copies of the play *Waiting For Godot* early one Monday morning when the sun was shining through the classroom window directly on my face.

It was just a couple of weeks into the semester. So like end of September.

"Normally I'd do this later in the year," Megiddo said as he passed out the books, "but there's going to be a live production of *Godot* here in Los Angeles and I'm trying get us group tickets to go see it and I want us to have read it first."

We read the play out loud in class, with Megiddo playing Vladimir, Claude Moss as the perfect Estragon, Miranda Savitch as Pozzo, and, in an inspired bit of casting, Buzzy Lagniappe doing Lucky's monologue. Gina Dichlich was the Boy.

"That line where Pozzo says, *They give birth astride of a grave, the light gleams an instant, then it's night once more* . . . What does he mean by that?" Megiddo asked us.

"As soon as you're born you've got one foot in the grave," said Manny.

"Elaborate on that."

"Each moment you're alive brings you one step closer to death."

"Correct. And true. What about the rest of it? *The light gleams an instant, then it's night once more* . . ."

"Temporariness," said Miranda.

"Yes. Impermanence. Life is this brief light that shines in that one stride from birth to death. Poof. And then Vladimir reiterates later, *Astride of a grave and a difficult birth. Down in the hole, lingeringly, the gravedigger puts on the forceps.*"

The sad fact of time moving irreversibly forward, I thought to myself.

Godot was another skull-splitting nexus for me, another lightning strike between the ears.

One could render the reality of existence in language and in the process highlight all its humorous truth. It was possible.

I copied quotes into my notebook and stared at them.

There's no lack of void.

We are all born mad. Some remain so.

We have time to grow old. The air is full of our cries. But habit is a great deadener.

The essential doesn't change.

All Mankind is us whether we like it or not.

That's how it is on this bitch of an earth.

We all attended a Thursday night performance of *Waiting For Godot* up on Santa Monica Blvd.

Donald Moffat and Dana Elcar were Estragon and Vladimir.

Pozzo was played by Ralph Waite.

"Daddy Walton!" somebody said out loud upon his first entrance while the rest of us thought the same thing independently.

The set was just a tree and a stone and small dunes of real sand.

I sat next to Emily Wolf because that's how she made it work out.

"When my dad goes out of town I throw these dinner parties," she said while we were waiting for the play to start, "You should come to one."

"Like a literary salon type situation?"

"Uhh, sort of?" she half-asked.

"Like Gertrude Stein's apartment."

"More like Ancient Rome," Emily said.

"You mean a toga party?" I went the dork route.

"Haha. Not exactly," she said, "You'll come to one and see for yourself someday. I can't really explain it."

As I was leaving with Gina Dichlich (who'd given me a ride), Emily asked, "You want to go see a movie sometime?"

"Yeah, sure, that'd be cool," I said.

"*Julia*? Next Friday night?" she got right to it.

"Like a week from Friday."

"Yeah, I'm not around this weekend."

"Uhh, yeah, OK," I said, a moment too late to take it back.

And bang, dude, just like that I had a date with Emily Wolf.

All that week I read up on Spinoza in the school library because I knew she was into him.

While I was trying to make sense of Spinoza's *Ethics*, which was cool in some respects but in other ways it was like reading geometry proofs, Jim Lord joined me at the table.

"What're you reading?"

"Spinoza."

"Getting heady?"

"I plan to be, yeah," I smirked and I think also blushed.

"With whom?" he looked puzzled.

"Emily Wolf herself."

"No shit?"

"Yeah, man. She asked me out."

"You're in, dude."

"We'll see," I shrugged.

"You are in, dude. *She* asked *you*."

"I guess."

"You understand Spinoza?" he took *Ethics* from me and looked at a page.

"Not really," I said, "but I just need the gist of it to moisten the maiden. Emily's really into him."

"Right on," said Jim and he gave me five.

"I read the entry on him in the *Jewish Encyclopedia* and got the basic ideas. I was just reading *Ethics* to find some primary text to throw around."

"Chicks dig primary text, dude. Quote the shit of her."

"Zackly," I took the book back, "I need a hook, a way in."

"Pick a sentence."

"*In other words, God is a thinking thing,*" I read.

"That's perfect. She'll swoon. Say those words out loud while you're licking her cunt."

"Tssh-tssh," warned Mrs. Tisk, "Don't be turkey-butts."

"Sorry," Jim said, and then quietly to me, "Say those words out loud while you're licking her vagina."

"Did you dig *Godot*?" I asked.

"Oh yeah, man. Tremendous. Reading it *and* seeing the production. It's

53

amazing how hilarious it is. I felt weird laughing because the vision is so bleak."

"Is it bleak, really? I don't know."

"It's like a . . . how do I describe it? . . . We just sit and wait for something to happen and it never does. And that's all life is. Waiting for a thing that never happens. That's not bleak?"

"I think it's pretty inspiring," I said as someone whose ongoing central life-motif is waiting for things that never happen, "I wrote a parody the other night."

"A parody of *Godot*?"

"Yeah."

"That's a weird idea."

"I don't think so. It came to me pretty quickly."

"How do you satirize the absurd?"

"By turning it in on itself."

"I don't get that."

"I don't either, really. But here, take a gander," I pulled the wrinkled script from my backpack, "I'm thinking it'd be fun to perform at the Fall Drama Festival at Birmingham, in the Original Works category."

"Yeah, let me check it out. It'd be cool not to do just some predictable Tennessee Williams monologue or something," Jim said.

"Here," I said. "Give it a read."

"Like right now?"

"Yeah. It's short. I'm just going to sit here and stare at Heaven Sender's ass which is situated directly in front of me right now while she's looking something up in the card catalogue."

"Hey, that's Buzzy's crush."

"Buzzy's obsession with Heaven Sender does in no way prohibit my staring at her ass."

"Indeed. You're right," Jim said and turned his attention to the play.

It Can't Possibly . . .

(Curtain. Dark Stage. The lights dim up.

Stage left, a man [Mortimer] covered by a white sheet.

Another man [Livingston] enters stage right, walking backwards as if eluding pursuit. He looks toward the audience and falls in surprise.

Livingston stands back up and sees the white sheet, walks over and cautiously removes the sheet.

Revealed is Mortimer, standing on his head, eyes closed, apparently sleeping.

Livingston begins to walk away.)

Mort.: (opening his eyes) You have some nerve. (Liv. is startled. He halts and turns slowly). I was trying to sleep.

Liv.: I'm sorry

Mort.: No matter. (gets to his feet) It's time to let the blood circulate anyway.

Liv.: You sleep like that?

Mort.: More often than not, yes.

Liv.: You don't have a bed?

Mort.: More often that not, no.

(Pause)

Liv.: I don't suppose you could tell me where I am? (Pause). I've never been here before.

Mort.: How can you be sure?

Liv.: I simply don't remember this place.

Mort.: There are plenty of people who wake up in the same place every morning and have that exact same problem. Don't jump to conclusions.

Liv.: I'm not.

Mort.: You are.

Liv.: What?

Mort.: It's all in how you look at things.

(Pause)

Liv.: I'm scared.

Mort.: You shouldn't be.

Liv.: It's my God-given right, and I'm scared. (Mort. chuckles). I don't find it funny. (Mort. continues to chuckle). They were always getting laughs at my expense.

Mort.: (stops laughing) I'm sorry. I have to apologize. It's just that it's so rare, and . . . well, here, why don't we sit down and you can relate the horrors of your obviously hopeless situation.

Liv.: If I knew I would tell you.

Mort.: Here's a question: How did you die?

Liv.: I'm not dead.

Mort.: Pardon me. I presumed. (Pause). I am.

Liv.: Dead?

Mort.: Yes.

Liv.: How did you die?

Mort.: I suffocated

Liv.: Why?

Mort.: Because there was no air.

(Pause)

Liv.: I guess there's no way out.

Mort.: That was true once.

Liv.: Once? Don't you mean always and still?

Mort.: When it meant something I was happy.

Liv.: Now?

Mort.: I cry daily.

Liv.: For what?

Mort.: For whom.

Liv.: Sorry. For whom?

Mort.: My mother.

Liv.: Your mother? Why your mother?

Mort.: She's all alone.

Liv.: So? Isn't everybody?

Mort.: She's alone. I cry for her.

Liv.: Aren't you alone also?

Mort.: Not at the moment.

Liv.: But generally, usually.

Mort.: Yes.

Liv.: And you don't cry for yourself?

Mort.: No.

Liv.: Why not?

Mort.: I'm dead.

Liv.: And?

Mort: Dead people don't need to be cried for.

Liv.: But you cry for your mother!

Mort.: She's alive.

Liv.: Oh. (Pause). You're not lonely?

Mort.: Of course I'm lonely.

Liv.: What do you do?

Mort.: Do?

Liv.: For fun.

Mort.: Fun?

Liv.: For laughs.

Mort.: Laughs?

Liv.: Yes.

Mort.: What do I do for laughs?

Liv.: Yes.

Mort.: I laugh.

Liv.: How often?

Mort.: Sometimes.

Liv.: Tell the truth.

Mort.: I am.

Liv.: Sometimes?

Mort.: Once in a while.

Liv.: Rarely?

Mort.: Once in a while.

Liv.: Every six months?

Mort.: Once in a while!

Liv.: Be specific!

Mort.: I never laugh.

(Pause)

Liv.: Do you remember the pain?

Mort.: I haven't got time for it.

Liv.: But you ARE dead?

Mort.: Yes. Most definitely.

Liv.: So what did it feel like?

Mort.: You don't want to know.

Liv.: I do.

Mort.: Believe me, it will make you miserable.

Liv.: It can't possibly make me more miserable than I am now.

Mort.: Don't be too sure.

(Pause)

Liv.: (sobbing) It was unfair.

Mort.: You're crying.

Liv.: Yes.

Mort.: For your mother?

Liv.: No.

Mort.: For yourself?

Liv.: No.

Mort.: For who then?

Liv.: For whom.

Mort: Yes.

Liv.: Forget it. You don't want to know.

Mort.: I do.

Liv.: It will make you miserable.

Mort.: It can't possibly make me more miserable than I am now.

Liv.: Don't be too sure.

Mort.: I get the feeling we've been this route.

Liv.: Yes, but the roles are reversed.

Mort.: Not really.

Liv.: What do you mean? Of course they are.

Mort.: No. There are no roles to reverse. We're the same person.

Liv.: That's impossible.

Mort.: Not entirely.

Liv.: How so?

Mort.: It's unimportant.

Liv.: Please?

Mort.: It's irrelevant.

Liv.: So is everything else. Since when does relevance matter? Please, I beg of you. Tell me.

Mort.: I refuse.

Liv.: Grant me this one wish.

Mort.: No.

Liv.: What's it worth to you?

Mort.: Money is of no concern to me.

Liv.: Everybody has a price.

Mort.: It does no good here.

Liv.: But still I—

Mort.: —so why did you bring it up?

Liv.: I really don't know. It was something to talk about I guess.

(Pause)

Mort.: You did. I could tell.

Liv.: I did what?

Mort.: Really want to know.

Liv.: About what?

Mort.: *You don't remember?*

Liv.: *No.*

Mort.: *You were just on your knees begging me for the secret of life.*

Liv.: *Was I?*

Mort.: *Yes you were.*

Liv.: *And did you tell me? (Mort. begins laughing). Why are you laughing?*

Mort.: *I just realized.*

Liv.: *What?*

Mort.: *The irony.*

Liv.: *Huh?*

Mort.: *The futility.*

Liv.: *I don't get it.*

Mort.: *It's absurd!*

Liv.: *What is?*

Mort.: *You were asking me, a dead man, for the secret of life!*

Liv.: *I don't find it funny.*

Mort.: *Asking a dead man for the secret of life doesn't strike you as funny?*

Liv.: *No. Who else would know?*

Mort.: *(ceases laughing) True.*

Liv.: *I thought you said you never laugh.*

Mort.: *I never did. Until now.*

Liv.: *Did you ever tell me the secret of life?*

Mort.: No.

Liv.: Why not?

Mort.: I'm not allowed.

Liv.: Who prevents you?

Mort.: Nobody prevents me.

Liv.: Somebody must or you would tell me.

Mort.: Not necessarily.

Liv.: Your master, this person who has control: What's his name?

Mort.: He isn't my master.

Liv.: Then there IS somebody!

Mort.: Isn't there always?

Liv.: What is he?

Mort.: Whatever you want him to be.

Liv.: God?

Mort.: If you like.

Liv.: What is he to you?

Mort.: The boy before the man came.

Liv.: What does he look like?

Mort.: The fat kid from Willy Wonka & The Chocolate Factory. What's his name? Buzzy?—

Liv.: Augustus--

Mort.: —Lagniappe?

Liv.: --Gloop. Augustus Gloop.

Mort.: I thought it was Buzzy Lagniappe.

Liv.: Augustus Gloop is the fat kid from Willy Wonka & The Chocolate Factory.

Mort.: Then who in Hades is Buzzy Lagniappe?

Liv.: Well actually I lived next door to a guy named Buzzy Lagniappe and his real name is Augustus and he used to be fat.

Mort.: Well, maybe it's the same guy. Like us.

(Pause)

Liv.: What does it feel like to die?

Mort.: I already told you: You don't want to know.

Liv.: I do.

Mort.: Believe me it will make you miserable.

Liv.: It can't possibly make me more miserable than I am now.

Mort.: It feels like you're hiding, trying to elude capture.

Liv.: I wish I had a way to kill myself.

Mort.: Suicide is redundant.

Liv.: I suppose you're right.

Mort.: You are always already dead.

Liv.: That's reassuring.

Mort.: There is a way out.

Liv.: But, let me guess: I don't want to know because it'll make me miserable.

Mort.: It can't possibly make you more miserable than you are now, so here's how it's done: Click your heels together three times—

Liv.: —Uhh, I'm not wearing ruby slippers, Mr. Wizard, sir.

Mort.: Hmm, well then that won't work.

Liv: I've been taught to pay no attention to the man behind the curtain.

(Pause)

Mort: You could always try getting up and leaving.

Liv.: You think that'll work?

Mort.: And if it doesn't?

Liv.: True. Why not try it.

(Liv. stands up, looks back briefly at Mort., shrugs, and exits stage left. Mort rises, picks up the white sheet and wraps it around himself)

Mort.: Now I stand me up to sleep. I give the Lord my soul to keep. And if I wake before I die . . .

(Mort. covers himself. Pause. Liv. enters stage right walking backwards as if eluding capture. He turns, sees the audience, looks at Mort. under the sheet, gazes back at audience)

Dim lights.

Curtain.

"I will absolutely be in this with you. Far out shit," Jim Lord looked up from the script. I love that you got Buzzy Lagniappe's name into it. That is excellent. Hilarious."

"We should probably cut that part though for the festival."

"Yeah. Too inside. Let's tell Van Poole and start rehearsing."

"She'll want to read it first of course."

"Van Poole will dig the shit out of it. See you in 6th," Jim left for the quad when the lunch bell rang.

I went to hang out in Madame Couchée's room and started telling her about seeing *Godot* and about doing my Beckett parody for the drama festival.

"*Formidable*," she said, "You will let me read it sometime *j'espère*."

"For sure, I said. I need it right now but definitely eventually."

"Lovely," she said. "What are you reading with Mr. Megiddo right now?"

"We're about to start *Madame Bovary*," I said.

"*Ah, oui. Le meilleur. Absolument extraordinaire.* You will love it. You especially."

I looked at her in question.

"You'll see what I mean," she smiled.

Later, when Friday night arrived, I sat on the front porch waiting for Emily to pick me up for our date.

I had boned up enough on Spinoza to maybe get my bone up in Emily Wolf, though I supposed the first date would merely lay the groundwork for later.

We went to see *Julia* in Westwood.

She wore her hair down, a departure from her usual tight ponytail or bun.

"So who are your ex-girlfriends?" she got right to it, as per usual, while we were driving, "Catch me up on all the Lance gossip. I'm at a social disadvantage without it. I have to suss out the competition."

"Haha."

"No I'm serious. You seem like someone who has lots of ex-girlfriends."

"Thank you so much."

"Tell me."

"Uhhm, OK. Uh, do you know Claire Farnaway?"

"Yeah, she's in my calculus class."

"So her for a while."

"Ah."

"And Lorelei Lux."

"From French? She's in my calc class too actually now that I think of it," Emily paused, "Really? Lorelei?"

"Yeah."

"Hm. Interesting. Anybody else?"

"This girl named Candy Stoner who goes to Beverly now. We frenched for about 3 weeks in 8th Grade."

"3 weeks straight?"

"Haha."

"Who else?"

"Nyeah, outside of school maybe a few dalliances."

"A few meaning a lot."

"No not at all. Just like a couple. Maybe 3 people. Or 4. Wait . . ." I counted.

"What about Miranda Savitch?"

"Nyeah, I don't know if that qualifies."

"It's so bloody obvious something has gone on between you two. I'm hypersensitive to electro-magnetism. I pick up on that stuff."

"I don't know. It was more like this thing that never happened."

"You guys never?"

"Even kissed, no. Not for real, anyway. Our lips touched in a kissing game once."

The stiffness of our interactions didn't distract from my sexual desire for Emily Wolf.

Was she picking up on that magnetism?

I was in the vulnerable position of revealing my romantic history, a position she'd put me in, and I was trying to figure out why she'd done that. I had no interest in hers.

Although I knew on that first date there was something essential missing that would preclude our ever being much of a match, I was just bothered enough by the lack of girlness in my intimate sphere to seek contact with the enigmatic complexity and sexy intellect of Emily Wolf.

After the film we went to Stan's Donuts and ate our bounty while walking around the Village.

"Homo Erectus," Emily said unprompted.

"What'd you call me?"

"You heard me," she said as a smidgen of custard from her eclair dripped down her chin. I dabbed it away with my napkin.

"Have I done something cavemannish?" I asked.

"Nope," she said, "Just a thought that crossed my mind. I don't know why I love that term."

"Homo Erectus."

"Mmmyeah," she chewed. "Can I taste your apple fritter?" she asked as she pinched off a piece.

"Why sure," I said after she'd already started chewing it, "Go ahead."

She gave me a thumbs up.

"That's yum," she swallowed.

I pushed her up against the wall outside Yesterdays and tried to kiss her on the mouth.

She kept me at elbow's length, both elbows actually, and I relented immediately sensing how much she meant it.

"Sorry," I said.

"Maybe I should get you home," she answered, "I got up really early this morning to finish reading for the outside novel essay in Megiddo's."

"What did you do it on?" I tried to skid past the awkward kissing attempt.

"*Les Liaisons Dangereuses*," she said as we started walking to her car.

"Good?"

"I loved it. Just the right amount of naughty."

"I should check it out then."

"You should. I usually read philosophy, but I love fiction too when it's good like that."

"You're into Spinoza, right?"

"Yes. Very much. I don't know, I just get his non-dualistic vision. I kind of feel that way about the cosmos. Like it's all one substance, one consciousness, or whatever."

"Like we're living in a giant brain or something," I tried to keep up. She was way too smart for me. I couldn't crack Spinoza at all.

"No, we *are* the cosmic brain. We're not living in it, we *are* it."

She sounded a little like Manny.

"Yeah, that reminds me of that line in *Ethics*," I boasted, ready to spring the one Spinoza quote I'd memorized on her, "I was reading it in the library the other day—"

"—You read Spinoza?"

"Yeah, of course . . . but the line was something like *In other words, God is a thinking thing*. Something like that?"

"Yes," she touched my arm and smiled and you could tell she thought it was cool I read Spinoza even though she didn't want to kiss me.

Chicks dig primary text, man. Quote the shit out of her . . .

"Aren't you just loving *Bovary*?" I asked.

"Oh yes it is amazing. I love the *book*, but I'm working very hard to like Emma, I find."

"For sure," I said. "She cheats on her husband shamelessly. . . "

"Actually I don't give a shit about that," Emily said, "She can do whatever, or whomever, she wants. What bugs me is how she makes other people responsible for her happiness. She doesn't realize happiness originates within."

That's the kind of talk that made me fall in love with Emily Wolf even though I knew all along we had no future together.

"Aren't most people guilty of that, though?"

"Exactly, that's what I'm saying. Emma is all of us. That's what makes it so painful. She's everything we hate about ourselves. Like that Oscar Wilde quote Megiddo is always using about how nothing bugs us more than—"

"—our own sins writ large in others," I finished.

"That one, yeah."

We shared a bashful smile.

"I just realized my name is like the adverbial form of Emma," Emily said.

"To do things Emily is to do things in an Emma-like way. Emma-ly"

70

"Emma as in Emma Bovary."

"I mostly relate to Justin."

"You would."

"I think Justin grows up to be a priest."

"No, a monk."

"Yes. Even better. That's it."

On the way home we talked a little about *Julia*.

"That's such a betrayal at the end of that movie," Emily said, "The way Julia's family doesn't want anything to do with her daughter and wants to just sort of remove Julia from the family history."

"Nyeah, it's weird to think how quickly and easily the memory of your existence can be erased. It just takes one generation for it to pass away completely."

"Unless you've created something permanent, a work of art, some great action on the world stage, an idea that takes hold, something that will be remembered after the people who knew you personally are gone."

"Totally," I said, "Cheating death."

"I think culture comes from primitive man's need to archive memories. It was a necessity in the wild with our weak bodies. We had to remember what happened before in order to move forward and know what to be on the lookout for. The only way to be ready is to to have prior knowledge."

"So art is the result of a survival instinct."

"Yes. Or, well, it evolved into a much more complex response to the reality of existence, obviously. I mean, you read Spinoza."

"Totally," I said because it was the only way to hide my lostness. I hoped she wasn't going to bring up Spinoza anymore because I was out of ammo.

She pulled up in front of my house, and I leaned in to kiss her on the mouth but she turned and gave me cheek.

"You know what I'd like?" she asked.

"What," I said, keeping my face close to hers.

"I'd like to do this again," she said and kissed me back on the cheek.

"Cool," I said and got out of the car.

"Call me later?" she asked through the window.

Dang, dude.

"Probably not. I have some stuff to do," I shuffled and shook my head.

"Well, go get your work done, young man," she said. I couldn't tell whether she was annoyed or not due to that subtle sarcasm girls use to let you know you've made the wrong decision (I provoke it often), "See you in Megiddo's on Monday."

I waved as she drove off.

My dad was sitting on the front porch having a smoke.

"What's this one called?" he asked.

"Emily."

"You are racking up quite a collection there, son," he said in his Andy Griffith voice.

I shrugged, "Nyeah, I love girls. They are a pain in the ass but they keep hooking me with their eyes and their minds and their mouths and I can't decide which one I want because I want all of them."

"At once?"

"One at a time," I said, "in chronological order."

I didn't know what I meant by that and my dad didn't laugh. He wasn't much into riffing. Manny and I would've run with the chronological order thing and the inevitable double-entendre puns that would follow for at least

10 minutes until either becoming an idea for a sit-com or until one of us would say in devil voice, "*Your mother sucks cocks in hell.*"

"It's nice to have one special girl," my dad said.

"I guess."

"So you like Emily."

"Nyeah, I do, intensely, but I don't feel like she's really into it, or me, at least not in that way. She said she wanted to go out again just now so. I dunno, it's confusing. I also kind of have this thing for my friend Gina. But she's a lesbian."

"I know how that one goes."

I looked at my dad. I hadn't heard that saga.

"You fell in love with a gay woman?"

"I did. Once upon a time."

"So you know how much it sucks."

"You don't get to pick who you fall in love with," my dad said.

"I'd love to hear the story someday."

"Someday, perhaps," he watched his smoke ring dissipate.

And we just sort of dropped it and started talking about the Dodgers and the upcoming playoffs, blissfully ignorant of their impending trip to the World Series where they would lose to the Yankees.

Fucking Reggie Jackson.

Dang, dude.

The baseball gods are not Dodger fans.

It was Gina who first picked up on my brewing hotness for Emily.

"So. Emily Wolf. I see you talking to her a lot. Especially lately," she said one afternoon after school when we got pizza at Damiano's on Fairfax because she was starving.

"Nyeah," I said, "I guess."

"How's Dolly?"

"I haven't heard from her since she left. I ran into her dad in Farmers Market and he said she's doing great and that she said she was going to write to me but she hasn't."

"Hmm. That's weird. I thought you guys were 'best friends,'" Gina said with a twinge of bitterness.

"Does that bother you?"

"I don't know. It kind of bothers me a little that you're my best friend and I'm not your best friend.

I shrugged, "To all intents and purposes you are my best friend, G. Really. You're my favorite human to hang out with."

Gina smiled, satisfied, "So, Emily Wolf," she picked it back up.

"I dunno. Yeah. We talk. We hang. We went to see *Julia* together last Friday."

"I was there when she asked you."

"Oh yeah, huh."

"So, was it like a date, or what?"

"I don't really know."

"What do you mean you don't really know? Did you make out after? Or during?"

"No, not really."

"What does that mean, not really?"

"We didn't make out. She seems like she's not into it."

"With you? Or in general?"

"I dunno, she seems kind of like weird about it or something."

"Sure that's not just some Lorelei residue in your own head?"

"May be. I tried to kiss her but she held me at bay with her elbows. I don't really know, G."

"I like when you call me G. You're the only person who does that."

"G. is short for Gigi. Gigi Dichlich," I said.

"No."

"Gigi, am I a fool without a mind or have I simply been too blind to realize? Oh Gigi," I crooned to her across the table. I wanted to kiss her but she'd've been annoyed so I didn't.

"Great film," she said, "However, no."

"I can't call you Gigi?"

"You may not."

"Poo on you, Miss Deetchleetch, uh, Ditchlitch, uh, Dyke-like,"

"There ya go."

"Oh, man, girl, every year on the first day of school when you correct all the teachers mispronouncing your name . . . "

"What about it?"

"The way you say, 'It's DICK LICK.'"

"Yeah? That's how my name is pronounced."

"It's erotic. You are amazingly sexy, G."

"I like to be sexy. To girls."

"Does it freak you out when I tell you I think you're sexy?"

"Think about it this way. How would you feel if a guy friend of yours told you you were amazingly sexy?"

"I'd totally want to fuck him."

"Come on, Lance," she said and threw a pepperoni at me.

"I'd be uncomfortable," I said, eating the pepperoni she'd thrown.

"OK, uncomfortable."

"Yeah. Like decidedly disinclined, for sure."

"And there we have it. Feel that feeling, of a male friend hitting on you, and then you'll know what I'm feeling when you say stuff like that to me."

"Ah, so," I sighed wisely like Hashimoto-San, "I grok the fullness," though I would continue my admittedly futile come-ons to her. It would evolve into a humorous part of our shtick together eventually.

"Unless you are really a fag and just deeply in denial," she kicked the side of my leg, laughing, "and that's why you're uncomfortable with the thought of a male friend hitting on you? Hmm?"

"Nah I'm into pussy, dude. 100%."

"Me too," she said as we paused to exchange nods.

"I grok it even fuller," I said.

Another joint moment of total knowing with Gina Dichlich. That was basically our thing together.

"Do your parents know you're a lesbotarian?"

"Nyeah, they do. They're trying to be calm about it in that just a phase kind of way. My dad is more freaked out about it than my mom, I think. My mom just goes, 'But you're so girly!'"

"You are," I said.

"Shut up. And then I just go, 'Yeah 'cause that's how I like to dress and I'm into the kinds of girls who get off on the girly thing.'"

"My mission in life is to win you over to my side of the sexual divide," I said, "I will break you, Gigi Dyke-like.

"Suck my cock," Gina said.

"I love you."

"S'anyway Emily Wolf," Gina threw another pepperoni at me.

"We'll see what happens I guess."

"Are you going to go out with her again?"

"She said she wants to. So, if she asks, yeah."

"Oh, *she* has to ask *you*."

"Yeah. That's how it is. She's the one who asked me to go see *Julia* with her. So the dynamic is established."

"So there might be a second date."

"Seems like it," I said."

"You open to it being real?"

"It's not. I don't know. She confuses me."

"And there's the Dolly problem."

"This is true."

I got a letter from Dolly just a couple of days after I told Gina I hadn't heard from her yet.

Dear Lance,

I bet you thought I had forgotten you, but the opposite is actually true. I think about you every day and wish you were here to see this splendid city in all its autumn crispness.

Rouen is lovely and even bustling in its own way. You've seen the Cathedral, of course, because of the Monet paintings we looked at in Megiddo's class last year, but, jeez-o-man, mon dieu, it is even more majestic in person. Sometimes I find time to take a break from everything and sit in the Cathedral and I always think of that funny story you told me about ditching Confirmation class to go to mass across the street. I love the empty silence of the cathedral. How grand and vast and eternal it is. The reason I haven't been able to write you a letter until now is that I've been, as you can imagine, quite busy. Keeping up with classes is hard enough, but remember: all of my classes are taught IN FRENCH also! So, you see, I have been running twice as fast just to stay in one place as Alice herself might say. Luckily, the Çafille family are gracious hosts and really supportive. Anne-Marie, my "sister", is my age and super smart and we have most of our classes together, so she helps me with my homework, but it's also annoying because her boyfriend Donal is always over and distracting her. The dad, Louis, is an engineer, so he's a good resource for math help. Calculus in French! Merde, alors!

And I've also been, well . . . I've been preoccupied in other ways . . . OK, dude, I know I'm not supposed to include this subject in our correspondence, but you are my best friend and I have to bring you up to date. There is a boy here, Georges (but I call him Georgie), and I have become romantically involved with him and I might even be "in love" (whatever that means. Ugh.). I hope it's ok that I'm telling you this instead of keeping it a secret. I'd be holding back my happiness and I know you would not want me to do that. "Feel it all the way," you said to me once when we were hanging out at the Tar Pits and I'm taking your advice now. I promise to spare you the gory details, as per your request, but I thought it important that you should know about this latest development in my heart and in my life. Please feel free to share any of your multiple female obsessions of which I'm sure there are currently several going on simultaneously because there are always several going on simultaneously in your horny mind. We can gloat together like best chums do.

I miss you SO much, Lance, and I hate that I can't just pick up the phone and gab with you all night about everything like always. I hope that you'll write to me really really soon with all kinds of wonderful Lance-doings. What's the Fall play? How's the new drama teacher? Who are you thinking about these days (or nights)? Do tell!

Avec beaucoup d'amour toujours,

Dolly

I lay the letter down on my nightstand and thought about having sex with Emily in her car while parked in front of my house, like right where the girl got stabbed that time.

5

The next long pause between songs settled on the restless crowd at the Shrine.

"What the fuck are they doing?" Manny said in the lull.

"Figuring out what to play next," said this dude in front of us who'd turned around with a look of disdain just to tell us that.

The Deadheads were hooting and then laughing at the hooting and then hooting again and laughing again until finally the band rolled into its next number.

I have seen where the wolf has slept by the silver stream
I can tell by the mark he left you were in his dream
Ah, child of countless trees
Ah, child of boundless seas
What you are, what you're meant to be

"Do you want a Coke or something?" Gina asked us, "How are you guys feeling?"

"I've become part of the invisible spectrum, to the left of ultra-violet, to the right of infrared, the point at which they overlap and intersect and give birth to everything we see," said Manny, gesturing like a yogi, "A Coke would be good."

"Lance?"

"Nahm fine," I waved her off, "Just grooving on the holy whatnot," I said, trying to be profound like Manny.

Gina descended into the lobby to get herself and Manny a Coke.

Manny stood up and was making hand gestures in conjunction with the music.

"You know what I was thinking, dude?" Manny said as he danced. I stood up to hear him better.

"What, man?"

"Like the ancients, dude. Like the people who figured out the difference between planets and stars. How'd they come up with that shit? I look up in the sky and it all looks the same to me. How'd we figure anything out, dude? Not like tools and weapons but like molecules and atoms and elements and photosynthesis and symbiosis and medicine and the existence of microscopic life and the shape of the earth and its rotation and revolution and electro-magnetism and the size of the universe. I mean, dude, these are miracles. Not the things themselves, but the fact that we figured them out. Miracles. Human beings observing and realizing. Where does that come from?"

"It starts as a survival skill and evolves into a luxury and by-product of leisure time."

"You don't believe we're divinely inspired?"

"I'm of two minds," I said, as usual when this topic would arise, "On the one hand our ability to reason and remember makes perfect evolutionary sense, but on the other hand I know the Muses are real 'cause I'm visited by them. I think people of the future will look back on these times as caveman days. Just dark and barbaric. 'How could they live like that?' 'How could they believe those things?' will be their prevailing questions about us."

I was thinking about when I first read the parts of *Madame Bovary* that take place in Rouen, especially the scene in the cathedral, and how reading about

Rouen made me think of Dolly which made me sad and how even thinking about it months later at a Grateful Dead show still made me sad.

Would Dolly become a part of my past only? Was her life in Rouen the start of an irreversible path away from me?

Not long after I'd gotten the letter from Dolly, I wrote her back about school stuff mostly but also wished her well with her new beau.

Dahlia dahling,

It was so great to hear from you finally. I admit I had fears that you were forgetting me. Sigh. I can't imagine how difficult it must be to be taking all your classes in French. Flagrant, dude. Anne-Marie Çafille seems cool. Now you'll get a taste of what it's like to have a sister. Remember: I have two. So I know that situation intimately.

Senior year is pretty fine so far. Megiddo's class is amazing. We read Waiting For Godot and then went to see a live production of it up in Hollywood. We're currently reading Madame Bovary, some of which takes place in Rouen, so I have been thinking about you a lot, young lady.

The new drama teacher is Ms. Van Poole. Her first name is Francesca. She's really into Commedia Dell'Arte, so the fall play is Scapino, the Moliere parody. Remember we saw it in 9th Grade, the whole class went, at the Huntington Hartford? Anyway, that's what we're doing and . . . ready? . . . I am playing Scapino. Yes, dear, I got the fucking lead. What on earth? The auditions were really weird. We all did scenes from other plays, not Scapino, and then she asked us a bunch of questions we had to respond to in writing. She cast the play from that. So, yeah, I'm playing Scapino. Jim Lord and David Harkins are the two old men. The two female leads are Lorelei Lux and Diana Hitchcock. Yes, Diana is back in school and in action. I have a kissing scene with her. Hubba hubba. Their male love interests are being played by Ricky Tang and Xeno Cortez. My sister is one of the waitresses. Sharon Rose is the nurse. Sasha Sherlock and Bart Scribner have two small roles but Van Poole hasn't decided who's going to play which one yet so they both rehearse both parts. She is really into the stylized Commedia Dell-Arte style blocking so I have to do some pretty acrobatic things on stage. The set is a bunch of risers of all different heights. Lots of jumping around.

As to female obsessions, well, surprisingly few. There's this new girl Emily Wolf that I'm

81

pretty into. She transferred from Hami. We actually went out on a date and will probably go out on another one. Not much chemistry really, but at least she's someone to think about. Blah blah blah. I feel like my well has run dry, D.

But your well certainly hasn't! Mazel Tov on the boyfriend. I hope you have a blast with Georges. Feel it all the way, for sure.

I miss you most when I'm at the Tar Pits.

I Louvre You (like a work of art),

L.

I didn't expect a quick response and didn't get one.

I could feel Dolly leaving me behind.

6

Fare thee well now.
Let your life proceed by its own design.
Nothing to tell now.
Let the words be yours, I'm done with mine

The Grateful Dead were singing what I was thinking.

I stood up to engage more deeply. I was getting it.

The music made me feel the way I felt when I thought about Miranda, a mournful aching joy.

Back in late October in French class we'd started reading "Les Bijoux," the Guy de Maupassant story usually called in English "The False Gems."

I looked over at Miranda.

you remind me of the little prince! luv, miranda

Miranda patted the top of my head when she left class in acknowledgment of that memory.

The next day, a sunny Saturday, I was walking down Mansfield and saw Madame Couchée standing outside her house.

"*Bonjour, Monsieur,*" she nodded.

"*Bonjour, Madame,*" I nodded back.

"*Ça va?*"

"*Oui, ça va bien.*"

"*Bon.*"

We stood silent a moment.

"Would you like to come in for tea?" she asked.

I had nowhere else to go and I thought how trippy it'd be to hang out with a teacher, so I went in for tea.

We sat at her breakfast room table and drank tea and ate madeleines and it was supremely cool.

"I got the lead role in *Scapino.*"

"Ah, *Les Fourberies de Scapin! Formidable, monsieur!*"

"Well, it's a parody of the Moliere play, but yeah."

"Yes, I saw it when it was here several years ago."

"At the Huntington Hartford."

"Yes."

"I saw it there too."

"It was funny. but Moliere is better."

"*Bien sûr,*" I said, "and speaking of French literature, I'm reading *Lost Illusions* for my outside novel in Megiddo's."

"*Ah. Oui.* Balzac. Are you enjoying it?"

"Very much."

"It's a series of betrayals," she said.

"Yes, so far."

"But with love triumphant."

"I haven't gotten to that part yet. It's all pretty bleak where I'm reading. David's in hiding."

"*Ah, oui.* Yes."

"You know, I read 'Les Bijoux' in 7th Grade English class. After our discussion in class about it, I realize I hardly understood any of it. That's how I met Miranda Savitch, actually, doing a worksheet on that story."

"Miranda Savitch," Madame Couchée smiled.

"Yes?"

"Are you in love with Miranda Savitch?"

"What? I . . . no."

"I can tell by the way you look at her when she's not looking."

"You're reading into it."

"She looks at you the same way when you're not looking."

"We've come close a few times, but no," I said, "It reached futility a long time ago now."

"I didn't ask you if you were getting together with Miranda Savitch, I asked if you were in love with her. Getting together as a couple has nothing to do with being in love. Some couples aren't in love and yet have a beautiful life together. And some people are in love but can't make a daily relationship work. The world, all of history, is filled with both circumstances. *Non?*"

"Whatever I feel for Miranda does not enable me to engage with her romantically," I said stiffly.

"Meaning sexually."

"Nyeah, that too I guess."

"But I'm presuming you do engage with other girls romantically."

"I've had romantic experiences with several girls, yes."

"Are you still a virgin?"

I was caught by her frankness.

"This is kind of weird."

"Have you had sex yet?" she persisted.

She didn't seem to feel weird about it.

"Yes," I said, "several times."

"With how many different girls?"

"Just one," I said. "So far, haha."

"You are confident."

"Nyeah. Optimistic."

We smiled at each other. I was blushing hard.

"It's ok to still be in love with Miranda. Enjoy that feeling for what it is. It doesn't matter. Just feel it."

"It holds me back in this very subtle way, though, when I'm with anybody else."

"You have enough love for anybody who needs it," Madame Couchée said and looked at me in this very intense way that freaked me a little but also turned me on, "You have stars in your heart."

"I'm kind of into Emily Wolf right now. We went out on a date."

"Emily Wolf. *Très intelligente.*"

"*Ah oui*," I agreed.

"I don't feel the energy between you two, though."

"Nyeah me neither," I said, "She's not into the sex thing."

"*Au contraire.* You are misreading her," Madame Couchée insisted, "And *she* is misreading *you.*"

"I do like her though. I'm definitely infatuated with her brain."

"There's more to her than her brain. You seem to have thrown her off somehow. She knows she likes you but she doesn't know what to make of you. Her feelings for you have caught her off guard. I think she usually falls for a different type of boy."

"And you pick all this up from seeing us in class?"

"Well, you all do reveal tremendous amounts about yourselves when you talk about literature and when you interact with one another. It's like watching a play. Sometimes an Ionesco play, but a play nevertheless. But I also know Emily's family. Her father is an old friend of mine. So I have inside information. She has experienced a lot."

"I don't think I want to know."

"*D'accord*," she said.

And we left it at that.

The following week, Jim Lord and I performed *It Couldn't Possibly* in the

Drama Festival at Birmingham High, doing a 5-minute cutting we'd made from my original script.

We didn't even make it out of the first round.

The sting of being eliminated so early was mitigated by *Scapino* rehearsals which, by this time, were heating up and the production was becoming the new focal point of everything.

Diana and I had started joking around a lot in Play Production. One of us would say something vulgar—her favorite image was 'pig clits'—and the other would imitate Elmore E.D. Sedgwick, Jr. saying, "Perversion," hip thrusts and all.

Our first attempt at a stage kiss was stiff and awkward.

We just sort of touched lips, neither of us knowing how seriously our mouths were supposed to engage or how.

"Try again!" shouted Ms. Van Poole from the front row of the aud. "You don't have to really kiss, but it does have to be believable. Put your arms around each other. Mean it."

"Come on, we've done this for real before," Diana said.

"I remember."

"I thought maybe you were too drunk or something."

"Oh I was definitely too drunk. But not too drunk to remember. I did puke my guts out when I got home, though."

"And you tell me this right before you kiss me on stage in front of everybody."

"Get used to it," I smiled.

"I suppose I'll have to, whiteboy," she said.

"'Cause I'm like that," I said and started kissing Diana for real to the hoots of the rest of the cast watching from the audience while we ran the scene, though Ms. Van Poole wasn't pleased.

"Can you do it *with* the dialogue?" she instructed as we remained lip-locked, "I mean when you're all done with what you're doing up there. It doesn't have to be *that* believable. And the script doesn't go away, children!"

Diana and I looked at each other with a sweet smidgen of lust and moved on.

Every time we did that scene, though, rehearsal or performance, the kiss was real. And only we knew that.

The principal complained after watching the dress rehearsal.

She said the whole play was too risqué.

Ms. Van Poole smiled, apologized, and later told us to keep doing it the same way regardless.

That was why she only lasted one year as the drama teacher.

I remember feeling with great certainty during one of those kisses—it might have been opening night—that I would one day have all kinds of torrid sex with Diana Hitchcock.

I was still waiting for that to develop, though at the Dead show I became more aware that perhaps the coupling was truly inevitable.

Come all you pretty women
with your hair hanging down
Open up your windows 'cause
the Candyman's in town

"I want to fuck every girl here tonight," Manny said, not realizing how quiet the music had gotten.

Gina gave him a thumbs-up.

Several girls turned around and looked at him and, by association, me.

"I can't tell if they're scowling or prowling, dude," Manny said.

"What?"

"Never mind. Just a thing in my own head. I can't translate it for general audiences. I do want to fuck every single one of them, though. Don't you?"

"In random moments, I guess, yeah."

The guy standing in front of me turned around and gave us both five and Cali-drawled, "Right fucking on."

I'd had a similar conversation with Jim Lord in the library.

"You know those times when you catch yourself thinking of every single female sexually no matter what she looks like?" Jim said.

I assured him I understood the omnivorous nature of the promiscuous imagination for sure.

"I go through these phases where I want to fuck every girl I look at, it doesn't matter. Like I'll be watching *I Love Lucy* reruns and catch myself thinking about Ethel Mertz."

"Oh, you mean *those* kinds of times. Dude, of course."

"Like when FUCK is an entity unto itself."

"En*titty*."

"Nyeahzackly, heh. Titty Titty Milk Fuck."

"Starring Dick Fag Dyke."

"A porn sitcom. For those days you find yourself thinking, 'Dude, I just need to pound that shit.'"

"Did I ever tell you about how I learned what the word fuck meant?" I asked knowing I had.

"You might've," he said in an attempt to avoid hearing about it again.

That didn't stop me however.

I was 9 years old, in the 4th Grade at Melrose Avenue School, when I first noticed the word fuck being used a lot on the school yard.

It was just after I had become aware of my own mortality for the first time.

Unclear on the meaning of fuck (beyond it being a bad word only spoken by bad-ass kids), I asked a streetwise bully, a 6th Grader named Charles Baxter, whom everybody called Chuckles, to hip me to its meaning.

Chuckles would normally beat up on a gay golita 4th Grader like me, but for some reason he spared me his menace.

He was always giving Wayne Paul Nader a hard time, though.

But then Wayne was a pretty annoying kid so we all looked the other way and let Chuckles throttle him 'cause it'd always shut Wayne up for a while and he wouldn't be asking you to tickle his legs in the handball line.

Elementary school *realpolitik*.

One day during recess, right after he had just finished accusing Wayne Paul Nader of fucking his own mother, I asked Chuckles what fuck meant.

"When you fuck somebody, it's when you take your middle knuckle," Chuckles demonstrated by getting me in a headlock from behind and screwing his middle knuckle into the midway point of my lumbar vertebrae, "and stick it into their spine and twist and twist, so you fuck them *up*."

"So you use fucking to hurt people."

"Fucking is the worst kind of hurting, dipshit."

With this new knowledge, I decided I would wield it against a girl in my class I disliked immensely named Dolores Mizrahi.

I sat directly across from her at the same table in Mrs. Nipper's class.

Dolores was the kind of kid who would ask things like, "How'd ya like to lose a game of chess?" or "Why does your mother make you such crappy lunches?" or "Have you always stunk at math?"

The sorts of dick-shriveling questions to which there is no vindicating answer.

90

I hated her even as I was dropping my pencil on purpose, so I could scootch under the desk and look up her Girl Scout dress.

Dolores Mizrahi was also mean to Rose Benedict who sat next to me and who was pretty much my best friend at the time. I still miss Rose. She had green eyes and buck teeth and I loved hanging out with her.

But Dolores saved her meanest mean-stuff for me.

I now had a means of revenge. Fucking Dolores. One day after school I would fuck Dolores Mizrahi. I would come up behind her suddenly and fuck her and it would hurt and she'd say please stop fucking me and I'd say only if you stop being mean to me and she'd say ok only if you promise never to fuck me again and I'd say ok only if you stop being mean to Rose Benedict also. At least that's the way I thought of it.

After my tutoring session with Chuckles, I wrote Dolores a note:

Dear Dolores,
I want to fuck you.
Sincerely,
Lance Atlas

Dolores, who already knew the correct meaning of the word, gasped and showed the note to Mrs. Nipper, who posthaste sent me to the principal's office.

The principal, Mrs. Chaffee, a dowdy rich lady who dressed in furs, drove a Jaguar, and brought her Pomeranian to school with her, called my mother to come pick me up, and I was suspended for a day.

My mother was shocked that her little fella was capable of writing such a note, but she chose to wait until my father got home to dole out punishment.

In the meantime, angry at Dolores Mizrahi and angry at being sent home, I went into our garage, grabbed a bucket of purple paint we had left over from some household project, and proceeded to graffiti our garage door—visible to the street—with the following:

I want to fuck Dolores Mizrahi

Dolores Mizrahi is a fucker

Fuck Dolores Mizrahi

I was awakened from an unplanned nap by my father shouting my name from outside.

"Do you even know what that word means?" my dad asked when he paid a visit to my room (to which I was now officially confined until further notice).

"Yeah," I said, "Chuckles taught me."

"Who's that?"

"This 6th Grader."

"Named Chuckles?"

"His real name is Charles."

"What did Charles teach you?"

"That when you fuck somebody it's when you take your middle knuckle and twist it into their spine."

"That's not what the word means, Lance," my dad shook his head, "It's not ugly like that."

My father then proceeded to teach me the real meaning of fuck after which he went outside to paint over the vandalism and I lay there confused by cock-in-pussy thoughts unable to fully comprehend how it all worked.

I still sort of have that problem.

I remember looking out my window that evening and seeing my father out there, in the dark, rolling white paint across my graffiti when he would much rather have been doing the crossword puzzle or taking a dump or smoking a cigarette on the front porch or watching the Lakers on TV but instead was making things right with the world which is the ongoing task that dads have.

Jim Lord offered kind nods at this umpteenth repetition of the story.

"But you do want to fuck every girl in the world sometimes, right?" he found his moment to disengage.

"Of course. Dang, dude. Who doesn't?"

I told Mr. Megiddo I was going to read *Far From The Madding Crowd* for my next outside novel. We weren't required to get his approval, but I always liked bouncing titles off him and getting his advice that way. I wanted him to be impressed with what I was reading.

"If you're going to read *Far From The Madding Crowd*, definitely check out 'Elegy Written In A Country Churchyard.'"

"Thanks," I said, "Why?"

"You'll see when you read it," he held up a finger then dug into his filing cabinet for a copy which he retrieved and handed to me.

The mimeograph was pale purple and fading, but I could make out the lines as I scanned down the poem.

Mr. Megiddo pointed to the stanza in question:

Far from the madding crowd's ignoble strife,
Their sober wishes never learn'd to stray;
Along the cool sequester'd vale of life
They kept the noiseless tenor of their way.

"Ah," I said, "I see. I'll have to sit down with this and read it closely."

"It's a great one, that poem," Megiddo said.

On a down day just after we'd finished reading *Le Petit Prince* in French, I brought in the French bridge of the Talking Heads song "Psycho Killer" to translate for fun because Madame Couchée was always into that sort of stuff.

Ce que j'ai fais, ce soir la

"What I did that evening," Madame Couchée said.

Ce qu'elle a dit, ce soir la

"That's easy," she nudged us.

"What she said that evening," Miranda tried.

"*Bon*," said Madame Couchée.

Realisant mon espoir

"Realize my hope," said David Harkins.

"Realizing," Couchée corrected.

"Realizing my hope," David Harkins said and I looked over at Miranda who wasn't looking back, instead she was writing something.

Je me lance, vers la gloire

Nobody volunteered a translation for that line.

"Monsieur," she pointed to me, "You should get this one."

I looked around clueless.

"Your name is in it," said Miranda, "*Je me lance.*"

"It might be my name but I don't know what *lance* means in French."

"Throw," Madame Couchée mimed.

"I throw me—" I started.

"—myself—"

"I throw myself around—no—into. I throw myself into the river."

Madame Couchée laughed.

"An interesting image but not right."

"La gloire is not the river?"

"Glory," said Madame Couchée, "I throw myself toward—not into—I throw myself toward glory."

"I throw myself toward glory," I repeated.

"I like 'I throw myself into the river' better," Lorelei Lux said but didn't look at me.

"You were probably thinking of the Loire," said Madame Couchée.

Realisant mon espoir

After class Miranda left a note on my desk as she walked out.

95

I didn't open it until after school, sitting in the auditorium waiting for rehearsal to start.

It was short.

"For you it will be as if all the stars are laughing. You alone will have stars that laugh!"

    —*The Little Prince.*

I told Gina Dichlich about my increasingly recurrent thoughts of Miranda.

"But you know you guys don't click, dude. I know you can't just shut off your feelings for her, but you've got to find someplace to bury them or enshrine them."

"Like where?"

"Art, man. Turn it into stories and songs."

"Maybe."

"Do it . . . That's where she belongs. Not in your actual life. *Write* about your Miranda complex instead of *living* it."

Gina and I had gone to see *Looking For Mr. Goodbar* together, and then we hung out at Venice Beach for a while.

"I wish I had the courage to do erotic drawings," Gina Dichlich said as we sat getting high in her car.

"Do it, G. I can't wait to see those drawings. Hot girl-on-girl action."

"You like that idea, huh?"

"The only thing better than a girl moaning with sexual pleasure is two girls moaning with sexual pleasure."

"Ah. It's just simple arithmetic then."

"Yeahzackly."

"But drawings wouldn't have moaning in them."

"The moaning would be implied by their facial expressions and how their legs are positioned."

"Legs."

"Yes. It's all about the positioning of the legs."

"Thanks for the tip, girl," Gina chided as we got out of her car and started strolling the boardwalk which is really just pavement.

Buzzy Lagniappe was walking around by himself near Muscle Beach and we flagged him down.

He waved and wandered over.

"Hey, how's it going?" he asked.

"Pretty good," we both said out of unison.

"What're you doing down here?" Gina asked.

"Just checking it out," he said, "I dunno. I wanted to look at the ocean."

"Nice," I said, "except it's nighttime."

"The ocean is still there," Buzzy said.

"That it is."

"Flippy Killbones says the ocean is a comfort to the dying."

Gina and I caught eyes. We would attempt to rein him in.

"What're you reading for your outside novel right now?" she asked him.

"*Narcissus & Goldmund*," Buzzy said, "Hermann Hesse."

"*Siddhartha* had a huge effect on me," I said.

"I think *Narcissus* is better. And I loved *Siddhartha*," Buzzy said, "But yeah."

While we were talking to Buzzy we saw Heaven Sender pass by with one of the Dirth twins.

Buzzy obviously became aware of them first.

"Which one is that?" I asked.

"I can't tell them apart," Gina said.

"Godfrey," Buzzy said, "God. The man I want to be."

"Dang, dude, no, you do not want to be that guy, he's a dick," I said, "Come off it."

"Then I'd get to Heaven."

"Dude, she sleeps with everybody. You want to be with a girl like that?"

"I don't mind sharing so long as I also get my share too," he said in his old Kansas accent which had disappeared years before but now was back.

"You'd always know she's also fucking other guys. Dang, dude. That'd suck."

"Like I said, I don't mind sharing. As long as I get to be the last guy, at night, in bed, with the lights off and the first guy in the morning when the sun comes shining through the curtains."

Gina and I sort of traded glances.

"I am gonna get to Heaven one day," Buzzy said, watching Heaven's ass sway as she walked by with Godfrey Dirth.

"I'm gonna split," said Buzzy who then ventured off in the same direction Heaven and Godfrey were heading.

Gina and I stepped into the bookstore at the Sidewalk Café, and I bought a *Greetings From Venice Beach* postcard for Annie De Milo.

"Is that for your room?" Gina asked.

"No, it's for this girl I know in Wales."

"Ah, secret lover. I see."

"Haha, no. A great kid I met who's actually from here but her family moved to Wales."

"Ah. And you're sending her a postcard."

"She asked me to."

"Cool," Gina put back the Mark Rothko book she'd been thumbing through, "You know, that movie was really depressing," and we started walking back to her car.

"*Looking For Mr. Goodbar?* Well, yeah. But I loved how you couldn't tell whether she was really this mild-mannered schoolteacher looking for kicks or this depraved addict hiding in a schoolteacher persona."

"Yeah. Which one was the costume?"

"Maybe both," I said. "How can you ever tell something like that?"

"What's going on with you and Emily these days?" Gina asked.

"Permanent Limbo," I shrugged.

Permanent Limbo would also be a great title for something.

Permanent Limbo: Moribund Love of The Necessary Vagina

"Are you at least getting some good songs out of it?" Gina asked the essential question.

"Not really, no," I said. "I'm kind of blocked creatively at the moment. The Muses have been distant."

"You're not smoking enough weed."

"That's kind of true."

"Just kidding."

"I hate when the Muses are not moving through me."

"I dig, dude, big time. When did you write your first poem or whatever?"

"Oh, it was in 1st Grade, I think, Miss Trawley's class."

"Do you remember it?"

"Haha, my mother still has it on the refrigerator. So yeah."

"Recite it for me."

"OK. It was only two lines: *I like green. I wish everything was green.*"

"Aww, beautiful."

"But I dunno, I think my creativity was really born in 6th Grade. Miss Quimble's class."

"I loved Miss Quimble. Didn't she like used to be a nun or something and then met some guy somehow and decided she wanted to marry him so she left the convent then he dumped her?"

"Yeah yeah, I remember her telling us that story. She really stoked the fire and stirred up my juices. Remember studying Paul Klee?"

"Yeah, and and and Marc Chagall."

"Joan Miro."

"Vincent Van Gogh."

"And then listening to the Don McLean song."

"*Starry starry night, paint your canvas blue and gray* . . . Oh, yeah, and remember when we did that art project where we listened to Don McLean and made collages?"

"Yeah that was to 'American Pie.'"

"Right," Gina said, "Make your own American pie."

"Out of construction paper and glue."

"And the economy project that Quimble and Schnee had us do."

"Oh, man. Unforgettable."

Occasionally, projects done for school stick to the ribs (or the long term memory anyway), either because of their psycho-spiritual truth or because of their applicability to/preparation for real world social interaction.

One of those memorable school projects happened when Gina and I were in 6th Grade.

We the students of the 2 6th Grade classes—Miss Quimble's and Miss Schnee's—had to create a mock economy.

Three days a week, in the middle of the day was dedicated to the playing out of this economy in the form of business transactions and other activities of commerce, in two classrooms, for the 2 hours between recess and lunch.

Each of us chose a profession and had to learn how to keep track of our "money" and use it to survive on a budget which included rent and food and taxes.

We had to maintain a checking account but could also make transactions using cash, a currency referred to as "Bungalow Bills," as both 6th grade classes were in the bungalows across the yard from the main building.

Some people provided services like homework help or psychotherapy or message delivery.

This blond girl, Blythe Nelson, who didn't belong in public school and would always talk about how she was going to Marlborough starting in 7th Grade, put out a weekly newsletter paid for by the government (Miss Quimble and Miss Schnee). It was usually pretty boring. Mostly interviews with selected citizens about their businesses.

Jason Alioto set up a sports salon where you could talk about sports and bet on games. He always had that day's standings up on a bulletin board along with the previous night's results. Miss Quimble said it was okay because no actual money was changing hands (or so she thought). He made a fortune during the 33-game win streak off kids who bet against the Lakers.

Wayne Paul Nader had a petting zoo which was just 3 cages holding his hamster, his guinea pig, and his rat. Miss Quimble let him keep the animals in her classroom but he had to bring them home every weekend. Seemed like a pain to me. The hamster died about halfway through the semester but Wayne Paul's parents got him a new one as a replacement.

Gina and this epileptic girl named Dotty Pinkett created a museum of student artwork they charged a dollar to look at, which ended up being lucrative because the artists would each pay a buck to see their own work up. Hang everybody's art, everybody's gonna come at least once.

Manny Shepherd rented out *MAD* Magazines and *MAD* books at his pay-to-read lending library.

Sally Castro gave jump-rope and hopscotch lessons outside the bungalows.

In a masterpiece of miscasting, I was named Chief of Police.

I, who even at that age had an intense aversion to rules, was in charge of enforcing the law, a much mightier concept than rules.

I really wanted to have a radio station and just play records and charge money for advertising, but for a reason I can't even remember now Miss Quimble wouldn't let me, so I took the Police Chief gig and lived off taxpayer money for the entire term.

On mock economy days I would stroll back and forth between the two classrooms, aloof, not doing much of anything really other than getting Osvaldo to do the Bic 4-color pen commercial in Spanish yet again or trying to look up Gina Dichlich's dress when she was on a stool hanging up new art.

My innate Taoist approach to human social activity served me well in maintaining a peaceful, prosperous economic environment.

An Israeli girl named Daphne made money balancing people's check books for them, though if you slipped her a real $1 bill she'd kiss you behind the handball courts during lunch, recess or after school (prostitution in other words).

She tried to bribe me into looking the other way while she made her dollar kiss transactions, but I declined.

"Free kisses whenever you want," she promised, "anytime, anywhere."

"Can't do it, ma'am," I said like the cops I'd seen on TV.

As the Chief of Police I was legally obligated to bust her and take her to the hoosegow (a chair next to Miss Quimble's desk) where she'd be unable to participate in the mock economy for the day and get fined a bunch of money, but I chose instead to let her do her thing, mostly because after I turned down her bribe offer of free kisses anytime anywhere, she sent the two class tough guys, old nemesis Sid Yarnell and this new hillbilly kid named Beasley Slocum, to threaten an unholy ass-kicking if I were to "stick her in the pokey," (a phrase that fueled my bathtub fantasies for quite some time).

"Do yourself a favor and poke her in the sticky instead," giggled Yarnell, in an untypical moment of spooneristic cleverness.

"Yeah, or dick her in the pussy," chimed in Beastly (as we called him) with a more predictably sick image from his well-stocked grossery store, enough to make me blush (though it too rocked with its own sort of confusing fantasy fuel).

Instead, I ignored her handball games and kept my ass unbruised and my conscience clean despite the compromise.

Whitman Rust and Gus Lagniappe had a "game arcade" (i.e., darts, ring toss, Skittle Bowl, Twister, Mille Bornes, Husker Du, View-Master with 3-D pictures of Hoover Dam, the Grand Canyon, Niagara Falls, Yosemite) in the cloak room.

I always loved that archaic term "cloak room."

Nobody at that school had worn a fucking cloak in at least 4 decades.

I remember being in 1st Grade and hearing the teacher talk about the cloak room and thinking, "What's a cloak?"

Nobody knew.

But everybody still called it the cloak room.

In that whole mock economy thing, the guy with the coolest gig was this quiet and sensible chap named Lyle Kenway who operated a "tollbooth" between the two classrooms. He exacted a fee from each student for each crossing either direction.

"No surer way to make money than charging people for doing what they have to do, like the first guys that figured out how to charge money for water, man, those are my heroes," he'd say to me when I'd hang out with him while trying to nab kids who might attempt to cross without paying, though the only guys who ever did that were Yarnell and Beastly, Daphne's muscle, and I wasn't about to apprehend those two.

Manny Shepherd, Gus Lagniappe, Whitman Rust and I engaged in an unconscious rebellion, during most of 6th Grade, against our mock economy, through a secret lunchtime meeting place called "The Trading Post," where we bartered food from our various lunches, hung out, goofed around, competed (by actual demonstration) over who could piss the farthest, talked about The Lakers' 33-game win streak or Marlo Thomas or Dr. Demento or *Omega Man* or *Willy Wonka & The Chocolate Factory* or *All In The Family* or how great it was to watch all in a row on a Friday night *The Brady Bunch, The Partridge Family, Room 222, The Odd Couple,* and *Love American Style* and you didn't have to get up for school the next morning, and had those first discussions of noticing this or that girl or just girls in general but most often Gina Dichlich.

"Gina's wearing purple panties today," Whit said this one time, "I saw during kickball at recess. I popped a boner immediately. Right there in left field."

"More like left asphalt," I said.

"Heh, ass fault," snickered Whit, "like the skid marks in your jockey shorts, dude."

"Dang, dude," Gus said, "I pop a boner just from Gina's name."

"Do you think she knows how crazy she drives us?" Manny asked.

"Nah," I said, "To the girls we're just a bunch of goofball losers."

"Or gay golitas," Manny said.

"Oh, girls know, dude. They've been taught to know," Gus said.

"Gus is right," Whit said and reached over to attempt a titty twister on the left breast of Gus Lagniappe but Gus slapped him away.

"Oop oop, Augustus Gloop," Whit chanted, "slapping at me like a leetle girl."

The Trading Post took place in the boys bathroom in the 6th Grade bungalow on the southwest corner of the campus, across the yard from everything, including the designated covered eating area.

Our presence in that bathroom was forbidden during lunch, so every day we'd lag behind the 2 6th Grade classes going out to lunch and sneak, one at a time, into the corridor between the 2 classrooms and from there into the bathroom, staying out of eyeshot of the Safeties—student cops . . . essentially, our own little breed of Kapos—and the yard monitors, who were often moms.

The boys bathroom was our version of Tom Sawyer.

We'd sometimes peek into the deserted girls bathroom, at once disappointed with the lack of erotic charge in doing so and also pleased that it smelled just as bad as the boys bathroom did.

The Trading Post ended abruptly when this spaz named Clyde tried to force his way into our little klatsch and when we refused him entry he stormed off and finked on us to one of the yard monitors.

I recall looking out the bathroom door and seeing the principal and several moms heading our way.

For some reason, Manny tried to flush his lunch down the toilet, like it was a fucking drug bust or something, and of course the plumbing backed up and therefrom emerged a gargantuan ooze of water, blurry around the edges like in a movie dream.

We were all busted, even Clyde the Fink, only my second time in the principal's office.

I have no memory of what she said or how or if I was punished, nor do I have a memory of my parents being angry.

I don't recall any consequences really, other than gaining a wee bit of coolness cred with the tough guys.

Yarnell and Beastly gave me five when I got back to class and stopped leaning on me after that.

Getting in trouble wasn't as cataclysmic as I'd always feared it would be.

Although the Trading Post failed, our unintentional experiment in a non-currency based system of commerce, which defied what our teachers and the curriculum were teaching us, what remained of The Trading Post was the sweet fraternity of it all, the hint of rebellion, the visceral rush of secrecy, the renegade triumph of getting busted, its closeness to the way things should be.

"We might not get to hang out as much as we have been lately," Gina said as we sat on a bench and looked at the Venice night sky.

"Why?"

"I'm kind of seeing someone," she said.

"Corazon?" I asked.

"Yeah," Gina acknowledged.

"I thought so."

I'd been seeing her flirt with Corazon in Government class and a few times

I'd seen them hanging on the quad at Nutrition, looking pretty chummy.

Gina always liked her lady friends sassy and butch and Corazon De Leon certainly had plenty of that going on.

"Bite my flaps," she'd say to anyone who pissed her off or even slightly annoyed her.

"And Corazon wants more of your attention than you are giving her."

"Yup," Gina sighed.

"That's what happens."

"Yup."

"It's cool," I said, "I know how that goes."

Gina smiled at me.

"Yes you do," she said.

"You know, if you love me you'll let me watch you two going at it."

"Ew, you're disgusting," Gina said and then put her arm around me.

7

Firefly
Can you see me?
Shine on, glowing
Brief and brightly

The music inside the Shrine had become this visible swirling wave of color, like Dorothy landing in Oz.

All the Munchkins were bobbing to the beat.

I tapped Gina on the shoulder.

"Hey!" she smiled looking over at me after taking a last sip of Coke, "Feeling groovy?"

"Thus far," I nodded, "I am tripping on the motion of the air."

"I am tripping on this music," she pointed as I sidled up to her ear.

"I love you," I said.

"I love you too."

"I was thinking about that just now on the latest little foray into the psychotropic. Thank you for being our escort tonight. I know you'd've rather been hanging with Corazon."

"I'm exactly where I want to be," she said, kissed me on the cheek, and turned back to the music.

People were saying
The whole world is burning
Ashes were scattered
Too hard to turn

Upside out
Or inside down
False alarm, the only game in town
No man's land, the only game in town
Terrible, the only game in town

When I closed my eyes I saw the beach scene in the postcard that I'd sent to Annie the night I got home from hanging in Venice with Gina.

Dear Annie,

As per your request here is a postcard from Venice Beach. Hey, before I forget: I was at the circus a while back and I thought of you because the lion tamer was a woman named Cleo DIPCHUNK. Don't know if she's a relative or not but I knew I just had to tell you. And on a depressing note, I was at the performance where the 2 tightrope walkers, Clovis & Findhorn, fell to their deaths. Don't know if you heard about that over in Wales. And, yeah, sorry, kid, but it sure does sound like that boy Chad likes you. Like likes you likes you. Deal with it. The Once And Future King is great. I was really into King Arthur stuff too way back when. I still kind of am actually. Lance=Lancelot, duh. Anyway, that book tells the stories well. You should definitely read it. You'll be into it. Good luck with Chad!

wink wink,

Lance

With eyes closed I could still see the music.

The music looked like a thousand parachutes landing.

Garcia was sending out guitar lines like searchlights.

What is a man
Deep down inside
But a raging beast
With nothing to hide

We had been reading *The French Lieutenant's Woman* in Megiddo's class and one Sunday afternoon free of *Scapino* rehearsals I went over to Emily's house to hang out and maybe talk about the book but I thought maybe I would attempt to make out with her also.

She lived on Highland between 2nd & 3rd, so just a few blocks away from me.

"It's the pink house with the fancy arched window," she told me what to look for.

Emily was waiting for me out front and looked utterly edible in white velour pants and a pale yellow blouse underneath her perpetual brown v-neck sweater.

"This is your dad's place?" I asked as we walked into the house which sort of looked like the inside of a mushroom.

"Yeah. My mother lives in Beverlywood with my older sister. That's why I was going to Hamilton."

"Why'd you move in with your dad?"

"My mother and my sister are both slightly not right in the head and my dad thought it would be better for me to live with him and the court agreed. They are disturbed enough to be dangerous."

"Dang," I managed.

"I bet they miss me, though," Emily said of her mom and sis, "They don't have Dick Nixon to kick around anymore."

She flicked a fake cigar and raised her eyebrows. It's the only time I've ever seen a girl imitate Groucho Marx.

"Groucho Marx should've played Nixon in the movie if there'd been one," I said because I thought it sounded flippant and ironic.

"The avant-garde Nixon movie."

"Directed by Ken Russell."

"Brilliant."

"Yeah."

"Gorgeous."

"Like you," I said and moved toward her mouth.

"Groucho just died didn't he?" she resisted.

"Yeah. In August," I backed off, used to it, "Like 3 days after Elvis."

"Mercury must've been in retrograde," Emily said with a straight face but then started laughing.

"Ha, yeah, I didn't think you'd be into astrology."

"You think correctly, sir."

She held me by the hand and led me into her bedroom which had two full bookcases but only a small record collection, all classical, primarily Mendelssohn and Mahler.

"I love Mahler's Fifth," I said, pulling out the Herbert von Karajan/Berliner Philharmoniker recording.

"Fantastic, yes."

"The Adagietto."

"Sublime."

"I heard it at the Hollywood Bowl in August."

"That must have been a beautiful night."

"It was," I remembered, "consciousness altering. A major life event."

"All that from a symphony."

"Nyeah, yeah," I blushed.

"A symphony epiphany."

"Actually Desiree Stoner played the Adagietto naked for me on the cello after I fucked her poorly but went down on her quite excellently that night I lost my virginity," I couldn't say out loud to Emily because, dang, dude, I hadn't even really kissed her yet although in retrospect she probably would have gotten off on hearing that.

"I don't know Mendelssohn at all," I said. "Except the wedding thingy from *The Newlywed Game*."

Emily didn't laugh at the *Newlywed Game* reference. I don't know, I thought it was pretty funny.

"How come you always wear sweaters even on hot days?" I asked her because I'd been wondering about that.

"It's the wool. They're all made from wool my grandmother gave me before she got murdered."

Dang, dude.

This chick's life was a fucking freak show.

"Your grandmother got murdered."

"Yeah. When I was 9."

"What happened?"

"She was cheating on my grandfather with this other guy in their 4-plex over on Dunsmuir and her lover's wife caught them and shot my grandmother to death."

"What about the lover?"

"She didn't shoot him. She wanted to be with him after she got out of jail."

"Dang, dude. That's a movie."

"My grandfather's trying to option the story, actually. My dad's helping him. They're trying to prove that Tessie Hendel shouldn't be able to make money from the tragedy, nor should her husband, but rather the victim's family."

"Cray-zee."

"My life is that. Yes."

"But you're not."

"I believe myself to be quite sane despite the circumstances that surround me."

"So that wool is important. Like armor. Like a secret emblem or something."

"I'm the wolf in sheep's clothing," she said.

"Hah, nice," I pointed at her, "The better to eat me with," I said, testing how raunchy I could get with her.

Emily stared at me, neither fazed nor impressed, "I thought the point of this liaison was a discussion of *The French Lieutenant's Woman,* good sir."

"Absolutely," I went hands up like a suspect.

"Have you noticed how everything we've read in Megiddo's is about cheating and betrayal?" she asked.

"*Godot* doesn't really work, though."

"Yeah yeah but he did that 'cause of the production in town."

"This is twue," I held up my index finger.

"Maybe there's something going on in his personal life."

"You think his syllabus is autobiographical?"

"Could be . . ."

"I can ask Gina Dichlich," I said, "She's pretty close to him. They hang out and talk and stuff."

"Gina's a dyke, right?"

"I guess?"

"She doesn't look like a dyke, but she acts like one."

"What does that mean?"

"Sorry. I know you guys are best buds and stuff," Emily said with subtle disdain.

"We're good friends," I said, "But we're not hanging out as much these days."

"She's bumping cunts with Cory De Leon," Emily said to my great shock and titillation.

"I have no idea."

"Liar."

I was trying to figure out how to get her to say bumping cunts again.

"I love how the artist is God in *French Lieutenant's Woman*," I said.

"Totally. Transcending the illusions of time and separated consciousness," Emily said, "just being everything at once."

"Is that a Spinoza thing?"

"Yeah, a bit. But Fowles brings a more atheistic angle to it. Spinoza, even after being excommunicated by the rabbis, still kept that *a priori* assumption that God exists."

"Are you an atheist?"

"I call myself agnostic for now 'cause I've never seen proof that God doesn't exist either. But, yeah, I lean toward the Godless cosmos."

"Hmm."

"What about you?"

"I waver. Most of the time I just don't know."

"Have you ever had a personal experience of God?"

"No. Not really."

"Then what makes you waver?"

"The thought that maybe I'm misinterpreting the message, misperceiving God's presence. Like when I'm making music. Or swooning in love. Or looking at the night sky."

"But that's all just consciousness. Why mythologize it?"

I chose not to tell her about my convocations with Calliope and Euterpe.

We talked for quite a while about the novel until her dad came home and appeared in the bedroom doorway. He was with a girl I recognized from the Hollywood Bowl. She'd worked with Gina up on 3rd Prom.

"Hey, how's it going," she said to me in mutual recognition.

"Pretty good," I said.

"You two know each other?" Emily's dad asked.

"We worked together at he Hollywood Bowl last summer," she said.

"Eli," Emily's dad said to me and held out his hand.

"Lance," I said and shook it.

He was definitely the Jew part of her.

"What are you guys up to?" he asked.

"We were discussing *The French Lieutenant's Woman* and then veered off into God," Emily said.

"Sounds fun," said her dad. "Lisa and I are going to make a salad and watch the Kings game if you two want to join us."

"I was just getting ready to leave," I said.

"Well, nice to meet you."

"Go Kings Go," I said and he smiled and so did Lisa.

"Hockey fan."

"Oh yes," I bowed my head.

"Who's your favorite player?"

"Marcel Dionne."

"Hang on to this one," he said to Emily.

"We'll see," she drolled back.

Once they were out of earshot I had to ask, "What's the deal with Lisa?"

"She appears to be my dad's current girlfriend."

"But she's only, like—"

"—Yup. 2 years older than I am."

We walked out into the front courtyard and kissed goodbye awkwardly and briefly.

As I started to leave she pulled me back toward her.

"I find myself rather confused regarding the subject of *you* these days," she said.

I decided not to tell her how beautiful she was.

"I don't know . . . I'm not used to this . . ." she went on, "I like you. I'm maybe even somewhat crazy about you. But I can't seem to let it all out. Or let it all in. Or something."

"Try me," I said, slightly discomfited about what she might be hiding, what I might find out, "I'm not interested in hanging out with someone who's wearing a mask or a costume."

"Well, we're all doing that, my special friend, even you."

"Busted," I faked a guilty grin.

We both laughed then kissed awkwardly and briefly again and I left.

On the walk home I let the night air summon my Muses.

I hadn't been writing much at all and my psyche was suffering because of it.

I decided to get higher than *mahasamadhi* on this latest grass Bigelow Rust sold me called Metempsychosis and let the heavenly sisters sing through me some newness.

Once stewed to a delectable succulence, I climbed up onto the garage roof with my guitar and called upon my favorite ladies, begging their blessings.

Calliope and Euterpe danced among the stars and filled my head with messages.

A song unfurled in the dark.

To Every Season
(There Is A Turn)

Humanity enamored of laws
Your vanity demands a cause
Exquisite bliss this fix we're in
A consciousness that's always been

To every season there is a turn
Sometimes you freeze and sometimes you burn
Beyond all reason you can discern
To every season there is a turn turn turn
Around

No god in fact who looks like you
Not white not black not brown nor blue
The preacher serves an empty sky
With Jesus' words upholds the lie

To every season there is a turn
Sometimes you freeze and sometimes you burn
Beyond all reason you can discern
To every season there is a turn turn turn
Around

No time to any purpose and no heaven

There's only this one senseless escapade
Engage in some spontaneous creation
Congratulate yourself for getting made

Come take it in your brand new skin
All naked and immune to sin
A time to get both high and deep
A time for sex and food and sleep

To every season there is a turn
Sometimes you freeze and sometimes you burn
Beyond all reason you can discern
To every season there is a turn turn turn
Around

A time to know death
A time to forget
A time to unlearn
A time to return turn turn

I sang the tune through several dozen times, picturing myself onstage in front of an audience or even just one-on-one with Penelope Lagniappe right up there on the garage roof.

I knew Penelope was away at college but still had this unfounded hope she might scent my presence and climb up to join me.

I flagged that thought for possible masturbation later and went back to strumming the cool new tune as Calliope and Euterpe dissipated like a dying nebula and I was left with emptiness.

8

After another extended pause, the Dead had fallen into a song that featured their female back-up singer on lead vocals and Gina, having downed a large Coke, needed to make a trip to the bathroom.

"You guys should try to go too even if you think you don't have to. If anything it's really cool to pee while you're tripping. You'll feel like Shiva with the Ganges flowing out of his lingam."

"In a little bit," said Manny, who also had a bladder full of Coke, splayed in his chair, palms outstretched, like he was getting a blowjob from Parvati herself.

"OK," she said, "but soon. Really. I'll be back. You want another Coke, Manny?"

"Nahm cool," he waved as Gina split.

"This is one of the worst songs I've ever heard," Manny said.

"Pretty much. But it's like it doesn't matter really. I feel like I'm expanding outward in all directions right now," and I closed my eyes and floated farther and farther apart from myself like all matter is constantly doing.

"Do you have like a metallic taste in your mouth?" Manny asked.

"Yeah. Like silverware."

"Silverware from Bargain Circus," Manny laughed and looked at me. "I hope this acid isn't tainted with poison or some shit."

"Nah, man, it feels too good."

"Maybe poison feels good. Maybe we're dead already and haven't realized it yet."

"You think the afterlife is a Grateful Dead show?"

"Whoa shit. Never mind. I take that back. I've committed some sins in my life, for sure, dude, but nothing deserving of this."

"I dunno, man. This song most certainly sucks ass, but I've been kind of getting into what they're doing in places. It has definitely carried me into orbit several times already."

The Dead moved mercifully on to a new song just as Gina got back from the bathroom.

"Everything come out ok?" I teased.

"Ugh, the line was too long. I'll try later," she said and swung right back into grooving to the band. "Where you at?"

"I am all over," I said and placed my hand over her face.

"Stop," she swatted at me laughing but I held firm.

"I am everywhere at once," I said and removed my grip.

"It'd be wise to keep that fact hidden."

"My omnipresence? Whatever for?"

"If the government finds out they might want to use you as a weapon."

"I'm the God Bomb," I struck a Morrison pose, "I am the Wizard King. The man behind the curtain."

"You are tripping on acid. That's your current status as a sentient being on this spinning planet."

"This music is just totally rocking," I said facing the stage and bouncing involuntarily.

"See?" Gina said.

Goes to show you don't ever know
Watch each card you play and play it slow

Wait until your deal come round
Don't you let that deal go down

Jerry Garcia unleashed a blistering hot solo and I was sucked all the way into his thing as I once thought I'd be into Emily's, alas.

Garcia's guitar was telling a story about deception all clouded in the rocket's red glare.

I followed the wordless narrative until it landed back on the song which barreled to its conclusion like a freight train coming 'round the mountain when she comes.

They segued directly into the next song and I looked over to catch Manny also paying attention.

He was hip to the shift.

We looked at each other and nodded.

"Funky," Manny mouthed.

"Crisp," I mouthed back.

It's a rainbow full of sound
It's fireworks, calliopes and clowns
Everybody is dancing . . .

Gina reached over and put her hand on my shoulder and we were sort of dancing together.

They're a band beyond description,
Like Jehovah's favorite choir
People joining hand in hand
While the music plays the band

The crowd roared at the self-reference, both to the Grateful Dead and to the congregation of acolytes themselves.

When the music slowed into mystical timelessness Gina put her arm all the way around me.

I tingled a bit at that intimacy with her because of how much I wanted it.

We leaned our heads together and nuzzled in the quietness.

Then the floating tempo caught an updraft and we joined its ascent.

"I'm very happy to be here," Gina said in my ear and I put my arm around her and we swayed like during *Oseh Shalom* at the end of Shabbat services while Garcia went soaring heavenward and we all of us with him riding the cresting incandescence and the exploding nodes of consciousness like a stampede of ions etching themselves into flaming tablets spinning like pinwheels and I looked around at the yellowish vermicular multitude of Deadheads for whom Garcia had called down the Eucharist and we all lurched forward everybody together taking communion from Il Papa . . .

Manny joined us and we three shared a deep embrace.

Were they ever here at all?

Bob Weir said, "Thank you. We're gonna take a short break and you can too," and then the house lights came up.

"Dang, dude, there's more?" Manny said. "I feel like we've been here since dinosaur times."

"These *are* dinosaur times," Gina said.

"Come on, dude," I said, "The last two songs?"

Manny fidgeted, "OK, that was some rock and roll, I admit it. But still. More?"

"We should take this opportunity to pee," Gina interjected.

We ventured down the stairs, descending into the crowded lobby where we became but three trippers among thousands.

Everybody moved like ghosts, both flowing and floating.

The men's room line was long, but once Manny and I secured two urinals next to each other we loosed our dicks and let the plumbing function.

I closed my eyes and flashed back on being at the circus with Dolly when I had a similarly intoxicated urination, though the visual mythos of LSD blasted multifaceted imagery across my consciousness in a way that cannabis can't approach.

I tried to avoid reimagining the plunging deaths of Clovis & Findhorn and sought instead memories of Cleo Dipchunk the lion tamer or even better Dolly's face just before I kissed her that afternoon under the big top.

I had just gotten a postcard back from Annie but couldn't concentrate on what it said as peeing was taking up most of my headspace and Gina's suggestion re: feeling like Shiva was plugged into truth because I felt like I was standing paramount, atop the Himalayas, the source of Ma Ganga, filling the pool of life with sustaining waters.

I looked over at Manny who was standing at the urinal next to me, eyes closed, dick out.

His dick was bigger than I remembered it.

Maybe it was the acid.

"Dude," I poked him, "I think you're all done."

He opened his eyes, looked down, said, "Oh yeah, huh," and put his dick back in his pants and inhaled a laugh. "I am majorly tripping, dude."

On our journey back to the balcony we ran into the Deadhead kids we knew from Fairfax.

"Hey, how's it going?" I said to them as we passed them in the lobby and then stopped to talk even though we never really spoke at school.

"Pretty good," said Zeke West, a tall feller in overalls and long red hair.

"Fairfax High," said Holly Fox, someone I could fall in love with much too easily and pretty much started to right there.

"You were Scapino," added Amanda Chester, who had no bosom to speak of.

"That's right," I said.

"You were funny."

"Thank you."

"The play wasn't. But you were."

Zeke, Holly, and Amanda were there with the rest of the hippie contingent from school, Laura Story, Erica Heath, Beth Mason, and these two dudes Sonny Blue and Kensh Rutha who in 10th Grade were so stoned one day they fell asleep in P.E. class. Like, during calisthenics. How do you fall asleep while doing push-ups?

"Gina Dichlich," Sonny Blue said, pointing.

"Have we met?" Gina asked.

"Everybody knows your name," Kensh Rutha snickered and he and Sonny slapped hands.

"You guys are into the Dead?" Amanda Chester asked incredulously.

"Not really," said Manny.

"I'm pretty floored by what I'm hearing tonight," I said.

"I'm a convert," said Gina. "I loved the first set. I was with it all the way. Outside of tending to these two astral travelers."

"You guys tripping?" asked Holly Fox.

Manny and I bowed with folded hands.

"Second set is for peaking," Erica Heath said, nodding her head.

"It'll be out there for sure," said Laura Story.

"Jerry is ready for ascension," Zeke lifted his hands like a rocket ship leaving the atmosphere.

"You should hang out with us after the show," Holly said, "We're gonna crash in Zeke's van, smoke out, listen to Dead tapes."

"Nah, it's a school night," I said.

Everybody laughed, including Manny and Gina.

"Dude, you are not going to be sleeping tonight," Sonny Blue said, "That acid is gonna be zooming around in your system until tomorrow morning."

"Come party with us," Holly urged again and pulled at my sleeve, "We can all come down together. It'll be sweet."

Manny, Gina, and I looked at each other and knew.

"We have to decline," Gina said and grabbed me and Manny by the arms and we turned to leave.

"Well, come hang in the quad at lunch sometime. Join our picnic on the grass," Holly said and waved.

"Off to see the Wizard?" Zeke said as we journeyed forth.

"You're looking at him, dude," I saluted.

"Right on," Zeke nodded and probably half-believed me.

Gina led us to the balcony staircase.

"Going up?" she pointed.

"Already there," I began the climb, "but yeah. Let's."

"Totally," said Manny who followed.

And up we went again into the heavens.

I briefly lost track of the fact that I was at a Grateful Dead show and thought for some reason I was in the balcony of the Wiltern about to sit through all 5 *Planet of the Apes* movies.

But then the Dead came back out onstage for the second set and I realized my actual circumstance.

The futzing and tuning went on, again at excessive length, as had been the case between each song throughout the 1st set.

Eventually Bob Weir announced some kind of problem with "Jerry's equipment" and then they went back to fiddling.

Manny rolled his eyes and Gina was dancing as if they were already playing.

"So while we're fixing this I'm going to take this opportunity to tell you all a story," Bob Weir said.

The crowd yelled its approval.

"No, it works now, so we don't have to worry about all that," Weir backtracked, and they moved right into the first tune.

We can share the women, we can share the wine.
We can share what we got of yours 'cause we done shared all of mine

I closed my eyes to a view of liquefied purple geometry and let my mind flash itself in the mirror.

In a time-honored annual tradition we'd long heard of and finally got to experience first-hand as 12th Graders, Mr. Megiddo invited his AP students over to his house in Hancock Park for a costume party to which everybody must come dressed as literary figures, either authors or characters. Literary couples were welcomed if students wanted to do that.

Mr. Megiddo's house on Arden was much larger than we expected, and although he wasn't married, his student teacher from last year, Miss Dillard, appeared to be living there, we presumed as his girlfriend.

Emily had asked me if I wanted to go to the party together as a literary couple.

"Who'd you have in mind?"

"I thought Lillian Hellman and Dashiell Hammett," she smiled, "like in *Julia*," and it might have been the only time I ever saw Emily Wolf blush or seem embarrassed.

"Our first date," I smiled back. "That'd be kinda cool, but what could we do to make people know who we are? I think maybe they're not distinctive enough looking."

"That's true. Can you think of anyone else?"

"Henry Miller & Anais Nin," I said, "That'd be pretty easy. I'd just need one of those skull cap thingies. I've got the glasses. "I'm sure you could come up with a long dress and pull your hair back in a tight bun or curled on top of your head."

"I've never read Miller," Emily said, "but I like the Nin books I've read."

"*Delta of Venus?*"

"Hot stuff, I don't know, though, I think it'd be more interesting if we went as maybe Jean-Paul Sartre and Simone de Beauvoir."

"That's cool by me."

"Can you get a pipe?"

"I have several pipes," I said.

"A tobacco pipe," Emily clarified.

"Nyeah, that'll be harder to come by."

"But can you get one?"

"Yes, ma'am, I most certainly can."

"Don't disappoint me."

"Jawohl," I said like Sgt. Schultz which she sort of giggled at but I think it actually irked her.

Miranda and Freddy came as Jane Gallagher and Ward Stradlater from *Catcher In The Rye*.

"How could we not when I have a yearbook handsome boyfriend?" Miranda tore into my soul.

Claire Farnaway came as Cathy from *Wuthering Heights* and was there with this new guy she was dating named Santana Windsor who was dressed as Heathcliff.

Tom Studdard and Lorelei Lux came as F. Scott Fitzgerald & Zelda, though Tom looked and acted much more like his namesake Tom Buchanan than like the bratty man-child author of *The Great Gatsby*.

"You look dapper, Lance Atlas," said Lorelei Lux who hadn't been nice to me in a couple of months.

"Love the beret, guy," said Tom Studdard. "Very classy."

"And the pipe," said Lorelei who took the pipe out of my mouth and put it in her own.

"*Çeci n'est pas une pipe*," I said, taking it back.

"*No habla*," said Tom and headed to the drinks table to pour himself a root beer.

Jim Lord and Misty Winters came as Humbert Humbert & Lolita.

Misty was small enough to pull it off and did the Kubrick Lolita with heart-shaped glasses and lollipop.

"I love the pleated skirt and the saddle shoes," said Gina Dichlich who'd come as Virginia Woolf, "Hubba hubba."

"I'm taking it Corazon's not here."

"Cory doesn't have Megiddo."

"Duh," I winced, "I knew that."

Waldo Banks had come uncostumed and claimed to be dressed as the Invisible Man.

"But we can see you," said Misty Winters, "You aren't invisible."

"But as a black man in America I might as well be," he said.

"He's Ellison's *Invisible Man*," Jim Lord explained to Misty, "Not the one by H.G. Wells."

Manny came as Arthur Rimbaud and arrived with Whitman Rust and Buzzy Lagniappe who came in a single shared suit that Whit's mom had made for them.

"Who are you?" asked Miss Dillard when she greeted Whit and Buzzy at the door.

"Dr. Jekyll and Mr. Hyde," Whit said. "I'm the good doctor."

"And I'm the lunatic criminal," said Buzzy with a maniacal leer.

Rudy Tuesday and Xeno Cortez came as Oscar Wilde and Lord Alfred Douglas.

"Somebody has already mistaken us for W.H. Auden and Christopher Isherwood, oh and Waldo Banks just described us as James Baldwin and his Spanish boyfriend," said Rudy Tuesday.

"Did James Baldwin ever have a Spanish boyfriend?" Xeno asked.

"Does it even matter? We aren't them, ok?" Rudy slapped back, "I'm Oscar and you're Bosie."

"More like you're Oscar and I'm Felix."

"We should have come as Bert and Ernie. With me being Bert."

"Hell no. I'm the Bert in this relationship."

"Um, you're the one who still plays with a rubber ducky in the bathtub. Isn't that right? Or am I mistaken?"

"Unfair!" proclaimed Xeno, "but yes I suppose the rubber ducky does make me the Ernie."

"You are *so* the Ernie," said Rudy.

Xeno's music for *Scapino* was perfectly realized. Using a small ensemble— violin, viola, cello, piano, and percussion (both for the music and as sound effects for the Commedia slapstick). It ended up being the only good thing about the production.

The rehearsals were mostly dreadful. A lot of jumping around and cartoon antics with nothing to latch onto and make meaningful other than the daily stage kiss with Diana Hitchcock.

Part of the problem was Ms. Van Poole. As a director, she'd always be pressing us to make it believable, but then in her blocking she'd always go for a sight gag over genuine human exchange.

"Wrong again, moose-face," Ms. Van Poole would often say in reaction to whatever scene I had just run through, "You're playing it too sincerely. In this play, everyone is wearing a mask. The personality is a facade. And that's where the comedy happens, in that space where the audience sees both the real person and the mask he's wearing. Scapino doesn't mean anything he says."

"So mostly it's just irony then," I said.

"Commedia Dell'Farte," Ms. Van Poole said, "Yeah."

The food at Megiddo's party was a buffet that included *pate de foie gras*, caviar and crackers, quiche lorraine, dolmathes, baguette sandwiches with runny cheese, haricots vert in butter and garlic, sliced beef, and a salad of garbonzo beans and back olives. Food for grown-ups. The only thing missing was the wine.

I bummed a cigarette off Emily and stepped outside for a smoke while

Emily stayed inside and talked to Mr. Megiddo about Italy.

Lorelei Lux wandered out alone and stood next to me.

"Hey," I said, waving my cigarette.

"Friends," said Lorelei Lux, holding out her hand.

I took her hand and shook it.

"We are. Yes," I said.

It was weird seeing her without her notebook.

Lorelei had somehow become even more beautiful.

"I miss talking to you," Lorelei said as we continued shaking hands.

"Likewise."

Our eyes did not meet.

"You're in love now," I said.

"Could be," she said. "And you?"

"Me? Nyeah. You know."

"You and Emily aren't a thing?"

"At times. I dunno. The usual confusion. It's boring."

"You are always in love, Lance Atlas. You are always in love with everybody."

"May be," I said. "But I'd rather be in love with somebody."

"But you are that also," she said and turned to go back inside, "That's why it's so hard to be with you."

"Whom are you talking about, may I ask?"

Lorelei Lux smiled, "Duh, as you earthlings say."

I flicked my cigarette butt into the street and went back inside also where everyone was at the buffet table getting their food.

Emily signaled me from a couple of spots she'd snagged at a table in the corner of the back patio.

She had brought 2 plates of food to the table.

"I took two of each thing," she said and she was for that brief moment totally my girlfriend.

"I thought *The Second Sex* was amazing," said Emily out of nowhere while we sat and ate and grasped for things to say to each other.

"I beg your pardon?" I said like Barney Fife, "I'm still waiting for the first sex."

"The Beauvoir book. She writes about every kind of woman I don't want to be like. Brilliant. It's like *Struwwelpeter* for an awakened womanhood."

"*Struwwelpeter*, that's like the naughty little suck-a-thumb stuff with the scary illustrations?"

"Yeah yeah. The German kids book," she said and looked at me intently.

She started to say something several times and stopped herself.

"Do you really want to be here? Be honest," she finally said.

"I think it's cool to be at Megiddo's house," I said.

"And now you've seen it. So?"

I shrugged.

"There's nobody here I want to talk to," Emily said.

"Same here. Everywhere I walk at this party I get that sensation, like, you know that weird feeling you get when you pass by a house you used to live in and now someone else lives there?"

"I know it well, m'lad."

"So what I'm saying is we can leave if you want."

"You sure?"

"Absolutely, I'm in agony," I said and stood up. "Let's do it."

We moved inconspicuously toward the front door and then out to Emily's car.

I always feel better once I've left a party.

Mr. Megiddo lived a few blocks from John Burroughs Jr. High and I had Emily pull up in front so I could show her the brick building wherein so much foundation was laid.

"A lot happened in that place," I said.

"A lot happens every place," Emily said and pulled me toward her and we exchanged our most passionate kiss yet, touching tongues and everything.

She was far more practiced than I'd expected.

"You have a big mouth," I said afterward, having been lost in her lips.

"The better to eat you with, my dear," she said and put her head on my shoulder. "Alas, m'lad. I don't know what to do with ye."

After she parked in front of my house we dug into one last monster kiss, one of those perfectly met comminglings.

I got a brief whiff of her cunt in the stillness of the car air, which heightened my horniness, though when I reached between her legs she rebuffed my encroachment.

"I'm still trying to figure things out," she said and nudged my hand away.

"I understand," I said and started to get out of the car.

"Hey," she held onto my sleeve and tugged me back, kissing me on the mouth with scant passion. "I do like you, you know."

I nodded and opened the door.

"I'm sorry," she sort of winced as I said bye.

It was depressing but I jacked off about her anyway that night.

Sometimes you just have to.

9

Annie laid her head down in the roses.
She had ribbons, ribbons, ribbons, in her long brown hair.
I don't know, maybe it was the roses,
All I know I could not leave her there

The Dead were meandering their way through a very mellow tune.

I took a seat next to Manny and reclined in the space lounge, flashing on Annie's last postcard:

My Dear Lance,

Cleo Dipchunk is my aunt! I've only met her a couple of times, though. She ran away to join the circus when she was 16. She calls my mom when she needs money and my mom always sends it to her. We heard about the Clovis & Findhorn accident. It was in the newspaper. Very sad and upsetting. My mom tried to reach Aunt Cleo after we heard but couldn't find her. And shut up about Chad liking me because that is gross! You are wrong. But you are a nimnork so that is to be expected. Oh, I started reading The Once And Future King and I love it. Dwerp. Glurp. Shlurp. Pay no attention to the girl making funny gurgling sounds. She is only a figment of your imagination. Hey you're going to graduate in June, aren't you? You are OLD! Nah. Psych. You're the opposite. Haha. (I know your secret). Guess what? Cambria is another name for Wales. Isn't that just totally cray-zee? I mean, we met in Cambria and I live in Wales. Nutso!

OK, I just ran out of things to say.

Dang,

Annie

p.s. I don't care what kind of postcard you send next. Pick something neat.

"Well demanded, wench," I said out loud after reading the card.

I'd been using that line to myself ever since we'd done *The Tempest* in Megiddo's.

We read the play out loud in class, and I had been assigned the role of Ferdinand.

"Would having Miranda read Miranda be too obvious?" Megiddo asked.

Miranda started to volunteer but—

"—I can do Miranda," Emily Wolf said and Megiddo gave it to her.

I looked over at Miranda who appeared dashed all to pieces.

And so it went through Acts I and II. I was Ferdinand and Emily was Miranda. And Miranda was stewing in the back row having petulantly turned down other roles offered by Megiddo.

Then, the day we did Act III, Emily was absent and Megiddo knew what he had to do.

"Who am I to tell Miranda she can't be Miranda," Mr. Megiddo smiled.

"You did it once," Miranda retorted.

Megiddo nodded.

"Come up here and sit next to Lance. This is a big scene for you two coming up," he said, "Emily picked a bad day to be absent."

Miranda took Emily's seat next to me and we began.

"*Admir'd Miranda!*" I croaked and cleared my throat.

The first that e'er I sigh'd for

"Go on," said Mr. Megiddo.

I went forth unto the breach:

"Indeed, the top of admiration; worth
What's dearest to the world! Full many a lady
I have ey'd with best regard, and many a time
The harmony of their tongues hath into bondage
Brought my too diligent ear: for several virtues
Have I lik'd several women; never any
With so full soul but some defect in her
Did quarrel with the noblest grace she ow'd,
And put it to the foil: but you, O you!
So perfect and so peerless, are created
Of every creature's best."

Dang, dude.

Luckily we were reading so we didn't have to look at each other.

". . . I would not wish
Any companion in the world but you,
Nor can imagination form a shape,
Besides yourself, to like of," Miranda read.

And I replied, " *. . . Hear my soul speak:*
The very instant that I saw you, did
My heart fly to your service; there resides,
To make me slave to it."

"Do you love me?" Miranda asked.

I spoke my line slowly, *"I beyond all limit of what else i' the world*

Do love, prize, honour you . . ."

Megiddo, who was playing Prospero, read:
"Fair encounter
Of two most rare affections! Heavens rain grace
On that which breeds between them!"

"Wherefore weep you?" I took my turn.

"At mine unworthiness, that dare not offer
What I desire to give; and much less take
What I shall die to want . . ." Miranda started but then stopped short.

Megiddo let her gather herself.

"Hence, bashful cunning!" she spoke clearly,
"And prompt me, plain and holy innocence!
I am your wife, if you will marry me
If not, I'll die your maid: to be your fellow
You may deny me; but I'll be your servant,
Whether you will or no."

I bowed my head as did Ferdinand in a show of humility.

"My husband, then?" Miranda asked.

"Ay, with a heart as willing
As bondage e'er of freedom: here's my hand," I said but didn't move.

Music called me back to the Shrine.

In the midst of all that Dead drenching, I thought about how small punk rock songs really were.

My whole sense of proportion had changed.

While I was broadening my ears at the Dead show to better prepare me for the wide-path mind I aspired to, the Sex Pistols were making their doomed way across the United States.

They'd be ending up in San Francisco, where the end of the continent would also be the end of the road for them.

The Sex Pistols were brand new and yet already irrelevant.

And my mind was being pulled very powerfully into this more expansive perspective, toward epic music making.

The Dead were winning me over.

The Dead were something bigger, or at least the music they were making was.

Save for the interminable pauses between, it seemed like, every other song. That sucked.

"Only the Dead could get away with this," Manny said, "Because everybody in the audience is tripping so they're easily distracted by other things."

"Including silence," I added.

Eventually, the silence morphed into sound which then coalesced and became a song.

My time coming any day, don't worry about me, no

Weir strutted while the band stumbled their way into synch with him, and then the groove was on.

I was caught up in elastic strings hanging from the rafters, overlooking Kathmandu, and, on the horizon, Krakatoa (East of Java).

California, preaching on the burning shore
California, I'll be knocking on the golden door
Like an angel, standing in a shaft of light
Rising up to paradise, I know I'm gonna shine.

"Lance?" I heard a voice say my name from maybe behind me or maybe in front of me, "Lance Atlas?"

I looked toward the aisle and saw a familiar face.

It was that gnarly bitch Yocheved who sat next to me in Hebrew school.

"Hey. Yocheved. Long time. How's it going?"

"Pretty good," she gave me a thumbs up. "I didn't know you were into the Dead."

"Seems like it," I said.

"First time?"

"Second. First time getting what it's about though."

"Glad to hear it," she smiled and nodded and gave me another thumbs up.

Was Yocheved Levy really being nice to me?

Yocheved who always picked the seat next to me in Hebrew school every year and then would scowl at me and accuse me of cheating off her?

Yocheved who purposely spilled apple juice on my backpack once?

Yocheved whose father thought Rabbi Saks was the Moshiach?

Yocheved who smelled like bologna and mayonnaise?

Yocheved who used to listen to The DeFranco Family?

That Yocheved?

"I'm definitely on board," I said.

"And it looks like you're also on acid," Yocheved said and smiled.

"That too."

"How have you been? You didn't come to Hebrew High."

"Oh, I quite often came to Hebrew high."

"You know what I mean."

"Nyeah, I wasn't into it anymore. Kind of never was, to be honest."

"I'm president of USY this year," she said.

United Synagogue Youth was not my thing.

"Yeah, my sister told me you got elected. Mazel Tov on that."

"Thank you."

"*Yasher Koach*," I said and in that moment caught myself flirting with her.

Flirting With Yocheved would be a great title for something.

The sequel to *Reading Leviticus For Pleasure*.

"You go to Beverly, right?"

"I do," she said.

"Do you know Candy Stoner?"

"Candy Stoner? Oh yeah. Everybody knows who Candy is."

I presumed that was Yocheved's way of saying, "Duh, she's black."

"Well, say hi from me if you see her."

"I will, for sure."

"I fucked her older sister," I thought of saying but instead I said, "So, the president of USY drops acid at Grateful Dead concerts."

"Sometimes she does, yes," she smiled. "I love the Grateful Dead."

"You don't look like a Deadhead."

"I'm not a Deadhead. I just love the Grateful Dead. I love the music."

"What do you love about it?"

"I don't know. It makes me feel like I'm floating in water."

"I get what you're saying," I said, and, dang, dude, I was tripping pretty hard at that moment and was really weirded out that I was flirting with Yocheved Levy and her face kept changing into different people who all kind of looked like Barbra Streisand and that made me freak for real.

Plus, I couldn't even remember what we were talking about anymore.

"Nice to see you again," I said to her and let my attention drift back to the music, not really conscious of how rude I was being.

I suppose she just walked away at some point once she realized the conversation was over and what a dick I am.

You've all been asleep, you would not believe me
Them voices tellin' me, you will soon receive me
Standin' on the beach, the sea will part before me
Fire wheel burning in the air!

Garcia hitched himself to the tail of a comet and we were dragged along again for maybe the millionth time of the night.

And I had my palms extended, on the receiving end, open to the crisscross stigmata, letting the gods dance around me and then upon me and they are light like balloons, like feathers, like bags of leaves, and the journey is circuitous but scenic . . . I heard a flute . . . or something . . . I saw . . . pilgrims and pioneers . . .

The Friday of Thanksgiving weekend, Emily and I went to the movies together.

Emily didn't want to see *Pete's Dragon*, and neither did I really but Jim Dale was in it, the guy who created *Scapino* and starred in it.

We ended up going to see *The Turning Point* and Emily was enthralled.

"I love the ballet. It's so ordered and precise. And reliably traditional. It's one of my comforts."

"Do you dance?"

"I did. I wasn't very good though. I love to watch. And watching Mikhail Baryshnikov is a special treat for the eyes."

"'Cause of his dancing."

"Of course," she said, "What else would I be talking about?"

We sat and had coffee at Norms on La Cienega.

"Can I smoke in here?" Emily asked, pulling out her pack of Gitanes.

"Definitely," I said, gesturing that I'd like one.

"I feel like we're in a movie," she said as she lit my cigarette in her mouth and handed it to me.

"*Now, Voyager*," I said.

"What's that?"

"You've never seen *Now, Voyager*? Bette Davis? Paul Henreid? Utter amazingness?"

"And there is a cigarette lighting scene, I presume?"

"Several, yes. It's like a running shtick. Paul Henreid always lights two cigarettes in his mouth and then hands one to Bette Davis. There's a *Now, Voyager*/*Dark Victory* double bill at the Continental over on Melrose near Van Ness tomorrow night and Sunday also. If you want to go, I'm thinking of checking it out."

"I'm supposed to spend tomorrow and Sunday at my mom's house unfortunately."

"Oh, bum."

"*C'est la vie, mon ami*," she said with smoke wisping from between her lips.

We both stared into our coffee during an awkward lull.

"I don't know, I'm starting to feel like every story in the world is about betrayal these days."

"You mean, like, beyond the Megiddo reading list thing."

"Absolutely. Look at that movie. Anne Bancroft betrayed Shirley Maclaine to make sure she got the part of Anna. Shirley Maclaine cheated on Tom Skerrit. Mikhail Baryshnikov—sigh—used Leslie Browne for sex."

"I guess it's an important issue."

"Or a common one. But, I don't know. I mean, what's the big deal? Cheating is part of the game. I come from a family of cheaters so I know."

"Why is it even called cheating?"

"Exactly," she said, "All's fair in love and war."

"We, the great authorities on love and war, do declare it to be thus," I softly pounded my fist on the table.

"I have to pee," she said, getting up. "If the waitress comes I want blueberry pie a la mode. And more coffee."

"I will see 'tis done and done quickly, m'lady."

"Moi aussi," she said and headed to the ladies' room.

When Emily returned the waitress still hadn't come and I think she thought I was a wimp because I didn't get up and find the waitress and order her blueberry pie a la mode with vanilla and more coffee so that it would be waiting for her upon her return.

I wasn't even her boyfriend yet and already I was a bad boyfriend.

"Everything come out ok?"

"I bet you say that to all the girls," Emily pawed back.

"What are you reading for your next outside novel?" I asked.

"Hang, on . . . Excuse me," she flagged down the waitress, "Can I have blueberry pie a la mode, and more coffee? Do you want anything?" she asked me.

"More coffee?" I shriveled.

The waitress nodded.

"*Swann's Way*," Emily said and lit a new cigarette.

"How is it?"

"Gorgeous. Difficult. Profound."

"Like you," I flirted.

"You need to mellow out, m'lad," Emily said and offered me another cigarette which I declined because I was sort of nauseated, "You know. If it's meant to happen it'll happen between us. In the meantime just be here with me."

Our goodnight kiss as we sat in the car outside my house later was considerably more involved than just being there with her. It was long and deep and perfectly still. It jiggled my innards and stole my face right off my head.

Nothin' left to do but smile, smile, smile

The Dead wailed and the audience in its entirety wailed along and I was suddenly back with them.

I swayed to the lumbering cadence, slow and autumnal.

And, dang, dude, I'm just now realizing that was the amazing "Estimated Prophet"-into-"He's Gone" that Waldo was talking about at the party last night.

The end of November was a blur of *Scapino* rehearsals (we opened the first weekend in December) and filling out college applications in time to get a November 30 postmark before midnight at the 24 hour post office near LAX, standing in line with all the other procrastinators.

The *Scapino* performances were thankfully sparsely attended.

The debacle went mostly unnoticed.

Xeno's music was truly great, though. Melodic yet almost avant-garde in places.

"You should record that shit, dude," I told him after the production ended, "It's really brilliant."

We then got into a mutual love gush over Stephen Sondheim with him going nuts over the *Company* score and me enthusing about *A Little Night Music*.

"I got to see *Pacific Overtures* on Broadway last summer," Xeno said, "A work of genius. Sondheim does Kabuki. I have the Original Broadway Cast album if you ever want to hear it. I actually stole some ideas from it for my *Scapino* incidentals."

"Oh, man, that'd be great. I've read about *Pacific Overtures*, I haven't heard any of the actual music yet. Maybe over Christmas Vacation."

"Date," Xeno said and rushed off to his next activity, which could've been any of a hundred things.

Standing cliffside backed up against a steep incline, I perused a quivering cityscape below.

I was aware of the music scaling the incline above me and trying to drag me up with it but a voice held me where I was.

"Did you reap the seeds like a man stranded on Jupiter?" the voice murmured, and for a second I thought maybe Manny had said that in my ear but I looked over and he was in his seat with his eyes closed.

I feared that if I let myself slide down the sudden mountainside I'd land in space again and then just keep falling like a time I remembered from before and so I held on and looked up at the Shrine ceiling and piano notes were tinkling like the chandelier and then as my gaze fell back upon the stage the entire band had left except the drummers.

The drums placed me in Arabia, in the Arabia of Hollywood films.

Big-eyed girls were dancing and flaunting their curves and the twin illusions of availability and receptivity.

The vibration of the boom-boom made them smile like they'd just been riding horseback.

A winnowing away of the dancing girls left only two who approached me though at first I presumed they were moving toward somebody behind me.

They took hold on either side of me and led me to the center of the room.

Hundreds of people were sitting on pillows along the walls, watching.

The band lifted off right through the roof and we all got sucked up with them.

I ricocheted off other spinners, all of us gyrating in the sky.

My two girls were aloft with me.

Spanish lady come to me, she lays on me this rose

At a closer glance I realized how much one of the girls looked like Rose Benedict from elementary school.

"Calliope," she introduced herself.

"And Euterpe," said the other and then I recognized both of them. It was rare to see them that close up.

It rainbow spirals round and round,
It trembles and explodes

"You've been ignoring us," Calliope said.

"I've been busy."

"We need your attention."

"You sound like a magazine," I said and Calliope slapped me.

It left a smoking crater of my mind,
I like to blow away

"We are goddesses to be worshipped," Calliope held her own breasts.

"And the way you worship is by giving voice to the music we fill you with."

"Let us bear witness through you."

"And through us you shall also be heard," Euterpe cupped her crotch.

"The bliss is reciprocal."

Comin', comin', comin' around

Calliope and Euterpe warped with me into a wormhole and I couldn't find anything to hang onto and for a time there was nothing but a roller coaster and a scream that wouldn't come all the way out of me.

"This is where you need to go," Calliope pointed to the galaxies as we passed them.

"Your message is hidden out here," Euterpe said.

"And in there," Calliope pressed my chest.

"Give us a portion of each day."

"No vacations."

"No Sabbath."

"And we will guide you to the great discoveries which await you right where you're always standing," Calliope said and the two of them vanished, leaving me right where I was in the Shrine.

I had landed.

Escapin' through the lily fields
I came across an empty space
It trembled and exploded
Left a bus stop in its place
The bus came by and I got on
That's when it all began
There was cowboy Neal
At the wheel
Of a bus to never-ever land

Never-ever land stayed in my brain and I was stuck in that uncertainty as to the actual or imaginary existence of Peter Pan.

For a moment the air smelled like Cambria and I thought of the July 4th evening on the beach talking to Annie De Milo, the night Taryn Rust gave me a blowjob, the night my heart skipped a few too many beats.

It got me thinking too about Emily Wolf.

Once Christmas Vacation had arrived, that put more pressure on me to make an effort to see Emily now that school—for the next two weeks—was not the built-in easy option for hanging out.

She called me the night school let out for break and asked me if I wanted to go see *Saturday Night Fever* with her in Westwood the next night and I said yeah.

When we got to the Fox Theatre, *Saturday Night Fever* was sold out so we went across the street to the Bruin and saw *The Goodbye Girl* instead.

Richard Dreyfus reminded me of me, but I'm sure every Jewish guy in America felt that way.

I didn't absorb as much of the film as I'd've liked due to my sordid thoughts about Emily and how I'd like to peel away her restraint.

Emily wasn't uptight like Lorelei, but she *was* restrained.

I didn't make a move on her in the theatre because she once told me she hated that sort of thing—people making out in movie theatres—plus my growing confusion over what we were doing was getting me depressed, and with such depressions comes the inevitable loss of desire for a while.

My lust resurged after the movie when, looking through the hanging racks at Postermat, Emily said, "I think they should've showed them fucking."

"Who?" I asked.

"Richard Dreyfus and Marsha Mason."

"You mean like X-rated?"

"No. Just good steamy intimations. A moan or two. Heavy breathing. Bodies moving under the covers. Simultaneous orgasm. A hot kiss at the end. You know how the movies do."

"Nyeah, but—"

"—I think the best art, when you strip away the details and the materials, is really out to provoke a tasteful commingling of hard and wet."

That phrase was recited nightly for weeks afterward.

a tasteful commingling of hard and wet

I liked this version of Emily a whole lot.

"That movie was quite well done. But it didn't get any hardness or wetness going. Richard Dreyfus reminded me of you," I remembered her saying as Jerry Garcia's guitar lines did loop-de-loops through an epic soliloquy and intruded upon the memory of my night with Emily, but kept on thinking about how I declined going to Canter's and feigned a creeping ailment so that I could end the evening early and Emily didn't seem disappointed which both saddened and relieved me.

When she dropped me off at home, our lips did lock and our tongues engaged for what I thought was a very fine smooch indeed.

"You need to know me better," Emily said, "Before I suck you all the way into my thing, you know."

"I'd like to be sucked into your thing."

"It's a big thing."

"So's mine."

"I'd love it if you'd come to my Winter Solstice dinner party. My dad's out of town."

"Winter Solstice. That'd be cool. Are you cooking?"

"Haha, well there won't really be any dinner there."

"Ah. So more like snacks and stuff?"

"Eh, sort of," she smirked and added, "You are very sweet. Snacks and stuff. Oh my God are you cute."

Whenever Emily Wolf smirked I wanted to kiss her really hard on the mouth.

"Can I bring something?"

"Just bring what you've got," she said.

I had no idea what she meant by that so I figured I wouldn't bring anything.

10

The Shrine was in the throes of jubilation as the music rollicked and the walls pulsed with all the life inside them.

"One nation under GD!" a celebrant shouted and basked in the rapture.

I was starting to step back a little, winded and gobsmacked from my flight with the divine ladies.

It started to feel more like a regular concert.

Some come to laugh their past away
Some come to make it just one more day
Whichever way your pleasure tends
If you plant ice you're gonna harvest wind

Xeno Cortez invited me to go see the *A Little Night Music* movie with him and then go back to his house and listen to the *Pacific Overtures* cast album, but instead I went by myself to the new Gene Wilder movie, *The World's Greatest Lover* at the Egyptian up on Hollywood Blvd.

I went despite the wretched reviews because Gene Wilder was in it.

And I also went so I could wallow in a loneliness that went beyond the default built-in loneliness of going to the movies by yourself. It was the loneliness of not knowing. Love without an object. The kind of love that makes you feel like Jesus. On the one hand, that kind of love can be cool. Oh yeah for sure. But you're still lonely regardless.

As I walked down the aisle looking for a seat I passed Miranda, who was also alone.

"Hi, Lance!" she waved and I waved back.

She didn't invite me to go sit with her so I found a seat a few rows in front of her and dug into my popcorn.

During the closing credits she came over and sat next to me for a minute.

"What'd you think?" she asked.

I shrugged.

"Yeah, it pretty much sucked," she affirmed.

"Yeah."

"But I had to see it because it's Gene Wilder."

"Same here," I admitted.

We looked at each other for a few damn good seconds.

"I've gotta go," she said as she climbed slowly over me to get to the aisle, "Nice bumping into you."

"Yeah," I said and waved as she left.

I kept sitting there because I like to stay until the credits are over (which carries its own special kind of sadness, especially the copyright date in Roman numerals). It's like you're being left behind or something.

Miranda ran back in and kissed me on the top of the head, adding, "Bye,

Lance!" on her way out.

We never stopped rocking 'til the moon went down

The music charged into this double-time typhoon that required full bodily participation.

Gina started bumping asses with me and I savored every soft buffeting.

Manny was doing the twist, the swim, and the watusi in ironic rotation.

The three of us ended up jumping up and down and laughing like back in kindergarten.

When the music got quiet we bent our knees and got small and as the music started resurging we came back to full extension and pogo'd like punks up to and including the final chord.

When the Dead left the stage we stood sweating and exhilarated from a potent dose of all-consuming music.

After running into Miranda at the movies, I went over to Manny's house to get stoned and listen to the new Eno album.

"When's your sister coming home for break?" I asked as we smoked a bowl in his old playhouse in the backyard.

"Fuck if I know," Manny said.

"Just curious."

"Uh huh."

"Dang, dude, Penelope Lagniappe never comes home. I used to love getting high with her on the garage roof. We had some holy moments up there."

"Uh huh."

"No really."

"I heard Buzzy saying she eloped with some guy she met in college."

"No way."

"Sorry to bring you the bad news."

"Penelope Lagniappe is married?"

"I'm pretty sure that's what I heard."

"Dang, dude, that ruins everything," I said and sighed, "I feel like I would've heard about that. I mean, they live in the house next door. My mom is friends with their mom."

"I'm just saying what I heard. Did you think *you* were gonna marry her?"

"It's a hope thing."

"See, I'm just the opposite," he said, "I'm stoked by hopelessness. The more unattainable the girl, the hotter the fire."

"That's like Buzzy with Heaven."

"Maybe not that hopeless."

"Haha."

The Eno album came galloping out of the speakers like a liquid stallion.

It will shine and it will shudder as I guide it with my rudder
On its metal ways
It will cut the night before it as it leaves the day that saw it
On its metal ways
Nobody passes us in the deep quiet of the dark sky
Nobody sees us alone out here among the stars
In these metal ways
In these metal days

"This is already amazing," I said after the first verse.

"Sublime discovery."

And we both submerged.

"I feel like we're being boated through a robot swamp," Manny said.

"That's potentially accurate," I sort of agreed.

The instrumental center grabbed me like a trance. The looping guitar tones in the middle of the song that danced along into a funkish breakdown and back to the second verse.

"Is that Fred Frith or Robert Fripp?" Manny asked of the guitars.

"I don't know. Both maybe?"

"Trippy whoever."

"Dig it."

"I am digging, dude. Way down deep."

Through a fault of our designing we are lost among the windings
Of these metal ways
Back to silence back to minus with the purple sky behind us
In these metal ways
Nobody hears us when we're alone in the blue future
No one receiving the radio's splintered waves
In these metal ways
In these metal days

Dang, dude. Eno was speaking our minds.

Backwater!
We're sailing at the edges of time

"Hey, this song bounces like a heavy balloon," I said to Manny.

"Led Zeppelin."

"Ha."

"Hee Haw."

"Dang, dude, does anybody actually watch *Hee Haw* anymore?"

"Did they ever?"

"I can't believe it's still on," I said, "I caught it like on Channel 5 or something not long ago."

"I guess there's still a market for hillbilly humor."

"Beasley Slocum."

"Ha, yeah. I wonder if that dude's in jail. Do the girls still all look like Ellie May Clampett on that show?"

"I guess. I don't know."

"I'd watch it if it were just Buck Owens and Roy Clark jamming every week."

"That'd be flagrant."

"Hell yes."

The time I almost drowned came to mind as we spoke but I think it was because of the music.

I was with my grandparents at a motel where they were staying because their house was being remodeled.

I was around 3 years old I think.

I had been sitting on the top step of the motel pool, my grandfather sitting on the deck dangling his legs in the water and talking to my uncle.

I did not yet know how to swim.

Trying to stand up, I slipped off the first step and began to sink.

I paddled my arms and legs and could see the surface but I couldn't get there.

A dream I've had many times since.

Through the distorted film of the of the water's surface I could see my grandfather look down and thrust his arms into the water to grab me.

I remembered that when I paddled I wasn't panicked. I was calm. It was all right to be in the water.

But if you study the logistics
And heuristics of the mystics
You will find that their minds rarely move in a line

I did panic the time I was trying to impress Evelyn Childs with my body surfing skills and wiped out, bumping my head and losing my sense of up and down, not knowing which way the surface lay, plus the roil of the wave I was caught in and its subsequent undertow, afraid that I'd run out of breath and drown. It ended up being the wave itself that saved me, tossing me to the shore and leaving me there.

I so wanted to fuck somebody but I had no idea whom.

Miranda Savitch maybe. I tried to imagine myself on top of her, fucking her.

My mind couldn't make it happen.

Abandoned by the Muses.

Lying on my back I moved my hips to the funky bassline but it didn't make me horny.

I was being rendered sexless.

Miranda Savitch was the first girl I ever wanted to have sex with, the first one I ever thought about having sex with.

And still she drew me like an eternal return.

I used to love watching her read when we sat next to each other in Mr. Beauregard's class.

You knew the text was getting her closest regard and consideration.

I wanted that from her.

But every time she gave it to me I freaked out and turned into an android.

Dang, dude.

I hate moments of tragic insight.

All alone in Act IV, agonizing.

The rocking end of Side A had us both air drumming to the last beat and pulled me out of my self-inflicted bummery.

King's lead hat put the innocence inside her
It will come, it will come, it will surely come

"Rock and roll," Manny pointed at the speakers.

"Jamming," I kept the air-beat going.

The trippy recursive breakdown in the tune layered in upon itself and jiggered our thought patterns and might've made us cross-eyed, at least I'm pretty sure Manny was.

King's lead hat put the poker in her fire
It will come, it will come, it will surely come

"Dang, dude. Put the poker in her fire."

"*It will come, it will come—*"

"*—It will surely come,*" Manny said. "That'd be a great Bubba Free John song."

"Is Bubba Free John a songwriter?"

"He should be," Manny said and got up off his bed, "Recharge the batteries?" he pantomimed toking.

"Sure ting, mon," I said and pried myself vertical.

We took a stroll around the block when Side A ended so we could rekindle our smoldering brainwaves. I'd brought what I had left of the Metempsychosis weed which turned out to be the perfect complement to Side B of *Before And After Science.*

"I ran into Miranda Savitch at the movies today," I said, handing the joint to Manny.

"Yeah?"

"Yeah."

"And?"

"That's all."

"Was she there with Freddy?" Manny exhaled.

"No she was alone."

"They are hanging out separately a lot."

"Seems like it."

"What'd you see?"

"*The World's Greatest Lover.*"

"Dude. Why'd you go see that crap?"

"Willy Wonka's in it."

"That's not enough."

"It most definitely was not, no."

"Did you guys sit together?"

"Nah, she didn't invite me over when I said hi, so I kept walking to a couple of rows in front of her."

"You are a disgrace to the gender, dude."

"Nah, man, what you will one day realize is that I actually represent the gender. There are more guys like me wimping out at opportune moments than there are of Joe Pussy out there trying to bang every chick he comes into contact with."

"May be."

"She came and sat down next to me afterward, though."

"A sure sign that she wants to fuck you."

"Haha. No, we talked about how lame the movie was and then she left."

"That's lamer than the movie, dude, and I haven't even seen it. Nor will I ever."

"She did come back and kiss me on the top of the head."

"See, dude? She does want to fuck you."

"Nonsense."

"True love waits."

"Buddy Holly," I said and we both mock-salaamed.

When we got back to Manny's I stopped by Leah's room even though she was still not back from school for break. I was desperately seeking erection fodder and thought maybe her ambience might be powerful enough in the room that it could stoke something.

I flipped on the light and saw the tidy perfection of Leah's world, everything arranged just so like a window display, this beautiful girl made even more alluring by her fastidiousness.

But that didn't work either.

I sidled my way into Manny's room which was always a hassle because you had to pass through the dining room where the dining room furniture was too big for the space so it made walking awkward.

He turned off the light and we dove into Side B.

Here he comes
The boy who tried to vanish to the future or past
Is no longer here with his sad blue eyes.

Here he comes
He floated away and as he rose above reason
He rose above the clouds, he was seven feet high.

"Dang, dude, this song is about me," said Manny in the dark.

"You don't have sad blue eyes. Your eyes are the jewiest of jewy brown."

"Jewy Brown is going to be my stage name."

"Jewy Brown: The white Sammy Davis, Jr."

"Totally," Manny croaked inwardly.

"You sounded like Satan just now," I said.

"Your mother sucks cocks in Hell!" Manny gurgled and we fell into another prolonged silence.

I managed not to think of Miranda for most of it.

The music turned to atmosphere only.

And then a pulse, a heavenly pulse, rippled in the stillness.

Zero gravity.

I am on an open sea,
Just drifting as the hours go slowly by.
Julie with her open blouse
Is gazing up into the empty sky
Now it seems to be so strange here
Now it's so blue.
The still sea is darker than before...

"*Julie with her open blouse*," said Manny. "Eno is more sexual than usual on this album."

"*Put the poker in her fire.*"

"*It will come, it will come, it will surely come.*"

"This could be a Gilbert O'Sullivan song."

"Maybe if Gilbert O loosened up and smoked some weed," Manny said.

"I love Gilbert O'Sullivan."

"Dude, I know."

"That album *Himself*, man. I'm telling you."

"I've tried, dude. I'm sorry. But no."

I levitated away from Manny for a while. Not because of the insult to my musical taste but because the music had become a tendril that was lifting me.

Here we are
Stuck by this river,
You and I
Underneath a sky that's ever falling down, down, down
Ever falling down

"Haiku music," said Manny but I didn't answer because I was too busy listening, "Or Erik Satie with electric piano added."

Through the day
As if on an ocean
Waiting here,
Always failing to remember why we came, came, came:
I wonder why we came

I understood this song and I couldn't stop myself from thinking about Miranda Savitch, sitting with her at the Tar Pits by the little stream that don't hardly move none.

I would lean into her and kiss her and tell her something like, "We are sitting atop an ancient graveyard."

"And someday more highly evolved beings will be sitting atop us and wondering what our lives were like," Miranda would say in response and then I'd find some way to sabotage our connection.

This was our song. The one I'd never sing to her.

You talk to me

163

As if from a distance
And I reply
With impressions chosen from another time, time, time,
From another time

I wanted to sit someday with someone at the Tar Pits by the little stream that don't harldly move none.

I had given up hope that it would be with Miranda.

"This is not a river anymore," Manny said of the instrumental track going on beneath us as we floated, "This is a pond."

"And we are frogs?"

"We are one frog," Manny said. "Waiting."

"For a friend."

"For Hell to freeze over."

"For the end of the world."

"For our moment in the sun."

"For Lefty."

"For Godot."

"For the man behind the curtain to help get us home."

The spider and I
Sit watching the sky
On a world without sound

"This reminds me of Buzzy," Manny said.

"Flippy Killbones," I said and we both chuckled with sadness for our disintegrating friend.

We knit a web to catch
One little fly
For our world without sound

I thought (out loud apparently), "How come Sam the ice cream man never comes around with his Dinosaur Times truck anymore?"

"That dude got arrested for murder," Manny said.

"What?" I was taken aback both by his answer and the fact that he'd heard what I thought was just a thought.

"He got arrested for murder. That's what my dad said not that long ago."

"Holy shit. I wonder if it was—"

"What?"

"Remember that girl who got stabbed in front of my house?"

"Yeah of course."

"Dinosaur Times was abandoned on our street that night."

"Whoa. Yeah, actually I remember you telling me that."

"That was a long time ago, though."

"My dad didn't say *when* he got arrested."

"How come you always find about about shit that I never find out about? And I mean important shit. Like Penelope Lagniappe getting married. And Sam the ice cream man getting arrested for murder."

"It's because of my what's-it-called."

"Ah. Right. I remember. The what's-it-called."

"I've had it since the day I was what's-it-called."

"Hang on," I stopped him, "I want to listen to the what's-it-callled," pointing to Manny's stereo.

"This album is all about water," I said eventually, "All the songs have water imagery in them."

"I think it's all about magic."

"How so?"

"That which exists before and after science. Magic."

"Dang, dude. That is excellent."

We touched fingertips.

"Yup."

"But water is predominant too. It's tied into the magic thing somehow."

"Totally."

"I think we have to listen a few hundred more times to figure it out."

"Oh most definitely."

We sleep in the morning
We dream of a ship that sails away
A thousand miles away . . .

We were going to go see *High Anxiety* together after listening to the Eno record but I didn't really have any money and I kind of wanted to go home and wallow in sadness alone some more.

"We should go see the Grateful Dead when they're at the Shrine next month," Manny said as we stood in his driveway.

"I'm not into the Grateful Dead. I fell asleep when I saw them the first time."

"Yeah, same with me. But I heard it's really easy to get acid there."

And so a month later we went.

On the barely cold January night in downtown Los Angeles that was still in progress but winding down.

The Grateful Dead had come out for their encore.

I felt like I'd been there for days.

Red and white, blue suede shoes, I'm Uncle Sam, how do you do?

Gina and I danced face to face, her arms around my waist, mine around her neck.

"What should we name our children?" I said.

"Richard and Kat," Gina said, "And we can call them Dick and Pussy."

"I'm sure they'll thank us later."

"Exactly."

We smiled.

"But you do realize I'm not going to fuck you," Gina said, "so I hope you're coming to the marriage with a powerful syringe and very good aim."

Shake the hand that shook the hand of P.T. Barnum and Charlie Chan

I was encouraged that Gina was letting me joke about us being a couple.

It was like our own weird version of "taking it to the next level."

Wave that flag, wave it wide and high

I had forgotten the flagpole in Emily Wolf's front yard.

The first time I'd gone over her house, that day we talked about *The French Lieutenant's Woman*, at first I thought, oh no, Republicans, but when I looked up and saw not an American flag but instead a Jolly Roger flapping in the breeze, I thought, oh, all right, cool. Captain Hook. Peter Pan. Maybe it's real. Maybe it's not.

I got to Emily's Winter Solstice dinner party late because my mother made me go with her to the market to get something to give to the hostess.

"She told me to just bring myself," I said, "or something like that."

"It doesn't matter what she told you. It's always nice to bring something. Do they need drinks?" my mother asked. "Soda is good to bring."

"I think it's just snacks and stuff," I said, "I don't know. She didn't really say."

"Chex Party Mix," my mother decided as we pulled into the Ralphs lot, "That's what you should get. Chex Party Mix. The big bag. I think it even says 'Party Size' on it."

"Why would they make a Chex Party Mix that's not party size? I mean, since it's for parties?"

"Don't be a smart ass," she handed me $10 and waited in the car.

"Get two bags!" she yelled out the window, "You don't know how many kids are going to be there! One regular and one cheddar!"

Consequently, because I was already slow getting out of the house anyway, and the long line at Ralphs, I got to Emily's house nearly an hour late.

I rang the doorbell but no one answered, so I tried the knob and the door was in fact unlocked.

I stepped into the living room and saw—and heard—a couple dozen or so kids not just making out but in fact having sex everywhere, some fully clothed, some in varying states of dishabille, one girl completely naked.

In particular on the couch I saw Freddy Snow's bare butt humping the spread legs of someone who was not Miranda, and nearby Emily was on her knees sucking the cock of some guy I didn't recognize, and doing so like a seasoned veteran.

I watched in frozen fascination, two bags of Chex Party Mix in hand, the roomful of couples and threesomes having at each other, balls slapping asses and perinea as cocks pounded pussies and cunts danced a-grind on dicks in polyrhythmic fission, and I marveled at the beautiful shamelessness of the proceedings.

Freddy, as I mentioned, was plowing the field of some farmer's daughter on the big couch.

There was one couple over on the love seat, she giving him a blowjob while he fingered her from behind. At some point I looked back and he was on top and pouring himself into her.

All the way across the room a buxom lass had straddled a skinny-legged boy on the overstuffed chair and, dang, dude, she was riding that cock-horse to Banbury Cross.

On the floor two girls were making out and there was a half-clad dude stumbling over them taking polaroids.

A threesome was standing up in the corner, a girl giving two guys hand jobs simultaneously while one finger-fucked her and the other nibbled on her breasts. They took turns kissing her mouth. I watched that liaison for quite a while.

Back on the floor, one of the girls had started going down on her lady friend who was now, obviously, without pants on, and depending on how she moved, I could, off and on, see her vagina.

I was amazed at the talent and variety and skill.

I felt like I was at a carnival.

I presumed all these kids—with the exception of Freddy and Emily—went to Hamilton.

They obviously partied way differently over there.

At Fairfax parties we mostly just smoked weed and listened to music. Sometimes we'd play charades.

I returned my attention to Emily who was now taking it doggy style from a different partner.

The guy she'd just blown walked toward me, his half-hard dick still sticking out of his fly, and said, "Oh, cool, Chex Party Mix," took both bags and laid them on the dining room table. "Dive in!" he said as he disappeared into the kitchen.

I didn't know if he meant the orgy or the Chex Party Mix.

Emily was on all fours while the guy behind her, on his knees, pummeled her from behind like a jackhammer.

"Harder," Emily groaned, her hair loose and hanging over her face so that I couldn't see it. His right hand grabbed her hip for better leverage while he occasionally smacked her left butt cheek with his other hand which Emily seemed to dig quite a bit because she rasped 'yeah' every time he did it or maybe she just felt like she was supposed to react that way, I have no fucking idea.

Emily had on a silk blouse and a sleeveless suede vest but no pants.

Her ass was rounder than I'd imagined it through her jeans.

She still had her shoes on. The clunky Victorian ankle boots she always wore.

I thought about how awkward it must've been for her to get her pants off over her shoes, and I wondered how I'd missed seeing that happen.

I was pretty turned on by the rabid activities and sounds but not enough to take part.

Seeing Emily at that moment, naked and amorous and totally into cock, rattled my fancy and very much made me want to go home immediately and jerk off.

Finish the story that way because it always ends better than real life escapades do.

No hassles. No phone calls later.

I'd grown enamored of its efficiency.

Freddy Snow came gruntingly inside the girl he was fucking who'd been raising quite a thunderous ruckus herself.

I thought about the possibility that Emily and Freddy had fucked at some point and that bummed me out but I promised myself I'd never ask her.

After a series of intermittent potent orgasms exploding across the room, and fairly certain Emily'd been too preoccupied to notice I was even there, I skulked out the front door horny but heavy-hearted and into the night air which felt cool on my lungs just like the air outside the Shrine as we exited the venue after the Dead show.

Manny and I had both peaked but were definitely still tripping reasonably hard.

As we walked across the parking lot I saw Holly Fox making out with Sonny Blue and they were going at it pretty fiercely.

I was silent in Gina's car on the way home.

Manny lived closer to Gina so they dropped me off first.

"Thanks for being the ride and the guide," I said as I was getting out of the car.

"It was an honor, sir," she said. "You ok enough to face your parents?"

"My dad's probably still awake. But yeah I can maintain."

"Debrief tomorrow at school?"

"Oh yes. This was religious. I plugged into the music quite a bit."

"It looked like you were having a grand excursion."

"I was all the way up in it, yep," I grinned, "And still nicely switched on right now. I'd most definitely check them out again."

"Same here," Gina blew me a pinky kiss.

"Later, dude," I said to Manny who grunted from the back seat, "Enjoy the rest of it."

My dad was indeed awake watching TV in the living room, a peanut butter and butter sandwich on a plate in his lap when I got home.

"How was it?" he asked.

"Top flight," I said, both thumbs up like Yocheved Levy, and floated into my bedroom where I lay awake tripping less and less until dawn.

I did want to experience having an orgasm on LSD, but no one was resonating.

Every time I thought of Holly Fox I pictured her making out with Sonny Blue.

Every time I thought of Emily Wolf I pictured her sucking cock and taking it from behind at her dinner party.

Every time I thought of Gina Dichlich I'd picture her bumping cunts with Corazon De Leon.

And although that was fleetingly sexy, I couldn't translate it into an erection.

Every time I thought of Dolly Ferris I'd picture her in bed with her boy Georges.

Every time I thought of Taryn Rust, I'd picture her getting finger-fucked by Artie the music geek.

Every time I thought of Penelope Lagniappe, I'd picture her getting married in Vegas with a Liberace impersonator officiating.

Every time I thought of Desirée Stoner I'd picture her practicing the cello, her one true lover.

Every time I thought of Miranda Savitch I'd picture her finding out that Freddy was fucking someone else.

Every time I thought about Miranda Savitch it made me want to think some more about Miranda Savitch.

I abandoned my orgasm plan because my dick was just not interested, and instead I put on this weird record I feel like hearing occasionally, an album of music and readings from the horror soap opera *Dark Shadows*. My favorite track on the album is Jonathan Frid, who played the vampire Barnabas Collins, reciting Prospero's soliloquy from Act IV of *The Tempest*:

Our revels now are ended. These our actors,
As I foretold you, were all spirits and
Are melted into air, into thin air:
And, like the baseless fabric of this vision,
The cloud-capp'd towers, the gorgeous palaces,
The solemn temples, the great globe itself,
Yea all which it inherit, shall dissolve
And, like this insubstantial pageant faded,
Leave not a rack behind. We are such stuff
As dreams are made on, and our little life
Is rounded with a sleep.

For much of the rest of the night I lay in silence, a perfectly soft being, like a feather, *like an angel standing in a shaft of light*, floating in the midst of it, awakened and empty.

The ring of clarity focused my brain and body.

When streaks of red and pink in the eastern sky were visible through my window, I put on Side B of *Before & After Science*, the record that had not left my turntable for the past 4 weeks, and decided what I was going to wear to school that day. Jeans. Baseball shirt. Adidas. Powder blue zip-up sweatjacket, the one with the hood. The basic daily ensemble. The only variable really was which baseball shirt to wear, Dodgers or Angels.

The spider and I sit watching the sky on a world without sound

There was a glow in the waning darkness and above me in a corner of the ceiling I saw him.

"Flippy Killbones," I said, "Nice to meet you."

Buzzy's friend wanted me to know he was real. I could feel the friendly presence.

When the song was over I moved through the blue-gray light of the hallway and into the bathroom where I turned on the shower and urinated in the toilet while waiting for the water to warm up.

The urinary stream was no longer cosmic. The magic had vanished. I was alone and forlorn and loath to face the school day.

I sang to myself in the shower.

We sleep in the morning
We dream of a ship that sails away
A thousand miles away

I let the water cascade down my body and swirl into the drain.

I let it splash against my struggle with gravity and inertia and entropy.

I sagged in the slipstream.

All my energy left me.

All my emptiness opened.

All my girls had gone elsewhere.

Goodbye Yellow Brick Road

1

Levon Arrow loved everybody.

No matter how small or insignificant.

Levon's heart beat sometimes in fits and squiggles, but he'd grown accustomed to the flurries, even the occasional swoon.

Levon's mother always told him ever since he was a little boy, "There is a star in your heart for every person in the world."

"But won't it get filled up and burst?" he'd ask.

"No, that can't happen," his mother would assure him, "The heart just keeps on growing. You can never run out of love and there's always room for more."

"Sometimes my heart feels like it's going to burst, though," Levon would say back.

"Your heart's not going to burst. That's just a bunch of new stars being born," his mother promised.

I remember only the onset, not the aftermath.

Diana was saying, *"There can't be any feelings between the like of you and the like of me.*"

And then I couldn't do my next line.

"Not now," I thought as I felt the dizzy swim and shortness of breath creep up on me and everything went white.

After that, only a blankness like the blankness I beheld when I came in Taryn Rust's mouth that first time she gave me head up in Cambria.

I returned to awareness of myself and my surroundings while being lifted onto an emergency room bed by two Ethiopian guys.

A nurse began attaching me to elaborate machinery which was probably frighteningly expensive but which from my up-close bedridden perspective looked really plastic and chintzy like something from a toy store.

Machines don't look like machines anymore.

"Hey, you're with us," the nurse noticed me.

"And where would that be?" I queried.

"Tarzana," she answered.

"Is your name really Nurse Ratched?" I pointed to her badge.

"No, I just wear this to mess with people's heads," she said as she finished taking my blood pressure. "All your vital signs are normal, Mr., um . . ."

"B-B-Billy B-B-Bibbitt," I said.

"How original."

"Oh, I bet you say that to all the lunatics, Nurse Ratched,"

"Call me Queenie."

"Is that your roller derby name?"

"You are a smart-ass," Nurse Ratched wagged her finger as she left me.

"Only when I'm flirting," I shouted and I know I made her laugh because I could hear her trying to hide it.

A doctor stopped at my bed and looked at my chart.

"Lance Atlas," he said.

"What happened to me?"

"What do you remember?"

"I was doing a scene from *Pygmalion* in the first round of the Drama Festival at Birmingham High, and I started getting short of breath and everything got very bright."

He moved close enough that I could see his badge.

Dr. Fagot

Dang, dude.

My parents arrived at that moment and my mother pushed past everyone to reach my bedside.

"Little Fella," she said and held my face.

"Mr. Lance," my dad intoned like a man from Cleveland and then leaned toward the doctor's badge. "Dr.—"

"Fagot," the doctor confirmed the worst.

"Beg your pardon?" my father winced, no doubt seeking a mental fortress strong enough to restrain the cackling laughter dying to emerge (as were we all).

"You heard right," Dr. Fagot said, "Just be glad you weren't me in high school," and then he asked me, "Has this happened before, Lance?"

"At least twice before," my mother answered for me.

"So you've known about the arrhythmia," Dr. Fagot said.

"Yes, his pediatrician Dr. Gemara has been handling it."

"Solomon Gemara?"

"Yes."

"Ah, I know Solly. He's a dear friend. When was the last time this happened?"

"A couple of years ago?" my mother looked at me, "That time at the basketball game at Fairfax?"

I thought about saying, "Actually it was right after I got a blowjob from Taryn Rust when I stayed with them up in Cambria, and there have been a couple of other minor incidents since that I haven't mentioned," but instead I just ended up saying out loud, "Yeah."

"Are you on any medication?"

"No," I said.

"Well, I'll consult with Dr. Gemara and in the meantime," he turned toward my parents, "we're going to do some tests. Queenie?"

Nurse Ratched appeared at the curtain.

"Yes?" she said.

"I'm going to keep Lance overnight. After they're done down here we'll admit him to a room."

"There is apparently a very upset young lady outside insisting on seeing this particular young man," Nurse Ratched said.

"Is that the *schvartze* we saw crying?" my dad asked the entire corridor.

"Theo," my mother squelched him not quite soon enough.

"Diana probably," I said, "my acting partner. That's who I was doing the scene with when it happened. I'm sure she's freaking out."

179

"She can come visit you tomorrow. Come with me, Queenie," Dr. Fagot said as they departed.

"What happened?" my mother asked.

"Diana and I were doing our *Pygmalion* scene and I collapsed," I said. "I don't remember anything after that up until they put me in this bed."

"Did it feel like before?"

"Yeah."

"But you feel fine now."

"Yeah. Like always. It's nothing."

"Are you involved with that girl in the waiting room?" my father asked.

"I'm waiting to find that out," I said with a wicked grin.

"You think that would be a good idea?"

"Why not?"

"You'll be facing social problems," my father said.

"I have no idea what you mean by that."

"I mean interacting with your friends."

"What?"

"Theo," my mother intervened.

"You look at me like I'm crazy," he said.

"You don't get to pick who you fall in love with," I reminded him.

"Wise words," my father acknowledged his own once upon a time advice to me.

"From a wise man," I agreed.

I knew he'd drop it after that.

My dad had just enough coolness to get it.

After a battery of cardiac tests and the departure of my parents a familiar loneliness set in.

The hospital staff brought me food I was unable to eat because it smelled like the sadness I was trying to avoid.

I made an attempt to eat the jello but it just made me cry.

On the one hand I knew I was fine and would be going home the next day to resume all normal activities. On the other hand I wondered if perhaps this was going to become an increasingly limiting disability which would prohibit my full involvement in the world (which I had enough trouble maintaining even without the heart irregularity).

I stared at the hospital room ceiling and went back over the stresses that had led to my latest episode.

In recent days, as the Drama Festival approached, I kept wanting to tell Diana how I felt about her and that was making my pulse erratic for sure.

We'd be rehearsing our scene from *Pygmalion* and all I could think about was making out with her.

I decided I would express my feelings via a written note that I planned to give her the day of the Drama Festival.

But also, I was a little awry after an incident the night before, when I went to see *Death In Venice* with Xeno Cortez.

We had just read the Thomas Mann story in AP English and Megiddo recommended the Visconti film which was going to be showing at the NuArt.

Everything was cool until about halfway through the movie when Xeno kissed me on the cheek and laid his hand gently on my crotch as we watched.

I nudged his hand away.

"No?" Xeno asked.

"I'm not into it," I had to thwart his advance and I felt bad, "really."

"Sometimes you seem like you are," Xeno said.

"I like girls. Straight up, dude."

"I'll take your word for it," Xeno said and sat up straight.

"If you had a vagina I'd fuck you, if that's any consolation."

"Praising with faint damnation."

Although he said it wryly, I couldn't gauge his inward agony at the rejection.

We both went back to watching the movie.

Near the end of the film, when Aschenbach is watching Tadzio point to the farther shore, with the Adagietto from Mahler's Fifth in full crescendo, I felt a tachycardial premonition, a forewarning, a blip in the rhythm.

I couldn't tell if the glare was on the screen or in my head.

I had flashes of Desirée Stoner playing cello naked and also of Annie De Milo standing on the beach, pointing at the Cheshire moon in Cambria.

I didn't lose consciousness but I slumped over like Aschenbach in the beach chair when he finally reaches Olympus and passes into the mythic realm where billions upon billions of multiverses radiate the scope of eternity which is really just the condition of all possible dimensions being perceived at once.

When the movie was over Xeno shook me and asked me if I was OK.

"I'm cool," I said, a bit dazed.

"I think so too," Xeno smiled and sort of helped me up.

We left the NuArt to go check out Papa Bach across the street.

I bought a postcard there with an unusual illustration of Peter Pan. Crosshatched pen and ink.

I owed Annie De Milo a response anyway and thought she'd dig the picture of Peter Pan aloft at Wendy Darling's window, from Peter's perspective, on the outside looking in like always.

"I hear the new Sondheim musical is going to be some kind of Grand-Guignol horror opera," Xeno said as we stood among the stacks at Papa Bach.

"Wow. That's a whole different concept."

"Should be sensational," Xeno said, "I feel like I can already hear it."

I pulled a copy of *Come Back, Little Sheba* off the shelf.

"*I had that dream again, Doc,*" Xeno imitated Shirley Booth.

"That movie was unbearably sad."

"Painful, yeah. I love it, though. Shirley Booth and Burt Lancaster. Two great performances. But *Death In Venice* was also pretty darn sad, I'd say. I had an intense involvement with the story when we were reading it in class. I understood it on a very personal level."

"Primary text."

"Most assuredly."

"I thought Visconti visualized Aschenbach's artistic struggle in a cool way."

"It's also a sexual struggle, don't forget. It's not just that Tadzio is so young, it's also that he's a boy. Aschenbach is grappling with that and turning it into some kind of aesthetic mythos."

"Totally," I said. "Interesting idea to make him a quasi-Mahler figure."

"I think the Mahler music was really well suited to the story, so it made sense."

And so we just fell back into our natural rapport despite the awkward advance and rejection earlier.

Even though my relationship with Xeno after that night was unexpectedly normal, and we just sort of returned to sweet banterings in class or in Play Production about Sondheim and other wonders, the incident still skewed me enough in the immediate aftermath to have an effect the next day, I mean like really messing with my metronome in a major way.

2

Levon Arrow lived on a snail farm.

There were acres of snails in all directions.

Every horizon was a slimy gray wave.

In Levon Arrow's day, snails were used as rocket fuel. Nothing else was available to facilitate the final evacuation of the planet.

He knew he and his mom would be the last ones to leave because without the Arrows not enough snails would grow to combustible maturity.

Levon predicted he'd end up being left behind alone because the last snail to fuel the last rocket would be gone before his turn came, he was sure of it.

Levon Arrow was always last in line.

He always let other people cut in front of him because he loved them and he'd also been taught it was the considerate thing to do.

Every day at school the bell to end lunch would ring just as he was getting his tray.

Every dream would end just as he was about to kiss his beloved, in every dream the same beloved.

And every morning he would wake up with the heart pain one suffers whenever a star is born therein.

He knew eventually he'd be left alone on earth.

And he was cool with that.

Luckily or unluckily, my sexual attention at that time was all being sucked in one direction.

Yet another Charybdis ahead.

Dang, dude.

I didn't want to be into Diana Hitchcock because I had just sworn off girls, yet again, following the abrupt end to my stillborn romance with Emily Wolf.

Whatever horniness I'd harbored for Emily Wolf evaporated at her orgy back in December.

After walking in on the already well underway bacchanal in her living room that Solstice night and thereupon watching her give a rather adept blowjob to one guy and then, with another, get fucked to what seemed like or at least sounded like orgasm doggy-style, I found it difficult to ponder having a conversation with her, so, out of cowardice, I didn't call her all Christmas vacation.

"I was really sad you didn't come to my dinner party," Emily said that first day back at school after the break, "And then you didn't call either. What happened?"

"Yeah, I-um, my parents ended up not letting me go 'cause they sprung a family trip to Palm Springs on us and we were leaving early the next morning."

The Palm Springs part was approximately true.

My dad came home from work the day after the orgy and told us to pack a few pairs of underwear and some swimming gear because we were going to

Palm Springs for the next several days.

"What, like now?" Mimi complained.

"Soon. Within the hour I'd like to be on the road."

"What about dinner?" Mimi asked.

"We'll grab a bite somewhere. It'll be fun. We're staying at the Rivers of Babylon."

"Why are we going to Palm Springs?" I asked.

"To get away from Christmas," my dad said. "Where better to ignore Christmas than with a bunch of Jews in exile?"

I was not surprised to run into Miranda Savitch by the hotel pool. I knew her family went to Palm Springs every year around that time and that they stayed at the Rivers of Babylon also.

"Hi, Lance!" I saw her waving from the deep end.

"Hey, how's it going?" I said.

"Pretty good," she said, swimming over to the side of the pool where I sat down and dangled my legs, "So you're here too."

"Yeah."

"Welcome to Jewville. We usually come for New Years. We came earlier this year 'cause my dad was anxious to get out of town."

"My dad's all ootchie, too. Weird. We never go anywhere. And then suddenly he said we're going to the Rivers of Babylon right now. Cray zee."

"I've told you about this place," Miranda said.

"Yes yes, you have."

We stared off in opposite directions for a little while.

"What are you doing later?"

"I think we're doing the Chinese buffet thingy," I said.

"Of course. Us too. I'm planning to slip out after a while and sit out by the pool. It'll be empty."

"Good idea," I said.

And, indeed, later, after hanging briefly at the buffet, I wandered out to the pool which was, as she'd predicted, nearly deserted, save for Miranda herself, on a plastic lounge chair, looking up at the sky.

"Hey, hey, Ellie May," I drawled like Jethro.

"It's the secret chimp," she said and waved feebly, "Hi, Lance."

It looked like she'd been crying maybe.

"What's wrong?"

"Oh, I had a stupid fight with Freddy on the phone up in the room just now."

"Ah. I know those."

"Yeah. He's all pissed because I'm not going to be with him on Christmas."

"Isn't Freddy Jewish?"

"Yeah, but he's into that whole it's a day that's all about love and togetherness bullshit."

All I could think about was Freddy's pelvis vigorously pounding the pudendum of that girl-who-wasn't-Miranda on the couch at Emily Wolf's Winter Solstice dinner party.

But I maintained guy-code silence.

Never rat out a brother.

Even if he did steal the heart of the first girl you ever loved.

"It was embarrassing too 'cause my little brother was in the room with me," Miranda said.

"How is Jeremy?"

"He's 12 now. He goes to John Burroughs!" her spirits brightened a bit.

I sat in the chair next to her and offered her a hit from the mini-bong I'd smuggled into my travel bag.

"Hmm?" I held it up.

"Holy shit," she said, taking the bong, "Hell yes. Gimme."

She inhaled and I watched her breasts separate.

"Thai stick," she said as the sweet smoke pervaded her brain.

"Yeah. From Bigelow Rust. He's calling this one Misty Beethoven 'cause it really opens you up."

"I don't get it."

"Nyeah it's a reference to a porno movie."

"Ah. Not my thing."

"Nor mine," which wasn't entirely true but I said it anyway.

"Nice high, though, regardless."

"He really names his pot?"

"Yeah. Except for the Thai Stick, it's all the same stuff, but he says giving each batch a unique name increases consumer interest. He claims it's the future of marketing. He told me the other day, when I bought this stuff as a matter of fact, he said, 'This shit's gonna be legal one day and I'm gonna be ready to go into business. I'm gonna be the king of fucking everything.'"

"May be," Miranda said and took another puff of the magic dragon.

I further enhanced my head as well and we both sat silently, seeing much more of the Milky Way than Los Angeles ever allowed us.

"I remember sitting right here like 4 years ago or something and wondering if you were looking at the same stars I was."

"I was," I said, "I told you that way back when you first asked me that."

"Nyeah, I didn't know if you were being honest or not."

My silence probably confirmed her doubt.

"Man, I was so in love with you, dude," Miranda said, her face reflecting ripples from the pool water, "For like a long-ass time. Cray-zee," she shook her head and started to get up.

"Where are you going?" I asked.

"I should probably go back to the room and call Freddy."

"Ah. Make nice?"

"Nyeah. I guess," she said, "Thanks for sharing that bud."

"A pressure and a pilferage," I said like old Milt Spilkes and looked at her. "I should probably make a phone call too."

"Emily Wolf," Miranda said.

"Yeah."

"She's waiting and wondering right now."

"How would you know? You're not even friends with her."

"I devoted several years of my life to waiting for Lance Atlas to call. I empathize with the confusion she is now feeling."

"Confusion?"

"Yes. You are confusing."

"In what way."

"Just call her. Love is simple."

"I'll call her."

"No you won't," Miranda turned to leave. "Bye, Lance," she nodded and walked back into the hotel.

"Nice hanging with you," I said but she was beyond hearing by then.

"And you couldn't at least call me? Like maybe when you got back from Palm Springs?" Emily Wolf brought me back to the present tension.

"I'm sorry."

"I wanted to give you a chance to see the animal in her natural habitat."

"How was the dinner party?" I played innocent.

"Oh, it was reasonably entertaining. These two bags of Chex Party Mix magically appeared. According to my friend Richie some guy brought them over and then left," and she stared me down.

I got the feeling she knew it was me, that I was there and saw the lascivious doings and freaked out and left.

"Chex Party Mix," Emily grinned.

"That was thoughtful," I said and oh fuck yes she totally knew I was there.

"A tad on the dorky side. But cute."

"Like me," I tried to look adorable.

"Exactly like you," she nodded.

I knew she knew and now she probably knew I knew she knew and she was just going to be maddeningly patient and eventually milk a confession out of me no matter how long it took and so I had no choice but to hit the deep freeze which I am very good at doing when I need to. And plus I was pretty thrown off by seeing her getting it on with those two guys and being so into it.

I couldn't stop picturing it and hearing her.

3

"We call it the Minerva Syndrome," the doctor said of Levon's heartaches one year when Levon felt particularly weakened by his enlarging heart, "Do you know who Minerva is?"

"No."

"The Roman goddess of wisdom. The Greeks call her Athena."

"What does she have to do with my condition?"

"She is the product of her father's brain alone. Her brain is the only part of her body she cares about."

"I still don't see what this has to do with having stars in my heart."

"Minerva loves everybody, but she doesn't know what to do about it. She doesn't know how to use her heart. Her half-brother Bacchus has the opposite problem. He was born from his father's thigh. He doesn't know how to use his brain."

"I still don't understand," Levon Arrow said.

"Well," said Dr. Ferry, "When Minerva felt love for someone, meaning everyone, her heart would ache and flutter and burn and she said it felt like stars being born. So now, whenever someone is born with stars in his heart, like you, Levon Arrow, we hearken back to Minerva and the longing she can't fulfill."

"That fits," Levon said, "I grok it the most. And if someone is born with stars in his brain is that called the Bacchus Syndrome?"

"No, we have named that condition after the fat kid from <u>Willy Wonka & The Chocolate Factory</u>. What's his name? Buzzy—"

"Augustus--"

"—Lagniappe?"

"--Gloop."

"I thought it was Buzzy Lagniappe."

"Augustus Gloop is the fat kid from <u>Willy Wonka & The Chocolate Factory</u>."

"Then who in all the heights of Olympus is Buzzy Lagniappe?"

"Actually, I live next door to a kid named Buzzy Lagniappe and his real name is Augustus and he used to be fat."

"Ah, but there is another realm wherein exists another <u>Willy Wonka & The Chocolate Factory</u> in which there is another fat kid named Buzzy Lagniappe."

"I'd like to visit that realm. What is it called and where is it located?"

"It's called the Realm of All Things Possible, a place where everything you think of is true, and it's located all the way inside."

"Inside where?" Levon inquired.

"Just inside."

"I don't get it. How do you get there?"

"You don't get there. You just suddenly ARE there. And then you realize you've always been there. You've never been anywhere else."

"Is there like a sign or something?"

"You'll know. You can only see it with your eyes closed."

"Dang, dude," Levon Arrow said, "that is flagrant."

I turned inward and spent a lot of time alone that January.

Other than seeing the Grateful Dead at the Shrine that one night with Manny Shepherd and Gina Dichlich, I wasn't socializing at all.

Gina Dichlich was intensely and increasingly into her girlfriend Corazon and largely inaccessible although we sometimes found time to hang out, usually over pizza at Damiano's on Fairfax, after school, when we could, but the intimacy was less intense. She'd become more guarded. I was no longer her confidant and felt the loss that must always accompany such realizations. I could tell she was squeezing me in before she had to go hang with her lady.

"I hope you're drawing," I said to her this one time at Canter's because she wasn't in the mood for Damiano's that day.

"I am! More than I ever have."

"And the girlfriend lets you work?"

"Cory is so supportive of my art," Gina said, "and she's also the inspiration. You have to come over and see the new stuff. Pretty much every drawing I do now is us together. Or what I imagine we look like when we're making out."

"You should get a big mirror."

"I want to! But it freaks Cory out too much."

"You have to convince her."

"It's the only way to get it right. Right?"

"Right."

"Plus watching in the mirror has to be sexy as hell."

"I would imagine so. Yeah. I'd be into it, I guess."

"I could tell my mom it's for doing self-portraits. She'd totally buy me a large mirror."

"Do it."

"And I wouldn't even be lying really."

"Correct."

"Dude, I have to push this mirror idea."

"You must."

"Do you have time to come over and look at the new stuff?"

"Yeah yeah. Definitely. Let's do it," I said and she drove us over to her house.

The new drawings were subdued pastels of female bodies–Gina and Corazon–intertwined in various acts of passion.

"Look at the legs. The lines."

"It's all about the legs," I said.

"I learned that from you."

"Legs imply leverage."

"I see."

"And leverage implies arousal."

"Preach it, brother."

"And arousal implies a tasteful commingling of hard and wet."

"Amen."

"The goal of all art."

"Says who?"

"Emily Wolf."

"Ah, a name from your not too distant present. You still have never told me why you guys stopped seeing each other."

"And I never will."

"I thought maybe I could coax it out of you when you were tripping at the Dead show. But that didn't happen."

"I have a well-trained unconscious."

"Keyed into all of your neurotic conflicts."

"Yes indeed. My unconscious would never rat out a brother."

We stood in her bedroom looking at her art in silence for a while.

"I'm sorry I've been so absent," Gina said.

"You're deeply involved with someone. That's how it goes."

"I kind of just always want to be around her to the exclusion of everyone else."

"I've done it unto others, G. Just not for any extended period of time."

Gina had the new Warren Zevon album and we listened to that for a while in her room.

I'd been listening to *Excitable Boy* a lot lately myself.

I was hoping immersion in Warren Zevon would reignite my creative flame.

"Check out the assonance in the chorus," I said of "Accidentally Like A Martyr."

We made mad love shadow love
Random love and abandoned love
Accidentally like a martyr
The hurt gets worse and the heart gets harder

"Perfect," I said, "Assonance is my favorite literary device. Something about it soothes me."

"I get that. Assonance to me is the equivalent of how I blend colors on the paper while I'm working."

The song "Tenderness On The Block" made me think again of Emily's orgy. All those kids I saw fucking. Their parents thought they were at some innocent gathering talking to their friends about philosophy and literature. I mean, that's what *I* thought it was going to be too.

Despite the brilliance of the Zevon songs, the muses stayed away.

I had plenty of melodies, complete songs musically, but every attempt I made to whelp lyrics turned into a miscarriage or, at best, a still-birth.

One night, in search of inspiration, when I was out toking a strail (as we had come to call the practice of getting high while taking a stroll around the block) I ran into Buzzy Lagniappe coming the other direction, probably home from Whit's.

"How's it going," Buzzy said and offered me a hit off the joint he was smoking.

"Pretty good," I said, holding up my own joint in full acknowledgement.

"The only way to fly," Buzzy said.

He seemed cold in just a t-shirt.

It was one of those chilly L.A. nights in the middle of February where you really should be wearing at least a long-sleeve shirt.

I had on my Marcel Dionne jersey and was myself a little shivery, though that might've been the weed.

"So what're you up to these days?" Buzzy asked.

"I dunno, reading, listening to music, trying to write."

"Songs?"

"Yeah mostly. Nothing's coming though. I'm artistically constipated at the moment."

"Well, you know the cure for that, dude."

"Right here," I held up my diminishing joint.

"Nah, dude. Pussy."

"Nuh-uh, man, I find pussy has quite the opposite effect on me. Pussy is how I got myself into this condition. Fuck pussy."

Buzzy looked cockeyed at me. "In the figurative sense you mean," he said.

"Right. Obviously."

"Every girl has a pussy," Buzzy said, "Always remember that."

"I'm aware of this phenomenon, yes. But when it comes to dealing with a girl, dude, what I've found is that her pussy is actually the least of one's problems."

"My only problem with pussy is that I don't get any," Buzzy said.

"It's not worth the soul-killing agony of pretending to be something you're not. Believe me."

"Dang, dude. You are a cold and bitter young man."

"Nah. Just a guy with a small collection of particular experiences."

"Dang, I remember when you were a little gay golita who didn't even know what frenching was. Now you're all over that shit. How'd that happen, dude?"

"I knew it by the river," I feigned some inscrutable Mesmeresque prestidigitation gestures. "So is it true your sister got married?"

"Yeah, dude, she eloped with this guy from college. I don't even know his name. I don't even know if *she* knows his name."

"Flagrant," I said feeling just that much more despondent with the fact now verified. Penelope Lagniappe was married.

All my rooftop fantasies died in that moment.

Buzzy took another puff of the latest incarnation of Bigelow Rust's loco weed, a batch called "Mergatroyd" because it made you feel, according to Big, "like a gay mountain lion," but Buzzy thought it should be called High

Priest.

"'Cause if I can one day get to Heaven's heart," Buzzy said as he exhaled, "She'll be my keys to the Kingdom."

"The Kingdom?"

"The House Next Door."

"Oh, yeah yeah," I knew his longstanding alter-world.

"I think I've got a shot as long as Flippy doesn't fuck everything up."

"Flippy Killbones gets in the way," I said of the spider who inhabits Buzzy's brain off and on.

"Man, it's his favorite thing to do to me. I call him Floppy Cockbones when he derails my pursuit of pussy."

"You need to distract him."

"How?"

"Isn't there a lady spider for him to copulate with or something?"

"Nah, dude, Flippy's a recluse. And that's what he wants me to be. This one time he told me I'd be happiest living in a dungeon."

"Dang, dude. That's flagrant."

Buzzy paused to consider the spider in his mind.

"Nyeah, he just lives to fuck my shit up."

We were almost back at our respective neighboring abodes just as his thoughts were starting to skew schizo in a way I wouldn't be able to follow much longer and so I was able to head inside to see if any inspiration lay in wait for me and avoid the inevitable rant about the house next door.

I had lately been grooving on this really earthy sandalwood incense I'd gotten at The Bodhi Tree. Originally I bought it because of the triangular box and the Devanagari script all over the packaging. It was one of those products I knew only visually. I never knew what it was called. But I ended up loving the smell. It really stoked my soul.

I lit two sticks and placed them in my sitting-Buddha incense holder, also from The Bodhi Tree, and then summoned the Muses with my usual lonely groan.

They appeared together like twin shadows, permitting me to glimpse their silhouettes only, Calliope and Euterpe, letting their legs intertwine, granting me wafts of their heat.

"Where have you been?" they blended together.

"Outside trying to find you."

"That's the wrong place to look."

"I have been lost in the allure of the human female at times, I admit, though I have foresworn the sisterhood, mostly, and do intend to concoct some sort of immunity to their alchemical effect upon me."

"See, Georgie Porgie, it's not a matter of *us* being available to *you*, rather it's about *you* being available to *us*," Euterpe said.

"And then you come puling back to us with this same pussified excuse every time," Calliope finished for her.

"What can I say?"

"Dude, we are better than vagina and you know it," said Calliope.

"Rather, we are the best vagina you will ever have, and if you don't know that then what the fuck other reason could you possibly have for writing music?" Euterpe interjected.

"The Yoni is all Holiness," Calliope said.

"Thy health and thy wellspring."

"There is a great bounty in store for you here, with us."

"If you but splash my cervix with your hot cum on a regular and exclusive basis," Euterpe enjoined.

"What?" I attempted to make sure I wasn't dreaming because the air and the pace and the emotional disconnection had the vague tinge of Morpheus.

"Will you agree to love only us?" they said as one.

I wrote in answer to their query.

You can't understand it
You're not from this planet
Wingless bandits on the run

They turned their backs on me. Calliope and Euterpe were present but ignoring me like a couple of house cats.

Guiles to misguide us
Piles of detritus
Miles still left inside us when we're done

I briefly pictured the act of splashing Diana Hitchcock's cervix with my hot cum and then opened my eyes to a deep black celestial vacancy, a starless void that was more gone than here.

Genuflect in the direction of the monarch's severed chair
To resurrect the old reflection of a God who's never there
In all respect we're bent toward Mecca or Jerusalem in prayer
Not a trace or speck of Allah or of Yahweh anywhere

I was writing without passion, without dance, without magic, without love. I was using the inspiration the muses gave me to insult them.

When the heavenly denizens heard human heartbeats drumming
The gods in twilight knew that the apocalypse was coming
When the guardian of victory removed the sword imperial
All Valhalla trembled immaterial

Calliope and Euterpe rose away from me in scorn.

"That's just a lot of language," Calliope said.

"That's not a song," Euterpe followed.

They vanished after that and left me empty.

I addressed my absent muses with a final tag to a piece that was nothing but another nothing.

You can't understand it
You're not from this planet
The random mandate's cancelled out
Mirror abnegation
Zero sum equation
The fear of expiration spans all doubt

I crumpled up the paper and lay with it on my bed.

It was too cold outside to go up on the garage roof.

I stayed in bed and eventually found myself imagining piston coitus with Diana Hitchcock and then falling asleep thinking about how badly I wanted my cock inside her.

When I came, I wiped my seed onto the crumpled lyric sheet and threw it in the trash.

4

Levon Arrow loved everybody so much he had to stay away from them.

Levon Arrow took care of the snail farm most days but every once in a while he'd venture down to the frozen river to sit and watch its motionless flow.

People were always skating by on their way somewhere else.

Levon didn't talk to them unless he had to.

He wasn't averse to social interaction, he just never sought it out.

If someone wanted to hang out with him he'd partake, but that rarely happened.

One day he was sitting and watching the frozen river and the people skating by when someone came up behind him.

"Hi, Levon!" a deep female voice bellowed.

Levon thought this was pretty weird because he didn't really know anybody and therefore presumed that nobody knew him.

Yet here was somebody calling his name.

He pretended not to hear her.

He was good at doing that.

"Hi," she said and sat down beside him on the lonely hillside to ensure that he couldn't ignore her.

Levon nodded but didn't look at the girl yet.

"I'm Glenda," she said. "I'm trying to find whales."

"Like the good witch in <u>The Wizard Of Oz</u>?"

"That's Glinda. I'm Glenda. I love how you always pretend you don't know me. It's

cute."

"*I can help you with snails, not whales,*" *Levon said and looked at her.*

"*I need whales.*"

"*What for?*"

"*To save the world.*"

"*You're going to save the world with whales?*"

"*No, the whales are going to save the world.*"

"*How?*"

"*They'll figure out a way. They're smarter than we are.*"

And Levon believed her.

"*Give me a girl at an impressionable age, and she is mine for life,*" Mr. Megiddo quoted from *The Prime of Miss Jean Brodie*, but we all knew he was talking about himself. "The whole thing here is about control. Jean Brodie shapes these girls into her own image of what they should be, which is always . . . what?"

"Some version of Miss Jean Brodie," Miranda Savitch said. She had moved to the other side of the room second semester, so I got to look across at her even though she was farther away from me.

"Yes," Megiddo answered.

"That's what you meant when you said all art is autobiography," Miranda added.

"Yes. Exactly. And maybe so is politics when you think about it. Like I was saying, by shaping these girls into her own image of what they should be just look at the control she exerts over them. It's no wonder Jean Brodie's so fond of fascist dictators."

"'Cause she is one," said Manny Shepherd.

"Yes. She wants her protégés to be her clones," Megiddo said.

"Isn't that what everybody wants?" Gina Dichlich asked, "I think we're all just looking around for different versions of ourselves or someone we can shape into being that. Anyway that's what I feel like I'm doing a lot of the time."

"We've talked about the *anima* in here, haven't we? The counterpart soul?"

"We're all different versions of the same soul," Manny Shepherd sang his refrain.

"Oh God," Arabella Mayflower rolled her eyes.

"God. Yes. That's exactly who I'm talking about," Manny said to her.

"But do you think it's possible for one human being to utterly shape another human being?" Mr. Megiddo rescued us.

"Isn't that what teachers do? I mean like sat-gurus and people like that," Manny said.

"The concept of a mentor does carry with it some of those tendencies, yes," Mr. Megiddo said, "All teachers have a little Miss Jean Brodie in them."

"I think we're influenced by every person we interact with, even if it's from a distance," Miranda said.

"From the *hoi polloi* to the *crème de la crème*," Mr. Megiddo said.

"And sometimes the greater the distance the greater the influence," I said and looked across at Miranda who was thinking about something else.

I was so caught up in that heart lesson I missed the rest of the Jean Brodie discussion.

Eddie Gurges had a free 4th Period Spring semester and started hanging out with me and Jim Lord in the library.

"Have you ever seen Gina Dichlich's drawings?" I asked him while he was doing his own.

"The pastels? Yeah. She's doing great work right now. Everything I've seen has been lesbian lovemaking but with clothes on."

"Yeah, that's the stuff."

"Why have I not been shown these *in flagrante delicto* pictos?" Jim Lord interjected.

"Mr. Pettigrew was going on and on about them the other day in Advanced Drawing. They aren't porny at all. It's just beautiful. Her colors and curves remind me of Cezanne, but her geometry's slightly less precise."

"I saw a bunch of them the other day at her house. She's really tapped into something right now," I said.

"Yeah, Cory De Leon's vagina," Eddie joked.

"Gay, straight, pussy's always the muse," Jim Lord said and he and Eddie and I all touched fingertips in homage to the supreme truth.

"Pussy," we said together a little too loudly and touched fingertips again.

"Tssh tssh," Mrs. Tisk admonished.

"Vagina," we whispered but then laughed loud enough for Mrs. Tisk to come over to our table and wag her finger.

"If you're going to act like jackasses and turkey-butts you have to go do that out in the quad," she said to us but Jim couldn't stop. "What's your name, young man?" she asked him.

"Jethro Bodine," Jim's eyes watered with stifled laughter.

"The pig on *Green Acres?*"

"No, the pig on *Green Acres* is named Arnold," Jim corrected.

"I thought it was Jethro Bodine."

"Arnold. Arnold The Pig."

"Then who in the boondocks is Jethro Bodine?"

"Uncle Jed's nephew on *The Beverly Hillbillies*."

"I thought Augustus Gloop was Uncle Jed's nephew on *The Beverly Hillbillies*."

"Nope. Jethro Bodine."

I interjected, "Augustus Gloop is the fat kid from *Willy Wonka & The Chocolate Factory*."

"Now just a doggone minute here," Mrs. Tisk said, "I thought Buzzy Lagniappe was the fat kid from *Willy Wonka & The Chocolate Factory*."

"Nope. Augustus Gloop."

"Then who in the name of Jehoshaphat is Buzzy Lagniappe?"

"Buzzy Lagniappe is a student here. And his real name is Augustus. And he used to be fat."

"What does he look like?"

"Red hair. Freckles. Kind of a Danny Partridge-looking motherhubbard?"

"Oh, yes, I know who that is. The kid who talks to himself."

"Yes," I said, "that's him."

"I wish they'd keep it down, though."

"Who?"

"Danny Partridge and his friends."

"What friends?"

"The ones he's always talking to," she pointed to her head and twirled her finger.

After she left, I said, "It's weird to think that Mrs. Tisk has children."

"Yeah. Somebody fucked her," Jim Lord said.

"More than once," I added.

"Do you think Mrs. Tisk still fucks her husband?" Jim wondered.

"I've tried very hard *not* to think about that," I said.

"Can you still do it when you're that old?" Eddie asked.

The thing was, I had in fact fantasized numerous times about fucking Mrs. Tisk.

I bet most guys did.

Lying there in the glow of the hospital machinery, I remembered how the morning of the Drama Festival we all got up early and met at Fairfax then drove caravan-style over Laurel Canyon to Birmingham High in the Valley.

Normally I'd go in expecting our asses to get kicked by Chatsworth as always because their drama program was like professional level, but this time I knew Diana and I had a shot at winning something. Our scene was that good.

We'd been wanting to work together due to our great chemistry during *Scapino*, so the Drama Festival seemed the ideal opportunity.

When we first went to Ms. Van Poole for ideas, she suggested a scene from *Pygmalion*.

"The George Bernard Shaw play. You two'd be a good Henry and Eliza. Go check it out. The scene where she throws the slippers at him. I think it's the end of Act IV. Perfect for you guys."

"Any kissing?" I asked.

"With you two? Definitely not," Ms. Van Poole said, "most definitely not. I will not be a party to that again."

We checked out Ms. Van Poole's suggestion and agreed it was a good fit.

Usually we'd rehearse at school during Play Production but as the festival got closer, we started doing additional work at Diana's house over in Carthay Circle.

Her brother's bedroom was vacant so it made for a conducive creative atmosphere.

"You'd like my brother Phillip," she said, "He's smart. Like you. He worships Bob Dylan."

"Where is he?"

"New York."

"Doing what?"

"I don't know. Just living I guess. He's got some job I don't even know what it is. And he's in this band called One-Eyed Sammy. Five black guys playing punk rock. They've got this one song called 'Black Punks On Rope' which I love. It's like druggy and hilarious and also political at the same time."

"Great title. Take off on the Tubes song."

"With lynching references thrown in."

"Wow."

"Yeah. But I don't know, other than that he just hangs out. He goes to museums a lot. He's into art and foreign films and literature and all that shit."

"You mean white people shit."

"Like I said, you'd be into him."

We had a good long stare.

"So should we do this?" I asked.

"Do what?" she wondered, holding my gaze.

"Rehearse," I broke it.

"I guess."

"We have to block that confrontational moment, the *'Claws in, you cat'* part."

"Yeah yeah. Let's do it," Diana said and readied herself.

"Claws in, you cat. How dare you show your temper to me? Sit down and be quiet," I said and pushed Diana down onto her brother's bed.

"What's to become of me? What's to become of me?" Diana lay supine.

I decided not to pounce.

I had taken a vow.

"Oh God! I wish I was dead," said Diana.

"Why? in heaven's name, why? Listen to me, Eliza. All this irritation is purely subjective," I climbed on top of her, vows be damned, and she wrapped her legs around me.

"I don't understand. I'm too ignorant," she said as I lay on her, neither of us making a move to separate, *"I'm sorry. I'm only a common ignorant girl; and in my station I have to be careful. There can't be any feelings between the like of you and the like of me. Please will you tell me what belongs to me and what doesn't?"*

We used a pause to disengage.

I stood and helped Diana up.

"We need to block this for real now," she said.

"What was that, just now?"

"I don't know," she said, "But it wasn't blocking. We're running out of time. The festival's coming up."

"Yeah yeah. I think I should lunge at you and you stop me with your line."

"Don't you hit me?"

"Yeah."

I advanced as Higgins.

"*Don't you hit me,*" Diana warded me off.

"*Hit you! You infamous creature, how dare you accuse me of such a thing? It is you who have hit me. You have wounded me to the heart,*" I said and tried to look wounded.

"That's not the face of heartbreak," Diana said, out of character, "You're playing it more sexy beast."

"I'm at my sexiest when I'm heartbroken. That's the problem."

"Seems a little bit backwards, yeah."

"It tends to attract really warped females."

"Oh does it?"

"Pretty much every time, yup."

"Like Lorelei Lux."

"Bingo."

"I see," Diana nodded

"Let's finish," I said. "I want to do some reading later."

"You *want* to read?" Diana was incredulous.

"I want to read. Yes."

"That's a foreign concept to me."

"I love reading. It's my favorite thing to do."

"For real? You like it better than having an orgasm?"

"Orgasms are cool, totally love them, try to experience them daily, but, yeah, I like reading better."

"That is weird."

"You don't like to read?"

"Not really. I pretty much do it only when I have to."

"See, to me *that's* weird."

"I read the Bible," she said, "I like doing that I guess. But yeah let's finish this."

"Damn you; and damn my own folly in having lavished my hard-earned knowledge and the treasure of my regard and intimacy on a heartless guttersnipe," I said and sort of broke character because the way she was looking at me made me want to laugh.

"Say that again," Diana smiled.

"Heartless guttersnipe."

"Mmm," she said. "Say it again."

"Heartless guttersnipe."

She acted a shiver.

"What?"

"Damn, figure it out," Diana scolded and walked out of the room then poked her head back in, "You are one slow-on-the-uptake whiteboy, whiteboy."

She had begun the process of reeling me in. Or maybe I was doing the reeling. I'm never sure which is which.

Diana was really into Jesus and I didn't know what that would mean down the line, me being a godless communist Jew and all, I just knew I wanted to mate with her right there on her brother's bed.

"The way I see it, God is the architect, and we are the builders," Diana said as we sat in her car outside my house later.

"So, God needs our help, in other words," I said.

Diana looked over at me.

"I've always thought that's kind of strange," I finished, "People who believe in God's omnipotence yet at the same time think God needs their help. Don't you think that's strange?"

Diana kept looking at me.

"I think of it more that God doesn't *really* need our help, he just wants to see what we're made of, if we're serious about serving his will," she said.

"That's an interesting perspective."

"*That's an interesting perspective,*" Diana mocked.

I couldn't tell if she was flirting with me or not.

"Brainy boy," she held my gaze and it felt deliberate, "Sexual intellectual."

"Tomorrow we have to finish blocking."

"Maybe we should work at school. I have a feeling we'll get more done that way."

"Definitely," I said, and, dang, dude, I can't remember how that conversation ended, but what I can remember is that we came very close to kissing right there in the car.

I almost told her in that moment of my powerful attraction as we sat in the glow of moon and porchlight.

Instead I went inside and attempted to do my homework.

I had trouble concentrating on the French grammar exercises I was supposed to be doing and then later trying to finish up *Death In Venice* for Megiddo's class because Diana's face kept hovering.

Over the next several days I deliberated with myself and decided I would give Diana a written confession of my attraction instead of saying it out loud.

I wrote my confession on a piece of notebook paper which I then folded into eighths and ended up giving to her right before we did our scene at the Drama Festival and told her to open it afterward.

Diana, I don't really know what I mean by this other than I can't stop thinking about you. You may or may not reciprocate these feelings but I just had to bring up the subject because really you're all that's on my mind these days. I do believe we've had our moments of mutual recognition but that could just be wishful thinking on my part too. Anyway, I hope this doesn't ruin anything because I love hanging out with you regardless.

Your Pard'ner,

Lance

I lay alone in the hospital room wondering if she'd read the note amid all the chaos of my collapse.

The night nurse came in to check on things.

"Can't sleep?"

"Not really. I keep thinking my heart is going to stop if I go to sleep."

"Your heart doesn't need your help," she pointed to the monitor, "See? Calm and steady."

"It's just weird not being in my own bed," I said, "I'm not used to it."

"Most people aren't. Let me give you something that'll help you sleep," she said and left the room, returning with 2 paper cups on a tray.

"What is this?"

"A mild sedative. Just enough to make you not care that you're not in your own bed."

I did fall asleep quite easily after that and dreamed that I was looking at what I first thought was a frozen ocean but it turned out to be a frozen river.

People were skating past and I thought, what an amazing way to travel.

But I had no desire to travel with them.

I preferred to stay put and look at the frozen river.

"What are you gonna do for food?" a person who was my friend in the dream said as he laced up his skates and began his tramp down to the river.

"I don't know," I said without concern.

"Well if you ever want to come find me, just head thataway and follow the jello thick load to the Realm of All Things Possible," my unknown friend said skating off beyond my vantage.

I haven't dreamed of him since.

I'm pretty sure I knew his name in the dream but now I can't remember it.

I continued to watch the frozen river and wonder why.

5

Levon Arrow didn't like having to pay attention to any one person in particular because it got in the way of his ability to pay attention to everyone else.

But Glenda wouldn't stop harping on whales and so he had to pay attention to her.

"If I can get to the sea I will find the whales I'm looking for," she said.

"How would one get to the sea from here?"

"Skate the river."

"Skate all the way to the ocean you mean."

"Yep. That's where everybody's heading. Notice how everybody is going in the same

direction?"

Levon knew they were all going somewhere but he didn't know where.

"That explains a lot of things," Levon said even though it only explained one thing maybe.

He didn't want to hang out with her or be into her or anything like that, but he did want her to think he was deep.

"Do you want to come with me?"

He did not wish to go anywhere.

"I don't have skates," he said.

"We have an extra pair in the shed that'd probly fit you."

"Anyway my mother wouldn't let me."

"Don't tell her."

"She'd freak. I have this condition called the Minerva Syndrome."

"What's that?"

"I have stars in my heart."

"Like the Little Prince!" she said.

"Who's he?"

"Just a character in a book. You should read it. It'd remind you of yourself."

Levon Arrow pondered the possibility of skating to the ocean in search of whales.

"I'd rather stay here," Levon said.

"Bad choice," Glenda replied and got up to leave.

"Where are you going?"

"To get my skates!" she said and walked off, "Bye, Levon!"

Levon watched her ass for as long as he could.

Sunday morning I awoke in my hospital room and stared out the window at the ochre sky above the Valley.

I still had the chill of the frozen river on me.

"Lance?" I heard a girl say.

I turned and saw Naomi Richter standing in the doorway.

"Hey," I said, puzzled by her sudden incongruous appearance.

"I saw your name on the little card in the door and had to see if it was you."

"You think there's another Lance Atlas?"

"What happened?"

"I have a bad heart," I said.

"What's wrong with it?"

"Irregular heartbeat."

"You never told me about that."

"I never told you lots of things."

"I'm really happy to see you," Naomi said, "Not in a hospital of course. But still. What are you doing out here in the Valley?"

"I collapsed while I was performing at the Drama Festival over on the Birmingham High campus. What are *you* doing out here?"

"My bubby had brain surgery. She lives in Encino so—"

"—She going to be ok?"

"She'll be the same pain she's always been, I'm sure. Unless they were able to remove the bitch lobe."

"Why, Ms. Richter, what a thing to say about your bubby. A bubby who's just had brain surgery yet. *Lashon Hara* and all that."

"Sometimes you have to call a bitch a bitch," Naomi said and grinned like she used to do in the library when she knew she was being naughty, a smile I hadn't seen since right before I tried to finger-fuck her while she was on her period. "Are you going to be ok?"

"Nyeah, of course," I said, "They did a bunch of tests yesterday and it sounds like I'm just going to go on this medication. I'm supposedly going home later today."

"*Baruch HaShem*. I'm glad."

"Are you in college now?"

"Yeah I'm at Brandeis."

"Brandeis. I'm shocked to hear this news."

"You thought maybe Brigham Young? I flew home to be here for bubby's surgery. She's been in her own room for a couple of days now, so I'm going back to Boston tomorrow."

"And you're not married yet I take it. Or are you? I know how it is with you people."

"I am not married," she pawed faintly, "You are bad."

"A *shondeh*, such a *shayne maidl*," I patted her on the hand, "What are you, 18? You want to be an old maid?"

"Stop," she said, "You are *bad*."

"You told me that already."

She didn't take her hand away.

"You cross my thoughts sometimes," Naomi said.

"Likewise."

"Liar."

"I'm not—"

"—I've seen you around here and there in the company of several different girls, especially that one who wears the short skirts. I've seen you two a bunch of times on Fairfax."

I grinned.

"Ha, that's Gina Dichlich and yes that's her real name. I don't see her that much anymore because she has an intense girlfriend right now."

"Oh my," Naomi reeled.

"And if you see me you should totally come up and say hi."

"I'm always too shy to do that."

"What about you? Any foxy *yeshiva-buchers* on the horizon?"

"No," she said, pausing, "But there are a few Reform boys I have my eyes on. That's all your fault."

"My fault?"

"For setting a precedent," she said and for a few ephemeral seconds we completely had our old library rhythm back again.

"I think I can avoid a *yeshiva-bucher* as long as I bring home a boy who is some kind of Jewish. My dad is coming to accept that he has a weirdo brainiac daughter who is going to do what she wants."

"So, he'd be cool even if you came home with a a Persian Jew?"

"*Nisht du gedacht*, no."

"Falasha?"

"*Kein ahora*," she laughed.

She was really sexy when she said *kein ahora*. Like when Ms. Cummings used to say *onomatopoeia* back in 9th Grade English. Same idea.

"Anyway, I need to go. I'm glad it's not serious," Naomi said and started to back out.

"Me too," I said and blew her a kiss which embarrassed her I think. "Have a good rest of semester. And next time you see me on Fairfax say hi."

"I will," she said and looked behind down the hall, "I better go. It's really good to see you. *Sei gesund,*" she rushed off.

Naomi faded into the yellow light but I heard her a few moments later echoing, "Bubby, what are you doing out walking in the hall? You just had brain surgery. Bubby, no . . . Ow! That hurt!"

About noon, Diana walked into my room and held my hand.

"Hey, pard'ner," she said, her wide shock of hair blocking out the light behind.

"Hey."

"How are you feeling?"

"Fine. Normal."

"You mean normal for *you.*"

"Well, yes that goes without saying."

She leaned in close to me.

"I read your note."

"Ah, good," I blushed.

"So . . ." she smiled, " . . . Yeah . . ." and she took my hands.

"So you like me?"

"You are dense."

"I have a bad heart . . . But, so, you like me."

"Yes, Lance, I like you."

"For real?"

"Dude, I want to rape you. OK? I want to make you forget there's anyone else in the world."

Her lips were almost on me when I held firm in resistance.

"That might kill me at this point," I pointed to the hospital machinery that surrounded me.

"A little one."

"Nyeah, not right now. I'm too afraid of my heart going haywire."

"Haywire?"

"Yeah. You know. Kerflooey."

"Kerflooey."

"Kerflooey. Yeah."

"You make *my* heart go kerflooey," Diana said.

"Ah yes, in my hospital gown and nappy hair. I must be ravishing."

"Right here," she pointed to both our eyes, "This is where the sexy's at."

We were happening. The agony was over. For a time.

"When I'm out of here we should do something together," I said.

"I can think of two or three things."

"Like dinner, a movie, and then dessert after."

"Exactly," she said, "I like dessert."

"But dinner and a movie first. Think of something you want to see."

"No you decide."

And so I did.

For reasons inexplicable and yet typical, on our first date I took Diana Hitchcock to see Bob Dylan's 4-hour avant-garde film *Renaldo & Clara* at the Regent Theater in Westwood.

In advance, she was excited to see it because she liked Bob Dylan herself and also her brother was a Dylan devotee and she loved everything having to do with her brother.

However, once the film was underway, I could tell Diana wasn't enjoying it because she spent a lot of time going to the bathroom, buying Cokes which then made her have to go to the bathroom again, fidgeting, sighing, nibbling on my earlobe, snoring on purpose, playing Whoops-Johnny on both of my hands, running her fingers up my thigh stopping just shy of my arched hard penis, meditating in the lotus position, practicing her time step from a sitting position, putting her head on my shoulder and sucking her thumb, sticking her wet thumb in my nostril, wiping her thumb on my face, braiding my hair, motor-boating my neck, and playing rock-paper-scissors with herself.

Four hours later neither of us felt like hanging out so Diana drove me home.

"Films like that make me feel bad," she said.

"Why?"

"They make me feel stupid."

"How so?"

"Like, I had no idea what was going on in that fucking movie, and I felt like everybody else did."

"All 12 of them in attendance."

"No, for real. Including you."

"There wasn't much 'going on' really. It was just amazing concert footage interspersed with a bunch of vignettes, some random, some semi-scripted. There were themes being played out."

"Hmm."

"To me it was a film about a whole bunch of cool people hanging out together, doing some improv acting, playing pranks, and making some very kick-ass music."

"I guess I like a story."

I held her hand while she shifted.

"I've never really paid that much attention in school," Diana said as we sat parked outside my house, "I mean, enough to pass and all that. But it never caught my attention the way performing does. Dance class, voice coach, acting workshops, those are what have always taken up my time and focus. But I want to be smart and know stuff too."

"Carve out some time to read. We should get together on Saturday, pick a spot, and spend all day reading. It's a glorious thing to do."

"I don't have anything to read."

"I'll bring you something. We can read it together and talk about it."

"A picnic," she smiled.

"Yeah."

"Griffith Park. We can hike up to the Observatory too."

"The idea is to read all day," I said.

"Oh, poo. You're no fun," she said and we began kissing like we'd kissed at Mr. Hill's wedding, kissing like we'd kissed when we were doing *Scapino*, kissing like we'd been wanting to ever since, kissing like we were meant to be kissing all along, all this time.

I unbuttoned her pants and reached in.

"Mmm," she murmured.

She'd already moistened and my finger slid to her clit gently and easily, barely glancing, my palm against her pubis, her pants tight against my hand, now two fingers playing inside her.

I was finger-fucking my new girlfriend.

Dang, dude.

Diana held on tight.

"Who's no fun?" I asked her.

"Dang, look how steamed up the windows are," Diana said, sitting back up in the driver's seat when she'd had enough.

"I wonder why."

"You had me making vapor, dude."

We kissed wetly again.

"See you later," I said.

We kissed some more.

"Next time . . ." she said.

"Next time what?"

"Next time we read."

"Deal," I said and stuck out my hand for a shake but Diana bombed my mouth and we smooched the windows all foggy again.

We were ravenously in love, the hungriest I'd ever been.

6

Several nanocenturies later Glenda returned with two pairs of skates.

She dropped one pair at Levon's side, sat down to put on her own skates, then continued to the river.

"Last chance!" she turned and waited.

Levon looked at her then at the skates then back at her.

"I'd rather stay here," he waved apologetically.

"Well," Glenda said, "You've got skates now in case you change your mind. I'll be heading thataway," and then she skated off out of view.

Levon Arrow figured that was the last he'd see of Glenda.

He wandered back to the snail farm in time to do the evening feeding.

The current generation of snails had evolved into carnivores and it was becoming difficult to scrounge up enough bugs to satiate the whole shrooming lot of them.

Levon began to worry they'd start eating each other, preying on the weak and the small.

His main problem with that was there'd be that much less rocket fuel if cannibalism took hold.

He must have been worrying out loud without realizing it because one of the snails said, "We'd never do something like that."

Levon looked around to see which snail had spoken.

"Toby is the name," the voice said, "Toby Snail."

Levon saw a snail moving toward him and sat on the ground to greet him.

"That's S-N-Apostrophe-A-I-L Sn'ail," Toby said.

"Why the apostrophe?"

"It's a contraction."

"Huh?"

"For snot trail."

"I feel like I've dreamed you before," Levon said.

"Entirely likely, given the set of all possible circumstances. But anyway we'd never eat our own. We are not cannibals. We are just diversifying. The broader our diet, the less likely we are to starve. It's a simple equation."

Levon's heart fluttered and he thought he should hurry into the house and lie down.

"Where you off to?" Toby called out to the retreating Levon.

"A star is born," Levon said and pointed to his heart.

"And Mrs. Norman Maine has lit out for the territories."

"Huh?" Levon stopped.

"You should be following that girl wherever she takes you."

"Glenda? I have no idea who she even is or how she knows me. She's on some crazy-ass trip looking for whales. Plus, I need to stay here and tend to you guys."

"No, you need to go find that girl and kiss her really hard on the mouth. And, see, dude, here's the thing, and I'm speaking on behalf of the entire sn'ail continuum: We don't need you anymore. We're just gonna end up as rocket fuel anyway. So who gives a roach's ass what we do?"

"The sn'ail farm is the only work I know," Levon said, vowing to spell the word right in his head from then on, "The rest of the time I'm just staring at shit for no reason. What am I supposed to do now?"

"Put on those skates and go find that girl," said Toby Sn'ail.

And Levon Arrow thought yes he just might do that.

Back in my room, I saw the Peter Pan postcard sitting on my desk and decided to write to Annie De Milo before fantasizing about Diana and heading off to sleep.

Dear Miss De Milo,

That is pretty crazy about Cambria being the old name for Wales. I just finished reading a book called <u>Death In Venice</u> which I liked very much. I also saw the movie version which is great too. In fact, I bought this Peter Pan postcard at Papa Bach bookstore across the street from the NuArt Theatre right after I saw the <u>Death In Venice</u> movie. I thought it would be something you'd like. Didn't you tell me that you like Peter Pan stuff? Papa Bach is a very cool place. The next time you are in L.A. you should definitely check it out. Are you guys ever going to visit L.A.? If you do we will definitely go to Papa Bach together. How is your parents' bookstore doing? What kinds of books do they sell there? Do you have a special secret book there that you hope never gets sold because you want it for yourself?

Let me know these things.

Lance

After I finished writing the card to Annie, I lay in the dark and fantasized that Diana and I had kept on going and fucked in her car outside my house while my parents were home.

It was an especially potent session because I could still smell her on my fingers.

On Saturday Diana and I went to Fern Dell in Griffith Park and had a picnic.

I had brought *The Little Prince* along because I thought she'd get into it, but after we ate the turkey sandwiches she'd made and then took a stroll along the shadowy creek that runs through Fern Dell, we ended up just making out on the blanket most of the day.

We were utterly a couple.

"You know what we should do now?" she gooped her eyes at me and smiled later in the afternoon.

"What?"

I wanted to hear her say fuck.

"We should hike up to the Observatory," she got to her feet and ran toward the trail laughing.

I knew it was one of those things where I was supposed to chase her and tackle her or something, but I'm not into doing stuff just because it's expected and I feel silly and embarrassed when I perform conditioned human responses like doing what I'm supposed to do because I'm the boy.

I hate shit like that.

"This trail leads all the way up to the top. I've done it before," Diana said, wanting to take the hike, "You come out right in the Observatory parking lot."

I had too many ghosts up there, especially the residue of that penultimate fuck-up with Miranda Savitch.

"Nyeah, I'm not really into it," I said.

"Poo on you. I want to have some fun."

"There are better ways to do that."

"Yeah? Name 3."

"We could stay up late and watch *You Bet Your Life* and *Twilight Zone* reruns."

"Remember when *Fractured Flickers* used to come on after *Twilight Zone*?"

"Or was it after *You Bet Your Life*?"

"I can't remember now. OK, name 2 more."

"We could get high and pig out on Count Chocula and half-and-half."

"Do you have all of those ingredients at your house?"

"I've got some pot and half a quart of half-and-half."

"But no Count Chocula."

"No."

"That's racist. How can you not have Count Chocula?"

"We usually do. We ran out. Bad timing."

"So that leaves option 3. Which is?"

"We could stay here and read."

Diana didn't like that idea, so we decided instead to go to my house and make out on my bed.

We had to pick out which music we were going to use to disguise the sounds of love.

I had just gotten Lou Reed's *Street Hassle* album and I put it on the stereo before we started fooling around.

Oh, gimme, gimme, gimme some good times
Oh, gimme, gimme, gimme some pain

As Lou Reed summed up most romantic relationships, our lips met and our hands were on each other's everything all over.

We were conjuring a vision and a rhythm together, finding our way, discovering our magic.

I got my hand inside her pants and rather than finger-fuck her that way I pulled her pants down and then all the way off so she could move her legs freely as the feelings fueled her. She hooked her leg around me as I got a finger up inside her and began the proceedings fervently, atwirl and then plunging, up and in and down-across, sometimes leaving it, pressing against the underside, my thumb up top on her clit eddying like a rotor.

And cascading slowly, he lifted her wholly
and boldly out of this world

I don't know if she came or not but she shuddered and gently pushed my
hand away.

Kissing me while unbuttoning my jeans, she reached within to free my pent
up cock and helped me kick my own pants off.

We were both still wearing our shirts.

I wanted to ask Diana if she came but decided not to because I'd have no
way of knowing if she was lying or not so it wasn't worth it.

Instead I kissed her very hard on the mouth as she gripped my dick.

"What have we here?"

"Dick."

"Mmmm, hi, Dick."

"That's Richard to you."

"Ri*chard*," she said with a French accent.

"And who are these guys," she took my balls in her hand.

"The twins. Castor and Pollox. The Gemini Twins."

"I don't like those names. Even though I *am* a Gemini."

"What would you rather call them?"

"Le*nard* and Tyrone," she stroked me slowly and nibbled on my earlobe.

My nipples hardened and I think I groaned a little.

She made her way down my body until her mouth was on my cock, first
just tongue and then lips and then she was bobbing on it.

229

I put my hand on her head and felt her motion.

I kind of looked at her sucking my cock but I also kind of didn't want to because I don't know why it just felt weird like I was watching it on television or something.

I closed my eyes and tried real hard not to think of other people.

This was a different mouth from Taryn's, from Desirée's.

My mind thought mouth, my cock thought pussy.

I loved this mouth, this girl, this person.

Gathering toward climax, I pulled myself away and panted a laugh to signal my imminent discharge.

Diana kept her mouth on me.

"But then we'll have to wait a while. You know," I held her back.

"I'm sure you can find a way to occupy me while your batteries recharge," she said and started sucking me off again until a few seconds later I came in her mouth so intensely my balls retracted and seemed to want to come out too in the geyser.

Diana let me ejaculate all the way before spitting my jism onto the Liberty Bell quilt I'd had since 4th Grade.

"A different kind of wet spot," Diana said and nestled into me. "You like that, baby?"

I smiled.

"You called me baby."

"That OK? I've never called anyone baby before."

"I love it," I said even though I knew eventually it'd bug me.

I started to peel her top off and she yanked it over her head the rest of the way as I got my lips and tongue and teeth on her breasts.

Like Lorelei Lux, Diana didn't wear a bra. A fashion choice I always wholeheartedly approve of.

Diana's breasts were small and alert to the touch.

Sha-la-la, man

She began to yank at my shirt to pull it off and I paused in my breast play to get the thing off me and be all the way naked with m'lady.

I palmed her pubis and let my middle finger rest on her slit while I alternated nipples with my mouth.

Diana grabbed hold of my surprisingly rigid-again dick.

"Mmm, somebody woke up early," she said and wedged herself under me, using her hand to aid with the angle of my dangle and via this coordinated effort we found ourselves quite soothingly and beautifully fucking.

And then sha-la-la-la-la, he entered her slowly
and showed her where he was coming from
And then sha-la-la-la-la, he made love to her gently
it was like she'd never ever come

"I don't have a rubber," I said for some ridiculous reason given the fact that my penis was already buried rather cozily in her vagina.

"We're cool," Diana whispered as her cunt churned like an Osterizer.

I'd never imagined anything like it before.

I pictured my dick coming out afterward looking like a polished rock, like all topaz and shit.

I wanna be black, have natural rhythm
Shoot twenty foot of jism too
and fuck up the jews

"What the heck?" Diana exclaimed, pushing me off of her.

"He got both of us," I said.

I wanna be black, I wanna be a panther
Have a girlfriend named Samantha
and have a stable of foxy whores

I wanna be black, wanna be like Martin Luther King
And get myself shot in the spring

"That is not right," she said, shaking her head.

I wanna be black, I wanna be like Malcolm X
And cast a hex
over President Kennedy's tomb
and have a big prick, too

Diana sat cross-legged and naked on my bed.

It was clear the fucking was over.

I took the music off and sat cross-legged facing her.

She held out her hands for me and I clenched them both.

We leaned into each other and kissed sweetly.

"Sorry," she shook her head.

"No, I'm sorry. That was fucked up. Obviously, it's my first time hearing the album so I didn't know."

"Bad timing."

"He is being sarcastic, you know."

"I know," she nodded. "It's still not right. Sarcasm or not."

"I'm sorry."

"We had it going on though, boy," she smiled, "Damn."

I smiled back and squeezed both her hands.

"I love you," she cupped my head.

"I love you, too," I felt an ache like missing someone.

Diana laid back and pulled me on top of her.

"Wance," she cooed in baby-talk and we started kissing.

"Lance?" my dad said while knocking on my bedroom door at that moment.

"Yeah," I croaked.

"It's time for your little friend to go home."

"OK," I said as Diana and I stifled our laughter.

I finished myself off after she left.

There was this one moment during the brief time we were fucking, right before the Lou Reed disruption, when I really wanted to come. We'd had a vigorous rhythm going and our legs were all scrunched up and spread wide and banging hard, and I was definitely trying to get back to that spot while jacking off.

Afterward, instead of reading, I fell asleep thinking of Diana and dreamed that I was helping her with her homework.

7

First Levon Arrow went inside to lie down on his bed and let his palpitations subside.

As he lay atop his wool blanket he thought about how to tell his mother he was leaving the sn'ail farm in order to follow some girl who's looking for whales.

"What will happen if you have a Minerva Syndrome attack God knows where and you need help?" was his mother's initial response upon hearing Levon's plans.

"I've learned how to rest and let the starburst settle. I can do that anywhere."

"I won't know how you're doing," she said mournfully, "I will live in a state of constant wondering."

"There's nobody left in the world to harm me. You needn't worry about my safety. One of the cool things about global entropy is the vanishing crime rate. There's nothing to gain in harming others anymore. Everyone's too busy en route to wherever they think their happiness is hiding. I guess I'm joining them."

"You think you will find happiness with this girl?"

"I don't know," Levon said, "But when I was out in the sn'ail fields I realized how much I'd be missing if I didn't at least try."

"But what about everybody else who needs your love?"

"I guess I'm going to have to figure out a way to love them too. Maybe Glenda will be cool with that."

"Glenda," said Levon's mother, "That's her name."

Levon Arrow stood up to leave.

"You're really doing this," she said rising also to hug him goodbye.

"I will find her and bring her back here."

"You will or you won't. I don't believe in promises."

"At least promise that if you have an opportunity to get on one of the rockets, and I'm not back yet, that you'll go without me."

"I told you. No promises."

"Just this one promise. Please."

"Be safe. Find a way to let me know how you're doing," his mother said, hugged him tightly to her breast, and then, as she had to, let him go.

Levon Arrow trudged across the tundra toward the frozen river, stopping briefly to say farewell to Toby Sn'ail.

"Thank you for spurring my journey. You made me aware of my own destiny," Levon told the dapper gastropod.

"May your travels be fruitful and result in many satisfying sexual experiences," Toby offered his best wishes.

"Do you have any words of wisdom that I might carry with me in my quest for fulfillment?"

"Surround yourself with beautiful women."

"You sound like my father."

"Maybe I am."

"My father is dead."

"Metempsychosis, baby."

"And how do I keep all those beautiful women satisfied?"

"Make each one feel like she is your favorite."

"That's it?"

"You accomplish that and you will own the world," Toby said and retreated into his shell lest the pestiferous farm boy keep on asking annoying questions.

Levon Arrow sat along the bank of the frozen river lacing the skates up tightly.

Glenda said she'd be heading thataway and so Levon Arrow hoisted himself to commence his journey onward.

At first he was caught off balance by the frozen ripples that wrinkled the ice, but once he caught on to their heavily regular pattern he glided quite gracefully across the gelid estuary.

Everybody was going in the same direction, but just to make sure Levon skated over to the wooden sign that stood tilted on the farther bank.

THATAWAY —> the crudely chiseled sign pointed.

Levon Arrow thereupon joined the pilgrimage.

We had just finished *Heart of Darkness* in A.P. English.

Megiddo was going over some of the key passages for us to remember for our unit test the next day.

"The usual. 5 short answer ID questions on various quotes, one essay with several topics to choose from," he said in response to Gina's question about the format of the test.

"Pay attention to this passage for sure," Megiddo said, "One of those many moments in the book when Marlow directly addresses the other men on the boat in the Thames where he is—all along don't forget—narrating the story, and calls into question the possibility of any true communication at all: *Do you see the story? Do you see anything? It seems to me I am trying to tell you a dream—making a vain attempt, because no relation of a dream can convey the dream-sensation, that commingling of absurdity, surprise, and bewilderment in a tremor of struggling revolt, that notion of being captured by the incredible which is of the very essence of dreams. . . . No, it is impossible; it is impossible to convey the life-sensation of any given epoch of one's existence,—that which makes its truth, its meaning—its subtle and penetrating essence. It is impossible. We live, as we dream—alone. . ."*

That last line followed me around everywhere for days.

We live, as we dream—alone . . .

I knew that vacuum well.

"The idea that you are never truly connected to another human being," Megiddo continued, "There's always that place of separateness, the secret you keep from everybody, the one thing no one can ever completely know, and therefore we are all ultimately alone."

"That's depressing," said Sharon Rose, looking up for a predictably brief moment.

"What's love then?" Miranda Savitch asked.

"A survival mechanism," Emily Wolf said. "We're more successful as a species when we bond and work together. Love entices us into doing that. It's the same reason sex feels good. So we will *want* to do it."

"You would know," Arabella Mayflower said.

"Doggy style," Buddy Feigenbaum chortled.

I guess word had gotten around somehow.

"You can choose to live in your idealized Emerald City if you want and roll around in the illusion," Emily said, "but I prefer Kansas because that's where we all are anyway, and I think it's better to face reality directly. I don't want to live an illusion."

"Auntie Em," Claude Moss coughed.

"All separateness is an illusion," Manny said but no one reacted, "Marlow's got it wrong. It's not connection that's the illusion, it's separateness. Maya. We are one consciousness constantly manifesting in myriad forms."

"That's deep," Claude Moss said, somehow sounding sarcastic and yet sincere at the same time without knowing the difference.

"And what about that decision Marlow makes at the end? When he lies to the Intended. *The last word he pronounced was—your name.*'"

"The whore!, the whore!" Jim Lord whispered like Kurtz.

"Marlow was telling the truth," Claude Moss got scattered laughs.

"Funny," Megiddo pointed at Claude and Jim, "but really, why does he lie to her?"

"'Cause she would've freaked if she knew how Kurtz ended up," Miranda said.

"*It would have been too dark altogether,*" I said.

"Way too dark," Megiddo nodded.

"So it's better to live oblivious to truth?" Emily asked.

"What do you think?" Megiddo challenged her.

"I think it's better to see clearly. How else can you lead a real life instead of some fairy tale?"

"Oh, fairy tales are pretty darn dark also, don't forget," Megiddo said.

"You know what I mean though."

"And what do you think Marlow thinks?"

"That it doesn't matter," Miranda said.

"That what doesn't matter?"

"Living a lie for the sake of sanity. That it's preferable sometimes."

"Only if you're a girl," Gina Dichlich said.

"*They—the women, I mean—are out of it—should be out of it. We must help them to stay in that beautiful world of their own, lest ours gets worse,*" Megiddo read and

238

looked at the class.

"See?" Gina said.

"Marlow is saying the opposite of what Emily was saying earlier," Megiddo said, looking for the sentence in the text, "Here . . . *The heavens do not fall for such a trifle*, Marlow says. The universe didn't cave in because he told a lie to protect the innocence of this young woman."

"The illusion is comforting," Miranda answered. "I mean, if we're all going to die anyway and merge with a blank nothingness, why not enjoy a beautiful hallucination while we're alive? Why not live in Oz? What's wrong with the Emerald City?"

"There's no place like home," said Sharon Rose like Glinda the Good Witch.

"Either way you're alone," Emily said, "Whether you choose to admit the darkness or not."

I asked Diana later which she thought was better, harsh truth or beautiful illusion, right after I'd finished going down on her for the first time.

She went with what she called "The beautiful truth of Jesus Christ."

We had gone to see the film *Coming Home* earlier that evening, and in the middle of the cunnilingus scene, right when Jane Fonda is climaxing, Diana whispered to me, "Try this at home, kids," and we did just that in her bedroom with Tom Waits's *The Heart Of Saturday Night* playing loud enough that her parents couldn't hear Diana's perorations at the grand finale.

"Dang, girl, you're gonna graduate Summa Cum Loudly."

"From the School of Hard, um–"

"That feel good?"

"No," she said and bit my cheek.

"What's coming like for you? What does it feel like?" I asked.

"Probably around the same as it feels for you. I don't know."

"Yeah, but I think it's also different."

"How could anybody really know that? I guess it's still the same energy that swells and then reaches a peak. For me it's like riding a wave. You let yourself be drawn into this accumulating energy and then go full on abandon, rocking with it, all the way overboard, cresting and crashing and ebbing back like an undertow. It's all about riding that wave for as long as you can."

"Is there some climactic moment, like an explosion? Or an implosion? Although I also know the wave you're talking about for sure. That's the best place to stay."

"Sometimes there can be an explosive moment. Sometimes it's just a really great long wave. I kind of like those better actually. The long waves. That's when it feels like real lovemaking, when there's just this ever shifting wave of pleasure, sometimes really slight, sometimes intense, back and forth, up and down, fast and slow, but it's all heavenly. I think of sex as a prayer of thanks to the Lord."

"That explains the 'Oh God' thing you do."

"Shut up," Diana slapped me.

"Now I know."

"Shut. Up," she demanded while pinching my left nipple, "You are disgusting," pushing me off and turning away, "And blasphemous."

I spooned against her.

My dick, beginning to re-harden, wedged into her ass crack.

"St. Peter's at the Furry Gates," I whispered to her and she elbowed me.

"Stop," she said.

"I have an idea," I twitched my dick.

"Hmm . . . Let me guess."

"We can make popcorn and watch *Twilight Zone* reruns."

"That was not going to be my guess."

"How about making passionate love on the living room couch?"

"My parents are home, baby."

"Let's get high and pig out on Count Chocula and half-and-half."

"I could actually go for some Count Chocula and half-and-half right now," she said and reached around to grab my cock.

"From now on, Di-licious, you are to call my dick Count Chocula."

"That name does not really work. Frankenberry is more fitting."

"I can definitely supply the half-and-half, though."

She turned to face me.

Her breasts were nestled against my own jiggling pecs.

"I suppose you want me to fuck you," I mock sighed.

"No, Dicklicious, I . . ." she said, pushing me onto my back and straddling me, "am going to fuck . . ." finagling me into her slit and lowering herself onto my shaft, "you."

I always got way deep inside Diana when she was on top. The tip of my dick would touch her upper insides, and I would get an extra 'ooh' from her when that happened.

If I hoisted my hips a bit occasionally, that would intensify the penetration and contact.

Or so she told me once.

Sometimes she would lean way forward, a-dangle over me, and grind my cock hard against her upper wall like a peppermill, or, actually, more like a cheese grater, because, dang, dude, she could shred my dick like parmesan.

"Jesus fucking Christ, yeah," I moaned that night we were listening to Tom Waits.

"Don't," she moaned atop my cock, "take, mmm," her eyes closed, "the Lord's name . . . in va— God yeah," she prayed as she fell straight back and pulled me on top of her for a trenchant humping to finish the business and all I could think of was that scene in *The Exorcist* where Linda Blair rapes herself with the crucifix.

There's no way her parents didn't hear us.

When I got home from Diana's later there was a letter from Dolly waiting for me on the dining room table.

She apologized for taking so long to reply to my last letter but school was consuming much of her time and the rest was taken up by stuff about her boyfriend Georges. As she described it: *"Georgie and I are all the way in love and it's beautiful."*

I marveled at the swiftness of our distancing. After a year of intense intimacy and best-friendship in 11th Grade. It felt like a permanent divergence, like I would never really have her back in my gravity, like I hardly knew who she was anymore.

I replied immediately because I knew if I waited I might never write back.

Hello, Dolly.

I'm so happy to hear of your happiness with your beau Georges. I have a similar situation to report. I'm deeply into a full-blown love affair with Diana Hitchcock. It'd been brewing for quite some time, like ever since the D-Lux/Mr. Hill wedding, but now we are, to use your words, all the way in love, and, yes, I totally grok the beautifulness you wrote of in your letter. I am just bonkers in love with Diana. To the point where my grades are suffering because all I want to do is be with her and so I'm way behind in my homework and reading for Megiddo. Do you know what I mean? Wanting to say your beloved's name over and over again? Picturing your adult life together? Unfortunately, it also means I haven't been writing any songs and find myself just devoid of ideas. Love has lobotomized me in a way. Creative blocks almost always have to do with girls. And yet girls are also the source of my inspiration. You know. The usual.

Diana is playing Dorothy in The Wizard Of Oz which Xeno Cortez talked Ms. Van

Poole into doing as the Spring musical. I'm the Tin Man, which is fine, even though I wanted Scarecrow and even sang "If I Only Had A Brain" at my audition. Van Poole gave Scarecrow to David Harkins, and I can see now the wisdom of that. He's got that lanky rubbery body. So I'm cool with Tin Man (even though it does remind me of this one time Miranda told me I was the Tin Man and she didn't mean it as a compliment). Sharon Rose will be perfect as Glinda but is trying to convince Van Poole to let her do it campy Brooklyn like Barbra Streisand. Xeno's doing the Cowardly Lion (of course) and Lorelei Lux is the Wicked Witch.

Otherwise just reading and writing for Megiddo, though not as much as I should, and getting by, at times barely, in my other classes, such as they are (Play Production, Stagecraft, Econ & French). French is still great. We're reading L'Etranger right now. I hung out and had tea with Madame Couchée a while back. She told me to call her Sofia when we aren't at school.

Anyway, I hope your happiness continues to grow and that your love for Georges just keeps getting deeper and stronger.

Love from way too great a distance,

Lance

8

Levon Arrow skated through a kind of Himalayan canyon--or how he imagined the Himalayas might look if they were in a frozen California--paying attention to as many girls as possible.

All of them would be his favorite.

There was this one chick in a long furry skirt whose name was Hedda.

Hedda spoke a form of Norse that predated even the Vikings.

For a stretch of miles Levon and Hedda spent their nights together camping in the open air and kissing until the fire went out.

Hedda would say things to him in Norse which he did not understand.

Likewise she did not understand his language.

It hardly mattered.

They loved the sound of each other's voices.

Hedda had blue eyes the color that the sky used to be.

When Levon Arrow would look into Hedda's eyes he'd forget other girls for a while.

When Levon Arrow would look into Hedda's eyes he'd forget where he came from.

Levon and Hedda slept facing each other.

"You're my favorite," Levon said to her each night before falling asleep despite her inability to understand. She would smile as if she knew.

One time instead of saying, "You're my favorite," Levon said on a lark, "I want to fuck you really hard in the vagina," at which Hedda slapped his face and turned away from him.

This was the moment Levon Arrow learned that girls understand everything.

After that Hedda didn't skate or sleep with Levon Arrow anymore, though she did keep him in her peripheral vision always.

During an early *Wizard Of Oz* rehearsal, while Diana and David were working on their first number together, I sat halfway back in the aud reading for Megiddo.

Right after we'd finished *Heart of Darkness* in AP English, the class started looking at "The Hollow Men" by T.S. Eliot, a poem I already sort of knew because Mr. Beauregard had given me a copy of it back in 10th Grade.

The epigraph, meaningless to me then, now gained full resonance.

Mistah Kurtz—he dead

I smiled to myself and loved the Beauregard/Megiddo legacy.

We are the hollow men
We are the stuffed men
Leaning together
Headpiece filled with straw.

I had wanted to be the Scarecrow but instead was cast as the Tin Man.

"The Tin Man is also hollow," I told myself as some kind of lame consolation.

I thought of standing with Miranda on my front lawn beneath the sycamore trees that summer afternoon it all ended.

Shadows of leaves trembled on her face.

A sweet breeze made her beauty perfect.

Was that day as sad and final for her as it was for me?

"You are the Tin Man," Miranda had said and knocked on my chest.

I wondered if she'd remember enough of that exchange to enjoy the irony once she found out I'd be playing the Tin Man in the musical.

I could see her smirk already.

She wouldn't even have to say anything to me.

Shape without form, shade without colour,
Paralysed force, gesture without motion

Watching David Harkins, though, I accepted that Ms. Van Poole had made the right casting choice.

He danced the role in all of its gangly looseness. He embodied it in a way I couldn't have.

My moves are too uptight, no matter how hard I try, or perhaps *because* of how hard I try.

Plus, David and Diana had an undeniable chemistry together which is essential to the success of that story. If Dorothy and Scarecrow don't hit it off, there is no Yellow Brick Road.

It did pang at my heart a bit seeing them be so good together but I was surprised at just how little it panged me and maybe that sad reality panged me even more.

While I pondered weak and weary, Lorelei Lux came and sat down next to me.

"Greetings, Lance Atlas," she said, placing her notebook in her lap and resting her hands on her knees.

"You digging being the Wicked Witch?" I asked her.

"It's quite satisfying, though I am still struggling with finding my own voice instead of merely imitating Margaret Hamilton."

"Yeah, she really does define the role."

"Indeed. I'm working with different intonations and mannerisms. I'll find the witch within. I will. Are you happy with being Tin Man?"

"I wanted to be Scarecrow, but, yeah. I think I'm going to have a blast dancing mechanically. It'll be like doing the robot at Junior High parties."

"I remember you were good at that."

"I've got the android thing down, yeah."

"And how are *you* you? The real you."

"Pretty good," I said. "Hot and heavy with Diana."

"Don't mess it up."

"I'm all the way in love with her," I said.

"No you're not."

"I am. I'm gaga."

"She is just another distraction."

"From what?"

Lorelei Lux wrote something in her notebook.

"How would you know anyway?" I asked.

"Because I was one."

"What?"

"One of your distractions."

"Huh? Distraction from what?"

"From whom."

"I'm not into this cryptic shit," I said.

Lorelei closed her book.

"You aren't the Tin Man," she said.

"No?" I said and knew I was about to be Lorelei'd.

"No."

"Then who am I?"

"You are Professor Marvel. Oz himself, Lance Atlas. By creating the outward illusion that he is great and powerful, Marvel never has to actually deal with anybody individually."

"In the book he's named Oscar Diggs."

"One and the same."

"And you're saying that's what I do."

"Yes. Your mask enables you to stay separate. You're very good at making it seem like you're paying attention to each of us but you're really not. I have observed this behavior for many years now and recently figured out what you were up to."

"I try to pay attention to everyone."

"That's a sweet little rationale you've invented. But I don't buy it. I don't buy it at all, Lance Atlas. Unless it's become so pathological you have started to believe in your own delusion. That's possible," she said and wrote something else down in her notebook.

"So, you still keep track of me in there?"

Lorelei looked at me and didn't answer.

"Nice talking to you, Lance Atlas," she said and shook my hand, "I'm needed on stage, my pretty."

In this last of meeting places
We grope together
And avoid speech
Gathered on this beach of the tumid river

A common dreamscape for me since 10th Grade, a ravaged planet, a lost humanity with nothing left to claim.

This is the way the world ends
Not with a bang but a whimper

My dreams remain predominantly end-of-the-world scenarios and in these dreams I am always astonished at how quiet it is.

Not the apocalypse Diana was always quoting from the Book of Revelations, but rather an inconsequential fizzle in the midst of all that has been forgotten and has ceased to matter.

It is there, and only there, in these dreams, that I am able to kiss Miranda Savitch.

I see her, I grab her, I kiss her.

A few days later Diana and I caught a double bill of *Coma* and *The Betsy*, both of which sucked (though I have to admit seeing Laurence Olivier's old flabby ass banging that chick on the bed almost made *The Betsy* kind of worth it, and also Kathleen Beller's tits were quite awesome), after which we felt like getting high so we went over to the Rust house to see if Whit or Big were feeling generous because we didn't really have any money.

"This weed is called Starship Enterprise," said Bigelow Rust, holding up a baggie, "Need I say more? Warp speed, Mr. Sulu."

"It's all the same weed though, right?" Diana asked, pointing to the other bags.

"Yeah. Well. Sometimes I've got Mexican, sometimes it's Columbian, occasionally Thai stick. I'm hearing about this Hawaiian shit called Maui Wowie starting to come through, though. See, a special name makes people feel like they're getting something different."

"Even if it's basically the same shit," Diana said.

"Brand names are a placebo," Big said.

As we walked past Taryn's old bedroom I peeked in discreetly to glimpse the site of that first great flirtation listening to *Aladdin Sane*, not knowing then I was being initiated into satsang with my sex guru.

Big and Diana and I went downstairs to sample some of the Starship Enterprise, and, coincidentally, as it turned out, to watch *Star Trek* with Whit, who was strewn across the den couch, obviously already buzzed.

"Hey, how's it going?" I said to Whit.

"Pretty good," he recited, "Check it out: it's the episode where Kirk has to tame that alien chick."

"Lame one," I said, "but we should watch it anyway. Have you seen it?" I asked Diana even though I knew she didn't like Star Trek that much.

"No, but I guess I'm going to," Diana said and took a hit off the spliff Big had rolled. "As long as nobody tells me I look like Uhura we'll be cool."

"This episode might possibly have the worst acting in the entire series. Everybody sucks," Whit said.

"Unbelievably bad performances, yeah," I agreed.

"Shatner sinks to new depths. Oh and that green-faced alien. Dang, dude."

"Aw, man, why's she gotta be black?" Diana said of the Dohlman of Elaas when she appeared in the transporter.

"You kind of look like her," I nudged.

"Fuck you," Diana kicked me and took another hit off the spliff.

"She is such a total bitch," Whit said.

"Of course," Diana said, "The black girl's gotta be the bitch."

"Uhura's not a bitch," Whit said.

"That's 'cause Uhura's the house negro," Diana said. "You know she is secretly fucking Massa Kirk."

"That radio isn't the only knob she's twisting," said Whit and held out his hand to give Diana five.

In one scene, the Dohlman rejects her welcoming gifts from Troyilus, throwing a pair of shoes at the Ambassador.

"Look, it's like Liza throwing the slippers! From our scene!" Diana kissed me on the cheek and put her head on my shoulder.

A little bit later in the episode, when Kirk tries to teach the Dohlman some manners, the two exchange blows.

"Dang, dude, he slapped that bitch back," Whit said of Kirk, "Go Kirk."

"She needs to be spanked," I said when Kirk threatened the Dohlman with such.

"She wants to be spanked," Diana said. "She's doing everything she can to make that happen."

I wanted to kiss her really hard on the mouth when she said that but not in front of Whit and Big, so I just smacked her on the ass instead.

"Women cast a spell," said Bigelow, shaking his head.

"Yeah they do," said Diana and rubbed my semi-hard cock through my jeans but stopped when Mildred Rust walked in.

"You guys watching *Star Trek*?"

"Get lost, Milly Dreadful," Whit snarled.

"But I love this one."

"All right, but no annoying commentary, nerd breath."

"I'll be cool," she turned to me, "Hey, Lance, how's it going?"

"Pretty good," I said, "This is Diana."

"Hey," Mildred half-waved.

"How's it going?"

"Pretty good," Mildred looked my way, "Hey, my friend Annie says you guys are pen pals."

"Uh, yeah," I nodded and Diana looked at me.

"Don't worry, I won't tell her you have a girlfriend," Mildred said and, dang, dude, did I hear about it on the walk back to my house afterward.

"Pen pal?"

"Annie is like 11-years-old."

"You have an 11-year-old pen pal?"

"I do."

"Oh kay, dude, that is kind of slightly creepy."

"She's a great kid. You'd like her."

"You could have told me about her. It. Whatever."

"I didn't think it was important."

"You write regularly to a girl and you think it's not important?"

"She's just this kid. I suggest books for her to read. What does it matter?"

"I want to know everything about you. I'm your girlfriend. No secrets."

"It isn't a secret. I just didn't think it was anything worth mentioning."

"From now on, if it happens, if it exists, it's worth mentioning."

"OK," I said.

"Do you write to Dolly also?"

"Nyeah, a couple of times."

"Ugh. Who else?"

"Nobody else."

"Swear?"

"Swear. Jeez."

I was sure Diana had secrets too, but the difference was I didn't really want to know about them.

People should be allowed to have their secrets.

Mostly because they're going to have them anyway, whether allowed or not, so why not make it easy on both parties and just be cool about the fact.

It removes a layer of unenforceable human nature.

We live, as we dream—alone . . .

Diana and I were still pretty high when we got back to my house, and we went inside intending to have torrential sex, but we were both a little bit too stoned to get it going right away.

"You know what I realized this morning when I woke up and was thinking about you?" Diana asked me.

Our eyes were fucking even though our bodies were incapable of it at the moment.

"Tell me."

"I realized that I can say I love you and know what those words mean. For the first time. And I also realized that I'm happy. And there's nowhere else I want to be right now. And I also can't believe I'm saying corny things like this."

She looked at me steadfastly.

"I love you," Diana said and kissed the tip of my nose.

"I love you too."

We both closed our eyes and enjoyed the high separately together.

Diana said at some point, "I'm not black, I'm Abyssinian."

"What does that mean?"

"I have no idea," she wheezed with her eyes closed.

"You are an abyss anyway," I said. And she was at times.

"An abscess?"

"An abbess. Get thee to a nunnery. Go."

"Then I'll be married to Jesus."

"Well you might as well stay right here then," I said as I rolled on top of her.

"Heathen," she said while wrapping her legs around my backside, "Blasphemer."

"You forgot Christ Killer," I said as I went in unto to her and knew her.

Diana Hitchcock occupied all my awareness.

Nothing else was necessary.

Our lives very quickly became completely enmeshed.

Every free moment was spent together.

And, for several weeks, I liked it.

Sometimes, even when I had a paper due for Megiddo, Diana would come over anyway and—while I was working in my room—would have coffee with my mom in the kitchen or a cigarette with my dad on the porch.

She was completely absorbed into my family.

I was equally embraced by her parents.

Her dad, Gerald, shared Lakers season tickets with a group of his pals and brought me to a few games, always introducing me to the other regulars in his section as "my daughter's white boyfriend," which made everybody laugh especially the white people.

"That core of Kareem, Norm Nixon, and Jamaal Wilkes," Gerald said, "I think that's a championship formula. They just need a couple more pieces."

"They're not going all the way this year."

"No. Not like '72."

"'72," I echoed fondly.

"Wilt. Jerry West."

"Gail Goodrich."

"Happy Hairston."

"Elgin Baylor. Sort of."

"Jim McMillan."

We shared that Lakers fan bond of '72. The 33 Game Win Streak. Jerry West's 55-footer. The Championship series against the Knicks.

"Next year. Year after. They'll be champs," he said and patted me dadly on the back, "They just need a little magic."

One weekend I slept over at Diana's house because her parents were in Vegas.

We had sex in myriad locations from early that Saturday afternoon into the wee hours of the night.

On the living room couch, in the pool, in the egg-shaped music chair thingy, on the kitchen table, while taking a bubble bath, reverse cowgirl on the floor of the entry hall, and finally in her parents' bed.

"I want to be a star," Diana said as we lay depleted side by side listening to the new Patti Smith album.

"You already are," I said.

"No, really. Like a famous star."

"Why?"

"So people remember me."

"I'd rather be a legend," I said, "But, yeah, the same idea."

"What's the difference really?"

"I don't know. Stars shine brightly and legends lurk in the shadows maybe. A legend's origins are mysterious. His whereabouts unknown. You don't know if he's real or imagined. Like Peter Pan."

"Uh, dude, Peter Pan is definitely fictional."

"I'm not so sure."

"You are stoned."

"Yes I am. But that doesn't negate the Peter Pan thing. Ever since I was little I've been confused about Peter Pan. A part of me thinks he's real. At least occasionally."

"You are so fucking weird," Diana started nibbling on my earlobe.

"Deal with it," I said a-tingle and reached for her breasts.

"That's what I'm attempting to do she said and found my mouth.

Dang, dude, did I really have another session left in me?

I wasn't completely sure. My dick was raw.

Penis tartare.

"You'll be a legend and I'll be a star," she said and began nudging my hand toward her crotch.

I obliged begrudgingly, afraid I wouldn't be able to finish.

"One day everybody will know who we are," she whispered and kissed me.

I don't fuck much with the past but I fuck plenty with the future

Patti Smith intruded upon our intimacy in that moment.

Baby was a black sheep
Baby was a whore
Baby got big and she's gonna get bigger
Baby wants something
Baby wants more
Baby baby baby was a rock 'n' roll nigger

"What the hell?" Diana pushed my hand away once the lyrics crossed her consciousness.

Jimi Hendrix was a nigger.
Jesus Christ and Grandma, too

"No no no no no no," Diana said and got up off the bed to take the record off.

Jackson Pollock was a nigger.
Nigger, nigger, nigger, nigger,
nigger, nigger, nigger

Diana stood there at the stereo for a moment.

"Horrible."

"I think you're misunderstanding how she's using the word."

"She doesn't get to use that word in any form."

"It's a metaphor."

"Slavery was not a metaphor."

"You are right," I said in hopes of preempting a longer rant.

Diana crawled back into bed with me.

"Well, I've done it again," I said, "I'm glad I didn't put on 'Woman Is Nigger of the World,'" I said, trying to get a laugh out of her, but she didn't respond.

"What did I just say about using that word? Whatever," she turned away from me, adding, "You never get to pick the sex soundtrack again. I'm taking over that duty."

I wasn't going to argue.

Even though I knew it meant that next time we'd probably be making love to Gino Vannelli.

Dang, dude.

"What time is it?" I asked.

"Almost 11."

"*Twilight Zone* is coming on," I said, guiltily relieved that we weren't going to finish having sex one more time.

Diana got up to turn on the TV.

She was very into *The Twilight Zone*, so she knew which episode it was immediately.

"It's the one about the writer who makes his characters come alive by describing them."

"Yeah yeah."

"It has kind of a corny ending, though."

"What is it again?"

"When it turns out that even Rod Serling is a character he narrated into his tape recorder."

"Oh yeah yeah."

"But otherwise it's cool."

We lay in the radiating glow of the episode we'd both seen multiple times but it doesn't really matter how many times you see a *Twilight Zone* episode.

I played gently with her nipples.

"I wish we could do this every night," she said.

"What, lie here and watch TV?"

"Yeah. Or whatever. Hang out. Listen to music. Fuck. Work on our crafts. Just our own place and nobody else. Wouldn't that be far out?"

"Yeah, it would," I said even though I didn't really like the sound of that scenario much.

I think we were both asleep before Rod Serling was made to disappear at the end of the episode.

9

Then into Levon Arrow's skate-girl loving life rode this other young lady named Ariel who wore tight pants and spoke Levon's language.

Ariel claimed to be descended from people who came from another planet.

One night Levon tried to take Ariel's clothes off but she wouldn't let him.

"Tell me a story, Levon Arrow," Ariel said.

And then Levon would make some shit up hoping it'd get him laid but it never did.

But that was cool with Levon for the time being.

Long days skating and holding hands with Ariel were filled with conversations about dying planets and other profound ruminations.

"My ancestors came here because our home planet was becoming uninhabitable. And now here I am, their descendant, skating across yet another dying planet."

"What planet are your people from?"

"They never told me. They thought if I didn't know its name I wouldn't be sad that it's gone."

Ariel had a preternatural sadness, a sadness beyond Levon's ken.

"I can't be certain, but it is possible I'm the last of my kind," she said.

Levon Arrow put his arm around Ariel and touched his head to hers.

"Do you want some soup?" Ariel asked and pulled a can out of her satchel.

A fire was made, the tomato soup brought to a perfect hotness, a pair of spoons provided.

"It's entirely possible that I love you," Ariel said and held Levon's hand as they shared the soup.

Levon took that as an invitation to reach into her pants but she yanked his hand away.

"That is not what I meant at all," Ariel sighed, "That is not it at all."

She turned to face the wind.

I was becoming obsessively engaged in my reading of *A Portrait of the Artist as a Young Man*, whose protagonist I related to more precisely than any I'd read of before, even Gabriel Oak who had been my most recent fictional soul brother.

"If you're having trouble following what's going on in Joyce thus far," Megiddo said and looked around at numerous nods of acknowledgement, "try to think of the narration this way: instead of a series of chronological events, you're seeing the ripples of what happens when a pebble is dropped into a still pond. The events are emanating outward in all directions, propelled not by cause and effect but by association."

He looked around the room.

"I like how it starts off with the most cliché opening," I said.

"*Once upon a time*," Megiddo said, "Yes. And then you realize fairly quickly it's not what you think it is. So how do we tackle this kind of narration?"

Nobody said anything.

Megiddo continued, "I think the three essential myths we get from Greek literature are Pygmalion, Narcissus, and Daedalus. And I'd like you to think about what ties those three figures together on a fundamental level," Megiddo said, "and how they tie into the deeper aspects of *Portrait*, or at least what we've read of it so far. OK, the Daedalus myth is easier than the other two, but see what you make of it. Discuss for a few minutes with your neighbor and toss some ideas around. It'll be a first stab at our method for reading Joyce. And then of course we have to add the Blessed Virgin Mary into that mix. Not to confuse you or anything."

Emily Wolf and I were always partners in these discussions, though this time she passed me a note before we started talking.

I know you were there, the note said.

I wrote back, *Huh?*

She crumpled up the sliver of notebook paper.

"Can we talk later? Like at Nutrition or something?"

"I have to hang out with Diana at Nutrition or she gets cranky with me."

261

"Gotcha."

I had reached that point of Diana saturation in which her demands on my time and attention became greater than the level I was capable of providing, than I wanted to provide, to be more honest. She had begun pouting if she saw me talking to other people, especially girls.

"I'm to have no contact with the outside world," I told Emily.

"Jealousy," she sighed and rolled her eyes.

"Insecurity," I corrected her.

"Same thing," Emily said and I totally pictured us fucking in her bedroom. "How about on the phone then? Or has she had your line tapped also?"

"I think I can manage to make a discreet phone call."

"I'm around tonight. You do still have my number, don't you?"

"Embedded in my memory," I said and was most definitely flirting with her, even though I wasn't entirely sure I actually did have her number anymore.

As it turned out, I did not in fact have her number but luckily she ended up calling me instead.

"You forgot my number, didn't you?"

"Nyeah."

"I figured," she let the menacing silence shame me. "Hey, so my note."

"Yeah."

"OK. So, I know you were at my Solstice shindig."

I nodded to myself.

"You brought the Chex Party Mix," she said.

"That was me, yeah."

"You saw me on all fours with the Persian boy."

"That, yeah, and also the strapping lad with the daintily upturned penis you were sucking with great mastery beforehand."

"Richie. Nyeah. We went to elementary school together. I wanted you to see that. I wanted you to see who I am and what I do."

"Why?"

"To see if you'd be freaked out or be cool with it. I wanted you to be cool with it."

"Why?"

"I'm not sure exactly," she said. "I remain very confused by you. Or rather by my feelings for you. To me, it's like this: there's the guys you talk philosophy and literature with and there's the guys you fuck. I've always kept the two separate."

"I sort of have the same tendency."

"So this is weird for you too then. Wanting to fuck someone you also like discussing literature with."

"No it's not weird *wanting* to fuck someone I also like discussing literature with. That's the bulk of my sexual history right there. It's a question of being *able* to do that. Wanting and actually doing are two different things. Whenever I've made the attempt it all goes flat."

"Well I'm up for the valiant attempt," she said. "We should give it a try one day. Maybe it'll be revelatory for both of us."

"I watched that guy fucking you. I don't think I could make you come like that."

"That's OK, neither could he," she said.

"You seemed into it—"

"—Don't judge a girl by her sex sounds. Guys need more than just their dicks stroked," she went on.

263

Dang, dude.

"Anyway, think about it," Emily said. "We can do it in private if that's what you're worried about. It doesn't have to be at a dinner party."

"We're leaving out the fact that I have a girlfriend."

"So?"

"SO? You think that doesn't matter?"

"Have you ever promised her that you're not going to fuck other people?"

"No, but I think that's pretty much implied."

"But you've never promised her you wouldn't fuck anybody else."

"No. Not officially."

"So, like I said, think about it. You're not violating any spoken oath or anything. Right? You didn't swear on the Bible."

"Eh, that was sort of implied too. Diana's into the Bible. It's the living word of God to her."

The next time Diana and I had sex I suggested doggy-style on my bedroom floor and for some of it I pretended I was fucking Emily at her orgy, hitting that shit like Xerxes himself.

"*I just wanna stop*," Gino Vannelli belted as Diana and I took turns coming in our signature two-part harmony along with him.

Afterwards, I started talking about *Portrait* which I was doing all the time and Diana was getting sick of it.

"The way Stephen Dedalus is with the girls he likes, the way he can't act on his impulses toward some girls because it shames him, yet he has no trouble having sex with prostitutes, I dunno, I kind of relate to that."

"What does that say about me?"

"No no, this has nothing to do with you."

"Um, yes it does," Diana said and promptly faced the opposite wall.

"No, I was just making the comparison because it reminded me of how I always acted around Miranda. In fact all the female characters in *Portrait* remind me of Miranda, or at least my relationship with her."

"It seems like everything reminds you of Miranda."

"Not true."

"Or Claire Farnaway. Or Lori Lux. Or your little Dolly Ferris Wheel. Or any of the other girls you've had sex with."

"What the hell?" I started to sit up. "Where the fuck is this coming from?"

"Sometimes during Period 1 I get the hall pass from Miss Turner to go to the bathroom and I walk by Megiddo's room so I can peek in the window and see you because all I ever want to do is see you and the other day I looked in and saw you passing a note to that yellow-haired girl, the one you were dating for a while."

"Emily Wolf."

"That know-it-all bitch, yeah," Diana said, "The suede-oh intellectual."

"It's sood-oh. Pseudo-intellectual."

"Whatever," Diana said, one of her many euphemisms for fuck you, "I heard she's a slut anyway. Some people here think she's a goody-goody only 'cause they don't know that all the guys she fucks go to Hamilton. Except for you of course."

"Jesus fucking Christ."

"Don't take the Lord's name in vain."

"Sorry . . . Emily Wolf and I have never had sex."

"Uh huh."

"We didn't do much of anything other than talk about literature and kiss a bit. That's it. I swear. Di. Really."

"From what I've heard, she's not the kind of person who just holds hands and kisses."

"Where are you getting your information from?"

"Lori told me. During Oz rehearsal."

"You listen to Lorelei Lux?"

"Yeah. She's very observant and nosy. She knows everything that's going on."

"Lorelei Lux is mentally ill. She spies on people. And yet she didn't even know that her own sister was fucking Mr. Hill," I submitted as evidence.

"Yes she did."

"That's not what she told me. And we were together at the time."

"I know you were. What can I say? Girls are strategic. Boys are oblivious."

"Well, I don't know what to say, Di, other than I've never had sex with Emily Wolf," I whined defensively, my heart churning with futility.

After a turbulent silence, Diana said, "Doggy-style felt really good, baby. Do me like that again next time," and fell asleep for a while.

I turned on my lamp and read Joyce until she woke up.

When it was announced that Bob Dylan would be playing 7 shows at the Universal Amphitheater, I asked my parents if that could be my birthday present, and they agreed to give me the money for tickets, though in order to get them I'd have to wait in line at the Amphitheater box office, probably overnight, but it was Dylan, so Manny Shepherd and I decided we were going to brave the elements and camp out.

Tickets went on sale at 10am on the Monday of Easter vacation, mid-March, for the June shows.

Manny and I got there on Sunday night around 8pm for our overnight stint.

Because of Diana, I hadn't been hanging out with Manny at all which in a way was good because I wasn't writing any music and I was ashamed of my artistic lapse and I knew Manny would give me a hard time about that.

When Manny and I arrived at the Universal parking lot there were already people in line, but not too many, so we gave each other five realizing we'd be getting great seats, just not 1st row.

We brought a blanket to sit on and some weed but that was it.

Diana said she would come up on Monday morning and bring us food and coffee and stuff before the box office opened.

We smoked some of Big's "Misty Beethoven" weed and settled in for a long haul made awesome by a cannabis fueled discussion of art, consciousness, God, music, David Bowie, Francois Truffaut, professional wrestling, the apotheosis of Alfred E. Neumann, wicked sin, infinity, Paris, Bob Dylan of course, Kierkegaard, the Torah, and the new Elvis Costello record *This Year's Model* which I had gotten at Aron's but hadn't listened to yet because school had been grueling, and, of course, vagina.

"That was funny when Mr. Megiddo was talking about *The Opening of Misty Beethoven* the other day."

"Yeah. That was great. The way he tied it into the Pygmalion story," I said, "and *Taming of the Shrew*."

"He said it was actually a good movie."

"No, he said he *heard* it was a good movie," I smiled and we both laughed.

"That's right," Manny said. "'Cause he'd never himself go see such a film."

"Right."

"Megiddo is so fuckin' cool."

"The coolest."

"Oh, and when Whit made the connection between *Taming of the Shrew* and the *Elaan of Troylis* episode of *Star Trek*."

"That was very Whit."

"What'd he say again?"

"'Kirk smacked that bitch down!'"

"That's right."

As we were descending into a sweet stoned sleep Manny asked me what it was like having someone to fuck whenever I wanted.

"Makes life easier in some obvious ways," I said.

"Duh."

"But you pay a price for it," I admonished, not wanting to elaborate on the demands on one's time and attention that go along with it.

"No such thing as free pussy."

"It saps all the other juices as well," I said.

"Dang, dude," mumbled Manny as he segued into sleep.

I listened to the diminishing conversations in line as I myself drifted dreamward, the occasional chortles and guffaws.

It was nice knowing some people wouldn't be going to sleep.

They would be our sentries.

My dreams were disjointed, the hard pavement having an effect, mostly of Diana in various states of being pissed at me but I never knew why.

Between dreams I'd awaken to the comfort of voices standing guard over the foggy March night.

When we rose at dawn with sore backs and heads, the line stretched beyond the parking lot exit all the way down the hill to Lankershim.

Manny went and looked.

There were two vending machines near the box office where Manny got us each a cup of shitty coffee.

We had run out of stuff to talk about so we were just kind of standing around girl-watching.

"Hi, Lance!" I heard Miranda's voice and there she was with Arabella Mayflower walking in our direction.

"Hey, how's it going?" I said.

"Pretty good," the girls said together.

"You've got a primo spot in line," Miranda said.

"We've been here a long-ass time," Manny said. "Since last night."

"Ooh," Arabella winced.

"Are you guys just getting here?" I asked.

"We got here like 20 minutes ago, nyeah," Arabella said, "The boys are holding the place in line while we take a stroll."

"Or toke a strail," Manny said and inhaled a laugh.

"Nah, just girl talk," Miranda said.

"And coffee," Arabella added.

"And some funky stuff," I said but Arabella didn't remember the reference.

Arabella was going out with Levi Cohen.

"I'm worried we're too far back to get tickets. We should've gotten here last night. I told Freddy and he just said nah we can get there in the morning. Right."

"He's doing 7 concerts, though. You'll get something."

"But there's a bunch of nights I can't go."

"I know, me too, 'cause of the musical. So Diana and I have to go on June 1 'cause there won't be a rehearsal that night. We have no other options."

"Same with me," Manny said, "Orchestra in the musical."

"Yeah, that's right, we'll be doing full run-throughs by then."

"I can go on June 1 if you happen to end up with extras," Miranda said, "Hint hint."

"Well, if I can score 4 of them you can buy my extra pair off me."

"Same with me," Manny said, which he totally didn't have to do.

"Bitchin'," Arabella said.

"Thanks!" Miranda added and leaned forward to hug me but it was somehow too stiff and too loose at the same time. Completely out of sync.

As Miranda and I were embracing, Diana arrived with Hostess Cupcakes and hot chocolate in a thermos.

"Well, that's cute," she said as Miranda and I separated.

"Hey, Di. you know Miranda, right?"

"Yeah, sort of. Hey," Diana said to Miranda, "I hear a lot about you from this guy."

Among Diana Hitchcock's many talents was being friendly and hostile at the same time.

"Here," Diana said and handed me the cupcakes and thermos.

"Oh, groovy, let's go sit on the blanket," I said.

"Nah, I'm gonna head home," Diana said.

"But I thought the plan was you were gonna hang with us until the box office opens."

"I didn't know you were going to have guests," she started back to her car.

I walked along with her like a dutiful boyfriend, enduring the silence.

As she climbed into the front seat, she finally said, "I bring you a care package and I arrive to find you hugging Miranda Savitch. Kind of kills my desire to hang out with you."

"I'm sorry. She and Arabella had just come up to us to say hello. They're way back in line."

"It's fine," she gave fake conciliation and held my hand, "We should hang out later."

"I'll call you when I'm back home," and we kissed goodbye like our parents do.

I did go over to her house later and engaged in some decidedly passionate lovemaking but at the same time something was broken and getting brokener.

The next day I got a letter, a regular letter, in an envelope, from Annie De Milo.

Dear Sir Lanceypants,

Goodness gracious, how did you know about my special secret book that I hope never gets sold because I want it for myself? I do have such a book. But I'm not going to tell you what it is. You have to figure it out. That is your new mission. When you figure it out you'll know everything about me. Maybe if you're a good boy I will give you some clues now and then. Do you know who Kate Bush is? She has a song called "Wuthering Heights" that has inspired me to read the book. My mother thinks I'm too young to understand it. What do you think? And there's also another song on the Kate Bush album that makes me think about you, but I'm not going to tell you which one so you have to get the album and figure that out too. Then you'll know everything about YOU! I'm giving you all these mysteries to solve! It's all part of my evil plan . . . (If you were here right now you would be able to hear my sinister laugh which is kind of like the Wicked Witch of the West). Oh, I got to go for a weeklong trip with my class to London. We went to see the RSC do Romeo And Juliet. I think I didn't understand a lot of it but what I did understand was very sad. I'd like to learn more about Shakespeare. I don't know when we are next visiting L.A., but we'll have to visit my grandmother sooner or later, I suppose. I would dearly love to see you.

The Peter Pan postcard is perfect! I will add it to the collection on my wall.

I'm writing you a letter instead of a postcard because I tried to write to you on a postcard but I ran out of room so I had to start over on notebook paper instead. I hope you don't mind.

The postcard was of Poet's Corner in Westminster Abbey. I got it on the London trip I just told you about. Instead of sending it to you I put it up on my wall with the cards you've sent me.

Somewhere over the rainbow in (the original) Cambria,

Annie

p.s. Boys are loco en la cabeza.

My rejection letter from UCLA and acceptance letter to CSUN both came on the same day in early April.

My future became just that much more clear.

I would not be a Bruin like my mother and my grandmother before me.

I would be a Matador.

Ole.

Cal State Northridge.

aaaaaah-ha, loser . . .

Dang, dude.

Getting older is a series of diminishing paths and narrowing options and fading possibilities.

Later that week, during a rehearsal of my number "If I Only Had A Heart," in a cosmic irony that would be considered hokum if it appeared in a work of fiction, I suffered a tachycardial episode that didn't land me in the hospital—I didn't lose consciousness—but which did prohibit me from continuing to be in the play.

"It would be a bad idea," was all Dr. Gemara had to say to my parents for them to forbid my participation.

I was replaced as the Tin Man by an 11th Grader who had transferred to Fairfax from Hollywood High, this Haitian kid named Eleazar Fontaine who somehow already knew all of Tin Man's lines and dance moves.

"I swear Eleazar used voodoo on you to give you that heart breakdown. He wanted that part," Diana said.

"That's silly."

"Dude, he'd already memorized all your lines and dance steps. Think about it."

"I thought Christians don't believe in voodoo."

"Oh, we believe that it exists, but it's Satanic. It's the Devil's power at work. Anyway, that's what I think."

"I don't know. I don't think so. I've had this heart problem for a long time."

"Well, anyway, I'm very sad we won't get to be in *Oz* together."

"I'm pretty bummed," I said.

Diana and I went out that night to see *Rabbit Test,* the Joan Rivers film about a guy who gets pregnant.

"This sucks," I said, not referring to the movie but to my circumstance re: the musical, though the movie sucked too.

"Baby, your health is more important than any dumb production. I keep telling you that."

"I know. But still."

"Yeah, baby, it sucks. I just want you to be alive and loving me."

Later that evening, after we had sex in my bedroom, Diana said, "what if I got pregnant?"

"You're on the pill," I said.

"Yeah, but who knows. Sometimes I forget to take them."

"You do?"

"Occasionally."

"Di—"

"—If I did get pregnant, by the time I'd have it we'd be out of high school. We could get married," Diana said.

"What about college?"

"We'd still go. Aren't you going to Northridge?"

"Yeah."

"We can get a place in the Valley. I'll go to Pierce."

"Who pays the rent?"

"Waah, you're being poopy," she frowned, "I want you to pway."

I didn't know if her baby talk meant play or pray.

"Pway?"

"Make bewieve we're gonna get mawwied."

Her clear vision for our domestic togetherness grabbed me by the windpipe and the stranglehold discomfited my every sensibility.

I went into gradual retreat after that.

In retrospect I wonder if that's what she wanted to happen.

10

Levon Arrow noticed this girl Alice and decided to place himself in her proximity.

Levon Arrow would have skated faster to catch up with Alice and get her to talk to him, but he was too much enjoying skating behind her.

Levon couldn't figure out how Alice didn't freeze her ass off sporting a skirt that barely made it over the hump of her butt. Not that he was complaining or anything.

Every turn or stride revealed the promise.

"I'll remain at this exquisite distance just a little longer," thought Levon, occasionally doing knee-bends to accentuate his view.

To his surprise, Alice suddenly turned to face him—skating backwards—too quickly for him to feign indifference.

"What are you looking at, horndog?"

"Your backpack."

"Uh huh," said Alice.

"No really. What do you have in there?"

"In my backpack? Provisions. And some of my drawings."

"You draw?"

"Yeah. Well, I used to. I ran out of supplies a while back."

"I'd love to look at your drawings."

"Maybe later," she said and turned back around.

That afternoon Levon and Alice sat by the riverside and looked at her charcoal sketches.

Some of them seemed abstract to him, or maybe she just sucked, but then he did come upon one that spoke to him.

"That looks like—"

"—A vagina."

"Yes."

"It is."

"Ah."

"You like?"

"Vagina? Yes. I think so."

"Me too," she said, "but I meant the art. You think it's good?"

"Oh, yeah yeah, this stuff is excellent," Levon said but he wasn't sure what she meant about liking vagina too so he didn't pursue it, and he also didn't have a whole lot to say about the art beyond what he thought might get him laid.

Levon decided he wouldn't make a move on her but rather wait for her to make a move on him.

Several weeks went by in platonic bliss until Alice's attention was called away by an attractive female named Xochitl who skated by one crisp morning in the now perpetual winter.

When Alice told Levon she'd be spending all her time with her new old lady, he responded by asking if he could watch them make out sometime and Alice said, "Totally."

He never ended up doing it though.

Diana had *Oz* rehearsal on my birthday, so I went out to dinner with my parents and my sisters at Moonshadows on PCH.

"Happy birthday to my little fella," my mother toasted with her wine.

My sisters and I held up our water glasses.

"I remember what I was doing 17 years ago tonight," she went on.

"That was also a Thursday," my father said.

"Theo, how do you even remember that?" my mother challenged him.

"I remember I had to cancel my regular Thursday appointment with Mrs. Fleetwood. She'd been coming to me every Thursday since I opened my practice. It was raining that day. Do you remember?"

"I was inside the whole time," my mother said, "and just a little bit busy."

"Giving birth to our first born child," my father beamed and raised his wine glass and my sisters and I raised our water glasses again, "When you were born, the doctor said, 'He's all nose and hose.' Here's to Temple Hospital and the beautiful boy it gave us."

"Sorry Diana couldn't make it tonight," my mother said, "We do love her so."

"That's show-biz," I said. "I like that it's just the Atlas Family Club tonight."

"The Atlas Family Club," my father started singing the dumb-ass song he wrote when he started The Atlas Family Club—back when I was like 10— which consisted of the 5 of us sitting in the living room on Sunday evenings having a meeting about the family and each getting our allowance for the week. "In it we have such fun," my dad continued singing to the tune of the Jingle Bells, the dashing through the snow part.

My dad was really into parliamentary procedure.

He actually used a gavel that he got from Toastmasters to conduct the Atlas Family Club meetings.

"First on the agenda: is there any old business?" he began that first meeting as chairman of the Atlas Family Club.

We all shook our heads.

"How can we have old business when it's the first meeting?" Mimi raised a legitimate point.

"Address the chairman and ask for the floor if you want to speak."

"Ask for the floor?" Joy laughed.

"Say, 'May I have the floor, Mr. Chairman?'"

"May I have the floor, Mr. Chairman?" Mimi rolled her eyes.

"The Chair recognizes Mimi Atlas." my father said.

"Which chair?" Joy wanted to know.

"Joy, quiet," my mother told her, "Daddy is the chair."

Joy burst out laughing, "Daddy's not a chair!" and buried her face in the couch pillow.

"Mimi, you have the floor," my father pointed with his gavel.

"Where does she have the floor?" Joy inadvertently became Chico Marx.

"Joy, shush," my mother said.

"How can we have old business when it's the first meeting?" Mimi asked.

"Good point," my father said, "I move we table old business and move on to new business. Does anybody second?"

"I second the motion," my mother said enthusiastically.

"The motion is seconded. All in favor?"

We raised our hands.

"No, you have to say aye."

"Aye," we all said and then Joy said, "Aye aye, captain," and saluted.

"You are such a mongoloid," Mimi said.

"I am a Down Syndrome child," Joy corrected her and then,

"Hoskitapookity," she conjured with her hands.

"Hoskitapookity? Is that some kind of mongoloid voodoo?"

"Mimi," my dad stopped her.

"Hocus Pocus," I said.

Joy affirmed, "I'm tryna make Mimi disinappear."

"Is there any new business?"

Mimi raised her hand.

"I have a question," she said.

"Request for information," my dad said.

"Whatever."

"Say, 'Point of information, Mr. Chairman.'"

"For real?"

"'Point of information, Mr. Chairman.'"

"Ugh. Point of information, Mr. Chairman," Mimi rolled her eyes.

"The chair recognizes Mimi Atlas."

"I can't remember what I wanted to ask—oh yeah: At the next meeting is old business going to mean talking about everything we're talking about at this meeting?"

"Only if something is left unresolved when the meeting is adjourned."

"Just wondering."

After 3 weeks, the meetings began skipping straight from the Atlas Family Club Theme Song to the distribution of allowances and a motion to adjourn.

"So how about the Soviets bringing down that Korean airliner?" my dad said, "How's that for a birthday present?"

"Cray-zee, yeah."

"Do they know why it happened?" my mother asked..

"We'll find out eventually," my father said.

"Or some version of it anyway," Mimi said.

I was happy to be with my dorky family and with a view of the ocean out the window which was exquisite even at night, especially with the Cheshire moon reflected against it, just as impermanent as everything else.

Later that night, Diana came over after rehearsal and brought me a present, a powder blue sweatshirt with the word LEGEND across the front in white letters.

"Happy birthday, baby," she said and kissed me on the cheek.

I thought perhaps we'd have a round of sex to celebrate my birthday, but Diana pled exhaustion, kissed me on the cheek again, and went home.

As *Oz* rehearsals got longer and more frequent I had to choose between sitting through them from the audience or not seeing Diana.

I opted for not seeing Diana.

When I wasn't reading I would go to the New Beverly Cinema which had just opened near my house a couple of weeks before and was a new cultural pipeline for me.

It was like the NuArt but I could walk there.

One night I went to see *The Guns of Navarone* at the New Beverly and I saw Emily Wolf sitting by herself in the middle of the middle row.

"The lone wolf," I said and plopped down next to her..

"Not anymore," she replied. "How are you, tiger?"

"Without much of a roar these days."

"That's a wasteful shame," Emily said.

"At least now I have this place."

"I shall be here often too."

"This used to be a porno theatre."

"I remember."

"Gay porn. It was called *Eros*. The sign always turned me on."

"I knew you were gay," Emily smiled and faced me, "That's the real reason you don't want to have a passionate tryst with me."

"Busted," I said which made her smile, never an easy feat with Emily Wolf.

About halfway through the movie she put her head on my shoulder and I let it stay there.

After *Guns of Navarone* I walked her home.

Once we agreed that we both liked the film, neither of us had anything specific to say about it so we strolled in mostly silence.

"It's a nice night," Emily tried to take my arm but I pulled away.

"It is," I said, "Look at Orion."

"His head is Betelgeuse," she said, "And look, The Pleiades," she pointed, "You can barely see them, to the right and just down from Orion's belt. The Seven Sisters."

"You know about The Pleiades?"

"Of course."

How could I not fuck this girl?

When we arrived at the pink house with the huge arched window, I sagged in agony as we stood awkwardly at her front door.

"Come inside," she said.

"Nyeah."

"Come inside. Stop being such a little fag," she said and tugged at my sleeve.

"What about Diana?"

"You *are* interested, though. Right?"

"This is the part of me I hate most. Yes. I'm interested. But Diana."

"Pretend I'm her. I don't care."

"What?"

"It's all just masturbation ultimately. Don't you think?"

We live as we dream . . . Alone

"You mean like it doesn't matter who you're with."

"Whom."

"Whom you're with."

"Not ultimately, no. Your climax is yours alone."

"You don't think that orgasm is a more cosmic connection to another person?"

"Has that ever once been what you think about while you're coming? Be honest. Aren't you really just in a momentary state of amazing brainless sensations that have nothing whatsoever to do with the other person?"

"When I come I feel connected to everything."

"You're mythologizing. You've read too much Walt Whitman."

"And D.H. Lawrence. And Henry Miller."

"I'm with Conrad on this one," Emily said, "The essential you is ultimately private."

This was Emily Wolf's way of saying, "Fuck me."

"So it really doesn't matter how public you are with anything you do," she went on.

"But wait, how does that jive with your guy Spinoza though? God as the singular substance and all that? Aren't those two views contradictory?"

"I am large, I contain multitudes, as your guy Whitman would say."

The more Emily Wolf talked, the more desperately I wanted to kiss her very hard on the mouth.

And we could easily have done it that night, but I realized that I'd probably not be able to fuck Emily Wolf the way she wanted and liked to be fucked because I still had too much shame attached and then she'd end up thinking less of me for not fucking her right—plus there was the unbearable awkwardness and guilt around Diana that would certainly ensue—so I ended up nodding goodnight to her at her front door and making to leave.

Emily furrowed her brow at me.

"You're a conundrum," she said.

"I've been called that before."

"You're about as hard to reach as the guns of Navarone."

"Nyeah," I didn't know what else to say so I left.

When I got home after my short bemused walk from Emily's house, I couldn't concentrate on the reading I was supposed to do.

Megiddo wanted us to get some practice with older English in preparation for the AP exam, so we were reading and discussing *Taming of the Shrew* and *'Tis Pity She's A Whore*.

I put off deciding whether or not to procrastinate by writing a postcard to Annie De Milo.

When I was at Moonshadows I'd seen this postcard they were selling by the cash register next to the mints that showed Old Joe's, a popular surfing spot in Malibu, and so I bought it because I owed Annie a reply.

Greetings from Malibu!

I do now own the Kate Bush album whereof you speak. It is most excellent. That song "Wuthering Heights" is probably my favorite too. I know you are a good reader, but I kind of agree with your mother that you're probably too young to understand the novel. As to the mysteries you've assigned me to solve: I accept your challenge. There will come a day when I shall prove my worth, damsel. Until then, I tread the lonely hinterlands in search of answers. I wish you would've enclosed the Westminster Abbey postcard. I hope to visit England one day. I want to breathe the air that Shakespeare breathed. And speaking of Shakespeare, a really great introduction to the plays is Charles and Mary Lamb's Tales From Shakespeare. I'm getting ready to take the AP English exam in a couple of days. Yikes! It is going to kick my bloody bum as you Welsh rarebits say.

See you on the other side,

Lance

11

Levon Arrow was hoping that along the way he might bump into this girl he knew way back when named Camille.

Camille lived across the road and would come over to the sn'ail farm everyday and hang out with Levon.

Sometimes she'd just follow him around and they'd talk while he tended the sn'ails.

Sometimes they'd read a book together on the front porch, out loud, trading off paragraphs.

Sometimes they'd sit by the riverside and lie on their backs at night and realize they were just on a big rock spinning through space.

Sometimes if it was raining they'd take a walk, without umbrellas, in some random direction and feel the earth's beauty together.

Sometimes they'd go over to her house and have hot chocolate and stare at each other.

Sometimes they'd watch TV at night, back when there still was TV, sometimes sitting holding hands, sometimes snuggling horizontally.

Levon loved when Camille would kiss his hand and hold it to her cheek.

That's what they mean when they say 'romantic,' Levon said to himself whenever she did it.

Sometimes they'd end up kissing for a long time on the living room couch if Levon's mom wasn't home.

One time Levon's mom did come home to find them kissing but just went about her business putting groceries away.

Later though she warned him that kissing could trigger the Minerva Syndrome and that he should be alert to it.

But then Camille and her family moved away and he never heard from her again.

Camille was the last person Levon Arrow knew for a very long time.

Out on the frozen river he looked around thinking maybe she'd be skating toward the ocean like everybody else on earth and perhaps en route thataway their paths would intersect as their genitals had almost done once upon a time.

After a reasonably long while, though, Levon kind of gave up on finding her.

Camille was probably somewhere on the other side of the ocean very far away.

The multiple choice section of the AP English exam wasn't as difficult as I thought it would be. I didn't recognize any of the selections, but I felt like I mostly understood them and answered the questions correctly.

The poem in the essay section was W.H. Auden's "Law Like Love." We'd done some Auden in class, "Musée de Beaux Arts," "The Unknown Citizen," and "As I Walked Out One Evening," so I knew a little of what Auden was up to in his writing, but really it didn't matter because the prompt asked for a textual analysis that didn't require prior knowledge of the author.

The last lines of that poem really stuck with me even though I was in the heightened tension of trying to write the essay.

Like love we don't know where or why,
Like love we can't compel or fly,
Like love we often weep,
Like love we seldom keep

My waning passion for Diana brought me down and had me wondering whether all love was thus fleeting, whether it ever lasts beyond a small number of months, always ending up stuck somewhere in orbit around Miranda.

The prose essay was on an 18th Century piece by Samuel Johnson, in the archaic English Megiddo had warned us would appear on the test, Johnson's review of a book about evil by this dude named Soame Jenyns.

I did a pretty good job of bullshitting my way through that one. I don't even remember what the topic was anymore.

The last essay, the free-response prompt, asked us to deal with unrealistic elements in a work of literature and how those unrealistic elements comment on the real world we live in. I used *Waiting For Godot*, focusing on the tree sprouting leaves overnight and the scene in Act II when they are all on the ground and can't get up.

I walked away from the test fairly positive. It seemed like I knew my shit.

It was strange in Megiddo's room the day after the AP test because the class was essentially over but we still had like 5 weeks left of school.

He told us that mostly we'd be seeing films and writing about them, but he also gave us a more extended assignment.

"Instead of a term paper, I'm going to have you do something else. Something creative. I'm going to ask you to write a piece of autobiographical fiction, and by that I mean you're going to write about yourself but in a way that the main character is not recognizable as you."

"So it shouldn't be realistic," Emily Wolf said.

"Oh, it can be realistic. Just not identifiably *you*. It can't be obvious."

"But we can do fantasy," Miranda said.

"Yes, as long as it's autobiographical."

A lot of people looked confused.

"It can be fantasy, science fiction, horror, suspense, crime, mythology, fairy tale, fable, anything, the genre doesn't matter, as long as you're drawing upon personal thoughts and experiences but which are disguised to all but the most knowing friends. In other words I should be able to read it out loud to the class and no one will know who wrote it."

That night I got extremely high and attempted to start the project.

After many cannabis-led peregrinations, and two pages worth of cross-outs, I finally settled on the name *Levon Arrow* for my protagonist and proxy.

I wanted a name that would echo Stephen Hero.

Plus I was of late obsessed with The Band and Levon Helm's voice. *Music From Big Pink* was in exclusive rotation on my stereo.

And of course whenever I hear or see that name Levon I think of the Elton John song.

287

Who doesn't?

And so my main character would be Levon.

And he would be a good man.

When I told Gina Dichlich about the name, she said, "And an arrow is like a little lance," which I hadn't thought about but I pretended it was intentional.

Levon Arrow loved everybody.

I knew that would be the first sentence.

The rest would depend on Levon.

I had no idea where I was going to let Levon Arrow take me, how deeply I'd let him burrow into my secrets.

I only knew I would be true to it.

Otherwise, why bother.

I wrote until really late that night without the help of Calliope and Euterpe.

I didn't need them anymore.

I had tapped into a new unidentifiable current.

The new muse was dreamlike and supremely arbitrary, a silent voice from a farther shore.

It gave me the mythos I needed: a house, a hillside, a frozen river, and no desire to leave.

The project overtook my attention. All I wanted to be doing was working on it, pigging out on mucho mojo.

I took Diana to the New Beverly Cinema to see *The Discreet Charm of the*

Bourgeoisie on one of those very rare nights she had off from rehearsal.

For much of the evening I felt like she didn't even want to be there. Or maybe I was the one who didn't want to be there. Or maybe it was unmentionably mutual.

She later told me she was upset because I chose to bring her to a movie that takes place in a country called Miranda.

"It always comes back to her," Diana said.

"Who?" I said because sometimes she wouldn't bother to pursue it.

"Nothing," Diana snorted, and I knew I was safe this time.

We made out for a little while in the car later but then she didn't want to come inside or anything. She said she was wiped out from all the rehearsals again.

When Patti Smith played the Santa Monica Civic in the middle of May I went with Manny.

Evelyn Childs tagged along with us because David was also busy with *Oz* rehearsals.

Back in January, David and Evelyn had invited me and Manny to ride up to San Francisco with them to see the Sex Pistols—it was right after Manny and I had gone to the Dead show at the Shrine—but my parents wouldn't let me go because I'd be missing school and then when I couldn't go Manny backed out also.

I was bummed about it, but when Evelyn and David got back they were really pissed off about how bad the show was, which made me feel better about not going.

"What a bloody waste of time," David said. "Fuck the Sex Pistols. They're a joke."

"We got punked," Evelyn said, "In the bad way."

Desire is hunger is the fire I breathe
Love is the banquet on which I feed

Patti and Company came out of the gate slamming.

Evelyn and Manny and I danced as a trio for the first half of the show.

Watching Evelyn bounce up and down rekindled a vestige of the 10th Grade lust I felt for her and how during that time thoughts of her crotch held me captive.

We'd shared some cool moments together, Evelyn and I. The Starwood parking lot when the Runaways played there. Flirting at Sorrento Beach. Ditching High Holiday services together. Exchanging many significant sampler tapes of our favorite bands. I also couldn't forget when we saw Deirdre Lux and Mr. Hill walking across the quad together in 11th Grade and Evelyn said it was obvious that they were fucking and she ended up being right.

The music was elevating and Evelyn was still so damn sexy.

When Manny went to the bathroom, she said to me, "Hey, can we talk about something?"

"Yeah."

"Not here. Monday after school?"

"Sure," I said. "What's this about?"

"I just want to get your opinion about something."

"It sounds a little more urgent than needing my opinion."

"Well, it has to do with you too. With both of us."

"Just tell me."

"Nyeah. Not here," she hushed me as Manny rejoined us.

After Patti, on the drive home, Manny and I decided to get serious about

290

putting a band together.

"Let's do it, man. Let's make a demo this summer with a bunch of songs on it and see if we can get gigs," Manny said. "I'll talk to Yigal in Orchestra 'cause remember he knows that bass player, Alain, and also the guitar dude."

"Emmett."

"Yeah him."

"We are doing this."

"Totally. It's happening, dude."

We gave each other five.

Arriving home from the concert, high on thoughts about starting the band and wired from Patti's passion, I decided to mellow out with some reading, diving into what would become one of the central texts in my conscience.

For a long time I used to go to bed early . . .

I loved the irony of reading that opening line at 1am.

I was enthralled from that first sentence of *Swann's Way* and then the first paragraph and then the first page and then the entire opening meditation on sleep and consciousness and memory. Proust put a spell on me.

On Monday after school Evelyn and I met in the quad and went to sit in the football bleachers.

Whatever the issue was, she said it involved both of us.

Did she want me to help her sell drugs perhaps?

Was she planning a surprise birthday party for David?

Maybe she really did want to have a threesome with me and her sister Julia like I'd often fantasized and had several times tried to communicate to her telepathically to no avail.

"So," Evelyn said, as we both gazed across the field toward Walt Whitman Continuation School and Rosewood Avenue beyond it.

"I'm listening."

"I think something is going on between David and Diana."

My stomach churned in acknowledgement. I'd been sensing that too. Or some version of it. But I didn't know how much had to do with my own flagging interest.

"May be," I said.

"Like, I don't know about you, but I don't think they are 'rehearsing' as much as they say they are."

"You mean like they're going somewhere else and lying to us? No way. I'm in Play Production. I know the rehearsal schedule. Especially getting this close to opening night. They are definitely at school."

Evelyn nodded without saying anything.

"That doesn't mean they aren't fooling around though," I said. "I have been picking up on that vibe myself to be honest."

"Yeah. I figured."

"I've been trying to attribute it to the heat of the musical or even my own cooling off. But yeah."

"No sex anymore?"

"Affirmative."

"Same here."

We shook hands facing the deserted unkempt gridiron.

We both knew what was up.

To our left we could see Yigal Frumkin shagging flies out on the baseball field.

"Yigal's going to be the drummer in my band," I told Evelyn.

"Cool. I didn't know you were starting a band. What are you going to call it?"

"I haven't settled on a definite name yet. One idea is calling it Tin Man Alley."

"Ouch."

"I think it's funny."

"Dude. *Wizard Of Oz* imagery. Not cool with me these days. You know, the whole Dorothy and Scarecrow situation we've just been discussing."

"Oh, right. Sorry. Yeah. Bummer. I didn't connect the two. *The Wizard Of Oz* means something else to me."

I couldn't elaborate.

"What do you think we should do?" she asked, "Call them on it?"

I shrugged and wondered, "What, like set up a double date and then confront them?"

"Yeah. That's a great idea."

"No, that's a terrible idea."

"Yeah, I guess you're right," she mused a while, "What if we fuck?"

"Sorry?"

"What if we revenge fucked? It'd be like a double revenge fuck because we'd both be getting revenge."

"That's not such a good idea either."

"Come on. You know you want to, dude. Be honest."

"OK," I paused, "I would probably greatly enjoy doing that, but I still think it's a bad idea."

"Dang, dude."

"Now, you and your sister at the same time . . ."

"Hey, man, at this point? If it'll take the pain away? I'm into it."

"Really?"

"Psych," Evelyn said.

Aaaaah-ha . . . loser

"But, dude, what the fuck should we do? Just let it happen?"

"I don't know," I said, "Diana and I have been pretty distant the last few weeks since I had to drop out of the show. Maybe she's figuring out how to break up with me. Like in *Annie Hall*."

"So, you see yourself splitting up with Diana and not saying anything about David."

"Yeah."

"Pussy."

"Affirmative again, sir," I saluted.

"Nyeah, me too."

"You? You are a tough-ass bitch."

"Not really. I give the appearance of being a tough-ass bitch, but actually I'm more the submissive type when it comes to guys."

The air smelled like tar and taco sauce.

"So we both agree this Diana and David thing is real," Evelyn went on.

"Probably."

"And it appears we're going to do nothing about it."

"Other than break up? That's likely how I'm going to handle it."

"I remain undecided. There's a part of me that thinks you and I should fuck."

"For revenge."

"Whatever. For fuck's sake."

"Fuck for fuck's sake."

"I could definitely deal with something like that."

"I bet you say that to all the boyfriends of girls your boyfriend is cheating on you with."

"No no you my ony boyfren," she said like an Asian hooker.

"You sincerely want to have sex with me?"

"I said I could *deal with it.*"

"For real?" I asked, thinking maybe it might happen.

"Psych," Evelyn teased and I blushed in shame.

That night I finished my Megiddo project which I'd decided to entitle "The Minerva Syndrome," and then I celebrated by getting off on fantasies of fucking Evelyn Childs even though I had to use a bunch of imagery from my crush on her in 10th Grade like catching glimpses of her in Geometry or that one time she asked me if she could borrow my eraser, etc.

12

Bernadette liked to fuck.

Levon knew that from the beginning.

In fact the first thing he ever heard Bernadette say was, "There's nothing like having a big cock inside you," to a girl skating next to her.

This dude who'd also overheard said to Levon, "You must meet Bernadette. She fucks like a firefly," and then skated on.

Levon had been eavesdropping on Bernadette ever since he'd started skating near her and noticing she had a mouth he wouldn't mind kissing really hard.

"Remember when there were books everywhere?" Levon said to Bernadette one typically gray morning after several days of working up the courage to speak to her.

She turned her head to acknowledge him.

"Nobody has ever asked me that before," she said, inviting conversation.

"Why would they?"

"You have an exclusive on the question, do you?" she smiled.

"Nah, just trying to flirt with you ma'am," Levon blushed.

Bernadette hooked her arm around his.

"Keep talking," she said. "What do you do?"

"I skate. Like almost everybody these days. Just doing this global pilgrimage."

"But before skating. Before the pilgrimage. What did you do back in regular times?"

"I was a sn'ail farmer."

"Sorry, a snail farmer?"

"Yes'm. S-N-Apostrophe-A-I-L."

"Why the apostrophe?"

"It's a contraction. For snot trail."

"Really?"

"Honest Injun."

"You're not making that up? That's racist by the way."

"What is?"

"Honest Injun."

"How's that racist?"

"Calling Native Americans 'Injuns.'"

"It's just a figure of speech."

"It's racist, just like calling someone who gyps you an Indian-giver."

"Isn't 'gyp' also racist?"

Bernadette looked away.

"Sn'ail IS a contraction, though," Levon said to re-establish his flirting technique.

"Did you like being a sn'ail farmer?"

"It was a decent life, yeah."

"What did you do for pussy?"

"Pardon me?"

"Sex?"

"I didn't do that. I didn't have anybody to do it with."

"No way. You've never had sex?"

"No ma'am. I came close once or twice."

"Well, if you stick with me we'll change that status for sure."

Levon Arrow did want to fuck Bernadette, and he probably would have, except later that night he saw two other guys fucking her really hard, one, standing up, in the mouth and the other, doggy-style, in the vagina, and decided he didn't want be part of that.

Levon Arrow wasn't a joiner.

I went to the Bob Dylan concert with Diana on her last night off before the *Oz* run.

Manny was there with Yigal Frumkin, and the two of them must've gotten high in the car because they were laughing at even the stupidest shit.

We had amazing 5th row seats.

"Dude," Manny said, "We're seeing fucking Bob fucking Dylan!" and he held out his hand, "Fucking fuck."

I slapped him back enthusiastically but was bummed because I could tell Diana's mind was elsewhere even though she had her hand on the back of my neck.

Diana and I didn't say much to each other throughout the concert beyond, "Do you want a Coke?" or "I'm glad I brought a sweater."

The houselights went fast to black followed by hoots and yowls.

As the stage lights came up, the band started playing without Dylan on stage.

That's a big-ass band, jeez," Manny said.

"Female back-up singers," I pointed.

Finally, Dylan came out wearing a shirt unbuttoned to his chest and bell-bottom pants with sequined seams.

"He's dressed like Neil Diamond," Manny said, and, yeah, he was kind of right.

The arrangements made it difficult to recognize even the familiar tunes that night. Dylan was singing these weird melodies.

It's like that disorientation when you go to a different Reform synagogue from the one you're used to. The lyrics are the same but the melodies are different.

"Thank you," Dylan said, "Here's a song I wrote just a few years back. This one's the story of my life."

Eventually I figured out he was singing "Shelter From The Storm."

Diana had her eyes closed and harmonized with Dylan and his back-up singers every time they sang, *"Come in, she said, I'll give you shelter from the storm."*

Near the end of the song I could see Diana had started crying.

I put my arm around her and she leaned her head into mine.

"I love you," she said, but it both sounded and felt half-hearted.

I patted her on the head and didn't answer.

While Dylan was doing "Ballad Of A Thin Man" I thought of the films we'd been seeing in Megiddo's: *Jules Et Jim, Cries & Whispers, Marat/Sade.*

Because something is happening here but you don't know what it is

I thought too of Diana and me in the echoes of that line.

My head danced in ricochet from the music itself to meta-thoughts about the fact that I was seeing Bob fucking Dylan play live to über-meta-thoughts about the discomfort with Diana in said milieu.

When the lights came up at the intermission, I made eye contact with Miranda who was there with Freddy and Arabella and Levi.

Diana saw us share a wave.

I asked Diana if she wanted a Coke and she said, "Yeah, that'd be cool," and so I set off in search of the shortest concession line, though even that line took longer than I'd anticipated.

I scurried back into my seat with Cokes for me and Diana as the house lights dimmed for the 2nd set.

The band came out and started the chromatic intro to "Rainy Day Women #12 & 35" again without Dylan on stage.

He made his big entrance near the end of the tune.

The audience sang the lyrics along with the back-up singers and cheered each time.

Everybody must get stoned!

Diana managed some exuberance during that tune and for the rest of the set.

Really interesting versions of "One More Cup Of Coffee," "Blowin' In The Wind," "I Want You," (during which Diana dug her fingernails into my flank as she hugged me), "Masters Of War," "Just Like A Woman" (which I sang out loud as if to Diana).

"On the violin and mandolin we have the 12-year-old genius of the group," Dylan said, as he began to introduce the band.

"He looks older than 12," Diana said.

"Actually he's 20 years old," Dylan continued.

"There you go," I said to Diana.

"David Mansfield. He's the only one in the group that's available," Dylan joked.

"What is this? The Catskills? He's turning into Henny Youngman," Manny shouted over to me.

"This is called 'It's Alright Ma, I'm Only Bleeding,'" Dylan said and launched into maybe my favorite song of his.

I mouthed the words along with his singing, a melody which, like the rest of the songs that night, bore almost no resemblance to the tune I knew, not that "It's Alright Ma" has much of a tune anyway, but still.

I remembered always wanting to analyze those lyrics in Beauregard's class in 10th Grade during the era of my intensest Dylan worship.

At the end of the show Dylan bade farewell, "We're gonna get on out of here . . . we'll be here for six or seven nights I think? So maybe we'll see you again. Until then I will leave you with this message," and slipped gently into "Forever Young."

May God bless and keep you always
May your wishes all come true

Diana hugged me tightly and I her as we swayed to the poetry.

May your hands always be busy
May your feet always be swift
May you have a strong foundation
When the winds of changes shift
May your heart always be joyful
And may your song always be sung
May you stay forever young

I got caught up in dreaded visions of mortality and the impermanence of all things, especially love.

As Dylan left the stage and the audience stomped and hooted and clapped for more, Manny leaned over and said, "Fucking Dylan, man! We're fucking here! We saw that! Isn't that right fucking on?"

"Totally!" I said.

After the encore, "The Times They Are a-Changing," we gathered in the courtyard just outside the Amphitheatre briefly to say bye to everybody.

Miranda thanked me and gave me an awkward hug.

"Yes, dude, so kind of you," Freddy extended his limp hand and I shook it.

"No problem," I said.

"Can't wait for our first jam session, man," Yigal said, as he and Manny parted ways with us in the parking lot.

"What was Miranda thanking you for?" asked Diana in the car on the way home.

"Oh, I got her those tickets. That's what we were talking about when you saw us in the ticket line."

"She was hugging you then, too. Yes, I remember."

"She was way far back in line and afraid she wouldn't get tickets so I offered to sell her my 2 extras 'cause Manny and I were up near the front."

"Ah. Interesting you didn't tell me about that."

"I told you right when it happened."

"No you didn't."

"Di, I swear I told you," I started to argue but realized the futility because I probably didn't tell her knowing it would upset her and fuck man I knew this was going to be a thing for a while.

"I would remember something like that," she said.

"I didn't think it was important or something then, I guess," I sighed, preparing myself.

"It makes me wonder what else you're not telling me."

"Am I required to tell you everything that happens in my day?"

I could have thrown the David Harkins affair right up in her face but wussed out as usual.

"I'm your fucking girlfriend."

Used to be fucking I wanted to say.

"When we were making out in the car the other day you totally smelled like girl."

"What are you talking about?"

"Whoever it is you're fucking."

"Whomever."

"Whomever, whatever, I smelled her on you."

"Jesus fucking Christ."

"Hey. Not the Lord's name."

"Sorry. Blankus fucking Blankst."

Although Diana was for sure out of her mind in that moment (unless she smelled my thoughts), the next night I did in fact smell like girl, not Diana, in a really unexpected yet ultimately inevitable sexual liaison.

What had happened was between sets at the Dylan concert, when I was standing in line at the concession stand to buy our Cokes, Taryn Rust came up to me and said hey.

"Hey, how's it going?" I said back.

"Pretty good," she zeroed her bloodshot eyes on me.

"How've you been?"

"All right I guess. You digging the show? Dylan, dude!"

"It's cool to be seeing him, but, I don't know. These arrangements are kinda cornball at times," I said.

"A little," Taryn said. "I'm just amazed I'm seeing Bob Dylan live. Where are you sitting?"

"We're in the 5th row, stage right. Amazing seats. How about you?"

"We're way in the back," she said, "second to last row. But it's cool. The Amphitheater's not that big so."

"What else are you up to?" I asked.

"Eh, trying to get motivated to go back to school one of these days."

"Do it."

"Yeah, I want to do something with music but I don't know what."

"You'll figure it out," I said and smiled at her. "And you're still at Aron's."

"Yeah yeah. I don't know how much longer though. Getting restless."

"Definitely go back to school. Music's already your life. Map out a way to get paid for it."

"I should, huh," she said and the conversation stalled. She looked around uncomfortably and then said, "Well, anyway, it's good to see you," and started to walk away.

"You here with Artie?" I said.

Taryn stopped and walked back toward me.

"No, I'm here with my friend Desirée."

"Oh," I blushed, even though I knew it couldn't possibly be the same one but the music connection had me wondering.

"It didn't work out with Artie."

"Ah. Sorry."

"No, it's cool, man. We weren't cut out for each other. Or he didn't quite do it for me at least. But I'm pretty sure it was mutual though."

"Thanks again for the Tom Waits album that time," I said because I couldn't think of anything else and I wanted to keep looking at her.

I hadn't fantasized about Taryn Rust in eons.

I thought she was done with me.

"No problem," she said and got closer. "So are you into Bruce Springsteen?"

"*Born To Run* was a major moment in my listening. For sure."

"We've got his new one at the store."

"What's it called again?"

"*Darkness On The Edge Of Town*."

"It's not out yet, is it?"

"Next Tuesday. If you want a copy early I can bring one home from work tomorrow night. You around?"

"Uh, yeah, I guess. But I don't really have any money at the moment to be honest."

"No money necessary."

"I can't accept another gift."

"We'll work something out," she said.

We paused and gawked and grokked.

"Tomorrow night. Whatever time," she said.

"I'll be there."

Diana had *Oz* rehearsal, so that made it easy to go over to Taryn's place the next night.

We pretty much started kissing as soon as I walked in the door, somehow, once again, picking up where we left off.

Springsteen on the stereo of course.

Lights out tonight
Trouble in the heartland

We went three rounds that night on her couch.

I didn't come the first two times, we just went at it until she was done.

That'd been happening a lot with Diana too, back when we were still having sex, the not coming thing. I thought maybe it was the weed doing it.

"Don't you wanna come?" she said, after a second complete listening to *Darkness On The Edge Of Town* and that rallied me to jackhammer status, pumping unto a total paradisiacal annihilation culminating in a gargantuan blast after which I felt utterly alone.

"Om Shanti Om," I chanted and kissed her really hard on the mouth, letting myself intuit all the fundamentals of existence.

At some point, it might have been during Round 2, I pretended she was Miranda Savitch for a minute, and that worked kind of nicely until I felt the compound guilt of fucking someone while thinking of someone else *plus* having a girlfriend while fucking someone else (even though said girlfriend was, herself, probably fucking someone else too).

We lay on Taryn's couch for a while not really saying much until she eventually said, "Um, would you mind leaving?"

"Oh yeah, yeah. Of course. I'll skedaddle," I started to get up, trying to hide

306

my bewilderment. I felt kind of sick to my stomach. I thought she'd want to hang with me for a while, let our skin press together a bit longer.

"Skedaddle," she said, "I love that word," which I took as an invitation to round 4 and started climbing back on top of her trying to be irresistibly adorable (though coming off more like Harpo Marx), but she said, "Uh-uh. Closed for business," and sent me home.

We were doing *A Doll House* in AP as our final piece of literature together after all those films in a row.

"No better way to leave high school than with that door slamming at the end," Megiddo said.

The last scene was really intense because Miranda was reading the role of Nora, and she was way into it.

"*When I was at home with papa, he told me his opinion about everything, and so I had the same opinions; and if I differed from him I concealed the fact, because he would not have liked it. He called me his doll-child, and he played with me just as I used to play with my dolls. And then when I came to live with you,*" Miranda said and looked up at Megiddo who was reading Torvald.

"Nora's my hero," Miranda said after the famous door slammed shut. "*I believe that before all else I am a human being, just as you are,*" she quoted.

"That final scene," Megiddo said, "You read that wonderfully by the way."

"Thanks, but also her whole journey to that moment."

"Yes and Ibsen handles that beautifully too, doesn't he, that growth? How does he do that?"

Nobody answered.

"Through language," Megiddo said, "Her language changes along with her personality. That's how it's done. In fact," Megiddo said, "That's what I'm going to have you write about for the essay that's due the day after tomorrow," and we all groaned as he wrote the prompt on the chalkboard.

"*I must stand quite alone, if I am to understand myself and everything about me,*"

Miranda quoted again, unsolicited, for everybody to hear.

And it somehow felt directed at me and Megiddo and Freddy in absentia and I guess every other male in her life.

Like I said, she was way into it.

13

Levon Arrow first met Frances when she was singing and doing figure eights in the ice, miraculously avoiding all the skaters heading steadfastly thataway.

Levon made it very clear he wanted Frances to talk to him by skating into her line of sight as much as possible but not looking at her.

"Hey boy," she finally said after untold agonizing eons.

"Hey," he said and they skated side by side in silence for a while.

"You like my moves?"

"Y'and your voice. I've been listening to you sing."

"Thank you," she said, pleased, and they skated side by side in silence a while longer until she said, "I'm Frances," and Levon said, "Levon."

"I've seen you around, Levon," Frances said. "You like girls."

Levon Arrow blushed and the heat felt good.

"I noticed that about you," she smiled and he blushed some more.

She'd been watching him too.

"Where are you going?" he asked her.

"The ocean. Duh."

"Why is everybody going to the ocean?"

"'Cause maybe it's warmer there?"

"What if the ocean is frozen also?"

"Dude, if the ocean were frozen then everything would be frozen. The ocean would be the last thing to freeze."

Levon Arrow had no idea if that was true or not.

"I guess," he said.

"It's still far away."

"I have no idea."

He wished that instead of talking he could kiss her really hard on the mouth which he did in fact do later that evening.

They lay snuggled together for warmth and she felt his hard cock pressing against her.

"What's that?" she said grabbing at the bulge in his pants.

"You tell me."

"Feels like some big business."

"That it is," he said realizing he was probably going to have sexual relations with her momentarily.

Frances reached into his pants and got her coldish hands on his dick to liberate it.

"It feels like he wants to fuck me really hard in the vagina," she said and guided Levon's hand into her pants.

"Why don't you ask him?" Levon couldn't believe he actually said and pushed her head downward..

Frances went at his cock with her mouth briefly and then worked her way back up to his face.

"He said yeah he wants to fuck me really hard in the vagina," she reported back from nether regions, squirming out of her pants and into the freezing cold air.

"I'd be honored to fuck you really hard in the vagina," Levon submitted.

"No, dude, you will not be honored, you will be humbled," she said and guided his quivering dick into her.

He fucked her really hard in the vagina for an immeasurable amount of space-time until nothing but dreams remained.

As usual the stars were not visible in the perpetually cloud-infected sky, but the two of them stared into the gray scrim and were able to regain a joy almost gone extinct in the human animal.

"Your cock is like a frozen banana from Zody's."

"Wait. Are you?——" he shuddered.

"——Probably not who you're thinking of," she said.

"Who do you think I'm thinking of?"

"The fat kid from Willy Wonka & The Chocolate Factory . . . what's his name? . . . Buzzy——"

"Augustus Gloop."

——Lagniappe?"

"Augustus Gloop is the fat kid from Willy Wonka & The Chocolate Factory."

"I thought it was Buzzy Lagniappe."

"Augustus Gloop."

"Then who in the frozen ocean is Buzzy Lagniappe?"

"Well, actually I used to live next door to a kid named Buzzy Lagniappe and his real name is Augustus and he used to be fat."

After that Levon and Frances had sex every night over a longer span of time than Levon thought was possible.

Frances had been a singer near the end of civilization, but first both of her parents died in an act of random violence such as was common in the old cities, and then the Ice Age returned unexpectedly and its encroachment advanced more rapidly than humanity could keep up with (due an impasse over what it all meant), so now she was just another nomad skating on the frozen river toward what all hoped would be a liquid ocean and someplace habitable.

Levon Arrow loved listening to Frances talk and sing.

In fact, after a while he found he loved hearing her talk and sing more than he loved fucking her really hard in the vagina.

It was right around the same time that Levon noticed Frances had started spending more and more of her day skating with this guy named Sammy who also used to be a singer back in the other days.

One awfully cold twilight Frances told Levon that she was going to spend the night with Sammy because he was a singer too and she jived more with that than with a sn'ail farmer which made Levon a little sad but also came as a relief because he had to admit that he too had gotten a little bored with the situation.

The night was sleepless and shivery, but the next day the sun glowed through the overcast and Levon relished with melancholy his latest freedom.

When the musical finally opened, Diana soared as Dorothy, and the *Oz* production was a huge success. All 4 performances sold out.

I was backstage for all of them, not officially on the tech crew, but helping out as needed.

I spent a lot of time hanging in the light booth with Justine Balthazar.

It was a perfect perspective, as the booth was six feet off the ground, easy to keep an eye on Diana and David and their backstage doings.

I saw nothing untoward during the performances which I knew would disappoint Evelyn Childs whom I'd promised to report back to regarding any illicit activity between the two of them.

Other times I'd stand in the wings and marvel at Diana doing her thing.

Hearing that velvety alto, especially on "Somewhere Over The Rainbow," still made my wonky heart go pit-a-a-pit-pit-a-a-pat.

But once the run was over, the convenient distraction over, Diana and I were faced with a romance at ebb tide, though neither of us brought it up immediately.

Instead we went to Disneyland to celebrate the end of *Oz* with a group of her church friends, none of whom I'd met before.

It turned out they were all guys.

They had a prayer circle on Main Street when we first arrived—which I didn't participate in—and then we all went behind the caves on Tom Sawyer Island to get high.

"Cool," I said, "Smoke a joint for Jesus," which I thought was funny but nobody else did.

I was the über-Jew in that scarlet moment.

"Jesus was the first Christian," said this one guy named DeMarco.

"Jesus wasn't a Christian," I said because he was so very wrong and had to be corrected.

"Yes he was," DeMarco insisted, "He invented it."

"Jesus didn't invent Christianity. A Christian is someone who worships Jesus Christ. Jesus didn't worship himself, did he?"

DeMarco was silent for a moment, "What was he then?"

"Jesus was a Jew. He was the first Reform rabbi."

DeMarco knocked me to the ground for saying that.

"Hey," Diana said, "Cut that the fuck out, DeMarco. That's not cool."

"Nor very Christian," I said.

"And Jesus *was* a Jew you fucking retard," she finished.

DeMarco made like he was going to beat the crap out of me, but Diana threatened to kick him in the balls.

"I like it better when you lick me in the balls right in the middle of a blowjob," DeMarco answered, and then to me, "Isn't she great at sucking cock, dude?"

"DeMarco," Diana said.

"After choir practice, that's right," Demarco imagined and pantomimed.

Diana avoided eye contact with me.

Dang, dude.

Diana hadn't told me that DeMarco was an ex-boyfriend of hers.

The most recent ex-boyfriend.

There was a lot of stuff Diana didn't tell me.

"You OK?" DeMarco asked and offered a hand to pull me up.

"Yeah," I said, "I'm fine," and got up by myself.

"You're gonna be sore tomorrow."

"We're a stiff-necked people," I joked but he didn't get it.

DeMarco was one of those guys who'd memorized lots of Bible quotes but never actually read the Bible.

"Fellas, we're at fucking Disneyland. Let's go have some fun. Jesus," said this guy named Randolph who planned to be a pastor one day (he told me later when we were on the Adventure Through Inner Space ride in Tomorrowland).

"Hey," said DeMarco, "Don't use the Lord's name in vain."

"You mean Walt Disney?" I goofed like an idiot and DeMarco probably wanted to beat the crap out of me again but he just ignored me instead and asked Randolph if there was any goddamn weed left.

That night I slept over at Diana's because her parents had gone to Murrieta Hot Springs for the weekend.

We attempted sex while watching *My Fair Lady* on her parents' bed.

I remember realizing while we were in the act that our thing was over. I was paying more attention to the movie or else picturing Diana sucking DeMarco's cock or fucking David Harkins.

Her vagina was abrasively dry.

My dick went limp midway through. That had never happened before.

We turned away from each other and went to sleep with the TV still on.

The next day we had some Count Chocula and half-and-half for breakfast and then Diana put on the second John Dawson Read album.

There's one road for angels, one road for men . . .

We sat in her living room, Diana in the egg-shaped music chair, I at her knees on the floor.

"Is this all over?" I finally brought up the obvious.

Diana was starting to cry, a tear bubble over each eye.

"Seems like it," she shrugged and wiped her eyes and nose with her sleeve.

I put my hand on her knee.

"Don't," she said.

"Di—"

She pushed my hand away.

"What happened?"

"I don't know. *Oz*?" I said, "David?"

She nodded. It was the first time I'd brought their affair up.

"Don't put all of this on me. You were turning away. I felt it. I knew it."

"Nyeah. I don't know."

"You think I'm uninteresting."

She was dripping tears like crazy.

"I love you," she whimpered, "I've never loved anybody as much as I love you."

"You love people other than me," I contended weirdly.

"No. That is not true," she shook her head and started crying convulsively.

"You have sex with people other than me," I tried to hug her but she pushed me down.

"That's not love," she sobbed.

"Then why do it?"

"I dunno. I always feel like you think I'm not worth your time maybe. Not smart enough. But I'm an actress, I'm a dancer, I'm a singer. I'm just as much of an artist as you are."

"I know that."

Some people are crazy, when they never give in . . .

315

I had my head on Diana's knee and she was stroking my hair.

"So when were you together with DeMarco?"

"Last year," she sniffled and wiped her eyes on my sleeve.

"Like when you stopped coming to school?"

"And before that. He was the reason I was gone for a while."

"How?"

"Well, I got pregnant—"

"And DeMarco was the father."

She nodded.

"What did you do?"

"I got an abortion. And then I flipped a shit because I felt like a murderer."

"Like nervous breakdown flipping a shit?"

"Pretty much. I was at St. John's for a while. By the time I returned home it was stupid to come back to school. The semester was like halfway done."

"Do you have to make up those credits?"

"I've done a lot of it already. I was able to do independent study for English and History while I was out, and then I made up Algebra 2 in summer school last summer. So I'm going to graduate and all that."

"We've been together for like 5 months and you've never told me about this."

"I know."

"That's how we all are," I said.

We were both crying silently.

"Why were you into DeMarco?"

"He believes in the Lord," Diana said without pausing to think.

"David Harkins doesn't," I said, bringing up his name for the first time.

Diana wiped her tears with her sleeve.

"I presume it is David Harkins you're having sex with, yes?"

"Nyeah, I guess," she said.

"You guess?"

"OK, yes. A couple of times," she said, and then turned it back on me, "How about you?"

"I swear I am not fucking David Harkins."

She actually giggled at that.

"Dang, dude. And *you* were always suspicious of *me*," I said.

"Didn't I have a reason to be?"

"Reason? Feels more like projection to me. Our own sins, et cetera."

"But still. Didn't I have a reason to be?"

"Maybe."

"With who."

"Whom."

She flipped me off with her eyes.

"Not Emily Wolf."

"Who then?"

"This girl named Taryn. You don't know her."

"I could've sworn you were having sex with Emily Wolf."

"Nope. Taryn. She's been kind of like my guru. Taryn taught me all that stuff you like."

"I'll be sure to write her a thank you card. How often?"

"It depends how you define often."

"How many times did you fuck her?"

"Full on sexual intercourse? Just once. Technically."

"Technically?"

"Well, three times. But they were all part of the same encounter. So yeah. Once. Technically."

"I don't really believe you," she said, "but it also doesn't really matter 'cause," and she got out of the chair and went into the kitchen to do the dishes.

I followed her into the kitchen, not sure of how to act or what to say.

"I think you should leave," she said.

"OK. Yeah."

She turned off the water, dried her hands, and walked with me to her front door.

We stood a moment facing each other but both looking down.

"I'm sad," she said.

"Me too," I replied.

"I don't really understand how this happened."

I made no move to leave but stood swaying on the welcome mat. My knees hurt.

"Bye—" she finally said and closed the front door slowly in my face.

I heard her start crying inside the house and I placed my hand on the front door for a moment, almost knocking, but then walked away.

I had to turn on, as Joyce puts it, "the spiritual-heroic refrigerating apparatus."

Getting home from where she lived was kind of a pain in the ass because there were no buses on San Vicente, but I couldn't go back and knock on the door and ask Diana for a ride, duh, so I walked over to Fairfax and then down to the Tar Pits to sit for a while and ruminate on yet another romantic failure.

It already smelled like summer.

I sat in my favorite spot on the lawn near 6th Street looking at the algae collecting along the banks of the little stream that hardly moves.

I pulled some folded up scratch paper from my back pocket, always there for just such an occasion (terribly rare in recent months), and started penning lyrics to a song, my first one in ages, a tune I'd been gestating for a while called "Stained Glass Windows."

Conscious dreams are dying young
Dream your conscious dreams
Along the threadbare seams
A ragged patch of promised land
The garden's been outgrown
Gotta head out on your own

Shattered stained glass windows
Congregations sing the blues
A ball of conclusions
Hesitate before you choose
You've got a lifetime left to lose

Conscious dreams are dying young
Attraction brings collision
Indifferent precision
True clowns don't speak and seldom rhyme

Alienation is a style
Laugh without a smile

Shattered stained glass windows
Vital memories tightly spun
Given life earn living
You might curse the damage done
You're not the only one

Conscious dreams are dying young
Better learn to pay
It's graduation day
Conscious dreams are dying young
Buried as infants this morning
It's the third world warning

Shattered stained glass windows
Congregations sing the blues
A ball of conclusions
Hesitate before you choose
You've got a lifetime left to lose

Shattered stained glass windows
Vital memories tightly spun
Given life earn living
You might curse the damage done
You're not the only one

14

Levon Arrow couldn't decide if it was a good sign that one never saw people skating back in the other direction away from the ocean (like perhaps they'd all found what they were looking for when they reached the coast), or if it was a very bad sign (like perhaps they met some gruesome end there).

Aside from human conversation among the skaters and the swish of the skates themselves, the air had mostly hung with silence since the beginning of his journey.

Therefore, the rippling of ocean water in the near distance came as both a shock and a comfort for he knew his trek was almost at an end.

Soon he would see the sea and Glenda.

When at last he skated his way to a descending slope and cascaded down to the grayish shoreline, he came to rest at the water's edge where thousands upon thousands of his fellow pilgrims were encamped.

Where would Glenda be amid all this disparate humanity?

The air was charcoal dark but the water was warm compared to the snow and ice.

The sand was damp but also warmer than elsewhere.

He didn't know why this was.

One might even be able to sleep without a fire. A comfort he barely remembered.

Levon took off his skates and let his feet feel the warm-cold of the sand.

His heart tingled in a mild spasm.

Perhaps another onset of the Minerva Syndrome.

"Hi, Levon!" he heard his name called and turned to see Glenda waving to him from the water.

She was swimming next to a whale.

"I was hoping you'd come! Welcome to the warmest place on earth!"

She gestured Levon to join her in the water which felt more like a lake than what Levon imagined the ocean to be.

"Look what I found," she said.

"A whale."

"THE whale. He says he's pretty sure he's the only one left."

"He told you?"

"Yeps."

"He talks?"

"In a manner of speaking."

"He's able to communicate with you and you with him."

"Yes. His name is Elijah."

"Elijah the whale."

"Yes. He's being pursued by a crazy king and queen who think he is the embodiment of all evil when really he's the embodiment of all that is good and true in what's left of this world. He's always going on and on about the queen and how she hates him and fears him. He's always on the move."

"How long has he been here?"

"A few weeks, like me. He says it's almost like we were fated to end up on this beach at the same time."

"How much longer is he going to stay?"

"He needs to get going, actually."

"Where's he off to next?"

"He says he doesn't know. He asked me to come with him."

"Dude, that's intense. What'd you say?"

"That I'd think about it."

Levon Arrow cocked his head because he couldn't read her expression.

"What are you thinking?"

"That depends on what you're thinking," she said.

Levon Arrow didn't know what she meant but instead thought to himself that this whale resembled the whale from Pinocchio and also the one at the entrance to the Fish Shanty on La Cienega.

"Do you think I should go off with him, or do you want me to stay here with you?"

"I think you should do whatever you want."

"Ugh. You're imposterous. I hate guys sometimes."

Levon Arrow saw fit to satisfy a curiosity.

"I've skated all this way to find you, and I'm not even sure how you know me. Where did we meet?" he asked Glenda as they sat on the darkening shore together.

Glenda pointed skyward.

"Up there," she said.

"We really know each other from before the time you introduced yourself?"

"Way before. Before the story even started. Up there," she pointed again.

They slept next to each other that night and the next morning, they lay beneath the leaden firmament.

"I am truly amazed that you haven't kissed me yet," Glenda said after a long dry silence.

"I've been thinking about it."

"That's your problem right there."

"What?"

"Kissing is the opposite of thinking."

Levon Arrow sat up and looked at Glenda.

Instead of telling her he wanted to kiss her really hard on the mouth, he said, "I think you have to decide for yourself whether you're going to stay here or go with Elijah the whale."

"Thank you, you just made up my mind for me."

"How?"

"By giving me a choice."

She teared up.

Levon Arrow didn't know what he was supposed to do.

And so he just sat there with her and let her cry.

Occasionally he patted her on the head.

At the beginning of class, Megiddo brought out the stack of graded autobiographical fiction projects to hand back.

To my relief and delight, I received 99/100 and a nice comment from Mr. Megiddo:

Lance, I'm so glad I saved this one to read last. "The Minerva Syndrome" is strange and funny, deeply insightful into the awkwardness of human relations, and a frighteningly accurate vision of our collective future. Bravo to the bravery. I would've given you a perfect score, but I do need to point out that you betray yourself by invoking Buzzy Lagniappe's name (in 2 different scenes), even though I sort of understand the joky nature of the reference. Still, the assignment asked you to create an unrecognizable disguise, and I have to ding you ever so slightly for the crack in your mask. Other than that, though, you have done astonishing work. Keep doing this sort of thing as often as possible.

Always craving Megiddo's approval, I bathed in his praise and read the comment over and over at school and then again that night in bed.

Jim Lord got a 98/100 for his screamingly funny story of a young stand up comic who ends up getting a drunken handjob from Phyllis Diller in the alley behind the Improv.

Jim let me read it in the library during 4th Period later that day and I was busting up throughout the whole thing.

His main character, Frummy Bandersnatch, is having a drink with Phyllis Diller at the Improv bar and he piques her romantic interest when he tells her that the best thing she ever did was *Mad Monster Party*.

Reading the scene where Frummy ejaculates all over Phyllis Diller's turtleneck dress I cackled so furiously Mrs. Tisk thought someone had brought an animal into the library.

"Tssh-tssh. Who's the jackass?" she whispered.

I couldn't resist reading out loud, "*My throbbing cock jazzed a Jackson Pollock design on her turtleneck schmatte while I grabbed at her wizened tits through the dress and said, 'Yeah, baby, that's right, lick it all up.*"

I gave him five across the table for not selling out his genius.

Eddie Gurges was there too, drawing while Jim and I read each other's stories.

"I'm glad I don't have AP English," Eddie shook his head as he noted the length of our stories, "I don't have the patience to write stuff that long."

"Megiddo would probably have let you draw it instead. It was intended to be a creative project," I said.

"That'd've been cool," Eddie said and went back to his sketchbook.

Eddie had gone directly from doing all the illustrations for the yearbook to designing the poster and program for *The Wizard of Oz*, and had now gotten back to doing his own pieces.

Eddie was always working on something.

I had lost the splendor of constant creativity for a while, but writing "The Minerva Syndrome" got me re-attuned.

I looked forward to a summer of full-time art making.

The day before Prom I went over to Taryn Rust's apartment because she invited me to hear the new Rolling Stones album before it officially came out—it'd become our thing—but of course we ended up having sex on her couch again.

"*Black girls wanna get fucked all night, I just ain't got that much jam,*" Mick Jagger conceded as Taryn and I lay in post-coital cuddlage listening to the new record.

"Is that true?" Taryn Rust asked.

"What?"

"Black girls wanting to get fucked all night."

"Why are you asking me that question?"

"Just making idle chit chat," she said and lit a cigarette.

"I wouldn't know."

"Nyeah, you've fucked two black girls, so I know you know."

"Two?"

"So I've been told."

"Somebody is telling lies about me."

"You're the one telling lies, loverboy. I'm friends with Desirée Stoner," Taryn said and blew a perfect smoke ring.

"Oh," I blushed. It *was* the same Desirée.

"Yuh huh. So? Is it true?"

"OK, I admit to having sex with Desirée Stoner."

"Six times."

"She told you that too."

"Yes."

"Well if she gave you that much information then you already know I was never able to fuck her all night."

"'Cause you ain't got that much jam?" Taryn teased reaching for my limp dick.

"No, actually because she was usually more interested in playing the cello the few times I went over to her place. We'd always get right to having sex, but once she climaxed, she'd lose interest and moved on to other things."

"Yeah, Desi's like that in other ways too."

"Great cello player."

"She is. How's *your* music going?"

"I'm going to be making a demo this summer. Manny Shepherd and I put together a band. We're having our first jam session this Saturday."

The first rehearsal of Tin Man Alley took place in Yigal Frumkin's garage, and the band consisted of me on vocals, Manny playing Fender-Rhodes and singing also, Alain Yehudian on bass, Yigal on drums, and this cat named Emmett Beall, described to me as a guitarist who sounded like Robert Fripp-Meets-Duane Allman, so in my mind I expected either some dapper English art-boy or a longhaired stoner to come walking into the studio rather than the shy chubby black guy who entered, said, "Hey how's it going," plugged in his guitar and proceeded to blow our minds.

Yigal and Alain had both played with Emmett in this band called Roaming Empyre and said he was amazing but that he only played music he liked so that first rehearsal was really an audition. We were auditioning for *him*.

The songs I had chosen to do for the demo were "Manifest Destiny & Beyond," "The Divine Tragedy," "When Shall We Be Free," "Frailty and the Naked Wrist," and this new tune I'd written called "Art For Sale," a song about commodification, heavily influenced by Talking Heads with a little Devo thrown in:

Voice is raised, message clear
Churn it out is fair play here
For art's sake art is not
It's the sake for which I fought

Art for sale
Art for sale
In my own backyard
I'll paint you a picture
I'll write you a book
I'm selling my art
Come and take a look

I have vision, I have stance
I need time, I need a chance
Stormy brain is on the brink
Of another much-missed link

Art for sale
Art for sale
In my own backyard
I'll paint you a picture
I'll write you a book
I'm selling my art
Come and take a look

Now reduced to peddling wares

Masterpieces come in pairs
Buy these two and get one free
Masterpieces come in threes

Art for sale
Art for sale
In my own backyard
I'll paint you a picture
I'll write you a book
I'm selling my art
Come and take a look

European artist
Commands a fantasy
Provided subsidy
Is respected
Is protected
American artist
Struggles street-wise
Perfects a compromise
Business deal
Mass appeal

I have vision, I have stance
I need time, I need a chance
For art's sake art is not
It's the sake for which I fought

Art for sale
Art for sale
In my own backyard
I'll paint you a picture
I'll write you a book
I'm selling my art
Come and take a look

When we were all done, we waited for Emmett's appraisal.

"I'm in," he said and that was it. Tin Man Alley was a band.

After the jam, we got high and listened to music.

Emmett had brought XTC's album *White Music* to rehearsal because he was at the time proselytizing for XTC and we were fresh ears to share it with.

Having moved to Yigal's bedroom, we all smoked a bowl and listened to the record.

"This is my current favorite album. I love the title," Emmett said.

"*White Music*," Alain Yehudian smiled and nodded.

"The title's ironic of course," Emmett said.

"How?" Yigal asked, shirtless and rubbing his own chest hair like drummers are wont to do.

"'Cause there's no such thing as white music," Emmett explained.

"Dude, that's not true," I countered, "ABBA?"

Emmett pondered a moment.

"I have to think about that one."

"The Mike Curb Congregation," Yigal offered.

"Toto!" Manny Shepherd croaked and Emmett cackled from his supine position on the floor.

"You know if Toto was even a little bit cool they'd do a cover version of 'Goodbye Yellow Brick Road,'" I said.

"Yeah, but they are not even a little bit cool," Emmett answered and then we all started cackling loudly enough that Yigal's dad knocked on the door and asked what the hell was going on.

Manny laid out a timeline for rehearsing and then eventually going into an 8-track studio to record the demo.

We were hoping to get it all done before school started.

Alain would be attending UCLA, and Manny, Yigal, and I were all going to Northridge.

Emmett was only in 11th Grade so he still had another year of high school.

He told us he'd be going to Hamilton instead of Fairfax next year.

"You know a chick named Emily Wolf, right?" he asked me.

"Yeah," I sort of drawled.

"This guy on my block who goes to Hami was telling me about these dinner parties she throws."

"Persian?" I asked.

"Yeah, dude. How did you know?"

"I'm psychic," I said and pictured Emily Wolf pantless and panting doggy-style on her living room rug.

I loved that she'd kept her shirt on.

15

Levon Arrow stood facing Glenda at the shoreline, the placid sea lapping at their feet.

"You're off then," Levon said, resigned to fate.

"Nyeah. There's nothing left here."

"Is there anything left anywhere?"

"There is. I'm going there."

"Where?"

"The perfect place to live."

"Where's that?"

"Inside Elijah."

"You're going to live in a whale?"

"The future of humanity is living in whales."

"But there is only this one whale left."

"For now."

Levon wasn't sure what she meant by that.

"So wherever Elijah goes you will go."

"Yes."

"But what if the king and queen he's afraid of find you guys?"

"I might come to some harm, yes. But no more than I'd likewise be exposed to here amid this slowly starving anarchy on the beach."

"You guys should go to Atlantis," Levon said, "That's totally where I'd go if I was living in a whale."

"Maybe we'll do that," Glenda said but didn't in the leastways mean.

"You will see the world," Levon said with a great growing formality which made the parting more bearable.

"From a certain perspective, yes. But where will you go?"

"I think I'm gonna stay on this side of the ocean," Levon said. "Maybe go back to the sn'ail farm. Live with my mom if she's still on the planet. If not, just with the sn'ails."

"I understand," said Glenda. "Thank you for coming all this way just to see me. I was hoping you would. At least I'll always know where to find you."

"I hope you do come visit one day if the earth allows it."

"If I can, I will."

"You will always do what you want. I know that."

Glenda hugged Levon goodbye and said affectionately in his ear, "Tu deviens responsable pour toujours de ce que tu as apprivoisé."

"I don't know what that means," said Levon.

"You become responsible, forever, for what you have tamed," said Glenda, "It's from The Little Prince."

Elijah opened his mouth wide and Glenda walked across his tongue and into her new life in the belly of the whale.

"Bye, Levon!" Glenda said before she vanished down Elijah's gullet.

Levon Arrow turned to face the masses skating toward him and decided for sure that, yeah, he was going to skate in the opposite direction.

When I was getting dressed for the Prom I came upon the rock from Asteroid B-612 I'd found on the beach in Cambria and which had been languishing in my underwear drawer ever since.

I put it in my pocket that night just in case I was moved to bequeath it finally.

After Diana and I broke up she kept the Prom tickets so I figured I wasn't going, but then Buzzy and Whit and Claude and Manny came up to me on the quad saying they'd heard I'd broken up with Diana and proposed what they called a 'Stag Attack' and also a 'Stallion Battalion,' or in other words 5 dorky guys showing up to prom together without dates.

We actually went out and rented matching tuxes over the objections of Whit who claimed it would be "way too gay."

"But that's what'll be so cool about it," said Buzzy, "The utter and obvious faghood of the thing."

"Speaking of gay, I heard Rudy Tuesday is going to prom with Gina Dichlich," Claude said.

"That's true," I said, "and Corazon is going with Xeno."

"That's hilarious," Manny croaked, "I get it."

"So the real gay people are trying to hide it, and 5 deeply hetero dudes are going to show up as some kind of faux-faggot entourage," Whit said.

"It's an interesting bit of theatre," I replied.

"And that's what makes it even faggier," Whit said.

Claude drove the 5 of us in his mom's station wagon.

We had planned to get high in the car before going into the Prom but when we pulled up in front of the Beverly Hills Hotel it turned out to be valet-parking-only which made that impossible.

"Dang, dude," Buzzy said, "We are going to have to make it through the Prom totally straight."

"Not possible," said Whit.

Claude added, in robot voice, "That does not compute."

"There's got to be somewhere we can toke a strail," I said looking around, but there were security guards everywhere, on the lookout for wayward youth.

"Fuck it, let's go in," Buzzy said and we followed.

When we entered the ballroom, I was struck by how vastly many people in our graduating class I didn't know at all, neither their names nor their faces.

"Have we really been in school with these kids for 3 years?" Whit asked.

We scouted around for the familiar, though I was hoping not to see Diana who, I'd heard, was coming with David Harkins.

Lorelei Lux was there with Tim Studdard who turned out over the course of the school year to be a much cooler guy than I gave him credit for when I first met him.

We saw Claire Farnaway and Santana Windsor posing for their official prom photo with these totally fake smiles which would no doubt horrify them when they actually saw the pictures.

Rudy, Gina, Corazon, and Xeno arrived together with a splash. Rudy had on a powder blue tux and Gina's dress was the shortest thing long enough to be legal. I nursed my recurring lust for her with quiet desperation. Xeno's tux did not include a jacket but instead only a vest and cummerbund over his pleated white shirt. Corazon had on a black and white pantsuit designed to look sort of like a tuxedo.

The foursome gave a great appearance of double-dating. In fact they were double-dating, just not in the configuration you saw in the prom pictures.

Rudy and Xeno did in fact try to take a prom picture together as did Gina and Corazon, but the photographer said that wasn't allowed which was really fucked up and Gina, being Gina, let them know.

"That's really fucked up," she said, at which Assistant Principal Tierny, overhearing, warned Gina to watch her mouth, or, to use his words, "Tighten your lips, young lady," which Gina resisted answering 'cause it'd just be too easy and, then, too difficult to ask, "Which ones?"

Jim Lord and Misty Winters were holding hands and laughing together at one of the many round tables that surrounded the dance floor.

Eddie Gurges, sketchbook in hand and open, was talking to Madeline Baker, though I don't think they were there together because Madeline, at least the last time I'd heard, was going with Sandy Clay, though I didn't see Sandy anywhere so who knows. I can't keep up with that stuff.

Justine Balthazar was with Moe Roth. We all figured they'd been, as Jim Lord put it, rocking and rolling, for quite some time.

Heaven Sender's date was Godfrey Dirth, and some girl I didn't know came with his twin brother Willoughby.

Arabella Mayflower, Levi Cohen, Freddy Snow, and Miranda Savitch had come as a quartet. That seemed to be their standard configuration of late.

The theme of the prom was "Always & Forever," a product of that song's popularity among the members of Student Council, specifically the Senior Class Officers, who made all of the decisions about Prom, from where it would be held to the color theme to the food to the music.

I could have sworn the lead singer of the band said, "Here's one for all the white people," just before they started playing "Goodbye Yellow Brick Road."

Miranda walked over to me, grabbed my hands and pulled me onto the dance floor without saying anything and I knew I had no choice but to dance with her.

"Hi, Lance," she said, swaying slowly.

"Hey, how's it going?" I said as we held each other stiffly, barely moving.

"Pretty good."

"Nice."

And it *was* nice to be looking so closely at her face again.

"I remember doing this once before," she said.

I nodded and felt like I was going to cry or something.

I was dancing with Miranda.

She went on, "Your Bar Mitzvah was the only time we ever danced."

"Until now."

"Isn't that weird?"

"I don't know. It's just what happened," I said, "or didn't happen."

I knew those deep brown eyes and beheld them long and long beneath the spinning disco ball as we swayed past David Harkins who was dancing alone.

"We should have had a thousand dances," Miranda said and looked down sort of shaking her head.

She still had that crooked close-mouthed smile of years ago.

"That's not how it turned out," I said.

So goodbye Yellow Brick Road
Where the dogs of society howl

I could easily have kissed her really hard on the mouth with my hands on her ass but of course I didn't do either of those things because that's the nature of our story.

Miranda touched her forehead to my forehead and was breathing loudly and slowly through her nose.

Oh I've finally decided my future lies beyond the Yellow Brick Ro-oa-oad . . .

She looked at me as if she were about to say something but that was right

337

when the song was ending and I guess it killed her moment because she just hugged me and that was it.

"You going to the After Prom?" she asked as we walked off the dance floor.

"Yeah, pretty sure."

"Maybe we can talk some more there," Miranda suggested and headed back to Freddy and Arabella and Levi, "Bye, Lance!"

The After Prom was at Dillon's disco in Westwood which had a wing with a separate entrance for kids under 21.

En route we had pulled down a side street off Sunset and smoked a couple of bowls of some righteous Thai stick courtesy of Bigelow Rust.

"He calls this shit Grandfather Clock," Whit said, "because it makes you feel like you're on an episode of *Captain Kangaroo*."

"If I was on *Captain Kangaroo*, I'd be Mr. Green Jeans," I said, "I always dug his vibe."

"Dancing Bear," Manny said, raising his hand.

"I guess that makes me the rabbit that steals his carrots," Buzzy said.

"Miss Mary-Ann was a fox," Claude said.

"That's *Romper Room*, zit brain," Buzzy said.

"But still. Miss Mary-Ann was a fox," Claude said. "Not as foxy as Mary-Ann from *Gilligan's Island*. But still."

Due to our spacing out for a bit in the car for longer than we thought, and given the fact that Claude was driving like 10 miles an hour even though he kept saying, "I drive better when I'm stoned," we arrived at the After Prom much later than everybody else.

Once we found our way inside Dillon's from the parking lot, which should have been a far less complicated journey than we made it, I caught sight of Miranda Savitch standing alone and walked over to say hey.

"Hi, Lance," she said and it seemed like she was slightly crying.

"Where's Freddy?" I said.

"Dancing with someone else," she nodded toward the dance floor.

"Aw, man. That sucks," I felt the karmic justice. "How's everything going between you two?" I asked.

"Oh, not so good," she said and gestured toward the dance floor again, "Duh."

"Come hang with me on the couch," I said, leading her to a cluster of black sofas near the back of the room.

She sort of held onto my sleeve with her thumb and index finger as we walked.

"Do you want a Coke or something?" I asked as she sat down at the end of the couch.

"No, I'm cool. I'm cool. This alone is cheering me up already," she said.

"I'm glad," I said, followed by a long silence of looking around.

"You should read *Swann's Way*," I told her, "It's great," as always retreating into literary talk.

A familiar panic tactic.

"I'll take it under advisement, sir," she said.

We looked at each other as if in a staring contest on a school bus long ago.

"Did you get a chance to see *The Wizard Of Oz*?" I asked.

"I did," she said. "I loved it. Diana was amazing. But I was a little disoriented 'cause I thought you were supposed to be the Tin Man."

"I was."

"You should have been," she smirked, "What happened?"

"A heart episode. My doctor thought it'd be better for me to bow out."

"Is that thing getting worse?"

"The heart murmur? I don't know," I said tersely because I hated the subject.

"You have to be OK," she said. "In every way."

I nodded.

"You will always be a special person to me," Miranda said.

"Likewise," I replied because I thought I was supposed to but also because I really meant it. I meant it more than anything.

Whit, Claude, Buzzy, and Manny walked by us making blowjob gestures behind Miranda's back.

I remained expressionless, as if gazing into some blank middle-distance, careful neither to laugh nor reprimand.

Maintain steadfast quietude, I told myself, know it by the river.

"You're the first boy I ever loved," Miranda said.

"The first," I acted surprised.

"You can never replace the first," she said, "It leaves an indelible imprint. You move on, yeah, but you never replace the first."

"I concur," I said and there pressed an agony on my heart without precedent.

The rock from Asteroid B-612 rested ready in my pocket. It would've been the perfect moment to give it to her and seal that eternal connection.

Freddy Snow came stumbling over and sat down on Miranda's lap.

"Hey, how's it going?" he said to me.

"Pretty good," I said.

He looked at Miranda and said, "Bella and Levi wanna split and go to Ships. You ready?"

Then Miranda turned to me and said, "I've got to go."

I nodded as she and Freddy struggled to their feet.

Miranda leaned forward and hurried, "Bye, Lance!" as Freddy dragged her off.

I sat there touching the rock in my pocket for a while but then I got too bummed out so I went to find my pals.

I had no idea where Buzzy, Whit, and Claude had gone and fell into a little stoned paranoid freakout that maybe they'd left me stranded.

It was like 2:00am by then. Dillon's would be closing soon.

I ventured desperate out into the parking lot where I came upon all three of them passing the peace pipe in Claude's mom's station wagon.

"Dang, dudes," I said, "I thought you'd marooned me."

"We didn't want to intrude on your move," Whit said, I supposed referring to my brief respite with Miranda on the couch.

"Coitus interrupts us," said Buzzy without opening his eyes.

"I wasn't going to be putting a move on Miranda Savitch. Please. That was a long time ago."

Was it really?

The following Monday I got a letter back from Annie De Milo.

Dearest Lance,

I'm pleased you have accepted my challenge, good knight. Listen to Kate Bush some more. Figure it out. In the meantime, I will think of you out there among the lonely hinterlands searching for answers. Oh, that postcard of the beach at Malibu was beautiful. I feel like

341

I've seen that place before. I can send you the Westminster Abbey postcard if you want.
You have to ignore what I wrote on it because it's really just the first part of the letter I
ended up sending you last time. Or maybe I can give it to you in person if we come to Los
Angeles this summer. But that's a big IF. But you know really I'd rather keep the
postcard because it looks good on my wall. By now you have already taken the AP
English exam. I have no idea what that is but it sounds hard. I hope you kicked ITS
bum instead of the other way around. Tell me what the AP English exam is. What does
AP stand for? Is it like A-Levels here, I wonder? Thanks for the <u>Tales from</u>
<u>Shakespeare</u> suggestion! I will look for it. If we don't have it in our store I'm sure I can
find it elsewhere in town. I am going to have a ton to read this summer in advance of the
fall term, so I might not get to it until later in the year. But thank you again!

See you soon maybe,

Antlers De Musso

And a couple of days after that I got a letter from Dolly:

Mon Cher Lance,

I can't believe that I'm going to be home in 3 weeks, that in less than a month I will see
you again. I'll be in L.A. for all of July and August. Then I'm going to be coming back
to France. I wanted you to know I've made the decision to do college here, or in Paris to
be more precise. Georges and I are planning to get an apartment and live together there in
the Fall . . .

There was more in the letter, but I would have to digest it another time.

I experienced a degree of despondency and palpitations at this news,
enough to need to toke a strail and unleash my mind on the cosmos.

Dolly had flown even farther away.

I anticipated discomfort in her impending presence.

What I had long looked forward to I found myself dreading instead.

16

Levon Arrow's journey back to the sn'ail farm was quicker than his journey away, the opposite of how most trips go, mainly because he didn't lose time messing around with girls on the return trek.

Levon Arrow had sworn off girls forever.

By the time he was nearing home, the river had become desolate, not a pilgrim left heading to Mecca.

Swearing off girls is easy when there are none around.

The house was also deserted.

The furniture was still there, but his mother was gone.

Levon Arrow figured she was probably dead, but there was no evidence either way anywhere.

Levon realized that after he died nobody would know his mother had ever even existed.

Levon Arrow wondered how many millions of saints there have been whose miracles have gone unrecognized, whose existences have been forgotten altogether because the witnesses died silent.

All the greatness we know nothing about.

He wasn't sure exactly how long he'd been away, whether it had been months or years.

He seemed to be fine food-wise. The cupboard was still stocked full of canned soup. If he had a little of that every few days it'd be years before he'd starve to death.

To his chagrin, the fields were devoid of sn'ails.

He thought perhaps they'd eaten each other.

Toby Sn'ail was still around—having sought refuge inside the house—and living on dust and snow in the window sill.

Toby was pleased to see that Levon had returned albeit alone.

"The prodigal son," Toby said and bowed his antennae.

"I'm back to stay. Where is everybody?"

"The last rocket ship has departed."

"Was my mother on it?"

"She was. She gathered up the last of the sn'ail harvest, brought it to the fueling center, and boarded the final departing space-lift out of here. I was living in the house already 'cause of all the fucking cannibalism going on out there."

"So my mother's not dead."

"That I would have no idea about. She did get herself onto that last rocket though. I'm reasonably sure of that. And what about you?"

"Me?"

"I take it you failed to find the young lady," Toby said.

"Oh, I found her," Levon said.

"And?"

"We hung out briefly."

"That's it?"

"Pretty much."

"Did you at least fuck her really hard in the vagina?" Toby asked.

"Dude, I didn't even kiss her really hard on the mouth."

"What the huh?"

"Nyeah, I dunno, I just couldn't bring myself to. It wasn't right. She had a different destiny."

"And what's that?"

"I'm not sure. It had something to do with living in whales. She was being all cryptic."

"I hate it when chicks pull that shit, dude."

"Don't they always?"

"That 'Why can't you read my mind?' bullcrap. Am I right? Tell me I'm not right."

"You got it, man. That's why I've sworn off 'em for keeps."

"That's a tough road, friend."

"I'm ready for the blissful silence."

And it was true.

Levon Arrow didn't need girls anymore.

He didn't really even need people anymore.

He looked forward to spending the rest of his days, however many that turned out to be, looking at the frozen river.

Levon Arrow smiled the smile of a self-styled messiah.

"Someday," he gloried, "I'll have the whole damned planet to myself."

The last day of school before graduation, we were all signing yearbooks in Mr. Megiddo's class.

When the bell rang at the end of Period 1, Mr. Megiddo asked me to come back and see him at Lunch, and when I returned to his room at Lunch, he was seated at his desk marking 10th Grade essays. The underclassmen still had another week of school.

345

"I have a graduation present for you," he handed me a bag from Pickwick Books.

"You like Pickwick," I said, "Cool."

"Of course. Open up the bag. Take a look."

First I read the card he attached to the outside:

Save these for later.

Cheers,

Harv Megiddo

Inside the bag were two books, *Finnegans Wake* and *Gravity's Rainbow*.

"Wow, thanks," I said. The only thing I knew about them is that they were difficult.

"You're not quite ready for those yet. But they are definitely in your future."

"How will I know when it's time?"

"They'll tell you," he said, pointing to the books, "Or rather they'll call to you."

"Hey, will you sign my yearbook?" I asked him.

"With pleasure," he said.

As he inscribed his note to me I wandered around Room 227.

Megiddo's classroom had been a portal of discovery as transporting as my own darkened bedroom or the garage roof or the Tar Pits or Miranda's eyes.

As far as relationships with teachers go I'd actually had more intimate personal conversations with Mr. Beauregard and Madame Couchée, but the literature we read and the shit we talked about in Megiddo's on a daily basis (there was never a single day in his class that wasn't interesting in some way), that's the stuff that transformed me, the juice that lured the muses to me.

When I got home from school there was a letter waiting for me, left on my pillow by my father, on his business letterhead.

Theo Atlas, DPM
Farmers Market Beauty Shop
3rd & Fairfax
Los Angeles CA

To my son on his graduation from high school,

As you approach a new phase in your life, and as the wonderful years of growing up and finishing school come to a closing time, I thought I would jot down a few of my feelings towards you.

From your very birth you have been a source of joy & wonderment to me. Part of your make-up is derived from the genetic material handed down from other generations & the rest is the uniqueness you have given to that material.

I hope your mother and I have given you some values that will serve as a source of strength in crises that may occur as you grow and mature further. By that I mean a sense of fair play, honesty, family, and compassion for those less fortunate than yourself.

Unfortunately I cannot bequeath to you large sums of material things. However there is no shame in those things, as long as they are accumulated honestly & are a reflection of your own abilities.

This old brain of mine is filled with a million dollars worth of memories of these wonderful years of our unique family, of which you have been an integral part.

As you go out into a bigger world and hopefully conquer a part of it (I know you will), remember your old man is behind you all the way. If at times you falter a little, don't let

347

it get you down. Just pull back & regroup and go out and get 'em again.

I won't go into all the highlights of your accomplishments thru the school years, but you know what they are, and I am looking forward to sharing in your future accomplishments.

So, onward & upward, polish those god-given talents and use them wisely & with gusto!

Lots of luck & all that sort of rot to my only son & carrier of the banner Atlas.

With Sincere Love,

Big Daddy Theo

My father at his profoundly simple best.

My saliva'd gone all salty from the tears.

Later that night I lay in bed and, as was my yearly ritual, read the signatures in my yearbook all at once.

I started with the faculty pages.

Megiddo signed next to his own picture.

Lance,

It couldn't have been more than a day or two when you set yourself off in my classes as someone who is a distinct person & unwilling to be treated as a number or as a face in the crowd. Having sensitivity and creativity that is sometimes awesome, sometimes scary, you must continue to explore those potentials within. So get out of here and be famous. But come back.

Harv Megiddo

On the same faculty page I found Madame Couchée's signature.

A un ami qui a des etoiles dans le coeur—
La renaissance personnelle perpétuelle et rire, rire, rire!
Car cette vie est une grosse comédie.

Amitié tendre,

Sofia C.

Xeno Cortez signed next to the Thespians group photo.

My Dear Mr. Atlas,

To walk away unscathed from a shambles like Scapino is a feat not to be taken lightly in this androgynous age. The original Scapino theme I composed and all the incidental music remains in my archives and you may consider it yours. I expect to read your stunning novel before the masses and quasi-intellectual critics take all the fun out of it so I can reassure you as to the infinite quality it will undoubtedly have and you will undoubtedly overlook.

Piously,

Rev. Xeno

Claude Moss left a message on the ROTC page.

Lance—

Sometimes I miss that brief period of time in 9th Grade when we were hanging out a lot and listening to music. And also making the movies in 9ᵗʰ & 11th. We haven't had that kind of connection in a long time, but I can't imagine having gone through all this madness without you. I am always rendered inarticulate at moments like this. Tar Pit

Kids Forever! I consider you a great friend.

Best of everything,

Claude

Eddie Gurges drew me in my *Scapino* costume next to his signature on a big white page near the back.

Lance!

Wow . . . we have come a long way together from Groucho to Monty Python . . . Now that's a long way . . . a long way . . . a very long way. How long was it? Glad you asked . . . I don't know. That's silly. You are a good—no GREAT— yes GREAT, SUPER, FANTASTIC, THE TOPS . . . well at least you are a good friend. NO . . . really a GREAT friend! I know we will become even better friends in the future . . . We only talk occasionally because I run and you act and in our most important works you WRITE while I DRAW. Call me in the summer, winter, spring, or fall . . . all you've got to do is call . . . and I'll be there. YOU TWIT! Sorry, I was getting too nice . . . you make me puuuuuuke! No. You are a legend.

Take care and I'll see you around,

Your Friend,

Eddie Gurges

Jim Lord had signed diagonally with diminishing space into the lower right hand corner of that very same page.

Lance,

Getting to know you backstage during <u>Guys & Dolls</u> and <u>Scapino</u> and even more in the library Period 4 (Tssh-Tssh!) has been a supreme pleasure. You are perhaps the only *person I know who would, if I wrote "dink-dink-dink-dink/ dink-dink-dink-dink" on a piece of paper, recognize it as the <u>Twilight Zone</u> theme. This alone would be enough to ensure our eternal friendship. But of course there is so much more; (<— notice the Beauregardian semicolon) however, I am not sentimental enough to even want to elaborate, other than to say I have no doubt our friendship will continue fondly into the future.*

Yours to fuck in any position you wish (but be gentle; it's my first time),

Jim Lord

Whitman Rust was predictably mocking and yet dear.

To my favorite little golita,

You will always be gay in my eyes, young man, no matter how fucking smart you are or how much pussy you conquer. But that is why I love you. Dang, dude, we were little kids together. We smoked our first joint together. We've been through it all. Sorry, no beaver. Schlitz. Baby getting kidnapped from Mr. Swanson's class. The Exorcist. Your mother sucks cocks in hell! The Sock Hop. Wiffle-ball on the front lawn. Farmers Market. Town & Country arcade. Nixon leaving the White House. Getting high at the Tar Pits. Dr. Demento. Laserium… So much crazy-ass shit, dude. We even managed to study enough to get good grades. How'd that happen? But really, dude, you are integral to who I am. I don't care how corny that sounds.

I love you, mang, (in the gayest way possible),

Whit

I wondered if Buzzy's entry was representative of the things he wrote in his spiral notebook:

Remember this, dude:

It is in despair that one knows the vanishing of fantasy, anticipation, drama, the future,
expectation, impossible dreams and aspirations, all the mitigating factors that act as a
barrier against your direct experience of reality. Let it all go. Be as unwarped and actual
as the earth's core in all its molten electromagnetic density. Be adrift in the winds of
infinity, untethered, aimless, a version of eternity that pivots around the most ordinary
emptiness. The only way is OUT, baby.

Your friend and neighbor in the house next door,

Augustus "Buzzy" Lagniappe

Manny wrote a long and sober message that took up much of an entire
page.

Lance—

12 years. It is quite odd (and yet old) how two people with the same roots: Fairfax—
Jewish—Middle Class—have both grown to attain such a high commitment to Art. For
instance if you look at all the great artists that came out of the Lower East Side of New
York it seems odd how an environment can form one's positive aesthetic aspirations.
What is needed is a community, a group of people, with genuine mutual interests in a
goal. Lance, you are are a definite part of the community that has nurtured my values
and goals. When I was living in a world of darkness and space (junior high) you seemed
to have been developing in a world of light and truth. I had to escape into this darkness
while you would find the darkness in the light. You have helped to bring me to this
consciousness throughout our high school years. I'm glad we have been able to rekindle our
closeness, the way it was in elementary school. I only hope that when we go to CSUN our
community will grow with people with new ideas that shall influence us more and project
our goals to the stars. Your imagination never ceases and you shall always carry the spirit
of a child. Perhaps the games that we played when we were little developed our being. It
seems that with each game we were more and more inventive. This process culminated
with the ultimate game of creating: our film, Judo Jew. I said that you've searched the
darkness within the light. This is reflected in your taste for music: Waits, Dylan, Cohen,
et al . . . There is such extreme darkness in the music. Depression, the darkness of

yourself. You have internalized. Perhaps this is much more injuring. But don't make the world around you dark. Use your love to fight the pain. In the meantime, let's make some great rock and roll this summer and beyond.

All my blessings,

Manny

p.s. Waiting in line for Dylan tickets was truly a cosmic experience

Lorelei Lux's signature came next.

Dear Lance Atlas,

I wish that the words to express how I feel would just spring out onto the page as perfectly as I feel them. There are so many things I want to say as there are two things that I once should have said but didn't. Do you get my drift so far? Look, I'll be straight with you. I realize there has grown a considerable distance between us, but I can't help feeling that I still really know you. You are a truly beautiful person and I will always love you. I don't ever want you to feel like you can't talk to me if you have a problem or something. I will always be there to listen. So, until we meet again . . . stay cool jewel and be profound always.

Love,

Lorelei Lux

p.s. I suggest that our grandchildren get together for a game of shuffleboard, okay?

Right below Lorelei's signature I recognized Emily Wolf's handwriting. She had in general over the past few months been veering toward a Victorian look in her wardrobe, but her handwriting had always seemed of that era, a wee bit floral, like what you'd see peeking into a Bronte diary.

Dear Lance,

I'm terribly glad I got the chance to know you this year. Sitting next to you in AP English and the few times we went out are sweet memories I will carry with me wherever I go. Unfortunately I won't have the opportunity for another dinner party before I go east for school. Maybe over winter break I'll have some people over to frolic. I really do think you'd enjoy yourself if you gave it a chance. I'm not sure exactly why we have been unable to connect all the way. I wish we had gotten closer than we did get but I must say what we did get was pretty damn good anyway. I love talking to you. I hope we will be able to stay in touch during our college years. We just simply have to. You have struck a chord, sir.

In psychic solidarity,

Emily

Gina Dichlich's message appeared right next to Emily's but I'm not sure who wrote first.

To my best friend and fellow slave to the Muses,

I know this isn't goodbye or anything because we'll be at CSUN together and of course we are bonded at the cellular level and are both embarked on this insane pilgrimage in the name of creative expression. Thank you for accepting me for who I am and not freaking out and running away when I told you EVERYTHING. Instead, you embraced me. You will never fully know how much that meant (and means) to me. I know I have been distracted by love lately, but you've been pretty elusive yourself this past school year, so let's just call it even and try to promise ourselves to spend more time together. We should totally camp out in my backyard this summer. Let's do it! We can stay up really late and talk about girls. And if you're ever into seeing the Grateful Dead again, I would love to do that with you too. That night at the Shrine was overwhelmingly inspiring. And I wasn't even tripping! Oh, and by the way: when you make your first album, I expect to get the call to do the cover. Or Else. And believe me you do not want to experience my Or Else, dude.

Sorry. You're stuck with me. Hope you can handle it.

Love on top of love,

Gina

Miranda had written hers on the last page, the inside back cover to be precise, so it was the last signature I got to.

But in truth I had already read it.

After signing my yearbook in Period 1 that morning, she'd handed it back to me open to where she'd written, and I couldn't resist taking a look immediately. In fact, it was almost as if she wanted me to.

I didn't find therein the profound confession or farewell I had hoped for. It was short, straightforward, and, I suppose, very true to Miranda.

Lance,

It's been great being able to watch you grow and change over the years. It seems like forever since I really knew you. I hope things are good for you now—and will be always. I look forward to the day we meet again and reminisce. I feel very much towards you—like I've told you before, you'll always be a special person to me. Good luck and goodbye.

I love you.

Yours always,

Miranda

p.s. ". . . pour moi, rien de l'univers n'est semblable . . ." —Le Petit Prince

By the time I'd finished reading and looked up to behold her loveliness, the bell had rung and Miranda had gone.

And I beheld in that sanctified moment all my eventual lifetimes, dozens of them, even the final one, the vanishing, the transcendence, as an Arhat blissed with highest perfect wisdom, beyond sentience, without the fear of being human, without the shame of wanting, without the rivering 'why' in why I couldn't kiss Miranda, why I allowed myself to reject her attentions and her willingness, repeatedly, there in the very birthplace.

I sometimes wonder if all those future lives are real.

Or just another preposterous mythology.

Afterlude

It's almost *Tisha B'Av* and apparently I'm supposed to be all freaked out about it.

Rabbi Meshuggenneh just now warned me to prepare because when bad stuff happens to Jews it is too often on that day.

The whole exchange happened a few seconds ago.

The sad fact is that time's actually moving irreversibly nowhere.

I hold firm to the earth in the midst of shifting differences and keep reminding myself that this is already eternity.

Things feel weird. Like Lautréamont weird. Like Lord Buckley weird. Like Ken Nordine weird. Like Professor Irwin Corey weird.

Rabbi Meshuggenneh doesn't typically visit the Tar Pits.

Has he come here to commingle with the primordial ooze of the bygone brothers beneath us, to entertain a heightened awareness of our own eventual circumstance, to contemplate the profound silence of the always present moment?

"All the past atrocities committed on *Tisha B'Av* were but foreshadowings of the worse destruction ahead. Beware the 9th of Av."

"Et tu, rabbi?"

"It is a bad day in the history and the future of the Jewish people. And yet I know *HaShem* means for us to daven in the 3rd Temple one day. So there is always hope. Remember that, Heshie."

Doggerel posing as dogma.

I try not to be flippant.

"Maybe death *is* the 3rd Temple or something," I offer.

He has this crazy blinking tic as he ponders.

"Death is meaningless. We continue in God's consciousness regardless of our material form. We are but numbers on a tree."

"Numbers on a tree . . ." I ponder it.

I like that numbers on a tree image, but I think I will ignore him rather than pursue any further madman poetry.

I swear he just said either "God has a vagina" or "God is a vagina," I'm not sure which, but definitely one or the other.

I don't know if he's talking to himself or to me.

"I was sorry to hear about your son," I attempt a maneuver.

His lip is trembling more rapidly than it usually does.

I've gotten through.

"*Zichrono L'vracha*," I muster lamely from memory.

"*Baruch HaShem*," he points upward, nods, and waddles off lugging his briefcase, slouching from sorrow and scripture.

God is a vagina

Dang, dude.

Now I have my thought for the day.

God is a vagina

It's true.

God is a vagina

Time to wallow in the matter.

Here in the aftermath of last night's tesseract.

I feel mostly reintegrated, though I fear I might've left a few molecules behind in the *chairos* upon reentry.

I know that after Waldo split the party at Madeline's house I was transported into timeless clarity while *The Best of Bread* was playing, and that when I opened my eyes I'm not sure how much later, I'd been joined on the couch by a cute girl I kind of recognized.

"You don't remember me," she said when she saw my eyes were open.

I tried to focus through the daze.

"I know enough to know I know you," I said, "or knew you."

"Dolores Mizrahi," she said, "We went to Melrose Avenue Elementary together."

Dang, dude.

Dolores Mizrahi got me suspended in 4th Grade.

Dolores Mizrahi hated my guts.

Dolores Mizrahi was the reason I learned what fuck meant.

"Dolores," I said through the haze, "Yes, I remember you. You left after 4th Grade."

"That's right. Good memory! My parents sent me to Jew school after that.

All the way through."

"Where are you now?"

"Loyola Marymount."

"LMU. The Jesuit school."

"That's the place."

"I see the yeshiva made a lasting impact. What are you studying?"

"I'm a Psych major."

"And what brings you to this party?"

"I know Madeline Baker from LMU."

Dang, dude, Dolores turned out beautiful.

"I've always felt bad about how mean I was to you in elementary school."

"I don't really remember."

I blushed because, dang, dude, she was most intensely fucksome.

"I have no recall of you being mean to me," I reiterated the lie.

I had no idea why I was lying to her.

Other than maybe it had something to do with the grooviness we had going on in that moment and I didn't want to drag it down.

However, none of that mattered because our ancient incipient sizzle got interrupted by Lily Adams, who'd been passed out on the green velveteen chair but had regained consciousness and subsequently found her way to my lap.

"Georgie Porgie," she said as she rolled into my arms.

Dolores Mizrahi nodded and got up.

"Nice to see you again, Lance," she said, "Oh, and I still have that note you sent me in 4th Grade."

"What note?" I feinted.

She shook her head and drifted elsewhere.

Probably better.

Dang, dude.

The note from 4th Grade.

I want to fuck you

The quaalude had definitely worn off and I wasn't tripping anymore from the dusted bud Waldo had shared with me.

"Hey, I'm going to be on the *Angel's Flight* staff next semester," Lily said, sticking her middle and index fingers in my mouth and I bit down just a little too hard which probably gave her the wrong impression.

Angel's Flight was the Cal State Northridge literary anthology.

"Editing?"

"Reading and evaluating poetry submissions."

"Isn't Tony Crumb going to be editor-in-chief next year?"

"Oui."

"Good move."

"Si."

"You'll be working closely with him."

"Ja," she smiled. "But in the meantime," she said, sort of crawling up my body.

I could most likely have had sex with Lily Adams last night, but I remained true to my now year-long vow of celibacy.

Instead of kissing her very hard on the mouth, I asked her because I'd long wanted to, "Did you ever go to Zody's when you were a kid?"

"Oh, hell yeah. I used to go all the time," she said. "Why?"

"I feel like I saw you there once. When we were like 11 or something."

Lily pondered the possibility.

"It'd be pretty freaky if that were true," she said.

"You don't have a similar memory?"

"No. Afraid not," she shook her head. "I saw lots of people at Zody's."

"Do you remember eating a frozen banana there maybe?"

"Definitely not. I don't like bananas. And definitely not a frozen one. Yuck."

A once teeming mythology gone instantly fallow.

I started scoping out exit routes.

"So," she looked at me, "are we going to go play somewhere?"

"I'm pretty wiped out," I said, "That shit Waldo turned me onto was monstrous. Plus the quaalude I dropped earlier. My head exploded. I had a quantum experience."

"In other words we aren't going to make it."

"Nyeah. I can't," I told her.

I had to stay true.

"Oh man," Lily groaned, "Georgie Porgie. How can you do this to me? I've been feeling you all night. I thought for sure we were gonna make it later."

"I am out of commission," I apologized decisively.

Lily started to get up because she knew I meant it even though she could probably also see my hard-on.

"All right, dude," she waved me off and shuffled away, "You're lying. But whatever. Your loss."

I'm not sure if she gave me the finger or not but she might've. I know I would've.

I floated over to the Hammond chord organ because I knew it would receive me without judgment.

I droned in C for a while, contemplating a return to "Blue Jay Way," but instead was moved to croon the song I never got to sing on stage, with eyes closed, to my audience of none.

When a man's an empty kettle
He should be on his mettle
And yet I'm torn apart
Just because I'm presumin'
That I could be a human
If I only had a heart

I was interrupted by two hands on my shoulders.

"Hey, so I'm getting ready to split."

It was Miranda.

I turned all the way around on the organ bench to face her.

She stood looking down at me.

"It was really really great seeing you again," Miranda said and we clutched hands.

"Likewise."

"I'll keep an ear out for your next show."

"We won't be playing again until the fall. Manny's in NYC for the summer. And Al's in Montreal. We have a gig at Club 88 in September, though. I can't remember the exact date."

"You guys are called Tin Man Alley."

"Right."

"Perfect. I will try to be there."

I already knew she'd forget all about it.

"I had a supremely weird and profound mental experience tonight," I said. "I don't know how to explain it. It was like some kind of psychic wormhole or something. Partially drug-induced, for sure. But there were other phenomena at work also. It involved you very intensely."

I surprised myself by saying those words out loud.

"Really," she paused and squeezed my hands, "Well now you have to tell me."

"Nyeah."

I wanted to tell her.

"Lancelot Link, Secret Chimp. You can't drop that on me and then withhold."

"It's the drugs," I said, "I'm kind of remembering it the way you remember a dream. Bits and pieces. Fragmented imagery. It doesn't make much sense. But I did learn something."

"Share your wisdom at least."

It was one last opportunity to confess my nevergone love for her, but instead I said, "Buzzy Lagniappe is not the fat kid from *Willy Wonka & The Chocolate Factory*," and shrugged.

"That's deep, Lance."

"Defenly," I jabbed, "May it alter the course of the rest of your life."

"Hey," she intensified her grip and looked at me fiercely, "Why do you seem so sad?"

"Always thinking of Doomsday, I guess."

"Be serious."

"I am being serious."

"Doomsday is a myth invented by people who can't bear the thought that the world will go on just fine without them. We've had that conversation. Several times."

"I'm realizing I might never see you again," I said, subtly freaking out.

"That may well be true," Miranda answered, "I kind of feel that way about everybody all the time these days."

I was trying not to cry.

"I-uh," I lulled and looked down.

"Say it."

"Nyeah, I," I shrugged.

"All you have to do is say it."

Give her the rock from Asteroid B-612, I thought.

I didn't look up.

I could feel her grip releasing.

"It was a long time ago, Lance," she said.

"And one day this will feel like a long time ago," I agreed and nodded, still focused on the floor.

Miranda unlatched her hands.

"Bye, Lance," she said and turned to leave.

I looked up long enough to catch a last glimpse of her ass in those white jeans.

Then I turned back around to finish the tune.

Just to register emotion, jealousy - devotion,
And really feel the part . . .

. . . and so I have come here to the Tar Pits this morning to bask in the midsummer day's reality, rock still in my pocket and the song still rattling around in my empty chest.

Picture me - a balcony. Above a voice sings low.
'Wherefore art thou, Romeo?'

"Lance Atlas," I hear someone behind me.

I lean my head back to identify the source.

It's Annie De Milo on roller skates.

"Hi, Lance!"

Annie sits down next to me.

Or rather she sort of falls backwards as the roller skates slip out from underneath her.

"Owie," she winces, "Owie kazowie."

"You OK?"

"Nyeah. Fine. My hands hurt worse than my butt."

"Did you just skate across the grass?"

"Yes I did."

"You could be a roller derby star. You could skate for the Thunderbirds."

"Who?"

"The L.A. Thunderbirds. Roller derby."

She doesn't get the reference.

"I saw you sitting here and wanted to say hi."

"How did you spot me?"

"Easy. You look like a Jewish Jesus."

"Jesus *was* Jewish."

"Oh yeah, huh. When we talked about the Tar Pits last night I decided I was going to come here after I got home from Ginger's house."

"And here you are."

"I am!"

"How was the sleepover?"

"Our plan was to get drunk on that punch but it didn't work so well."

"Why?"

"We fell asleep before we drank enough of it."

"Ah, but now you can enjoy this glorious Sunday and not have to deal with a hangover."

"I suppose."

"You should've written me that you were coming."

"I didn't know until too late. You probably wouldn't have gotten the postcard till like next week if I'd sent it. So I decided not to."

Annie points across the park.

"I was thinking of getting a frozen banana from Zody's."

"A what?"

I feel that familiar cold rush of shit to the heart.

"From Zody's ice cream truck. Over on Curson."

She means The Zodiac Chiller, an ice cream truck that's usually parked on Curson—in the spot where Sam the ice cream man used to park Dinosaur Times. The guy who runs it is named Zody, or at least that's what he calls himself.

We walk along the paved path that leads out of the park to Curson Avenue, avoiding the mimes by cutting across the grass when necessary along the way.

Annie nods toward a passing boy and whispers, "Augustus Gloop."

"I hope he doesn't think the tar is chocolate."

"I wouldn't mind drowning in a chocolate river."

"So you've said. Isn't that every chocolate lover's dream death?"

"Yeah what you want?" Zody snarls as we get to the front of the line.

I get a 50-50 bar.

"The frozen banana sign is gone," Annie gestures to the side of the truck.

I never knew there was one.

Annie turns to Zody.

"Wait, you don't have frozen bananas anymore?"

"Yes."

"Yes meaning you do have them or yes meaning you don't have them?"

"Yes, we have no bananas."

368

"But I had one yesterday."

"We have no bananas today."

"Oh, crumb."

"You get 50-50 bar. Like your boyfriend."

Annie looks at me and clears her throat and then turns back to Zody.

"OK. And can I also get an Everlasting Gobstopper?"

"A whuddy whuddy what whuddy?"

"An Everlasting Gobstopper. From Willy Wonka."

"We don't have no fairy tales here," Zody says and hands her a 50-50 bar.

We meander back to my usual spot on the north bank of the little stream that hardly moves.

Annie's almost my height with her roller skates on.

"I really wanted a frozen banana," she unwraps her 50-50 bar.

"You'll be into these though," I bite off a chunk of my own bar. "I love how it goes from the orange sherbet coating to the vanilla center. Very satisfying journey."

We regain our witness positions streamside and listen to the gurgling tar-water ooze by.

"When did you get your braces on?"

"November or something."

"Ah, you didn't tell me."

"I don't have to tell you everything."

"Correct, ma'am."

I finish up my 50-50 bar and run the stick along my teeth which gives Annie the shivers.

"Ew, criminy, don't do that."

"Ping?"

"What's ping?"

"Getting shivers from a sound."

"But it's not the sound. It's imagining what it feels like to make the sound. Ick. Shivers."

"Rakes on concrete do that to me," I hunch up my back.

"A fingertip on dirty car metal," she shivers again and makes a sound like "ghee."

"You are a nutball," I tell her.

"And you know what you are."

"Of course."

"A whuddy whuddy what whuddy."

"We don't have no fairy tales here."

"You are the one who's cuckoo bazookoo," Annie twirls her finger around her ear.

She finishes her 50-50 bar and takes my stick along with her own and puts them in her purse.

"What are you doing?"

"Souvenirs," she closes her purse.

"So, you guys are American. How did your parents come to own a bookstore in Wales?"

"My dad had this great aunt, Auntie Edan, and she was a writer who also owned this bookstore in Hay-On-Wye. When she died my dad was the only living relative. At first my parents were just going to sell it, but then they decided to move over there and run it. They both gave up writing for television out here in L.A. A couple of years ago you could really start to tell we didn't have as much money."

"Hence no more visits to Cambria."

"Nyeah. We're just here long enough to visit Nana."

"Your mom's mom."

"Yeah. Nana Dipchunk."

"Is your Nana cool? 'Cause some nanas are cool and some can be really mean-ass bitches."

"Nana's darling. She's this really sweet old lady who mostly watches game shows and does jigsaw puzzles. I love my Nana. She makes me sandwiches. And she always has Almond Roca."

Annie crosses her eyes and pokes her puffed up cheek.

"You've never told me what the bookstore is called."

"Borogoves," Annie says.

"From Jabberwocky."

"You're smart."

"Nyeah."

"For a nimnork."

I don't have a come-back line so we just sit in some more easy silence for a while, and in that silence I make a decision, there in the center of everything.

"Hey, remember this?" I reach into my pocket and pull out the rock from Asteroid B-612, "Speaking of Cambria."

"Yeah! Wow . . . It looks kind of like a 50-50 bar," Annie marvels at the old keepsake, "I still think about this rock sometimes."

"Why?"

"That was one of my favorite days of all time," her mouth gapes open, "The Cheshire moon. I couldn't believe I was talking to the boy from Angel's Flight. But I remember you said you were going to give it to someone."

"That's right," I place the rock from Asteroid B-612 in her hand, "I am."

"You said you were going to give it to a girl."

"Well, aren't you a girl?"

"I'm not always sure about that actually. Sometimes it's questionable."

"Well, this is for when you are sure."

"Oh man oh man oh man. Really? Thank you. This is bloody wonderful," she tucks the rock into her purse and lies on her back.

"You know we're sitting on top of an ancient graveyard," I say and cross my legs like a movie Injun.

"That's what I love about it," she replies.

Annie raises her hands to shield her eyes from the sun. "I want to live in a spaceship that never lands. That would be my dream house."

"Even if you were all alone?"

"Especially if I was all alone. As long as I had books to read? I'd be fine."

"You don't need other people?"

"Oh, I love people. I just don't like being around them for long periods of time all at once."

"Me too. And me neither."

I fling a pebble into the tar stream.

Annie grins.

"You know what?"

"What?"

"That's what.

"Haha."

"But really, you know what?"

"What?"

"I bet we'd build the same dream house."

"Mine wouldn't be a spaceship that never lands. Sorry."

"What would it be then?"

"My dream house would be by a river. But really it could be anywhere, I guess. As long as every room is a library and has comfortable sleeping arrangements."

"That sounds wonderful. I'm ready to move in now."

"Haha."

"No I'm being serious." She sort of pouts but I can't tell if it's part of a long play at psych-out humor or not, "We should build a dream house together and live there. I mean it. For real. Up on a hill. Overlooking a river."

"Why?"

"Yes it *could* be the River Wye if you want."

"Nyeah, no, I mean, why would you want to do that. It's a very weird idea."

"Why's it weird?"

"Because . . . um . . . let's start with the fact that you're 12 years old?" I say.

"What's the big deal? So are you."

"No, kiddo, I am not."

"Yes you are. I know your secret."

"What secret?"

"Your big secret."

"Oh yeah?"

"Your biggest secret."

"And what would that be?"

She motions me closer and her voice becomes a whisper, "You're a nimnork."

"That's not a secret."

She takes to punching my arm.

"But seriously."

She continues to jab me in the tricep with her fist.

"What."

"I know your secret," she almost sings it.

"Well, I must be keeping it from myself also because I have no idea what you are talking about."

"I know who you really are."

"Let me guess: the Little Prince."

"Who's that?" Annie giggles. "Guess again, Lanceypants."

"The Tin Man."

"Close."

"A hamburger."

"What? That's stupid."

"The fat kid from *Willy Wonka & The Chocolate Factory.*"

"No, you're not Augustus Gloop. Come on. Be serious."

"The boy from Angel's Flight."

"That's not a secret either. Keep trying."

"This could go on forever."

"Up to you. Guess again."

"I give up."

She motions me even closer than I already am.

I lower my ear to her. Again that whisper.

"You're Peter Pan."

I'm not sure if she's joshing or if she's actually onto me.

"You can't fool me, Peter," she sort of rasps.

I sit back up and tug at a clump of grass.

Annie starts singing.

"Ooh, he's here again . . ."

I recognize the song.

"Kate Bush," I say.

"Yups."

"That's the song you were talking about. The one that reminds you of me."

"Yups and yups again. You figured it out."

"Of course I did."

"That's one mystery solved," Annie sits back up and hugs her knees, "S'okay now to complete your mission, tell me the name of the secret book that I hope nobody buys because I want it for myself and you win the special prize."

I don't even have to think about it.

"No duh. *The Wizard of Oz*."

Annie looks straight ahead, across the stream, toward the big tar pit on Wilshire.

"That's right. Was it that obvious?"

"You've dropped a few flagrant hints along the way, yes. And plus I kept thinking about the *Oz* movie all frigging night last night, like in a dream."

"It's this beautiful leatherbound illustrated edition. I try to look at it at least once a day in the store. Just to make sure it's still there. I know it will be gone one day."

"Like everything."

Annie pulls a Band-Aid box out of her purse and opens it toward me.

"You win the special prize," she says.

"You still have the Band-Aid box."

"Yuh-huh. Take one. It's Juicy Fruit."

She takes a stick for herself.

I have to decline.

"Gum gives me a headache."

"Oh yeah. I forgot. I'll have to think up another special prize then."

Annie's eyes close as her mouth works the gum.

"Let's see now . . ."

I struggle to find an interruption.

"So you dug *The Tempest* in the Lamb book."

"Oh yeah."

"Who's your favorite character in *The Tempest*? Ariel I bet. The tricksy spirit. Just like you."

I bonk her gently on the top of the head and she sticks her wad of gum out at me.

"You have to guess."

"Of course I do," I look at her face in profile against the bronze morning.

"Well?"

"You've already said it's not Ariel."

"Nyep," she cracks her gum.

I already know the answer.

"Caliban," I play.

"Nyope."

"Prospero."

"Nyerp."

"Ferdinand."

"Nuh-uh."

I smile widely.

"Dang, dude," I shake my head.

"What?"

"Nothing."

"Tell me!"

I smile wider as her Cinderella golfball eyes are all bugging out at me.

"Talk to me," she starts digging her knuckle into my spine, "Don't be a nimnork noogie-noo."

"It's a long story," I swat her hand away.

"How long?"

"That's what I'm trying to figure out."

"Just tell me the story. Why's it so hard?"

"'Cause now *you're* in it."

I look over at Annie De Milo who has no idea what I'm talking about, or maybe she does, and everything feels eternal like the smell of that tar in the holy stream and infinite like a starry heart's capacity for love.

I wonder if she truly recognizes me or if it's just a million vague flutters and momentary notions and horrors that file across her antelope brainwaves without her even knowing it.

"Come on, Peter," Annie De Milo is tugging my sleeve, "Tell me the whole story."

Dang, dude.

It never ends.

ABOUT THE AUTHOR

Barry Smolin is a native of Los Angeles, California. He is the author of the novella *Wake Up In The Dreamhouse* (2011), *Always Be Madly In Love* (2011), selected poetry culled from the years 1988- 2010, and *Narcissus In The Dark* (2012), another novella, in addition to *The Miranda Complex Volumes 1 & 2 (2016,* 2017). Since 1995 he has been the host and producer of the radio shows *The Music Never Stops* (1995-2012) and *Head Room* (2012-present) on KPFK 90.7 FM in Los Angeles. He has also released five albums of original music under the name Mr. Smolin: *At Apogee* (2004), *The Crumbling Empire Of White People* (2007), *Bring Back The Real Don Steele* (2009), *Heaven's Not High* (2013), and *The Sooterkin Library (2017),* as well as setting chapter 1 of James Joyce's *Finnegans Wake* to music in collaboration with the band Double Naught Spy Car as part of the "Waywords and Meansigns Project" (2016) and on an instrumental album *That Tragoady Thundersday* (2016). His music was also featured on the Showtime television series "Weeds." He can be found online at www.mrsmolin.com

www.ingramcontent.com/pod-product-compliance
Lightning Source LLC
Chambersburg PA
CBHW071224250626
47163CB00001B/92